Before bec............................m was an
investigativ.........jour............erica, Australia
and Britain. As a journalist and writer he has investigated
notorious cases such as the serial killer couple Fred and
Rosemary West. He has worked with clinical and forensic

one million copie............nd the world..... the first of nine
novels featuring clinical psychologist Joe O'Loughlin, who
faces his own increasing battle with a debilitating disease.
Michael has also written five standalone thrillers. In 2015
he won the UK's prestigious Crime Writers' Association
Gold Dagger Award with his standalone thriller *Life or Death*.
He lives in Sydney.

Praise for *The Other Wife*:

'Robotham is one of the finest crime novelists on the planet.
Whether writing standalone novels or novels centered on
his recurring character, clinical psychologist Joe O'Loughlin,
Robotham grips the reader from the first page to the last'
Booktopian

'A past master at misdirection . . . he demonstrates the full
range of his skills here' *Crime Fiction Lover*

'As always, even Robotham's most extraordinary stories have
their basis in the kinds of things people really do . . . At its
heart, *The Other Wife* is all about what it means to be a
father. It's also a book about coming to terms with the past
in ways that allow us to move on' *The Age*

THE
OTHER WIFE
MICHAEL
ROBOTHAM

sphere

SPHERE

First published in Great Britain in 2018 by Sphere
This paperback edition published in 2019 by Sphere

1 3 5 7 9 10 8 6 4 2

A CIP catalogue record for this book is available from the British Library.

ISBN 978-0-7515-6280-4

Typeset in Bembo by Palimpsest Book Production Limited, Falkirk, Stirlingshire
Printed and bound in Great Britain by Clays Ltd, Elcograf S.p.A.

Papers used by Sphere are from well-managed forests
and other responsible sources.

Sphere
An imprint of
Little, Brown Book Group
Carmelite House
50 Victoria Embankment
London EC4Y 0DZ

An Hachette UK Company
www.hachette.co.uk

www.littlebrown.co.uk

For Ian Stevenson

Acknowledgements

When I introduced Professor Joe O'Loughlin in *The Suspect*, I had no idea that he would become my most enduring and best-loved character. Back then, one novel was the height of my ambition, and I imagined selling a dozen copies (with my mother buying eight of them).

Thirteen books later and the Professor is still with me – a man with a brilliant mind and a crumbling body, who has an incredible insight into the best and worst of human behaviour. Of all my characters, Joe is perhaps the most autobiographical, although he is far braver, cleverer, better-looking and wittier than I am. What is it with writers and wish fulfilment?

I am indebted as always to my wonderful editors, most notably Mark Lucas, my agent and friend, as well as Lucy Dauman, Rebecca Saunders and Richard Pine. I also wish to thank my wonderful publishing teams at Little, Brown Book Group UK, Hachette Australia, Goldmann in Germany and all the others around the world. In particular, I want to single out my translators, who work so hard to make my prose even better than the original.

I want to also mention Stuart Macdermid, a very generous man, who supported Parkinson's NSW in a charity auction and won the right to have a character named after him. Thank you, Stuart.

Customarily, at this point in every book I thank my family, most notably my wife, Vivien, who has come to expect a glowing tribute, which tends to make her friends jealous and puts me in the good books. Everything I've written about her is true. She has given me three beautiful daughters, thirty years of happy marriage and she still makes me smile. That's why I don't buy lottery tickets. I'm lucky enough.

Children begin by loving their parents;
as they grow older they judge them;
sometimes they forgive them.

Oscar Wilde,
The Picture of Dorian Gray

Day One

1

From the top of Primrose Hill, silhouetted against the arriving day, the spires and domes of London look like the painted backdrop of a Pinewood sound stage waiting for actors to take their places and an unseen director to yell '*Action*'.

I love this city. Built upon the ruins of the past, every square foot of it has been used, re-used, flattened, bombed, dismantled, rebuilt and flattened again until the layers of history are like sediments of rock that one day will be picked over by future archaeologists and treasure hunters.

I am no different – a broken man, built upon the wreckage of my past. It has been thirteen years since I was diagnosed with Parkinson's. It began with an unconscious, random flicker of my fingers on my left hand; a ghost movement that looked like a twitch, but read like a guilty verdict.

Unknown to me, working in secret, my body had begun a long, drawn-out separation from my mind; a divorce where nobody gets to keep the record collection or fights over who gets the dog.

That small rolling of the thumb and forefinger has now spread silently through my limbs until they no longer do my bidding without the assistance of drugs. When I'm medicated properly, I can appear to be almost symptom-free. A little stooped and more deliberate in my movements but normal in most respects. At other times, Mr Parkinson is a cruel puppeteer, tugging at invisible strings, making me dance to music that only he can hear.

There is no cure – not yet – but I live in hope that science will win the race. In the meantime, daily exercise is recommended. That's why I'm standing here, with all of London's mangled and magnificent history on display. My eyes sweep from east to west and settle on the curved rooftops and netting of London Zoo. Julianne and I bought our first house a few streets from here. We would lie in bed on warm nights when the curtains swayed from open windows, listening to the calls of lions and hyenas and animals we couldn't name.

It is sixteen months since she died. A surgical complication, they said; a blood clot that travelled from her groin to her heart and lodged in her left ventricle. She lived for a week on life support, lying on white sheets, looking tranquil and beautiful, but 'not at home', according to the neurologist. We turned off the machines and she slipped away like an empty rowing boat cut loose in the current.

The seasons since then have been like stages of grieving. Summer passed in denial and isolation, autumn brought anger, winter blame and by spring my depression had driven me to seek help.

I endure for the sake of my daughters, Charlie and Emma, because they deserve more than tragedy as their template and so much of Julianne lives within them; from the parting of their hair, to the inflection in their voices and the way they walk, frown and laugh.

We moved back to London a year ago, after selling the cottage in Somerset. I used the money from the sale and a bank loan to buy a top-floor flat in a mansion block called Wellington Court in Belsize Park, not far from Primrose Hill. Airy and bright, with high ceilings and a large bay window in the sitting room, it has three bedrooms and a small roof terrace, accessible from the kitchen window, where Emma and I sometimes watch the sun setting over London while sitting on deckchairs like passengers on an ocean liner.

Emma is twelve. I left her sleeping at the flat with an alarm set for school. No longer my little girl, she's on the cusp of womanhood, with green-grey eyes, curly hair and skin so pale it looks almost powdered like a kabuki dancer. In January she started at North Bridge House, an independent day school in North London with the sort of fees to make my eyes water. The scholarship came as a bonus and a surprise.

My eldest, Charlie, is in her second year at Oxford studying behavioural psychology. Parents are normally proud when children follow in their footsteps, but I take no pleasure in Charlie wanting to be a forensic psychologist, because I know where her fascination lies and how it started. She wants to understand why some people commit terrible acts and fantasise about even worse crimes; the psychopaths and sociopaths who haunt her nightmares.

Continuing down the hill, I cross the canal into Regent's Park. A young woman jogs past me, her buttocks hugged by Lycra and her ponytail bobbing on her back. I contemplate catching up with her. We could run together. Connect. I'm dreaming. She's gone.

I have an appointment this morning with Dr Victoria Naparstek at a café not far from her office in Harley Street. Victoria is a good-looking woman. Forty-something. Slim. Striking. I slept with her once when Julianne and I were separated. Victoria broke it off. When I asked her why, she said, 'You're still in love with your wife.' I asked her if that mattered. 'It does to me,' she replied.

She's waiting for me at a café in Portland Place. Dressed in an A-line skirt and matching jacket with a simple white blouse, open at the neck. She smiles and her dimples leave an impression on her cheeks.

'Professor O'Loughlin.'

'Dr Naparstek.'

'You're sweaty.'

'See what you do to me.'

We banter. Flirt a little. A waitress has come to take our order. Tea. Coffee. Toast. Jam.

Everybody told me that I should talk to someone after Julianne's death. I know the benefits of grief counselling, yet I fought against the idea until Victoria called me a 'fucking idiot' and a 'typical man' who shuts down and pretends the problem doesn't exist.

'You look good,' she says.

'I am.'

My first lie.

'Have you been sleeping?'

'Yes.'

Another one.

'And the dreams?'

'One or two.'

'Always the same?'

I nod.

This is part of our routine. Therapy without being therapy. She will quiz me, I will answer, and neither of us will feel under any obligation to reveal confidences or offer advice.

Victoria wants me to verbalise my worst fears, but I don't have to put them into words because I live them every day. I don't have to imagine being alone, or having an illness, or suddenly bursting into tears over a broken cup, or a dropped egg.

'How is Emma?' she asks.

'Good. Better. We spent yesterday painting her room and putting stencils on the walls.'

'Did she mention Julianne?'

'No.'

'What about the photographs?'

'She won't look at them.'

Emma hasn't cried or rebelled or asked questions about her mother's death. She won't visit Julianne's grave, or look at photographs of her, or reminisce about the past. This isn't about denial, or pretending nothing has changed. Emma knows that Julianne isn't coming back, but refuses to labour the point, or have it define our existence.

Some nights, I've found her hiding in her wardrobe, curled in a ball.

'What's wrong?'

'I can't sleep.'

'That's OK. Just rest your eyes.'

'What if I never sleep again?'

'You will.'

'What if I'm the only one awake? The whole world will be sleeping and I'll be on my own, in the dark . . . with nobody to help me.'

'I'll be here.'

'Promise you won't fall asleep until I do.'

'I promise.'

Emma worries about me because I am the last parent standing. When we cross the street, she insists on holding my hand – not to protect herself, but to protect me. She makes sure that I eat well and exercise and take my medication. I wake sometimes to find her leaning over my bed with her hand on my chest. She counts the number of breaths. Three sets of nine. Twenty-seven. Usually, that's enough to reassure her.

Our coffees have arrived. Victoria tears open a sachet of sugar and shakes the contents into the foam.

'Did you ask Emma if she'd talk to me?'

'She's not sold on the idea.'

'I understand.'

'I don't want to push her.'

'You shouldn't. Let her make the decision when she's ready.'

I've given the same advice to countless grieving parents

when they've visited my consulting rooms, but when it comes to my own flesh and blood I begin to question my thirty years of clinical experience as a psychologist.

My mobile phone is vibrating on the table. I don't recognise the number.

'Is that Professor O'Loughlin?' asks a female voice.

'Yes.'

'This is the registrar at St Mary's Hospital in Paddington. Your father, William O'Loughlin, has been admitted with serious head injuries.'

'Head injuries.'

'He underwent surgery six hours ago.'

'Surgery.'

'To relieve pressure on his brain. He was bleeding internally. Right now he's in a medically induced coma.'

'Coma.'

Why am I repeating everything she says?

The café has a shelf of bonsai plants, miniature trees with gnarled trunks and moss-covered branches. I find myself staring at the shrunken forest, no longer listening to what the registrar is saying. My knees are shaking.

'Are you there, Professor?'

'Yes. Sorry. What was my father doing in London?'

What difference does it make?

'I don't have that information,' replies the registrar.

Of course she doesn't! It's a stupid question.

'Does my mother know?'

'She's with him now.'

'Can I talk to her?'

'We don't allow mobile phones in the ICU.'

'I see. Right. Tell her I'm coming.'

I end the call and stare at the blank screen. I should call my sisters. No, Mum will have done that. I should catch a cab. Emma is at home. I'm supposed to walk her to school and then I have patients to see. I can cancel my appointments.

Victoria searches for her wallet. 'You go. Call me later.'

Within moments I'm on the pavement, looking for a cab. Three of them pass. Occupied. I start jogging, desperately trying to lift my feet and swing my arms in sequence. Traffic is backed up along Euston Road. I cut across Regent's Park and up Primrose Hill. My lungs hurt and lactic acid is building up in my legs.

Having climbed the stairs at Wellington Court, I'm ready to collapse.

'Did you run all the way?' asks Emma, who is sitting at the kitchen bench, in her school uniform – a striped dress, red cardigan, black tights and buckled shoes.

'Granddad . . . in hospital . . . I have to go.'

'What happened?'

'Some sort of accident. I need a shower.'

'Is he going to be OK?'

'He's in good hands.'

Emma follows me down the hallway. 'Bad things happen at hospitals.'

'What do you mean?'

'People die.' Her lips are pulled down at the corners and her tea-coloured eyes are shining.

'Not always. Most of them get better,' I say, knowing that my words sound hollow to someone who has lost her mother.

'I don't want you to go,' she says.

'Nothing is going to happen to me.'

'At least let me come.'

'You have school.'

'Who's going to take me?'

'I'll talk to the boys.'

The boys are men – Duncan and Arturo – a gay couple who live on the floor below. One works in advertising and the other runs an art gallery in Islington. Having showered and changed, I knock on their door. Duncan answers. He's wearing a short gown just long enough to brush the top of his thighs.

'Joseph,' he says excitedly, kissing both my cheeks. I bend in the middle to avoid groin-to-groin contact.

'My dad is in hospital. Can one of you take Emma to school?'

Duncan relays the message over his shoulder and Arturo replies, yelling from the kitchen. 'I can take her on the back of my bike.'

I want to say no. Duncan does it for me. 'You're not taking her on the bike. You ride like a maniac.'

'I did a safe-riding course.'

'With Evel Knievel.'

I've triggered a domestic dispute. Duncan waves me away. 'You go, I'll walk her. I hope your father is all right.'

Minutes later I'm in a cab, stuck in traffic on Edgware Road, listening to the talkback callers complaining about Brexit, 'fake news', immigrants and low wages. I've grown tired of politics and current affairs. I don't want to be informed by journalists or governed by politicians of any persuasion. Democracy has failed. Let's a try a benign dictatorship.

My father is in a coma. He turned eighty this year and I don't remember him ever being in hospital – not as a patient. I long ago labelled him 'God's-Personal-Physician-in-Waiting' because of his indefatigable energy and unrivalled self-belief. For more than fifty years he was a medical giant – a professor of surgery and public health; advisor to governments, founder of the International Trauma Research Unit, lecturer, author, commentator and philanthropist. Our family's charitable trust – the O'Loughlin Foundation – gives millions of pounds in research grants each year.

I saw Dad two weeks ago. We had lunch at his club in Mayfair; a pleasant enough two hours in a tweedy, pass-the-port sort of way. I don't remember what we spoke about. Nothing meaningful. He looked well. Happy. He spends most of his time at the farmhouse in Wales, but comes to London quite regularly for meetings and lectures.

The cab arrives at St Mary's and I hurry past a cluster of nurses and orderlies, smoking cigarettes on the pavement. The Major Trauma Ward is on the ninth floor. Waiting for the lift to arrive, I catch that hospital smell of antiseptic, floor polish and bodily fluids. Memories bubble up and scald my throat. Swallowing hard, I force them down, tasting the vomit.

I press a buzzer outside the ICU. A nursing sister answers, the heavy door sucking inwards like she's opening an airlock.

'My father is here. William O'Loughlin. My mother is with him.'

Her smile is encouraging. I wonder how long she's practised it.

'Please wash your hands,' she says, showing me to a sink with antibacterial soap and a paper towel dispenser. I follow her through a long dimly lit ward past rows of beds partitioned by machines and curtains. Each pool of light contains someone who is close to death, plugged in, taped up, filled and drained, hydrated and evacuated, medicated and sedated.

'He's the last cubicle,' says the nurse. 'Please don't try to wake him.'

I approach tentatively, catching my first glimpse of a broken man lying on a bed, imprisoned by tubing and cables. His head is heavily bandaged. An oxygen mask covers his mouth. IV bags hang above his head. Needles have been driven into his veins. Sensors are monitoring his vital signs.

I want to turn back and say, 'That's not my father. There's been a mistake,' but I know it's him.

A woman is sitting beside the bed, partially in shadow. She looks up as though startled, her eyes red-rimmed and bruised from lack of sleep.

Letting go of Dad's hand, she gets to her feet.

'It's Joseph, isn't it?'

I nod.

'I didn't want us to meet like this.'

'I don't understand. Where's my mother?'

'She's not here.'

'But I was told . . .'

'I asked the hospital to call you.'

'I'm sorry, but who are you?'

'I'm his other wife.'

2

How long do I stand there, unable to speak? I laugh uncomfortably, which is supposed to be her cue to say that she's joking. She doesn't take it. I look feeble and embarrassed, growing angry at her silence. What sort of cruel joke is this? Where are the hidden cameras? When will someone jump out and yell, '*April Fool!?*' Only it's November not April and I don't think I'm a fool.

The man in bandages is my father. The woman next to him is *not* my mother.

'I'm Olivia Blackmore,' she says, offering her hand.

I look at her outstretched fingers as though she's pointing a gun.

'I think you've made a mistake,' I say. 'How did you get my number?'

'William told me that if something like this happened, I was to call you first.'

'Something like what?'

'An accident or an emergency.'

In her forties with dark hair and the remnants of make-up, she has a slight accent, East European perhaps, which has faded over time. She's wearing high-heeled shoes, dark tights and a loosely belted trench coat.

'I was told my mother was here . . .'

'The nurse misunderstood me.'

I'm searching for words in vain. 'Is my mother coming?'

'No.'

I start again. 'What happened to him?'

'I found him at the bottom of the stairs.'

'What stairs?

'At the house.'

'Whose house?'

'Ours.'

'Who are you?'

'I'm his wife.'

'He's already married.'

'His other wife.'

'You're his mistress?'

'No.'

It's a fatuous conversation. I want to stop myself. Why am I deigning to talk to her? Clearly, she's crazy. How did she get past security?

I try again. 'He can only have *one* wife. Are you saying he's a bigamist?'

13

Olivia shakes her head. 'I'm sorry, Joseph, I'm not making myself very clear. I know this comes as a shock. Your father, William, made a commitment to me. We married in Bali. It was a Buddhist ceremony.'

'He's never been to Bali.'

'You're mistaken.'

'He isn't a Buddhist.'

'No,' she replies, 'but I am.'

Is a Buddhist marriage legally recognised in the UK, I wonder. My body chooses this moment to freeze. It does that occasionally – locks up or seizes completely as though playing a game of musical statues and someone has stopped the music.

'Do you need your medication?'

How does she know about that?

'I can get you some water.' She touches my forearm.

'No!' I snap, brushing her hand away.

Olivia steps back as though suddenly frightened of me. She resumes her seat, reaching across the sheet to hold Dad's hand.

'I don't want you touching him.'

'Excuse me?'

'Get your hands off him or I'll call the police.'

'Go ahead.'

It occurs to me that nobody has contacted my mother. I take out my phone.

'You can't use that in here,' says Olivia, pointing to a sign. 'You'll have to go outside.'

I step closer to the bed, whispering angrily, 'I don't know who you are, or why you're here, but my father and my

14

mother have been married for sixty years. He doesn't have "other wives".'

'Just me,' she says softly.

'I want you to leave,' I say, furious with her.

'Please don't raise your voice.'

'I'll do as I damn well please.'

An ICU nurse arrives, drawn by our argument. Moon-faced and pretty, with dreadlocked hair, she tells us both to be quiet.

'This woman is not my mother,' I tell her. 'She's tricked her way in.'

The nurse looks at Olivia suspiciously. 'Is that true?'

'No, I'm his wife.'

'I've never seen her before,' I say. 'I want her out of here.'

Olivia pleads: 'I know you're upset, Joseph, but don't do this. Go and call your mother. I'll sit with William.'

Her belted coat has fallen open. Underneath she's wearing a pale green cocktail dress stained by something darker.

'Is that blood?'

She closes the coat. 'I found him. He was lying at the bottom of the stairs.'

'Where?'

'I told you. At the house in Chiswick. It's where we live.'

I shake my head. 'No! No! No!'

'I'm telling you the truth.'

'You're delusional.'

The nurse has heard enough. 'I want you both to leave.'

'Please. We'll be quiet,' says Olivia.

'I'm calling security,' says the nurse. 'They can sort this out.'

'Somebody has to stay,' says Olivia, looking at Dad.

'No! Both of you get out.' She's not going to change her mind.

Olivia collects her handbag from beneath the chair. I wait for her to leave first in case she tries something. I don't know what I expect – she could sabotage the machines or smother Dad with a pillow.

The ICU doors close behind us. Olivia takes a tissue from her coat pocket and blows her nose. 'I have heard so many good things about you Joseph, but I didn't think you'd be so cruel.'

She pauses, making sure I've heard, before moving away and taking a seat further along the corridor. She searches her handbag and finds another tissue.

I call my mother's number. The phone rings. I picture her padding down the hallway at the farmhouse in Wales, picking up the receiver, using her posh-sounding phone voice. But there's no answer. She has a mobile phone. I try the number.

She answers, shouting to be heard above the background noise.

'Joseph?'

'Where are you?'

'I'm on the train.'

'Are you coming to London?'

'No. Why?'

'Dad is in hospital. Intensive care.'

I hear her sudden inhalation.

'He's in the ICU. They operated last night. I'm here now. I thought they might have called you.'

'No.' Her voice is trembling.

'He has head injuries. I don't know all the details. You should be here.'

'Yes, of course . . . I'll . . . I'll . . .'

'What was Dad doing in London?' I ask.

'He had a board meeting. He left yesterday. What happened?'

'I think he fell down the stairs.'

'Do the girls know?'

She's talking about my sisters: Lucy, Patricia and Rebecca.

'I'm going to call them.'

'Please don't leave your father alone,' she says. 'Stay with him.'

'I will.'

After ending the call, I glance up and see two police officers emerge from the lifts — one in uniform and the other in plain clothes. The detective is older and heavier with wire-rimmed glasses and Nordic features. He talks to a nurse, who points them along the corridor in my direction. I wait for them, but they're not looking for me. They stop at Olivia, who looks up from her phone. I can't hear the conversation, but I see her grow agitated. She's been busted! Exposed as a liar. Good! In the same instant I see hurt rather than fear in her eyes.

They're preparing to leave. Olivia looks at her feet, as though she might have dropped something.

'Where are you taking her?' I ask, having moved closer.

The detective turns to face me, setting his legs apart. 'What's your name, sir?'

'Joseph O'Loughlin.'

17

'Are you related to William O'Loughlin?'

'He's my father.'

'Can I see some identification?'

I show him my driver's licence.

He motions to Olivia Blackmore. 'Do you know this woman?'

'No.'

'Have you ever seen her before?'

'Never. Why?'

The detective ignores the question and turns away, walking towards the lift. I follow. 'What happened to him? Was it an accident?'

Neither officer breaks stride. They're at the lift. I stop the doors from closing.

'Did she do this?'

'Please, step back,' says the detective.

'Where are you taking her?'

'Chiswick police station.'

The doors are closing. Olivia raises her eyes to mine.

'If he wakes up, tell him . . . tell him . . . I love him.'

3

My eldest sister Lucy lives in Henley, west of London, with her husband Eric, an air-traffic controller, and their three children whose names I can never remember because they all end in the same 'ee' sound. I punch out her number and listen to it ringing.

Lucy answers. My left arm trembles. She's in the car. The school run.

'Can you talk?'

'I'm on the hands-free. What's wrong?'

'Dad is in hospital. He had some sort of accident. They operated last night to relieve pressure on his brain.'

Her voice changes, rising higher. 'Was he driving?'

'A fall, I think. He's at St Mary's in Paddington.'

'Have you talked to him?'

'He's in a coma.'

'Christ! Where's Mummy?'

'She's catching a train.'

'What about Patricia and Rebecca?'

'I called you first.'

Lucy is the natural leader among my siblings – the competent, organised figure who arranges family gatherings, remembers birthdays and coordinates our 'secret Santa' present-buying each Christmas. Patricia, my middle sister, lives in Cardiff with her husband Simon, a criminal barrister. Rebecca, the youngest girl, is a high achiever who works for the World Bank in Geneva. I'm the baby of the family – the long-awaited boy, although not the Little Prince. I abdicated that position when I chose to become a psychologist rather than a surgeon, ending a medical dynasty that dated back more than a century.

'I'll call Patricia,' says Lucy, taking charge. 'Rebecca is in South Sudan. You might reach her on her mobile. I'll be there as soon as I can.'

After Lucy hangs up, I call Rebecca's mobile and leave a message, giving her the briefest of details, telling her not to worry and to call me. What should I do next? There must be other friends or family I can contact, but I don't want to share the news, not yet. Functioning on a kind of autopilot, I stare out the window at a skyline dotted with cranes and half-built office towers. Pigeons wheel across a pale blue sky that is marked by the chalk-like smudges of jets travelling in the troposphere. A day like this should be darker and bleak. It should mirror the news or my mood.

Returning to the ICU, I sit beside Dad and take his hand

– something I haven't done since I was a child. *Did I do it as a child? I must have done.*

I study his face. His hair, so white and thick, was dyed until his mid-fifties, but turned white overnight when he threw away the bottle and aged as gracefully as he lived. A stranger might believe the wrinkles around his eyes were laughter lines, but the runnels are deepest where his skin has folded most often, perfectly illustrating his complaining nature and general dissatisfaction with people, particularly his children, most notably me.

This feels strange, being so intimate. I don't think in my entire life I have spent ten minutes alone with Dad when he didn't demean, belittle or insult me. Maybe that's an exaggeration, but his opinions were mostly disapproving or judgemental. Children were to be seen and not heard. Never mollycoddled or over-praised.

There is no lightness about my father, no play or mischief. Growing up, I don't remember him singing ditties or doing silly dances or acting the goat. He didn't chase us around the garden, or play hide and seek, or put on funny voices. He didn't get us dressed or make us breakfast or drop us at school, or drive us to sport, or listen to us practise piano, or help with our homework. When we fell over and hurt ourselves, none of us ran to Dad, or cried his name, or crawled on to his lap.

I'm not saying he neglected us. Others fulfilled these tasks: my mother, nannies, au pairs or housekeepers. Dad was needed elsewhere. Required by the wounded or broken or diseased. He saved lives. He pioneered surgical techniques. He battled infections that ate children and illnesses that tore families apart.

Some women are referred to being 'natural mothers' and men as being 'natural fathers'. I don't know what that means. My father is simply my father. Stiff. Self-conscious. Opinionated. Cantankerous. Demanding. Absent.

Even when home, he would spend long hours in his study. If we were playing in the garden, we knew to keep the noise down or risk having him open the window and bellow for us to be quiet. One time Rebecca peed her pants at the sound of his voice, although she was notorious for peeing her pants when she got too excited.

When I was eight or nine I complained of being hungry and Dad denied me food all day so I could experience deprivation and appreciate the most basic of elements. Another time, when I forgot to keep the wood-fired Aga alight, he made everyone eat a cold supper, insisting my sisters 'share' my punishment.

Where was my mother in all this? In the middle. Keeping the peace.

She hugged, kissed, bathed, bandaged and mended. She told us every day that Dad loved us and made us say prayers for him.

As a boy, I realised very quickly that Dad wasn't like other fathers.

At social gatherings, he didn't stand around the barbecue, drinking beer and turning sausages, talking cricket or rugby. He stood on the fringes, a glass of fizzy water in his hand, wearing black brogues and grey flannel trousers even in the height of summer.

Socially awkward, he was always on the margins, not so much a square peg in a round hole, as a square peg in a world full of round holes. On a father-and-son camping trip (I was astonished when he agreed to come) we were sitting around a campfire when one of the other fathers said that we only use ten per cent of our brains.

'That's incorrect,' Dad replied. 'A lot of people make that mistake. They think that geniuses like Albert Einstein and Stephen Hawking use more of their brain than the rest of us. It's an idea propagated by self-improvement hucksters and people who join Mensa, but it's not true. Doctors have imaged the brain tens of thousands of times with MRI and PET scans. There are no inactive areas.'

'And what makes you such an expert?' said the other father, his voice hardening.

'I'm not an expert, I'm a doctor.'

'And that makes you God's gift.'

'I don't believe in God.'

People laughed around the campfire.

The other father said Dad was a smartarse.

'Clearly, I've upset you,' he replied. 'I apologise. There are many medical myths. People believe that sweating gets rid of toxins, or that reading in poor light damages eyesight, or we shouldn't go swimming after eating, or shaving hair makes it grow back thicker and darker. It's not true. Cold weather doesn't give us more colds. Coffee doesn't sober us up. Your heart doesn't stop when you sneeze. And one arsehole isn't any smarter than another, although proctology isn't really my field.'

I thought Dad was going to get punched, but he has one brilliantly disarming feature – a laugh that opens his mouth wide, showing all his teeth, and releasing a joyous rumble that warms the heart. When he laughs, others follow. Problem solved.

In the semi–darkness of the ICU, I notice the same nurse sitting on a high stool behind the machines.

'Was I talking out loud?'

She nods and steps into the light, introducing herself as Henrietta. Her Jamaican accent makes the name sound musical.

'Is that really William O'Loughlin?' she asks.

'Yes.'

'The whole hospital is talking about him.'

'What are they saying?'

'He's a famous doctor.'

'Once. Yes.'

Henrietta says she is due to change his dressings. I offer to help. She hands me a polished steel tray containing scissors, cotton gauze and compression bandages. Unwrapping the progressively bloody layers, I see the stapled stitches where my father's shattered skull has been patched together. I can see the dome of his half–shaved head, which is no longer symmetrical, but concave on the right like the shell of a hard–boiled egg that has been cracked with a spoon.

The sheet has been pushed down to my father's pale chest and I notice deep bruises on his ribcage and sides. Clearly, they're not from any recent fall or attempts at resuscitation. Bruises change colour over time. Red, blue and purple are the early colours. Greens appear after four or five days and yellow comes after a week.

I take out my phone and turn on the camera.

'You're not supposed to take pictures,' says Henrietta.

'These weren't caused by falling downstairs,' I say, holding my fist over the darkest of the bruises. 'See the shape. This line of discolouration came from knuckles. Someone gave him a beating.'

Henrietta lets me finish. She rewraps Dad's skull, cradling his head gently.

'Professor O'Loughlin,' says another voice. I turn to find a nursing sister. 'The neurosurgeon has asked to speak to you.'

Taking a final look at Dad, I follow her through the ICU to a patient lounge opposite the main doors. The pastel-painted room has sofas, vending machines and a rack of magazines. The surgeon is counting coins in his hand. He reaches into the change bin, the way a child might.

'You don't have spare pound, do you?' he asks.

I find one in my jacket.

'Excellent. Low blood sugar. I get the shakes if I skip meals.' He feeds coins into the machine and presses a button. A chocolate bar drops into the tray with a *thunk*.

'I'm Pete Hannover,' he says, offering his hand. Warm and chipper, he's about my age, dressed in chinos and an open-necked shirt that clings to his pot belly. He takes a bite of the chocolate bar, chewing and talking. 'Your father lectured at my university when I was in pre-med. A remarkable man.'

The word 'remarkable' can have so many different meanings.

'Is he going to live?' I ask. The bluntness of the question dispenses with the need for small talk.

'Let's start at the beginning,' says Hannover, pointing me to a sofa. He sits opposite, showing his ankles when he crosses his legs.

'Your father arrived at the hospital just after midnight, suffering from catastrophic head injuries. Paramedics had intubated him at the scene and had to resuscitate him twice in transit. He was unconscious and bleeding from both ears. His right pupil was enlarged and unresponsive.'

The word 'unresponsive' bounces around inside my head and I recall how the specialists had talked about Julianne when she was on life support.

'An immediate CT scan revealed traumatic brain injuries and an acute subdural haematoma.'

'Bleeding.'

'Yes. I operated immediately to reduce the pressure in his cranium and managed to remove several clots in his anterior lobe. William is now in a medically induced coma. This is important in case the ruptured blood vessels are unable to deliver the usual amounts of oxygen to his brain. He's also receiving diuretics to reduce the fluid in his body, and anti-seizure drugs. Once the swelling goes down, we'll scan him again. This could be five or six days from now. Then we'll slowly lower the dosage of the drugs and bring him back.'

Crumpling the chocolate wrapper, Hannover tosses it overhead at a nearby bin. Missing. 'Don't worry. I'm a better surgeon than basketballer.'

'Will he recover?'

'The pressure on his brain was enormous and is likely to have caused multiple smaller haemorrhages. We won't know the extent of the damage for a while yet. I assume you've spoken to the police about the assault.'

'What assault?'

He frowns. 'Your father's head injuries were caused by blunt force trauma.'

'I was told he fell down the stairs.'

'That might be the case, but he was also struck from behind. Repeatedly. The blows were so violent that pieces of his skull were driven into his brain.'

My mind rushes to judgement. The woman – Olivia Blackmore – she was covered in his blood. That's why the police are questioning her. She attacked him and made up some story of him falling down the stairs.

Hannover's mobile begins chirruping. He takes the call. 'I'm afraid I have to go,' he says. 'Should William require more surgery, I'll talk to you again. In the meantime, a neurologist will manage his care.'

'Thank you,' I say, shaking his hand. I squeeze too hard and he flinches.

'Occupational hazard,' he explains. 'I have to look after these.' He holds up his childlike palms, showing me his delicate fingers and slender wrists. 'Fit for purpose. Who wants a brain surgeon with big hands?'

After he's gone, I find a men's room. Locking myself in a cubicle, I close the seat and sit down. I want to weep, but have no idea who the tears would be for – my father, my mother, my sisters or me.

Washing my face in the sink, I glance at my dripping reflection, trying to see what others see. I have my mother's eyes, lips and nose. What is there of my father? Our names blur into each other. He is William Joseph and I am Joseph William, but that's where the similarities end.

A door opens behind me. A young boy of eleven or twelve enters the men's room, wheeling a drip on an upright stand and wearing a surgical cap. I smile at the boy, who looks away nervously. He's been told not to talk to strange men, or acknowledge them, which is sensible, but also sad. I wonder what's wrong with him. Is he sicker than my father? Is his life worth more? Does youth trump brilliance? I feel guilty for having such thoughts.

Back in the ICU, I take a seat beside Dad, unable to bring myself to hold his hand again. I lost a wife a year ago. I cannot lose anyone else. I have paid my dues. I've given. It's someone else's turn.

In my imagination, I see my dad's eyes open.

'All this fuss,' he says. 'I must be dying.'

'You're going to be fine,' I reply.

'Don't kid me, Joseph. I'm a doctor.'

4

Lucy arrives shortly before eleven, out of breath and peeling off layers in the overheated hospital. She hugs me as though I've been away for years. When did she start to smell like my mother?

'How is he?'

'Not good.'

'Dying?'

'Fighting.'

I tell her the details, leaving out the part about 'blunt force trauma' and the mysterious woman I found sitting by his bed. I tell myself I'm protecting her, but I don't know exactly why. If Olivia Blackmore attacked our father, she won't remain a secret for long.

I warn Lucy about what to expect, but she's still shocked

by the sight of Dad – the tubes from his mouth and nose; the drips and cables. Someone has written on the white bandage around his head with a black marker pen: NO BONE FLAP.

'Silly old duffer. What have you done, making us worry like this?' asks Lucy, making it sound like Dad has grazed his knee. She kisses his cheek. Strokes his hand. Her questions begin: 'Where was he found? Who called the ambulance? How did you find out?'

Each one leads to another. 'Why was he in Chiswick? What friend? Who is she?'

I can't keep fobbing her off and obfuscating.

'Olivia Blackmore. She says that she's married to Dad.'

Lucy's eyes widen and she grabs my arm, pulling me away from the bed. 'Who is this woman? And why would she say such a thing?'

'I don't know.'

Lucy makes a scoffing sound. 'Did you call the police?'

I take a deep breath and tell her all that I know, glimpsing the attack in my mind, the paramedics, the sirens and flashing lights, hospital doors crashing open, the white coats and theatre lights.

'You say her dress was covered in blood.'

'Yes.'

'Did she attack him?'

'She denies it.'

'But the police have arrested her.'

'They're talking to her.'

Lucy looks nonplussed and strangely unsure of herself.

30

'I don't think we should say anything to Mummy or Patricia – not until we know more.'

'Agreed.'

My mother arrives mid-afternoon. As always, she looks the epitome of the country doctor's wife, dressed in her travelling clothes: a tweed skirt, white blouse and pearls. Her grey perm is cut short, framing a wedge-shaped face. We hug. She kisses my cheek. Calls me 'Joseph, darling'.

'What happened? Have you spoken to him?'

'He's in a coma.'

'Where are the doctors? What are they doing? Do they know who he is?'

'They know.'

She looks around, thinking she's lost her handbag, which is still looped over her shoulder. Turning full circle, she finds the bag and chides herself for being so foolish.

I take her into the ICU. Sighting my father, she lets out a soft cry and bustles to his bedside, kissing his forehead and straightening his fringe as though expecting a photographer to arrive at any moment. I feel embarrassed. My parents rarely display affection. I don't think I've ever witnessed more than a peck on a cheek or a squeeze of the hand.

'Are you making a nuisance of yourself?' she asks, fixing the top button of his pyjamas. 'It's the pretty nurses, isn't it? You want to be looked after.'

Lucy sniffles. I hand her a packet of tissues. Her eyes say, *I told you she'd be like this*.

My mother is still talking, barely pausing for breath,

explaining that she's brought his slippers and a toothbrush. 'And don't worry, Voula Pierce is looking after the dogs.'

She takes a seat. Holds his hand. It's the same chair that Olivia Blackmore occupied a few hours ago.

'Where is Patricia?' she asks.

'She's coming,' I reply.

'And Rebecca?'

'I left her a message.'

Henrietta comes down off her stool. Only two visitors are allowed per patient. One of us will have to leave.

I volunteer. There are things I need to do. Talking to the police is one. My mother hugs me goodbye and instantly the years drop away. I'm a child again, lost in the warmth of her bosom and the folds of her skirt. Mum seems to feel it too, touching my cheek with her fingers.

'Thank you, Joseph. You're a good boy.'

5

Chiswick police station is a red-brick and concrete building with blue painted doors, twin flagpoles and a bulletin board appealing for eyewitnesses and advertising crime prevention programmes.

The station sergeant closes a copy of the *Daily Mail* and gets tiredly to his feet, as though irritated by another interruption. His white shirt has a pen stain on the breast pocket which matches the colour of his epaulettes.

'And you have information about this alleged assault,' he says, taking down my name.

'I'm the victim's son. I was hoping to speak to the detective in charge.'

He makes a call. I wait. The station foyer has a dozen plastic chairs. Only one of them is taken by a bald man dressed in a turtleneck sweater that makes his head look like an egg in an eggcup. He nods to me. We don't make eye contact again.

Instead I focus my thoughts on Olivia Blackmore, trying to estimate her age. Mid-forties. Well groomed. Expensively dressed. Her cocktail dress clung to her curves, showing off her figure. I can imagine her turning heads, but not my father's. God's-Personal-Physician-in-Waiting is not some ageing Lothario. He doesn't chase skirt or chat up women. He's conservative. Predictable. Honourable. Upright. Beige.

A lot of men reach mid-life and lament the passing of their youth and unfulfilled dreams. Some succumb to sharp new clothes, sports cars, adventure holidays and the lure of younger women. That's not William O'Loughlin. I'm not exaggerating when I say that my father has always seemed to be asexual, or completely uninterested in women unless they're presenting some surgical challenge, anaesthetised on his operating table.

A junior detective steps from the lift and motions me to follow. I'm taken upstairs to an incident room where rumpled men are sitting at rumpled desks, with coats hanging off the back of their chairs and ties lowered to half-mast.

Detective Inspector Stuart Macdermid is forty-plus, prematurely grey, with a weathered face that hangs on his skull like a partially deflated balloon. His right hand is swollen and twisted in on itself. Arthritis. Early onset. Painful. Holding a phone to his ear, he motions to a chair. I sit down. The detective doesn't seem to be talking to anyone. Either he's listening to someone, or using the moment to study me. I do the same, glancing around the office. A hand-signed Glasgow Rangers shirt is framed on the wall, beside team photographs of them crowned as Scottish champions, holding the trophy aloft as ticker tape rains down on their heads. Elsewhere there's a small bronze statue of a racehorse in full flight with the jockey out of the saddle, whip hand raised.

Macdermid puts down the phone and cocks an eyebrow. 'You got my message, Professor O'Loughlin.'

'What message?'

'I asked you to come.'

'I came of my own accord.'

He frowns and lets it pass. 'Well, you're here now.'

Opening his laptop, he hits the keyboard with one finger as though it's operated by brute force.

'Do you know a woman called Olivia Blackmore?'

'I met her this morning.'

'She claims to be married to your father.'

'She's lying.'

'They live together.'

'That's *her* story.'

'Have you proof that she's lying?'

'She's half his age.'

'Is that what bothers you – the age difference?' His faint Glaswegian accent makes it sound like he's mocking me.

'Her dress was covered in blood,' I say.

'Yes. I asked her about that. She claims to have comforted him until the paramedics arrived. They confirm her story.'

'She still could have beaten him.'

'Yes, which is why she's a suspect – the obvious one – but so far she's been cooperating fully, providing us with

DNA samples and her fingerprints. She also claims to have an alibi, which we're checking out.'

I feel tension knotted between my shoulder blades. 'There are old bruises on my father's body – on his ribs and lower back.'

Macdermid leans forward. 'What bruises?'

I take out my phone and find the photographs. 'I took these at the hospital. They're at least a week old. See the knuckle marks?'

Macdermid studies the images. 'Any idea why someone would work him over?'

'No.'

He picks up a pen and makes a note. 'I'll have someone photograph the bruises.'

'It could have been Olivia Blackmore.'

'We'll investigate that. In the meantime, when did you last see your father?'

'Two weeks ago. We had lunch at his club.'

'When did you last speak to him?'

'Thursday or Friday.'

The truth is I don't remember. I phone my mother every few days, but rarely my father, who isn't one for small talk or regular catch-ups.

'Does your father have a mobile phone?'

'He doesn't see the point of them.'

'Phones?'

'He thinks people should make appointments and keep them without needing to constantly text to say they're running five minutes late or parking outside, or walking through the door.'

36

Macdermid nods in agreement, while glancing at the mobile phone near his left hand.

'Did you know your father was in London? According to Mrs Blackmore, he's here most weeks.'

'Not every week,' I say defensively.

The detective holds my gaze for a moment, neither of us blinking. He casts his pen aside and leans back, scratching his stomach.

'I went to my school reunion a few weeks ago. Twenty-five years since I graduated. I didn't recognise half my old classmates. They were older, fatter, greyer, balder. Most of them bore no resemblance to the people they used to be. Then I realised that I was no different – old and grey and growing fat. I caught up with guys who I was convinced were going to rule the world one day, who finished up delivering parcels for a living. Women who I thought were goddesses, who now had brittle hair, Botox smiles and spare tyres around their middles. Not all of them. Some had bloomed late. Girls that nobody looked at in school were strutting around that reunion like debutantes, new and improved by diet, or exercise, or surgery, or blessed with good genes. And didn't they know it.'

Where is he going with this?

'Then there were the nerdy guys – the ones who got bullied at school – the pseuds and the teacher's pets. Some of them finished up making a killing in the City, living in Surrey with wives who were fifteen years younger and drop-dead gorgeous. People change, Professor. You can't predict who they'll become. You might think you can, but that's bullshit. Your old man got himself a hot young mistress

37

and set up house. Even convinced her they were married. He's not the first and won't be the last.'

'She's lying.'

'Why would she do that?'

'She wants to blackmail us.'

'With what?'

'She could go to the papers and sell her story.'

'Is William O'Loughlin really that famous?'

Once perhaps. Not any more.

Macdermid continues. 'Can you think of anyone who might want to hurt him? Anyone with a grudge?'

'He's a retired doctor.'

'Surgeons make mistakes. One slip of the knife . . .'

'He lives in Wales. He tends the roses and does *The Times* crossword. He doesn't have a mistress. Ask my mother. Ask anyone.'

'Where is your mother?'

'At the hospital.'

'I'll need to speak to her.'

'Why? She doesn't know anything.'

'We'll have to confirm her whereabouts on Sunday night.'

'You can't seriously think she attacked him.'

My sarcasm annoys the detective. He jabs a gnarled finger in my direction. 'Where were you at midnight last night?'

'At home in bed.'

'Alone?'

'Yes.'

He shows me a photograph. 'Have you ever visited this house? It's in Barrowgate Road, Chiswick.'

'No.'

There's a knock on the door. A woman appears with a tray. Afternoon tea. Only one mug. Macdermid uses his left hand to pick it up. He takes a sip.

'We know your father caught the train from Wales yesterday afternoon. A black cab dropped him at the house at about eleven fifteen. Is he the type of person to let a stranger into the house?'

'No.'

'Could he have met someone on the train and invited them home?'

'My father doesn't make friends easily.'

Macdermid makes another note. 'It could have been a botched robbery, although there were no signs of a forced entry and nothing appears to have been taken. There have been several home invasions in West London, but this doesn't quite fit the pattern.'

'What pattern?'

'A gang usually targets couples – tying up the wife and pistol-whipping the husband until one of them gives up the combination of the safe or tells them where the valuables are hidden.' He sips his tea. 'We're working the usual areas – tracing your father's movements, his phone calls, investigating anyone who might have reason to attack him. We're also collecting CCTV footage from street cameras and neighbouring houses.'

'What about forensics?'

'SOCO pulled prints from the house and took samples. We'll run the results through the database, but any DNA won't be helpful unless we find a suspect.'

He changes tack. 'Let's assume, for argument's sake, that Olivia Blackmore is telling the truth.'

'She's not.'

'Who might know about your father's business affairs – his assets, life insurance policies, a will . . .'

'Kenneth Passage, my father's lawyer.'

'Would he be aware of William's double life?'

I hesitate before answering. Kenneth is my father's oldest friend. If anyone knew about Olivia, it would be him. I scroll through the contacts on my phone and find his number. Macdermid makes a further note and looks at his watch, before standing and moving to the door.

'Tell your mother that I'd like to speak to her.'

'She won't want to leave Dad.'

'He's not going anywhere.'

Macdermid holds out his left hand for me to shake. 'I'm sorry about your father, Professor. I hope he pulls through.'

'Where is Olivia Blackmore now?'

'She's been released.'

'Can you stop her visiting the hospital?'

'How am I supposed to do that?'

'Warn her off.'

Macdermid's gnarled hand turns the doorknob. 'Unless you have some evidence that she's a threat, I have no grounds for telling her to stay away.'

'Please,' I say. 'My mother doesn't know about her.'

'Well, you'd best go and tell her.'

6

Emma will be home from school by now. My housekeeper Andie will have met her at the east gate and taken her for hot chocolate at a café on the walk home. Andie is Australian and speaks with an Antipodean inflection that turns every sentence into a question; a habit Emma has started to pick up.

I call the flat. Emma answers. 'How's Granddad? Is he OK? Don't let him stay in hospital.'

'He can't be moved. Not yet.'

Emma wants to argue, but that would mean mentioning Julianne and acknowledging what happened. I change the subject, asking her about school. She goes quiet.

'Is everything OK?' I ask.

'Yes.'

I try to remember her best friend's name.

'Is Zoe having a party for her birthday?'

'Yes.'

'What's she doing?'

'I don't know. She didn't invite me.'

'Did you have a fight?'

'Not really.'

Emma doesn't sound too disappointed, but I feel for her. Julianne would know what to say. She was good at this sort of thing; sorting out problems or finding silver linings.

'Are you coming home?' Emma asks.

'Not yet, Squeak.'

'Can we get takeaway?'

'OK. Tell Andie I'll pay her back later. Do your homework?'

'It's done.'

'That's what you said last night.'

'Got to go.'

I walk along Shepherd's Bush Road, heading for Hammersmith tube station. Dark clouds have been gathering all afternoon, massing on the western front. Their first salvos arrive, sleeting rain falling diagonally, smiting my cheeks and clinging to my hair. Commuters clog the pavements, hurrying with their heads down, collars turned up and umbrellas unfurled.

I call Lucy from the station. She and Patricia have worked out a roster so that someone will be with Dad every hour of the day and night.

'Mum wants to do tonight,' says Lucy. 'Can you take over in the morning?'

'Sure.'

'Is six too early?'

'Six is fine.'

'Did you talk to the police?'

'They think it could have been a botched robbery or a case of mistaken identity.'

Lucy doesn't ask about Olivia Blackmore, which means my mother is probably within earshot. I offer to call her later and tell her more.

My train arrives, vibrating the rails and creating a pressure wave of rushing air. Doors open. Bodies press forward. Shoulder to shoulder in the crowded carriage, I wonder how many of these people are leading double lives or have secret families. I'm not shocked by the idea. I've read about such things – the Zumba instructor who moonlights as a call girl, or the glamorous estate agent unmasked as a Russian spy. Secrets are valuable. We lie to protect a relationship, or get a job, or keep the peace, or win the girl, or protect a child. In a deep psychological sense, we have no self unless we have a secret. We grab for them whenever we begin losing ourselves in our social group or work or marriage. We reassert our identity as somebody apart.

As a psychologist, I've counselled cross-dressers, transvestites, gender-conflicted teens, sex addicts and closet alcoholics – all of whom hid their secrets, sometimes from themselves. One of my friends had a father who died of AIDS. It was only afterwards that his family discovered his regular visits to gay clubs and steam rooms. A colleague at my first NHS hospital was extradited back to Argentina and convicted of running a death squad during the 'Dirty War'. These are life-changing secrets, not small white lies or sins of omission.

43

Up until now, I've never had reason to question my father's integrity or doubt his love for my mother. He is a man of his word, who has never asked me to uphold values or make sacrifices that he hasn't made himself.

I don't want to believe that he's a liar, a coward and a betrayer, but what if he is? Any man who keeps a separate family is sailing on a sea of lies, an ocean of untruths piled one upon the other until one day something triggers the tsunami and washes everything away.

It *cannot* be true.

It *must* not be true.

The train is pulling into Barons Court. Almost without thinking, I push my way off, apologising to my fellow travellers. I'm on the platform. I find the stairs and the street, now knowing what comes next.

7

The cab drops me at one end of Barrowgate Road and I walk the length of the tree-lined avenue, which is flanked by handsome Victorian houses, each with the same gabled red-tiled roof and white-painted windows. The sleet has turned to a misty rain, creating haloes around the streetlights that seem to float unsuspended above the ground, like helium balloons.

Thirty yards ahead of me I notice a woman seated on a low brick wall. Olivia Blackmore is wearing different clothes – a long skirt and oversized sweater. The police must have taken her dress and coat for analysis. Beads of rain cling to her shoulders and her hair.

'You're getting wet,' I say.

She looks up, surprised, and seems to reassemble herself before my eyes, straightening her back, thrusting out her chin defiantly. 'What are you doing here?'

'I thought we should talk.'

'Why, so you can insult me again?'

'I'm sorry for what I said at the hospital.'

Olivia can't maintain her anger, which transforms with a sigh into exhausted sadness. She glances at the house. I notice a set of keys in her bunched fist. Painted nails. One broken.

'How long have you been out here?'

'I can't go inside.'

'Why not?'

'It's where . . . I've seen . . .'

I understand now. 'Can you stay somewhere else?'

'No.'

'You must have friends . . . family . . .'

'I don't want to tell them, not yet. I want to wait until William wakes up.'

I reach down and take the keys from her. 'Come on.'

Unlocking the door, I push it open and look along the hallway. The forensic technicians have left their mark. Rugs have been rolled up and taken away. Blood splatters photographed and measured. Surfaces dusted and vacuumed.

At the bottom of the stairs, a large pool of blood has soaked into the hardwood floor like a permanent shadow. My stomach spasms and I swallow hard.

'I can call someone,' I say. 'There are companies that clean up after things like this.' I want to say suicides and murders, but hold my tongue.

'I don't want strangers coming here,' says Olivia, unable to cross the threshold.

'Give me your hand. Close your eyes.'

Stepping around the blood, I lead her deeper into the house to a modern kitchen with brushed steel appliances and marble benchtops. Making her sit down, I fill the electric kettle, setting it to boil. Mugs are found. Teabags. Sugar. Milk.

'When did you last eat?' I ask.

'I'm not hungry.'

Opening the fridge, I find an airtight plastic container with a selection of cheeses. I make up a plate and set it down on the table.

'How is William?' she asks.

'The same.'

'Is someone with him?'

'My mother and sisters.'

She takes a deeper breath. 'I want to see him.'

'That's not a good idea.'

'Please.'

Studying her more closely, I see a narrow face with prominent ears and traces of sun damage around her eyes. Her sleeves are pulled up, revealing tanned forearms, indicating that she works out of doors, or plays sport. Her tights are laddered near her left ankle. I doubt if she's noticed.

'How long have you lived here?' I ask.

'Fifteen years.'

'With my father?'

'Yes.'

'Mrs Blackmore.'

'Please, call me Olivia.'

'I hope you won't be offended, Olivia, if I treat everything you tell me with a degree of scepticism.'

'You think I'm lying?'

'I need convincing.'

She nods and tries not to look hurt. 'There are things you have to learn about William.'

'I *know* he's not a bigamist.'

'How often do you talk to him?'

'Every few weeks.'

'No. You talk to your mother, not your father.'

How can she possibly know that?

'This isn't about me,' I say. 'If you're living with my father, you must have evidence. Photographs. Letters. Emails.'

'Of course.'

'Let me see them.'

Olivia rises slowly and opens a cupboard above the fridge, taking out a bottle of Scotch and two glasses.

'Would you like one?'

I shake my head.

'Your medication . . . I forgot.'

Again . . . how does she know?

She splashes a finger of Scotch into a tumbler and swallows it in a gulp, flinching at the burn. She pours another and carries it back to the table. Having centred the glass between her forearms, she raises her eyes to mine.

'I will try to explain, but I will not tell you everything because there are details your father must choose to reveal . . . or not. William has a right to his privacy.' There it is again, a faint accent. Romanian or Hungarian, perhaps. 'If I fail to convince you of the truth, it will be my fault not his, but please do me the courtesy of not interrupting, or rolling your eyes or shaking your head. I will try not to skip ahead. I will lay down the pieces in their right order.'

Olivia takes another sip of Scotch.

'I married young and was widowed. I didn't intend to fall in love again. I was perfectly reconciled to being on my own. I may say this, but I have always had men looking after me. Does that make me weak?' She looks at me for an answer. I don't have one.

'I didn't intend falling in love with William. It just happened. But you must not blame your father. He is the same man today as he was yesterday. Kind. Gentle. Loving. We met in difficult circumstances. I was in a car accident. Bleeding. Broken. The fire brigade had cut me from the wreckage. I had a compound fracture of my right femur. Others wanted to amputate, but William insisted he could perform the operation. He saved my leg.'

Getting to her feet, she reaches for the hem of her skirt.

'Turn around.'

'What?'

She motions with her hand. I do as she asks, looking at the window.

'Look,' she says.

I turn back. Olivia has rolled down her tights and lifted her skirt to reveal her right knee, where puckered lines of scar tissue traverse the kneecap, running for ten inches down either side.

'He used metal pins and fused the bone,' she explains. 'I can walk because of William. I can run. I can work.'

Her raised skirt reveals the edge of her underwear. I

lower my eyes. She self-consciously drops the fabric, smoothing it down.

'William came to visit me when I woke up. "I know who you are," he said. "I once saw you play at Wimbledon. You were only fifteen." He remembered the match because I took a set off Martina Navratilova. That's why he wanted to save my leg. He knew what I'd been.'

'A tennis player?'

'Yes.'

'My father is a tennis tragic.'

Olivia laughs. 'That is a good description. If he's a tennis tragic, I am his tragic heroine.' I haven't seen her smile until now.

'I spent six weeks in hospital. William came to visit me almost every day. He asked about my career – why I didn't go further. "I thought you were going to win Wimbledon," he said. "You had such great hands." "You need more," I told him. "I didn't have enough."'

Olivia is staring into the glass. 'I had three more operations on my leg. William performed all of them. I thought I'd never play tennis or coach again, but William never doubted it. He suggested a physiotherapist who worked with elite athletes. I couldn't afford him, but William took care of the bills. I promised to repay him, but he refused. He said he only wanted one thing: a lesson.'

'Tennis?'

'Eight months after the accident, we hit up together at his tennis club. It became a regular thing. Once a week, sometimes more.'

'You were coaching him?'

'Yes. Maybe. Not really.'

'But it went further.'

'One day William asked me to dinner. He drove me home. We kissed. One thing led to another . . .'

'You knew he was married.'

'Yes.'

'But that didn't stop you.'

'It was too late.'

'How can it be too late?'

'I was in love.'

I stop myself making a scoffing sound, but Olivia can see my reaction.

'I did not ask William to leave your mother or abandon his children, or sacrifice his career. His secrets were his secrets. His life was his life.'

'He betrayed his wife.'

'He loved us both.'

'How do you know that?'

'He told me.'

Again, I want to laugh at her naivety, but she refuses to concede.

'Love does not have to be halved, Joseph. It can be doubled or tripled. Look at you and your sisters. Your father didn't love any of you less when another child was born.'

'You're right,' I reply. 'He was father of the year.'

Anger sparks in her eyes. 'Please do not insult him – not in this house, not in front of me.' Her knuckles have turned white on the empty glass. Would she throw it at me? Could she smash a man's skull?

'This affair – when did it start?'

'I was thirty-two.'

'And he was . . . ?'

'About your age.'

'He was old enough to be your father.'

'Are you saying you couldn't fall in love with a woman in her thirties?'

'This is not about me.'

'Are you sure?' she asks. 'Isn't it why you're here?'

I cannot hold her gaze.

'You're offended by my existence. You don't want to believe that your father fell in love with me, or that we made a life together. Why is it so strange? He had your mother in the country and me in London. He divided his time between us. I saw him most weeks. He would come down on Sunday and go back to Wales on Thursday or Friday. I wasn't jealous, or possessive. Sometimes, when he travelled, I went with him. He would introduce me as his assistant.'

'Weren't you worried that you'd bump into someone that knew my mother?'

'A couple of times it almost happened. Nine, maybe ten years ago, we went to Paris and met someone who went to school with you.'

'With me?'

Olivia nods. 'He saw William kissing me and knew that I wasn't your mother. I think he assumed that William had divorced and remarried. Another time we saw Rebecca in London.'

'You saw my sister?'

'We were leaving a restaurant off Sloane Square. Your

father introduced me as a former patient and told Rebecca we played mixed doubles together. She didn't bat an eyelid. I remember she complimented me on my dress. There were other near misses, but William and I have always been discreet. We don't go to charity balls, or big public events where there might be photographers or gossip columnists.'

'What about your family?'

'They're in Romania.'

'Do they know about my mother?'

'No. They like William because he makes me happy.'

So far everything Olivia has told me sounds perfectly plausible, but how does a man keep a second family secret for twenty years? How has he avoided letting things slip? It's one thing to erect walls, but another to compartmentalise every aspect of your life, so that nothing overlaps or pollutes or threatens your secrets.

'What am I going to do if he dies?' Olivia asks.

The question surprises me because it's so unexpected. People normally keep such dark thoughts to themselves, preferring to be stoic and optimistic in public at least. Olivia has set down her glass and lowered her head. Her shoulders are shaking and I hear a quiet sob.

A part of me wants to comfort her, while another part wants to recoil. This woman has dropped into my life like a grenade, causing nothing but chaos, yet she's distraught and alone.

'He's not going to die,' I say, shifting my chair and putting an arm around her shoulders.

'Did they tell you that – the doctors? Is he going to wake up? When?'

Unable to answer, I ask if she has a bucket and scrubbing brush. Maybe a mop.

Olivia wipes her eyes and shows me to the laundry where I fill a bucket with hot soapy water.

'You don't have to do that.'

'It's fine.'

Even as I say the words, I feel my stomach heave. I quit medical school because I couldn't stand the sight of blood. It's why I don't watch TV medical dramas or B-grade horror movies and why I once fainted in an A&E after Charlie fell off her bike and split open her forehead.

Carrying the bucket to the hallway, I kneel and scrub at the floorboards where the blood has settled into the grain of the wood like a birthmark. Olivia watches me from the kitchen. Her eyes are unnervingly changeable, as though capable of taking on the colour of her surroundings.

'Where were you last night?' I ask.

'At the theatre.'

'Were you expecting him?'

'William called me from the train. I had my phone turned off. I didn't get the message until later.'

'What time did you get home?'

'Midnight.'

'Were the lights on or off?'

'The house was dark. I thought he'd gone to bed.'

'You opened the door and turned on the hallway light.'

'Yes. I didn't see him straight away. I bent to pick up the note.'

'What note?'

'It was lying on the doormat beneath the letter plate.'

'What did it say?'

She tries to remember. 'Something like, *I can't do it. Find someone else.*'

'Can't do what?'

'I don't know.'

'Where is the note now?'

'The police took it.'

Olivia answers without hesitation or pause, almost taking comfort from the details. Either she's telling the truth, or has practised her story.

'I saw him lying at the bottom of the stairs. I thought he must have fallen. I called the ambulance and cradled his head. When he stopped breathing, I tried to resuscitate him until they arrived. There were four of them . . . paramedics. They opened syringes and put a tube down his throat and tried to find his heartbeat. They found it once, but lost it again. I remember one of them talking on a mobile phone, telling the hospital to contact the neurosurgeon. They put him on a trolley and took him out. I wanted to go with William but they wouldn't let me. I rode in the second ambulance. They took him straight into surgery. I had to fill out the paperwork. I gave them your number. I didn't know what else to do.'

Olivia squeezes her eyes shut, as though fearful the memory might bring the violence back. I push the bucket along the floorboards. Kneeling again, I notice a small circle of blood the size of a fifty-pence piece in the centre of the hallway. Three feet away there is another . . . then another . . . each fainter than the first.

'What was he wearing?' I ask.

She pauses to think. 'Trousers . . . a shirt . . . He only had one slipper, the left one. His other slipper was at the top of the stairs. I remember thinking his foot would get cold. I wanted to put it on him.'

Mentally, I'm picturing the scene, piecing together the attack. My father was hit from behind and fell forwards, tumbling down the stairs, bouncing between the wall and the bannister. His assailant followed and continued the attack, hitting him multiple times, raising something heavy above his or her head, spraying blood on the wallpaper and stairway runner.

Emptying and refilling the bucket, I begin again, using a mop to clean with fresh water; wiping down the walls, using a rag to get into the difficult corners between the bannisters.

Afterwards, I empty the bucket and take off the rubber gloves, propping the mop on the back steps, using the moment to check the locks. We're in the kitchen again. Olivia has gone quiet. Her long hair is bundled at the back of her neck, held in place by pins and clips. A strand has pulled loose. She brushes it away carelessly. It falls back again.

'You're more handsome in person,' she says, apropos of nothing. 'I've only ever seen you in photographs or on TV. I saw you on the roof of that hospital when you talked the boy down – the one with cancer.'

'Malcolm.'

'Do you remember all their names?'

'No.'

'Is Malcolm still alive?'

I shake my head.

Olivia blinks at me sadly. 'I once thought of making an appointment to see you. I was going to invent a phobia or some emotional problem.'

'Why?'

'Out of curiosity. William told me so much about you and your sisters – I wanted to meet you.'

'Really?'

'You sound surprised.'

'My father barely acknowledges my existence.'

'You're wrong. He loves you. He's always talking about you. He says you're quite brilliant.'

Are we talking about the same man?

'I feel at a disadvantage because I know so little about you.'

'You only have to ask.' Our eyes meet and she looks away. 'William says you're very good at reading people.'

'Does that bother you?'

'No. Yes. I don't know.'

'Tell me who you are.'

'I'm a loved woman and a wife.'

'My father has a wife.'

'He married both of us.'

'You keep saying that, but haven't shown me any proof. Where is the physical evidence – the photographs, the letters, a marriage certificate?'

Annoyance flashes across Olivia's face. 'Come with me.'

I follow her along the hallway to a sitting room furnished with squashy sofas, bookshelves and a French polished display cabinet with twin glass doors. Olivia opens a drawer and takes out a key. She unlocks the cabinet, revealing a shelf of bound notebooks. Dozens of them. Running her finger along the spines, she pulls one free.

'William keeps a journal. This isn't the most recent one – the police took that away – but one of his earlier ones. He likes to write down his thoughts and collect mementos. I'm not supposed to look at them, but, given the circumstances . . .'

Olivia opens the pages. Loose scraps of paper tumble out. She bends quickly to pick them up. There are ticket stubs, press clippings, photographs, receipts, brochures and theatre programmes. Olivia turns over a photograph and shows me. She and Dad are standing in a garden, each holding a glass of wine. He's dressed casually in linen trousers and a loose-fitting shirt. A pink cashmere sweater is knotted around his neck and his stone-coloured hair is swept back. Olivia has her arm tucked through his and has posed with the toe of her front foot pointing at the camera, raising her chin, mischief in her smile.

Since when did Dad start wearing loafers and pink sweaters?

'That was taken on William's sixtieth birthday,' she says. 'We had a drinks party in the garden.'

She hands me a second photograph, which shows a tennis foursome. Dad and Olivia are side by side at the net, holding a trophy. 'We won the mixed doubles six years in a row,' she explains, warming to her task. Taking a seat on the sofa next to me, she rests the journal on her knees. Another photograph shows them on a dance floor. My father has tipped Olivia back and is leaning in as though about to kiss her.

He never dances. He never kisses.

The next image is from a holiday in the Lake District. They're sitting on a drystone wall with the sun setting in the background, edging dark clouds with rays of light. Olivia is laughing, throwing back her head, flirting with the lens, aware of her beauty. I turn over the image and see the inscription: *Ten glorious years and getting more beautiful by the day.*

She selects another journal, opening the pages. There are more pictures of picnics, holidays, dinner parties and anniversaries.

'That was my fortieth,' says Olivia. My father is on his feet, making a toast. He's wearing a silly paper hat and drinking champagne. Dozens of glasses are raised. People I don't recognise. Her friends? His?

'Did they all know?' I ask.

'Know what?'

'That my father was already married.'

Olivia shrugs. 'I don't think people cared.'

I examine more photographs. One shows them on a cross-Channel ferry, standing at a railing as the wind blows their hair at all angles. Another is of Olivia alone on a beach, holding herself in an awkward pose, self-conscious about her bikini. My father has written: *Baggins, Portugal, 2004.*

'He calls me Baggins,' says Olivia.

'Why?'

'I have large feet. William says they make me look like a Hobbit.'

I glance at her feet and she grows self-conscious, tucking them under the sofa.

I ask her why she didn't find someone else. She's attractive. Well spoken. Elegant. 'You're half his age.'

'Thank you for the compliment, but I'm fifty-one.'

I calculate how old I must have been when my father met Olivia. Thirty-six. Married. Living in London. Charlie had been born a year earlier.

'Why choose my father?'

'Maybe he chose me.'

'That's not an answer.'

Olivia smiles. 'William made me laugh. He was kind. He came from a different world.'

'What do you mean by different?'

'Tennis is full of narcissists.'

'Medicine is the same.'

'Yes, but William didn't have to impress me. We weren't competing.'

I look around the sitting room – seeing it in a different light. Every single item is pregnant with meaning, revealing something new about my father. I can picture him here. I can see him pouring whisky into a cut-glass tumbler, reading a newspaper and chatting about the events of the day. Real-life scenes from an ordinary marriage.

Olivia's account jars at my senses, yet she has the evidence. She has made her case, exposing two decades of disassembling, lies and calculated deceit. We were loyal, but we've been abandoned. Orphaned. What was my father thinking? Did he honestly imagine he could keep his mistress a secret? And yet he's managed to do so for nearly twenty years.

Olivia seems to read my mind.

'Life is short, Joseph. I don't believe we are given any

second chances or do-overs. We grab happiness where we can. I love your father and he loves me.'

Night has fully arrived and rain streaks the windows. Olivia no longer seems nervous in the presence of a psychologist. Occasionally, she brushes away a question, saying, 'William must answer that.'

Several journals are stacked on the coffee table. I want to read them all in the hope that I might finally understand a man who has cast such a huge shadow over my life.

'Can I take them with me?' I ask.

'I don't think William would like that.'

'Have you read them?'

'No.'

She returns the journals to the cabinet and turns the key. I have more questions – like the bruising I found on Dad's body – but I won't press Olivia. I have nothing to gain from alienating her or making allegations that I can't substantiate.

Her phone begins ringing. She excuses herself and takes the call. I mouth the word, 'bathroom'. She points upstairs.

I climb to the first landing and discover the bathroom. Turning on a tap to mask the sound, I open the cabinet above the sink and search the medications, looking for a name on the pill bottles: *W. J. O'Loughlin*. Statins for his cholesterol. Iron tablets. Vitamins.

Leaving the tap running, I quietly open the door and cross the landing to the main bedroom. Olivia is still talking on the phone downstairs. Opening the double wardrobe, I examine the clothes. One side belongs to Olivia. The other has shelves of neatly arranged cashmere sweaters, polo shirts, tennis shorts, jeans and shoes. *I have never seen my father wear jeans.* His wardrobe in Wales is full of corduroy trousers and tweed jackets for casual wear and Savile Row suits and Jermyn Street shirts for business.

Reading glasses rest on a half-finished book by Ian McEwan on the bedside table. I open the top drawer and notice a strip of pills in foil packaging. Half of them are punched out. I recognise the brand. Viagra.

Walking around the bed, I open the drawers on Olivia's side. The top one has earplugs, night-creams, lip-balm and moisturisers. The lower one has nightdresses and lingerie. Some of the items are lacy and sheer. Did he choose them, or did she? I don't want to know.

Closing the drawer, I glance around the bedroom again and notice something at the top of the wardrobe, pushed out of sight, but still visible. I have to stand on a chair to reach the long, thin object, which is wrapped in an old cotton sheet. Heavier than I expect, I need both hands to pull it down. The fabric falls away, revealing a shotgun. My first reaction is to drop it, but I clutch it even tighter.

A floorboard creaks. I turn. Olivia's eyes go wide.

'What are you doing?'

I have no answer. No excuse. I expect her to be angry. She's not.

'Why do you have this?' I ask, still holding the shotgun.

'William insisted. He brought it from the farmhouse.'

'Why?'

'Protection.'

'From what?'

Olivia doesn't answer. Instead, she takes the shotgun from me and rolls it tightly in the sheet.

'My father hates guns,' I say.

'Yet still he owns one.'

I don't think she means to be flippant, but that's how it sounds.

Dad has always had two shotguns at the farm, which he keeps locked in a gun safe in the basement. He used them for pheasant hunting and to shoot clay pigeons at sporting fairs, but I can't recall the last time he did either.

'It should be locked away,' I say.

Olivia holds the shotgun out to me. 'Would you like to take it?'

I don't want to touch it.

There is a long silence. I can't tell if Olivia is challenging me or being sincere. When I don't respond, she stands on tiptoes and slides the gun on to the top of the wardrobe. I can still feel the oily residue on my fingertips.

'I think you've seen enough,' she says. 'I'm tired.'

Following me downstairs, she steps carefully across the newly cleaned floor. I collect my coat from a hook in the hallway.

'He dresses differently in London,' I say.

'Yes.'

'Is he a different person with you?'

'I don't know.' Olivia opens the front door, pulling it back and bracing her body against it. 'Do you believe me now?'

'Yes.'

'Please let me see William.'

'No.'

'I'll come anyway.'

'Let me talk to my mother. I'll call you tomorrow.'

She drops her head and draws in a ragged breath. I step outside, wondering how I should say goodbye. Olivia makes the decision for me, leaning forward, kissing my right cheek, then the left. She rests her head on my chest for a moment, as though listening to my heartbeat.

'We both love him, Joseph.'

Love him? I'm not sure if I even know him.

8

Scooping fried rice and chicken chow mein from waxed-paper boxes, I eat my reheated dinner at the kitchen bench. Emma is perched on the stool opposite, dressed in her pyjamas. Her top teeth are crooked, but the orthodontist wants to wait until the last of her milk teeth have fallen out before she gets braces.

'We saved you a fortune cookie,' she says, showing me the lone cookie on an enormous white plate.

'What did your cookie say?'

'Something I lost is going to turn up soon.'

'What have you lost?'

She shrugs. 'I won't know until I find it.'

Out of the mouths of babes . . .

Meanwhile, Andie is packing the dishwasher and wiping the kitchen benches. She's been fussing over me since I got home. Big and brash with sun-bleached hair and a raucous laugh, she's wearing skinny-legged jeans that cling so tightly to her curves that flesh spills over the waistband and occasionally becomes visible when she reaches up to a higher shelf.

'What was Granddad doing in London?' asks Emma.

'He had some business.'

'How's Grandma?'

'Sad.'

'Does Charlie know? We should call her.'

She's right. I completely forgot. I look at the clock and ponder Charlie's movements. She works three nights a week at a pub, collecting glasses and serving meals. Usually she calls when she's walking back to her digs because she feels safer that way. Not that Oxford is dangerous, but experience has taught Charlie to be careful.

'Will she come home?' asks Emma.

'I don't know.'

In truth, I know exactly what Charlie will do – catch the first bus or train to London. She loves her grandparents and her aunts and uncles. I wish I could protect her from this. I wish I could guarantee her a long life of unremitting happiness, but that's not realistic or even wise. We should wish our children full lives, jam-packed with triumph and tragedy, boredom and excitement, beautiful, messy, passionate and worth celebrating. I have spent my career treating people who believe that everybody around them is prettier, brighter, richer, happier and more fulfilled. My task is not to make them happier, but to manage their expectations; to help them cope.

Emma has gone quiet. I can tell when she's battling conflicting thoughts. Her forehead creases and goes smooth, as though she's conducting a silent argument with herself.

'Did something happen today?' I ask.

'No!'

Her answer is too quick and strident. The silence expands.

'I didn't do anything wrong,' she says. 'No matter what they say.'

'Who are they?'

'Nobody.'

'What do they say you did?'

'Nothing.'

'OK, that's good.'

I keep eating. With great reluctance, Emma goes to her schoolbag and takes out an official-looking envelope. Then she announces that she's tired and going to bed.

'Shouldn't we talk about this?'

'Tomorrow.'

She hugs me hard, before turning quickly and disappearing into her bedroom.

'Did you know about this?' I ask Andie.

She shakes her head.

Sliding my thumb under the flap of the envelope, I pull out a single sheet of paper.

Dear Professor O'Loughlin,
I write to you with mixed emotions. Regrettably, your daughter Emma was involved in an incident in the playground today which resulted in a child being taken to hospital. Thankfully,

Petra's injuries are relatively minor, but could have been much more serious. As you will appreciate, we make student safety our top priority at North Bridge House, which is why I'm writing to you.

This is not the first time Emma has been involved in an altercation with a fellow student. As a result, she is being placed on probation for the rest of the term. The conditions of this probation are:

1. The child must be able to be academically successful and willing to develop good work habits.
2. The child must be well disciplined.
3. The child must be respectful of teachers and fellow students.
4. Parents must be cooperative.

If Emma breaches any of these conditions over the remaining weeks of this term I will have no option but to exclude her from the school. I am also concerned that you have not responded to my two previous letters (15 September and 12 October) which requested a meeting between yourself and the school counsellor.

Yours sincerely,
Dr Christine Houten
Headmistress
Cc: Permanent File
Classroom teacher

What previous letters? I should summon Emma and demand an explanation, but it's late and I've had enough drama for one day. I'll sort it out tomorrow when I'm rested and medicated.

Charlie calls me when she's walking home from the pub. I can hear the raindrops hitting her umbrella and the swish of tyres on wet road. I tell her about her grandfather. She's annoyed that I didn't phone sooner.

'I'll catch a train in the morning.'

'There's nothing you can do.'

'I can visit him. I can hold his hand. I can help you look after Emma.'

'What about your lectures?'

'Most of them are recorded. I can talk to my tutors.'

I don't mention Olivia Blackmore because I know Charlie will quiz me for all the details. Instead, I ask about her course and her college and whether she's found a boyfriend.

'You don't have to do that,' she says.

'Do what?'

'Act like you're my mother.'

'Fathers can ask questions like that.'

'Yes, but they don't. Fathers are supposed to warn boyfriends off.'

'That's a cliché.'

'And how do clichés start?'

I hear a bicycle bell tinkling in the background. Charlie says hello to someone.

'I have to go.'

'Who's there?'

'A friend.' She hears the concern in my voice. 'He's not a rapist, Dad. He's in my psych classes.'

69

'What's his name?'

'Brendon. Do you want to have a word with him? You could tell him about your shotgun.'

'Very funny.'

'Love you. See you tomorrow.'

9

Andie is going to stay the night and take Emma to school in the morning. I can hear her now in Charlie's room, watching YouTube videos of *The Graham Norton Show* and snorting with laughter.

Opening my laptop on the kitchen table, I type 'Olivia Blackmore' into a search engine. The page refreshes. I look down the list. The top result is for the 'Blackmore Tennis Academy' – a coaching school in South London. Summoning the page, I read the history. The academy was founded by former British Davis Cup coach, Todd Blackmore, in 1984. Olivia Blackmore is the director of coaching. I click on her photograph and read her biography.

Born in Romania in 1967, Olivia Szabo was a tennis prodigy, who at the age of eleven became Romania's national under-fourteen champion and at fifteen won the junior singles title at

Wimbledon before turning professional in 1982. A former British number one, Olivia is now a top-rated coach who has mentored many of the UK's finest young tennis players.

I open more links and find a profile published in the *Guardian* in 1980. Olivia, aged thirteen, had just arrived in Britain on a tennis scholarship. The youngest of seven children, she had grown up in western Romania, as part of the German minority. 'I'm very happy to be here,' Olivia told the journalist. Asked about her ambitions, she said: 'I'm going to win Wimbledon and bring my family to England.'

Todd Blackmore had found Olivia playing in a junior tournament in Bucharest against boys almost twice her age. 'She is the purest ball striker I've ever seen,' he said. 'A once-in-a-generation player.'

The accompanying photograph shows Olivia in action, launching into a forehand with her legs braced apart, pigtail flying, her tennis skirt lifting off her thighs.

Her match against Martina Navratilova at Wimbledon captured the headlines with experts predicting a bright future for the girl from SW16. Sponsors came on board and she was photographed in her bedroom, surrounded by tennis trophies.

There are more stories, interviews and profiles. Victories in junior tournaments. A wild card into the French Open. Two paragraphs in *The Times* report her pulling out of the US Open due to injury. Another story refers to a comeback after an ankle operation.

In the months and years that followed there are fewer references. I search instead for the name 'Todd Blackmore' and come across a photograph in the social pages of *London Evening Standard*. Olivia is pictured standing on the steps of the Chelsea Registry Office. She has her head down, smiling shyly. Todd Blackmore has his arm around her. He's thirty-seven. She's eighteen. They're married.

The *Sun* picked up on the story. TENNIS COACH MARRIES STAR PUPIL is the headline above a photograph of Olivia and Todd Blackmore on court together. A second picture shows the ex-wife, Trudy, leaving a house in Wimbledon, refusing to comment on the divorce or wedding.

Moving forward, looking for Olivia's name, it's clear that she didn't resume her tennis career. Todd Blackmore set up his academy. Olivia taught alongside him. There are stories linking them to promising juniors, including a photograph of a young Andy Murray.

Opening a new link, I come across a photograph of a twisted car in a sea of smashed glass and spilled oil. The four-wheel-drive car is crumpled around the base of a concrete pillar, the driver's door has been torn off, airbags inflated and the passenger seat crushed by the dashboard.

Tennis Stars in Bridge Crash

Leading British tennis coach Todd Blackmore has died and his wife, former Wimbledon junior champion, Olivia Szabo, is fighting for her life after a horror smash in South London.

The couple's Jeep Cherokee left the dual carriageway and collided with a bridge pillar in the early hours of Friday morning, killing Mr Blackmore instantly. Olivia Szabo was pinned in the vehicle next to her dead husband for almost an hour before emergency crews managed to cut her from the wreckage.

Romanian-born, Szabo, a champion junior player, suffered extensive injuries to her legs and underwent emergency surgery at Guy's Hospital in London. A spokesman described her condition as critical but stable.

A later story reports her out of danger and that surgeons had saved her leg. All of this corresponds with what Olivia told me about the accident. A local newspaper covered Todd Blackmore's funeral, publishing a photograph of his children, a boy and a girl from his first marriage, who are walking behind his coffin. Olivia was still in hospital, where she spent another six weeks.

I close the computer, rubbing my eyes. It's late. I'm exhausted. On my way to the bathroom, I pass Charlie's bedroom door. Andie is still awake, talking to someone on the phone.

Turning on the shower, I step under the hot stream, washing away the sweat and disappointment of the day. My father is lying in the ICU. Someone attacked him – a defenceless old man – crushing his skull, leaving him to die.

I feel a cool waft of air as the door opens.

'I'm in the shower,' I say, thinking it might be Emma, half-asleep.

Nobody answers. The shower door has steamed up. I wipe it down and come face to face with Andie, wearing nothing but a towel and a smile.

'I thought you might want company,' she says, opening the shower door.

My hands go straight to my genitals.

'What? No!'

Andie drops her towel and steps inside. Full-breasted and

two-toned from years lying on Australian beaches, she stands on tiptoes and kisses me on the lips.

'Don't be scared.'

'You're the nanny.'

'We don't call ourselves nannies any more.'

'That's not the point.'

Andie has taken the soap and started lathering up my chest. My hands are still covering my genitals. Andie's fingers drift lower.

'Whoa! Let's not go there,' I say, trying to slip past her.

She blocks my way. 'I've seen you look at me.'

'No, I don't think you have.'

'Are you saying you don't fancy me?'

I'm shuffling sideways, trying not to brush against her.

'I'm very good you know – experienced.'

She throws her arms around my neck and kisses me fully on the mouth. Her tongue slides between my lips, her breasts flatten against my soapy chest.

She's half my age. Less than half. I could do the math if she didn't have one hand on my hardening penis.

I grab her shoulders and hold her at arm's length, telling her to stop.

'This isn't going to happen, Andie. It's not right.' I sound like I'm scolding a child.

'I don't think you really mean that,' she says, looking down.

My face glows. Pushing past her, I open the door and grab a towel, wrapping it around my waist. Andie steps out after me, but doesn't bother to cover up. Her nipples are large and dark. Julianne had such small neat nipples.

She puts her hands on her hips. 'What's the problem? You're lonely. I'm willing. We're both consenting adults.'

'I'm not consenting.'

'Well, I can hardly force you,' she says.

'Look, I think you're very attractive. And I appreciate the offer, but I'm not interested. What about your boyfriend?'

'He's a jerk! I know he's been seeing someone else.'

'Is that why you're here – to punish him?'

'No. Maybe just a little bit. But I like you, Joe. And I feel sorry for you – losing your wife, raising Emma on your own, and now your dad is sick. But don't get me wrong – this isn't a pity-fuck.'

'A pity-fuck?'

'It means what it says.' She has tied the towel around her chest, tucking it beneath her arms. It barely covers her crotch. I have a flashback. Andie had no pubic hair. I might never forget that detail.

She takes a second towel and wraps it around her wet hair. I reach inside the shower and turn off the taps before scooping up my clothes and taking them to the bedroom. Andie follows me once she's pulled on her jeans and her bra and buttoned her blouse.

'Well, that was pretty embarrassing,' she says, looking at herself in the mirror. 'Are we still OK?'

'In what sense?'

'We've seen each other's bits.' She gesticulates to my nether regions. 'Not that I mind. I'm always getting my tits out. But I don't want you to feel uncomfortable . . . having me around. Are you uncomfortable?'

'Not when you're fully clothed.'

'So, you don't want me to leave?'

'No.'

'Good. Well, I'm glad we cleared that up. Emma is adorable, if a little scary.'

'How is she scary?'

'Really, really smart.'

Andie yawns, stretches and wishes me goodnight. She stops in the doorway. 'One more thing. While you're in a good mood? I need a few weeks off.'

'Why?'

'My sister is getting married in Melbourne. Sorry for the short notice. I think she's up the duff. Shotgun wedding. Silly cow. Wants me to be the maid of honour. Old maid, more likely. I'm leaving Thursday. Is that OK? I know it's a bad time.'

'We'll manage.'

I listen to Andie padding barefoot down the hallway, calling Australia to give them the news. Crawling under the covers, I turn off the light and try not to think about her breasts against my chest and her lack of pubic hair and her tongue in my mouth. Soon the image transforms and I imagine that it's Julianne I'm holding and I dare not breathe in case she goes away.

Day Two

10

The cab drops me at St Mary's Hospital just before 6 a.m. and I take the lift to the ninth floor, where my mother will be waiting. How do I tell her about Olivia Blackmore?

Mum, a funny thing happened yesterday. I bumped into someone who knew Dad quite well.

Oh, yes, who was it?

His mistress . . . His lover . . . His other wife. She's surprisingly young and may have attacked him, but she otherwise seems quite nice. She wants to come and see him. Is that OK with you?

Nothing can sugar-coat this.

My mother is resting her head on my father's bed. I shake her gently by her shoulder, which feels brittle beneath my palm. Her eyes open. She touches her mussed-up hair. I take her hand. Her fingers are cold.

'Any change?' I ask.

'His eyelids fluttered. The nurse said it was involuntary, but I think he heard me talking to him.'

'That's good,' I say, trying to match her optimism. Meanwhile, Dad is as before – lying amid the tubes and cables.

'The police have some questions for you.'

'Me?'

'They want to know what Dad was doing in London?'

'He had a board meeting for the O'Loughlin Foundation.'

'That's not until tomorrow.'

'Oh.' She brushes lint from the shoulder of my jacket. 'Perhaps he had a lunch, or was meeting his chums for dinner. I don't pay much attention.'

'Where does he stay in London?'

'At his club.'

She means Home House in Portland Square.

'I called his club. He didn't make a reservation.'

Mum doesn't react, as if pretending not to hear me.

'He's been staying in Chiswick with a woman called Olivia Blackmore. Do you know her?'

Again nothing.

'She says she's Dad's wife.'

My mother spins around and slaps me hard across the face. The speed and firmness surprise me, not due to her age or small frame, but because I cannot recall her ever raising her hand to anyone, child or adult. The blow echoes in the quietness. She covers her mouth in shock. Tears forming. Turning away, she picks up her handbag and leaves the ICU.

I follow her outside, stopping her in the corridor. She

tries to step around me. I block her. 'We have to talk about this.'

'No.'

'Dad had a mistress. She called the ambulance. She was at the hospital when I arrived, sitting beside his bed.'

'Leave me alone,' she hisses.

'Her name is Olivia Blackmore,' I say.

'Do not use her name around me!'

She knows! Of course, she knows.

'Dad was cheating on you. You can't pretend she doesn't exist.'

Mum raises her hand as though ready to strike me again, but places it on my reddened cheek. Her voice vibrates through clenched teeth.

'I love you, Joseph. Your father does too. But if you ever disrespect him or demean him in my presence, I will never speak to you again.'

Stepping around me, she walks towards the lift.

Don't walk away. Don't hide from this.

'The police are going to ask you these questions,' I say.

'And I will answer them,' she replies coldly. 'I will not be interrogated by my son.'

The lift doors open and she steps inside. The doors close. Only her perfume remains.

How long has she known? How could she let it continue?

I didn't think it possible for my parents to surprise me. They're like an ageing double act, who finish each other's sentences or can sit in silence over dinner, having said everything that needs saying. I know the story of how they met as children, growing up as family friends, sharing baths as toddlers and attending the same primary school. 'I hated him,' my mother said. 'He was always pulling my pigtails and spoiling my tea parties.'

They met again at university. My father pretended he was worldly and experienced, but I suspect they were both virgins. My mother has always boasted the fact, telling my sisters to save themselves for 'Mr Right', as she did. Not that she 'saved' herself for long. She married at nineteen, fell pregnant, abandoned her degree and had four children in the next five years. *Catholicism will do that to you.* In the meantime, my father worked thirty-six-hour shifts, studying to be a surgeon.

What did she see in him? He wasn't particularly handsome or athletic, or charming or engaging. Maybe she admired his intellectual rigour or saw his potential as a surgical genius.

Each time Dad took a new position, Mum packed up the family and we moved with him, to Edinburgh, Manchester, Cardiff and London. She hated city living and missed the countryside, which is why they ultimately compromised and bought the farmhouse in Wales. Dad lived away during the week and came home on weekends when he didn't have surgeries to perform.

Did I miss him? I'm not sure it's possible to miss someone so rarely present. I know I wanted to impress him – to show *him* my school results and my debating trophies and my Bronze Medallion for swimming.

Despite his absence, my mother deferred to Dad on almost every major decision from holidays, to schools, to how short my sisters wore their skirts. What did that make

81

her? Contented but unfulfilled? A doormat? A weathervane, shifting in his wind?

She's walked away again, refusing to recognise the truth. I want to shake her by the shoulders and yell, 'Open your eyes! Your husband is an adulterer and a bigamist; a philanderer, a cheat!' He's a conman, who's fooled everyone into believing he's a fine, upstanding, English gentleman, steadfast and conservative, as predictable as a Hallmark card.

It's not anger that drives me, or disappointment. Instead I feel strangely vindicated – as though my father has suddenly become interesting because he has flaws that I can understand.

11

At midday Lucy arrives to take over. I stay for a while, watching her fuss over Dad. She is better at this than I am. She can find things to say, or questions to ask that don't require answers.

Outside I tug up my collar and feel the wind whip at my coat-tails. I make a phone call. Vincent Ruiz answers. I hear background noises. Plates. Cutlery.

'Are you eating?'

'Ordering.'

'Alone?'

'You make it sound like I have no friends.'

He's ten minutes away in Queensway at the Royal China.

'I'll buy you lunch,' I say.

'Good. I'll over-order.'

I find him at a table in the corner of the cavernous

dining room, which has the same black and gold lacquered walls that I remember from thirty years ago.

'What's with the suit and tie?' I ask.

'I'm working.'

'I thought you'd retired.'

'From the police force, but not from life. I'm now a corporate fraud investigator.' He hands me a business card.

'What do you know about corporate fraud?'

'The criminals have white collars.'

'That's a good start.'

I have known Ruiz for a dozen years, which makes him one of my oldest friends, a fact that I should find depressing but don't. Others have come and gone, particularly since Julianne's death, but Vincent has stuck by me. Barrel-chested, with cauliflower ears and hands the size of dinner plates, he's a former Scotland Yard detective, who was pushed into early retirement when a kidnapping case went wrong and left him with a permanent limp and a missing ring finger.

Ruiz is a man of simple, if disparate tastes – a lover of rugby, pork pies, spy novels, war movies, smutty jokes, Guinness and wide-hipped women. With equal passion, he dislikes football hooligans, abstract art, potpourri, Jeremy Clarkson, Elvis impersonators and people who say they're 'gender fluid'. I like him. He likes me. That's how friendships endure.

Plates of food begin arriving. Dumplings. Spare ribs. Pork buns.

'We'll have more chilli sauce and another lager,' Ruiz says to the waitress as he spears a dumpling with a chopstick. He pops the whole thing in his mouth and talks while he chews, asking about the girls, work and my love life, which is non-existent, unless I mention Andie's offer, which is too embarrassing.

'What exactly does a corporate fraud investigator do?' I ask.

He glances over my shoulder. 'Right now, I'm watching that attractive lady over there.'

I turn my head, trying not to make it obvious. A well-dressed woman in her late twenties is dining with a middle-aged man in a grey suit, who is topping up her wine glass.

'What's she done?'

'You see her handbag?' asks Ruiz, chewing thoughtfully.

'Louis Vuitton?'

'Worth four grand. Her earrings are from Cartier – six-carat diamonds, purchased in cash.' He sucks meat off a pork rib and points the bone. 'So how does a junior bank clerk earning twenty grand a year afford earrings that are worth six times that much?'

'How much has she stolen?'

'Half a million. Maybe more. She's been transferring money out of customer accounts into her own, withdrawing it from ATMs. The guy with her is her boss. I'm trying to ascertain if he's part of the problem or pussy-struck.'

Ruiz moves his chair closer to mine. 'Let's get a selfie.' He holds his mobile at arm's length and snaps a photograph. He shows it to me. My head is cut off but it clearly shows the couple dining in the background. He points to the last pork bun. 'You want that one?'

'It's yours.'

'What brings you here, Professor? And why do you look like you slept in that shirt?'

'My dad was bashed unconscious two nights ago. He's in a coma at St Mary's Hospital.'

The pork bun hovers near his mouth. 'Shit! I'm sorry. Why did you let me prattle on like that? Who bashed him?'

'No idea.'

'Where did it happen?'

'In Chiswick.'

'He doesn't live in Chiswick.'

'Exactly.' I take a deep breath. 'My father has a mistress in London. They share a house.'

Ruiz looks at me incredulously, the food forgotten. 'We're talking about the same person, right? God's–Personal–Physician–in–Waiting.'

I nod and tell him what I know about my father's second wife and secret life.

Ruiz whistles through his teeth. 'Give the man his due – that takes some doing. Two women. Two houses. Two beds.'

'You can shake his hand if he ever wakes up.'

Ruiz apologises for being insensitive. 'And you had no idea?'

'Not a clue.'

'What about your mother?'

'I think she knew, but she won't talk about it.'

Bunching his serviette into a ball, he tosses it on to the table. 'How can I help?'

'The police think it was a home invasion that went wrong, but nothing was taken.'

'Maybe they panicked.'

'It doesn't match the scene. The attacker cleaned up and turned off the lights.'

'You think it was a hit?'

'I don't know. I can't think why. Olivia Blackmore told police she went to the theatre on Sunday evening. She says she arrived home and she found him lying at the bottom of the stairs.'

'You don't believe her.'

'I think she's hiding something.'

'Like what?'

'Someone gave my father a beating about a week ago. I found evidence of old bruises on his back and chest. Fist marks.'

'A woman doesn't usually hit with her fists.'

'She's younger, fitter, stronger.'

'Why would she want to hurt him?'

'Jealousy. Greed. Money.'

'You're clutching at straws.'

'I have nothing else.'

Pushing back from the table, Ruiz takes a tin of boiled sweets from his suit pocket and unscrews the lid. Choosing carefully, he pops the rock candy into his mouth and swaps it from cheek to cheek as he sucks.

'Who's handling the case?'

'DI Stuart Macdermid. You know him?'

'Vaguely. I've heard good things.'

'You'd get on with him.'

'Why?'

'You're both reformed smokers, you drink too much,

you read *The Daily Mail*, you're mildly racist and sexist, but hide it cleverly; and you're indifferent to all things cultural.'

'Brother from another mother.'

'I hope not.'

A waitress brings the bill.

'You might want to be careful about making the mistress the villain,' says Ruiz.

'Why?'

'It's too easy. She's the outsider. Your family are going to want to close ranks – protect your father's name – which means isolating the one person who may have all the answers.'

'I'm not trying to protect anyone,' I say, aware of how hollow that sounds. Whatever my father is guilty of, I have to believe that he didn't deserve this.

12

My mother emerges from Chiswick police station, holding the railing as she descends the shallow ramp with small careful steps. She had a hip replacement two years ago and has never been as confident – not just with walking, but in other ways. Less sure of her driving and her memories.

Patricia offers to take Mum's arm, but the gesture is ignored. I've been waiting in a café across the road, wanting to know the outcome of the interview. Instead of calling out, I hold back and watch as Patricia hails a cab and opens the passenger door. They sit side by side, not speaking. The driver pulls away.

Entering the station, I ask to speak to DI Macdermid. The message is relayed and I'm escorted upstairs along near-deserted corridors. There are no ringing phones or humming printers. Maybe that's the difference between a

murder investigation and a serious assault – the energy level. Murder fires the blood because it's the only crime we cannot make amends for or take back. Lesser crimes like robbery and assault aren't worthy of the overtime or the resources.

Macdermid makes me follow him to the men's room, where I listen to him urinate. 'You went to see Olivia Blackmore,' he says, zipping his fly and adjusting his under-carriage. 'Perhaps I didn't make myself clear – you have no role in this investigation, Professor. You are not working for the police and have no authority to question witnesses or suspects.'

'She wants to visit my father. I need to know if she's dangerous. Is she?'

Macdermid pauses, as though debating how much to tell me.

'There are inconsistencies in her alibi.'

'Meaning?'

'A missing hour. The show at the theatre finished at ten thirty. She didn't arrive home until midnight. Her mobile phone was turned off during that time.'

'She's been lying.'

The detective shrugs ambivalently, before turning on a tap and squirting soap on to his hands.

'You should arrest her,' I say. 'You could hold her for forty-eight hours.'

'Perhaps you should talk to your mother before you start pointing your finger at other people.'

'What does that mean?'

'Ask her where she was on Sunday night?'

'She was in Wales.'

Macdermid shakes his head. 'We have CCTV footage of her arriving at Paddington station an hour after your father. She followed him to London.'

I try hard to disguise my surprise, but can feel the earth tilt. When I called my mother yesterday she was on a train. I didn't ask her where she was going or where she'd been. Why follow him?

Macdermid dries his hands on a paper towel and glances at the mirror. He's not studying himself, but looking at me.

'You might also warn your mother that obstructing a police investigation is a criminal offence.'

'She was just here.'

'Telling me a pack of lies. I asked her what clothes she was wearing yesterday. She couldn't remember. I said we'd need to confiscate them. Do you know what she said?'

I don't respond.

'She left her overnight bag on the train. How convenient.'

'I can guarantee she had nothing to do with this.'

Macdermid balls a paper towel in his fist and laughs, showing his teeth and gums and a pink epiglottis. 'You have one fucked-up family, Professor. And I won't hesitate to charge any one of you for obstructing or interfering with this investigation.'

'You'll have our full cooperation.'

'And your mother?'

'I'll bring her in tomorrow.'

'Will she be lawyered up by then?'

I want to say no, but I'm not sure any more. I'm following Macdermid back to his office. He sits behind his desk and looks up as if surprised that I'm still here.

'I know I can't officially assist work on the case, but you could use me. I could draw up a psychological profile . . . review the evidence.'

'Absolutely not.'

'Could I just look at the crime scene photographs?'

'Go home, Professor.'

'It wasn't a home invasion,' I say. 'Nothing was taken and there were no signs of forced entry. Whoever attacked my father was already in the house or he let them in. He was hit from behind. He fell down the stairs, bouncing off the wall and banisters. His assailant followed and continued the attack. Hitting him multiple times with a heavy object.'

Macdermid looks at me suspiciously. 'How do you know?'

'I saw the bloodstains. Whoever did this would have been covered in blood. They had to clean up – most likely in the laundry. They turned off the lights before they left.'

'So?'

'Home invasions tend to be quick and violent, designed to create maximum fear to frighten victims into giving up their valuables or account details. Whoever did this didn't terrorise or torture my father. Nor did they panic and run. They were comfortable in the house and seemed to know their way around.'

'You're not working this case.'

'What about the old bruises?'

'I'm not discussing it with you.'

'And the note inside the door.'

Macdermid puts his head out of the office and bellows across the incident room, summoning a female detective he calls Hawthorn.

'Please escort Professor O'Loughlin out of the station. Don't talk to him. Not even about the weather.'

The DI turns away. His right hand is cupped like a claw at his side.

The detective is waiting at the lifts. Dressed in a white blouse, her grey slacks hug her hips and flare slightly at the pointed ends of her boots. Her hair, parted, straight, cut sharp to just below her jawline, is a glossy chestnut colour, shot through with purplish red — some sort of henna. Her thick eyebrows are unplucked and a dusting of freckles covers her nose and cheeks. One of them is darker than the others, looking like a beauty mark.

She punches the lift button multiple times.

'It doesn't make them come any quicker,' I say.

'What?'

'Hitting the button. It's the same with pedestrian crossings. Traffic lights are on timers so it makes no difference how many times the button is pressed. That's why they're called "placebo buttons".'

The lift arrives. We step inside. She presses for the ground floor, pushing it only once. Pulling back her shoulders, she stands as though on a parade ground, not making eye contact. It gives her a lovely profile. Strong chin. High bust. Narrow waist.

'However, there is a trick to it,' I say. 'Next time you're waiting for a lift, try tapping the button three times and holding it for two seconds. Works like a charm.'

'Is that true?' she asks, finally deigning to speak to me.

'What do you think?'

Then it dawns on her that I'm joking. Her cheeks redden

and she frowns, annoyed at herself. The braces on her teeth make her look even younger, although she's probably in her late thirties.

The lift doors open and she escorts me past the front desk and down the steps.

'Have we met before?' I ask. 'You look very familiar.'

'No!'

'What's your first name?'

'Goodbye, Professor.'

Day Three

13

When I was seventeen I passed my driving test and took my mother's car to a party thrown by a girl whose parents were away for the weekend. I didn't come home at midnight, as arranged. It was after three when I rolled the car down the driveway with the headlights off and engine in neutral. I crept inside, navigating easily through the dark house up the stairs to my attic room. I found Dad asleep in a chair beside my bed. I thought perhaps I could slip past him and under the covers, pretending to be asleep, but his eyes opened.

I waited for him to read the riot act. I thought he'd smell my breath, or ban me from driving, or ground me for the holidays. Instead, he stood up and cinched his dressing gown and went off to bed. As he reached the door, he turned.

'Your mother has been worried sick.'

That was it. He didn't mention it again.

I don't know why I remember that. Perhaps I'm piecing together moments when I thought Dad might love me or at least care. Recollections like this seem like daydreams on the margins of fantasy, rather than real-life experiences. Another one comes to me. I'm sitting in the front seat of a beat-up Land Rover in the teeming rain. Dad hands me a mobile phone and a change of clothes, telling me to avoid the main roads and to pay for everything in cash. The police were looking for me, but Dad risked his reputation and safety to help me because he believed I was innocent.

'I know I'm not an easy man to love, Joseph,' he said. 'I don't give anything in return. But I will always be here for you.'

I began to understand that day that Dad was a product of his own upbringing, just as I am. He followed a career path that had been mapped out for him – the placements, tenures and specialisms. Doors were opened. Promotions were approved. I don't know if that's what he wanted. I suspect he felt trapped, or burdened by expectation in a family were filial obedience was a commandment and personal happiness a self-indulgence.

My phone is ringing. It's Lucy.

'Is Mummy with you?' she asks.

'No.'

'She left the hospital two hours ago, but hasn't shown up here.'

'Have you tried her mobile?'

'She gave her phone to the police.'

'I'll call you back.'

When I reach the hospital, I find Patricia sitting with Dad. She's been reading to him. Dickens. *Great Expectations*.

'I did consider reading to him from *Heat* or *Now*,' she says.

'He hates gossip magazines.'

'Exactly. If he wants me to stop, he'll have to wake up and tell me.' She laughs and looks at Dad lovingly. 'Remember when he used to read to us?'

'No.'

'He read us *Little Women* and *Charlotte's Web* and *The Hobbit*.'

'Are you sure?'

'When we hid under the covers he'd send the "tickling spider" to look for us. We laughed so much we begged him to stop.'

'Maybe I was too young,' I say, doubting everything she's saying.

Patricia is the quietest of my sisters. She married late and doesn't have children, but I get no sense of regret.

'Did Mum tell you where she was going?' I ask.

'To Lucy's.'

'What happened at the police station?'

'They wouldn't let me sit in on the interview.'

'How did Mum seem afterwards?'

'OK. Quiet. Why?'

'She took a train to London on Sunday night. The police think she followed Dad.'

'Why would she do that?'

'I don't know, but she's refusing to answer their questions.'

Patricia falls silent. Frowning. She's almost as tall as I am and looks more like my father with a high forehead and thick hair.

'Did you tell her about Olivia Blackmore?'

'She knew already.'

'How long has she known?'

'From the start.'

Patricia's pupils dilate and she shakes her head. Shocked. Adamant.

'Mummy would never hurt him.'

'No, but if she refuses to cooperate they'll charge her with obstruction, or worse. We need to find her.'

The silence is fraught rather than thoughtful. There are too many unanswered questions.

'Does she need a lawyer?' Patricia asks.

'I think maybe she does.'

14

A dozen polished brass plaques are bolted to the brickwork beside a heavy blue door that has been painted and repainted so often the surface is no longer smooth. I look down the list of names until I see Passage and Moore Solicitors.

Crossing the black-and-white chequerboard tiles in the foyer, I take the stairs to the third floor, climbing past an art deco chandelier suspended from the atrium ceiling.

'Can I help you?' asks a middle-aged woman sitting behind a glass-topped desk. Her gull-wing glasses and floral dress make her look like she's stepped from the set of *Mad Men*.

'I'm here to see Kenneth Passage.'

'You mean David,' she replies. 'Kenneth retired three years ago.' Almost in the same breath, she corrects herself. 'No, I'm mistaken. Four years ago. I should remember. I organised his farewell.'

'Kenneth left me a message,' I say. 'He told me two o'clock.'

The woman frowns and pushes her glasses higher on the bridge of her nose, before picking up the phone.

'I have a Joseph O'Loughlin to see Kenneth.' She listens. 'I see . . . No, I wasn't told . . . Certainly.' She puts down the handset. 'Mr Passage will see you shortly.'

I wait in a small anteroom with black-stained wooden chairs and bookcases that are lined with legal texts. A Matisse still-life hangs on the wall. I imagine it's a reproduction. Maybe I'm wrong.

Kenneth Passage has known my father since their university days when they played rugby together. Big and loud with a barrel-shaped body, I remember hearing stories about his exploits on the sporting field, how he'd charge into rucks with such ferocity that bodies would roll out beneath his boots. His teammates called him 'The Lion' because of his mane of hair and the way he roared when he made a tackle. He was tipped to play for England until injuries ended his career at club level. He married and had a family. My father was his best man and godfather to his eldest son.

What else do I know about Kenneth? He grew up in the tenements of Manchester where his father worked in an abattoir; and his mother made school dinners, but unlike a lot of working-class people, Kenneth has never romanticised his roots. He won scholarships to secondary school and to Oxford, where he lost his northern accent. Played rugby. Studied law. Met my father.

Most of my childhood summers were spent with the

Passage family. We rented neighbouring cottages in Cornwall. Kenneth came with his wife Rosie, and their two boys David and the newly minted Francis. Kenneth organised our daily itinerary activities, running things like a holiday camp, having us sailing, swimming, hiking, fishing and playing beach cricket.

Rosie was even more memorable with her Irish accent and her fabulous voluptuousness. I still get a frisson of excitement when I remember once walking in on her while she breastfed Francis. I don't think I'd ever seen a woman's breasts – not in the flesh. I didn't know where to look, but I knew I *wanted* to look; and I spent the rest of the holiday trying to orchestrate another opportunity.

When we played beach cricket at low tide, Rosie would tuck her floral skirt into her knickers and bowl over-arm, faster than any of the men. And she always found a reason to cool off with a swim, not caring how her wet clothes clung to her curves. I realise now that I lusted after Rosie before I knew what lust was, because she seemed more glamorous and exciting than other mothers, who smelled of talcum powder and scented soap. Rosie had a more primal and essential fragrance that affected me in places that Sunday school had taught me not to touch.

Francis joined the army straight out of school and did his officer training at Sandhurst. He died in an IRA bombing in Ulster on his twenty-second birthday – a loss that devastated both our families. I remember his flag-draped coffin being carried from the church, through an honour-guard of soldiers. My father sobbed. I had never seen him cry. Kenneth looked straight ahead, refusing to buckle under his grief. Rosie walked behind, her face hidden behind a black veil.

A door opens behind me. David Passage appears. Apologising. Smiling. Gripping my fist, he pulls me into an embrace; a proper man-hug, as if I'm being inducted into some secret order. Normally, I stiffen when someone takes me by surprise like this, but I feel myself soften and shudder in relief as though I've found someone who understands.

'How long's it been?' he asks. 'Ten years?'

'More,' I reply. 'You were working for an American bank in the City.'

'And now I'm here.'

David is still holding my hand and smiling, focusing on me with such compelling force that I feel myself drawing energy from him. Deep laughter lines are like parentheses around his mouth and his eyes sparkle with joy. In an instant, they change.

'How is William? It came as such a shock.'

'Who told you?'

'My mother called. Do they know what happened?'

'No.'

'If there's anything I can do. Please, just ask.'

'My mother might need a lawyer.'

'Why?'

'The police think she's a suspect.'

'That's ridiculous.' He makes a note. 'Get her to call me. I'll take care of things.'

David changes the subject and talks about school. We were both at Brighton College, although not at the same time. I'm a dozen years older, but we remember the same teachers, classrooms and dormitories. David went on to become a boarding school legend after getting caught *in flagrante delicto* with the headmaster's daughter in the cricket pavilion. Felicity, aged seventeen, had more curves than a scenic railway and by all reports had starred in countless adolescent fantasies among the boarders.

The headmaster, Mr Broughton, wanted David expelled. Kenneth stepped in, threatening to sue the college. Common sense prevailed. David was suspended for a term and Felicity banished to boarding school in Dorset, not even allowed home at weekends or mid-term.

The young lovers couldn't be denied. They married straight out of university and had two children – a boy and a girl.

'How is Felicity?' I ask.

David answers brightly. 'We're divorced. Eight years now. She's much happier.'

'And the kids?'

'I see them every second weekend. Marcus is at Brighton College. He's sixteen this year.'

'I thought you'd avoid the place.'

'Family ties, you know how it is.'

I do, but don't say as much.

'I've remarried,' said David, making it sound inevitable. 'A younger wife and a second family. I know that's prosaic and un-PC, but what can I say? I'm a shallow man.'

He rolls his hands out in a gesture of acceptance and gives me the same smile. David was always charming, which is probably why he survived the scandal. He points to a chair and circles the desk, unbuttoning his jacket. Light from the arched window reflects off the oil in his hair. He's wearing a lolly striped shirt and red tie that make him look like a mid-level account manager.

'I thought I was meeting Kenneth,' I say.

'He's on his way.'

As if on cue, the buzzer sounds. We both stand. I expect Kenneth to charge through the door and bear-hug me, but the man who arrives is a pale shadow of the giant I remember. The confident swagger has gone and his indestructible body has collapsed with age. Diminished and gaunt, he is wheeled through the door by a large middle-aged man with olive skin and hair the colour of steel wool, who could be a nurse or a minder.

'Joseph! Joseph! My boy, my boy!' says Kenneth, trying to stand. 'Help me! Help me!' he says to his carer, who lifts him easily to his feet. Kenneth pulls me into an embrace and I smell his age and aftershave. For a fleeting moment, I think I might cry. This man, this colossus, this force of nature has run out of puff and could be blown over by his own breeze.

Kenneth releases me. His eyes are shining. 'What news of William? How is he? I've been calling the hospital, but they won't tell me anything.'

'He's in a coma. They won't know the full extent of the damage until he wakes.'

'I must go and see him. I can make him wake up. He always listens to me.'

'Have you spoken to my mother?'

'Mary? Not since yesterday.'

'She's gone missing.'

Kenneth's face collapses as though leaking air. 'Missing? When? That doesn't sound like Mary.'

'She walked out of the hospital last night. I thought she might have called you.'

'No. What can I do? I have contacts in the Metropolitan Police. Commissioner Ferndale is a close friend.'

'I think he's retired,' says David, trying to be helpful.

Kenneth looks surprised. 'When?'

'Five or six years ago. There's a woman commissioner now.'

'A woman!'

Kenneth looks momentarily lost, uncertain of what he should know and how much he does know. He reaches for his wheelchair and lowers his frame. His carer holds his forearm and arranges a tartan blanket across his lap.

'You can leave us, Eugene,' David says. The carer waits for Kenneth to acknowledge the instruction before complying. He glances at me before leaving, tilting his head as though appraising what level of threat I might pose and finding me harmless.

'Is Eugene a nurse?' I ask once he's gone.

David shrugs. 'Nurse. Chauffeur. Gardener. Groundskeeper. Security guard. He was in the army with Francis. Served in the same regiment. He's been with the family ever since the funeral.'

'He doesn't say much.'

'No.'

Kenneth has perked up again. He motions me closer and takes my hand.

'How are you, Joseph? What about the girls? I haven't seen them since Julianne's funeral. Are they coping?'

'Yes, sir.'

'Please call me Kenneth.'

'Maybe I'll wait a few more years.'

He laughs and I feel good to be the cause of it because I've loved this man since I was a child. I used to wish that he and Rosie were my parents and we were like the Waltons, or the Brady Bunch, or the Ingalls from *Little House on the Prairie*.

Tea is offered and ordered. We ask after each other's children and grandchildren, as though purposely ignoring the elephant in the room. I confront the issue head-on.

'Did you know about Dad's other wife?'

Kenneth's eyelids close and a fan of fine lines concertinas around his mouth. 'William is a deeply private man.'

That's not an answer.

'How long have you known? Ten years? Fifteen?'

'What does it matter?'

'It matters to my mother.'

'I am William's lawyer.'

'You're our *family*'s lawyer. My mother is your friend. You've been a guest in her house. You have eaten her food. You are Lucy's godfather.'

Kenneth looks crestfallen. 'I'm sorry, Joseph. I love Mary and William. I would never do anything to knowingly hurt them. Olivia Blackmore has shared your father's life for the best part of two decades. I made my feelings known to William when he began their affair. I told him he was wrong. I said he should either leave Mary, or leave Olivia. He chose to do neither. But regardless of what has happened, he remains my friend; and I will not love him less.'

His watery eyes plead with me, but I will not apologise and forgive him.

'Olivia Blackmore claims to be married to Dad – is that the case?'

'She believes so.'

'What does that mean?'

'They had a ceremony, although I'm not sure if an English court would recognise the union. In my experience, judges generally try to accept foreign marriages as long as they meet certain criteria.'

'What criteria?' I ask.

'The marriage ceremony must be a valid form of marriage in the country it was performed in. It also has to comply with local law and have the relevant number of witnesses and the proper documentation.'

'What if the groom was already married under English law?'

'That would likely make any subsequent marriage invalid.'

'You mean illegal. She's not his wife. She has no rights.'

Tea arrives. Crushed leaves are infused with boiling water. Cups are allocated. David pours. Milk. Sugar. The pause restores equanimity.

Kenneth's hand shakes as he raises a cup to his lips, blowing across the surface.

'The law can be rather a blunt instrument when it comes to dealing with matters of the heart. William and Olivia were together in every way that counted. If it makes you feel any better, William has never shown favouritism between Olivia or Mary when it comes to financial support. Many years ago, I divided your father's assets into twin trusts that he set up to maintain his two families. He went to great lengths to keep each half separate. Occasionally the dividing wall would crack or spring a leak. It was my job to fix that wall and to make sure his worlds did not pollute one another in a legal or financial sense.'

'The house in Chiswick?'

'William signed a deed-of-trust giving Olivia ownership.'

'Life insurance?'

'He has two policies,' says David. 'Your mother is the beneficiary of one and Olivia the other. They were updated a few months ago.'

'There is a third policy,' adds Kenneth. 'The O'Loughlin Foundation has director's insurance. In case something happens to William.'

'Director's insurance?'

'A lot of companies insure their senior personnel,' explains David. 'We insured William because he's integral to the foundation – the chairman and figurehead. He has the contacts, the knowledge, the expertise . . .'

'How much are the insurance policies worth?' I ask.

David retrieves a folder from a filing cabinet and opens it on his desk.

'Your mother and Mrs Blackmore would each receive a million pounds, along with an annuity from their relevant trusts. The Foundation would get four million pounds.'

'Upon his death?'

'Yes.'

'What if the circumstances were suspicious?'

Kenneth raises a grey eyebrow. 'Is that likely?'

'Olivia Blackmore is a suspect.'

David interjects. 'I spoke to the detective leading the investigation this morning. He gave me no indication—'

'You spoke to DI Macdermid?'

'He asked if William has life insurance. I told him about the policies.'

'You said the will was updated recently. Why?'

'It was William's idea. He wanted to make a few minor changes,' says David.

'Who are the beneficiaries?'

Kenneth answers: 'The will is sealed.'

'You must know the contents.'

'William would have to give us his permission for it to be opened and read.'

'He's in a coma.'

Neither lawyer reacts.

'Are you refusing?'

'We're following our client's wishes.'

'This is ridiculous! I'm trying to discover why he was attacked and you're giving me semantics and hand-wringing.'

I'm surprised at how loud my voice sounds but I refuse to tone it down. I'm angry at these men for helping facilitate my father's dual life, for burying his secrets.

Kenneth Passage clears his throat in a phlegmy gurgle. 'You're upset, Joseph, understandably so. I am Mary's friend – and yours – but we act on William's behalf – not yours – and these are issues of lawyer–client privilege.'

The words seem to get caught in his throat and he begins coughing violently. Eugene is summoned; oxygen produced. Kenneth holds the mask over his mouth and nose, sucking in short gasps. His sunken cheeks are more pronounced than ever and I feel as though his skin would break into powdered fragments were I to touch him.

Kenneth begins breathing more normally, but the effort has exhausted him. David suggests that Eugene take him home. Kenneth wants to protest, but doesn't have the energy. He's wheeled from the office, arguing from behind the mask, waving his hands, as though delivering judgement. David follows and I watch him kiss the top of his father's head. Kenneth responds by stroking David's cheek. It's such an intimate moment between a father and son that it makes my heart ache.

David returns and apologises.

'What's wrong with him?' I ask.

'Congenital heart failure. He needs a new one, but he's too frail for a transplant.'

'And his legs?'

'A hip replacement. He should be walking by now, but still needs the chair or crutches.'

David seems more relaxed now that Kenneth has gone. The office is his.

'Have you met Olivia Blackmore?' I ask.

'Once or twice. She's come in to sign papers.'

'Has she seen my father's will?'

'William may have shown her a copy.'

'Would she know about the life insurance?'

'I have no idea.'

There is a pause. We both fall silent.

'You have to give him credit,' David says wistfully. 'Keeping two women happy for that long. I struggle to satisfy one wife.'

'You sound like you admire him.'

'I'm in awe of him.' He smiles apologetically.

'According to Dad's diary, he was due to meet you on Monday.'

'He wanted to discuss the O'Loughlin Foundation. There was an issue with the annual accounts.'

'What sort of issue?'

'We appointed a new treasurer four months ago. Samuel Rhodes. He arranged for the accounts to be forensically audited so he could get up to speed.'

'And he found something.'

'Apparently, although I don't know the details. I assumed that William would tell me when we met. I can give you Samuel's details. He works in the City.' Reaching across his desk, David takes a business card from a polished wooden box. He then glances at his phone. 'I have a meeting, but we should have lunch sometime. You should meet Maddie. She's a lovely old stick. Puts up with me.'

'I'd like that.'

'And when you see your mother – pass on my thoughts.'

'I will.'

We walk out of the office, along the corridor to the cage lift. He presses the button and we watch it ascend.

'It's really great to see you again, Joe.'

'You, too,' I reply, realising how much I enjoy his company.

'It was so sad about Julianne. We were in Portugal when I heard the news. I couldn't get a flight back for the funeral. Dad said it was the saddest one he'd ever seen.'

'I don't remember much about that day,' I say.

'That's understandable.'

111

The lift has arrived. David hugs me. My left arm jerks. He pretends not to notice. Pulling the doors closed, I press for the ground floor and the cage jerks into motion. David disappears bit by bit, first his head, then chest and legs. My eyes drop to his feet and a pair of white Adidas runners, which look incongruous compared to his business clothes.

Outside, I turn right and walk down Chancery Lane to Fleet Street. My left arm refuses to swing. I imagine people are staring at me. A week ago, my father was the great provider and part of a medical dynasty. Now he's a bigamist and an adulterer who may never recover his faculties.

Maybe he meant to leave my mother all those years ago when he first met Olivia, but time passed, time flowed, time eddied and swirled and washed over him, until his love was no longer urgent, or singular. I didn't tell Julianne when I was diagnosed with Parkinson's. I couldn't bring myself to utter the words. Instead I sought comfort in the arms of another woman. Is that any different? Maybe it's worse.

15

There are forty-six steps from the foyer of Wellington Court to the top floor. I know this because Emma insists on counting them every time she climbs the stairs to the flat. She's not with me today, but I feel her presence, as I pause on each landing, swapping bags of groceries between hands.

Andie left last night, which is why I'm shopping. She usually orders online and foodstuffs magically appear in our pantry and fridge, delivered by elves in brightly coloured vans, who flirt with Andie, and she with them.

'I'm home,' I say, as I close the door behind me. The hallway is in darkness.

'Charlie?'

No answer.

'Emma?'

The kitchen is empty. The clock ticks. A drip echoes in

the sink. Charlie caught a train down from Oxford at midday and promised to pick Emma up from school. Maybe they're still out, although it's after seven.

Charlie's overnight bag is sitting on her bed. Emma's schoolbooks are on her desk. I call Charlie's mobile. It connects. I can hear it ringing. The sound is coming from nearby. As I near the sitting room, I hear a whimper, which is suddenly muffled. I bet they're playing a game. Hide and seek. Emma always gives herself away.

'We're in here,' says Charlie, her voice tense.

'Why are you sitting in the dark?' I ask, seeing the square light of her phone on the coffee table.

'Don't touch the switch,' says a male voice.

I step into the room, my eyes trying to adjust. Charlie and Emma are huddled on the sofa, arms around each other, trying to make themselves smaller. Opposite them, sitting in an armchair, is a young man in filthy jeans and a hooded sweatshirt with a hole in the elbow.

Light from the hallway reveals half of his pale, narrow face; his lips as red as a wound and eyes dancing with chemical impatience. An object glints in his right hand. A blade.

Emma whimpers again. She could be in shock.

I look at the intruder, whose eyes jitter from side to side. He's high on something or suffering withdrawals.

'If it's money you want – take my wallet,' I say.

He wipes his mouth with the back of his hand and twists the point of the knife into the armrest. Anorexically thin, he has a concave chest and a buzz-cut hairstyle that shows every bump and hollow of his skull.

114

My mind is sprinting, trying to place him in my past. Is he a former patient? Did I have him committed? Has he come looking for me? His knees rock open and closed. He wipes his mouth again – a nervous habit.

I glance at the girls. 'Are you all right?'

Charlie nods. 'He forced his way in. I should have checked the peephole.'

'It's not your fault.'

'What does he want?'

He interrupts, telling us to stop whispering.

'Can I turn on the light?' I ask, reaching for the switch.

'No lights,' he says, pointing the knife.

I lower my hand and move further into the room. 'My name is Joe. What should I call you?'

'I'm the messenger.'

'Do you have a message for me?'

He frowns and slaps the side of his head with his open palm, as though trying to dislodge an answer. 'I must let go. I must let go. I must let go.'

'Let go of what?'

'All I hold dear.'

He's delusional or suffering a manic episode. Whatever happens, I must honour his sense of reality.

He's still muttering, 'I must let go. I must let go.' Suddenly, he points the knife at me. 'Are you working for them?'

'For who?'

'Them.'

'I don't know who you mean.'

'His name is Ewan,' says Emma, speaking for the first time. 'He told me.'

115

I glance at her. 'Have you met Ewan before?'

'He was outside my school,' she says nervously. 'I talked to him through the railings.'

I look again at Ewan in a different light, wondering if he's a paedophile who has targeted Emma.

'Can I sit down?' I ask.

Ewan doesn't answer. I choose a chair near the sofa, so I can intercept if he moves towards the girls.

'Why don't you put down the knife and we'll talk?'

He looks at the blade. 'Are you a believer?'

'I'm not sure.'

'Do you have faith?'

'I believe in the goodness of people.'

He thumps his chest. 'I have the faith of a thousand saints.'

'That's good.'

'I'm not Jesus but I lived at the same time. I'm not Christ either. People think they're the same person, but they're not. They're different. The gospels are wrong. They're fairy stories, written centuries after Jesus died. Do you know how old I am?'

'No.'

'Ancient. I'm older than the pyramids. I'm older than Stonehenge. I've been here longer than the Earth.'

He wants me to challenge these statements, but I try to ground him in the present. 'You've met Emma before, but not Charlie. She's my other daughter. You're frightening them with that knife, Ewan.'

Ewan rubs his eyes and blinks at them. 'I'm sorry.'

'When was the last time you slept?' I ask.

'I can't sleep.'

'Are you on medication?'

'Drugs and more drugs.'

'What drugs? Pharmaceuticals? Methamphetamines? Heroin?'

He's not listening to me. 'The Lord said, "Why do you despise your brother? For we will all stand before the seat of judgement."'

'I don't understand.'

'It means I should not despise you.' He cocks his head to one side. 'Do you hate me?'

'I don't even know you.'

'Am I my brother's keeper? Am I not my father's son? The Bible says everyone who hates his brother is a murderer and no murderer has eternal life abiding in him.'

He's quoting from the Bible, jumping between ideas that are ricocheting around in his mind, bouncing off each other. Yet somewhere in his madness will lie a kernel of truth.

'Do you have a brother?' I ask.

'You're my brother,' Ewan replies.

'I mean a proper brother, or a sister. You must have family.'

'Your father is my father.'

Is he still talking about God?

A thought detonates in the back of my mind, blowing cobwebs and dust from tea chests and sheet-covered furniture.

'What's your last name, Ewan?'

He hits his forehead again with the handle of the knife.

'You don't have to do that,' I say, moving closer, kneeling on the floor. 'What's your mother's name?'

117

'Don't tell her I'm here.'

My mouth has gone dry. 'Who is your father?'

'The good doctor raised me,' he says, before pointing to Charlie and Emma. 'Does that make you my nieces?'

A car horn sounds from the street. Ewan snaps his head to the side, staring at the window, as though he's seen a premonition or an apparition.

'They're listening.'

'Who?'

'They use the lights. Electricity. It's in the wires. That's why you can hear them humming. They're listening to us now.'

'Nobody is listening to us,' I say.

He points at Charlie. 'Are you one of them?'

Charlie looks at me, unsure of how to respond.

'Please make him leave,' says Emma, growing more agitated.

Ewan stares at the window again. 'They're watching us.'

'We're on the fourth floor, Ewan. Nobody can look in the window.'

'Are you calling me a liar?'

'I'll check,' says Charlie, edging past me, staying close to the fireplace until she reaches the window. She peers outside. 'I can't see anybody.'

'Are there cars?' Ewan asks.

'Yes.'

'Is anyone sitting in them?'

'The ones that are moving, yes.'

'What about the parked cars?'

'I don't think so. I see a woman walking her dog.'

'Does she have a phone?'

'I don't know.'

'They talk on their phones. They talk about me. Plotting. They want to kill me.'

'Why?' I ask.

'Because of what I've done.'

'What have you done?'

Ewan gets to his feet suddenly, bristling with a mixture of aggression and fear. 'They'll blame me.'

'What will they blame you for?'

He hits his head again. 'I must let go! I must let go!'

My mobile phone begins chirruping in my pocket. Ewan's head snaps up. He points the knife at me. 'You told them.'

'No.'

'They're coming.'

'I haven't told anyone.' I turn off my phone and toss it on to an armchair.

'Liar! You're like all the others.'

I step in front of Charlie and Emma, ready to protect them.

Emma screams. 'LEAVE US ALONE!'

Ewan blinks at her, shocked.

'YOU'RE A BAD MAN!' yells Emma. 'GO AWAY!'

Ewan opens his mouth, but doesn't know what to say.

Emma launches into an ear-splitting shriek that could shatter windows. She doesn't stop. She doesn't breathe. Charlie tries to calm her, but Emma won't be silenced.

Ewan's eyes skitter back and forth. He covers his ears and stumbles towards the door, flinging it open, pitching himself down the stairs.

Emma's face has turned a puce colour and her mouth is open so wide I can see her tonsils vibrating. Charlie is rocking her in her arms, telling her it's OK, we're safe. The bad man has gone.

'Call the police,' I say.

'Where are you going?' asks Charlie.

'After him.'

16

Ewan's boots echo on the stairs below me. I yell at him to stop but he carries on, crossing each landing and descending. Doors open on security chains. Faces appear. 'Stay inside,' I tell them.

I reach the foyer and pass the mailboxes and recycling bins, on to the pavement. Ewan is forty yards ahead of me, head down and hands deep in his pockets. He crosses the road without looking. A car brakes hard. The horn sounds. Ewan doesn't react. A figure steps from the shadows beneath the bare branches of a tree and joins him. Male? Female? I have no idea. They're both dressed in hooded tops, pulled up over their heads.

Moving quickly, they turn down Haverstock Hill towards Camden Town. The figure next to Ewan seems to be arguing with him. Ewan's movements are indecisive, as though uncertain whether he's running too slowly or walking too quickly.

I manage to keep up, dodging between pedestrians, pub patrons and diners. Olivia Blackmore didn't mention children. There were no photographs at the house in Chiswick; no evidence of a child-centred life.

Ewan must be in his late teens or early twenties. Delusional. Paranoid. Maybe both? He said he was going to be blamed for something. Perhaps he attacked Dad. He could be my half-brother. No! I can't accept that.

I turn the next corner and lose sight of them. Fighting the urge to run, I keep moving at the same pace, past restaurants, a bookmaker, a homewares store and dry cleaner's. I'm cold in my cotton shirt. I left my coat behind. My phone. Charlie will have called the police by now. How will they find me?

When I glimpse Ewan again, he's on his own – a shadowy figure lit momentarily by the headlights of a green double-decker that rumbles past. He stops, squats, head down, as though vomiting into the gutter. Wiping his mouth, he looks up at a bus which is slowing down, stopping. The front doors open. For a brief second, Ewan glances over his shoulder as though waiting for his companion. He steps on board and climbs the stairs. I run forward, waving at the driver, rapping my knuckles against the glass. He ignores me and pulls into the traffic. I contemplate running to the next stop. I'll never make it. A shape flashes towards me and I'm body-slammed from side-on, sent crashing into the bus shelter. Bouncing off the advertising hoarding I crumple to the ground. My attacker is on top of me. He gets to his feet, exuding heat and undisguised violence. White-haired. Skeletal. His boot swings towards my face. I cover my head and try to roll away. The boot connects with my back. A second blow sinks into my kidneys. Pain washes through me. I'm lying in the gutter, partially protected from the blows. A car horn blares. Someone yells. My attacker turns and runs, disappearing along the footpath.

Jammed hard against the gutter, I feel rainwater seeping into my clothes. Groaning, I manage to sit up. My left arm jerks. My head moves in sympathy. Mr Parkinson is tugging at my strings.

A woman at the bus stop ignores me, looking at her phone. She's listening to music through headphones, waiting for the next bus.

'Excuse me,' I say again, trying to get her attention.

She removes an earbud, pushing long hair off her face.

'Can I borrow your phone?' My left arm jerks. I hold it down with my other hand.

She steps further away.

'I have to call the police,' I say, slurring my words.

'Fuck off!' she hisses.

'You don't understand.' I try to stand.

The woman pulls something from her bag – a small can, some sort of aerosol. She aims the nozzle at my face. Sprays. My eyes close automatically, but it's too late. The pain is instantaneous. My whole face is on fire; my mouth, nose, eyes, even my hair follicles are burning. Blindly reaching out, I try to grab something solid to brace myself against. The woman is telling someone that I tried to steal her phone.

My eyes are streaming and my lungs are filling with liquid gunk. I ask for water. Plead for it. A man tells me to sit down. I fight for control but my limbs are in rebellion, jerking and twisting, forcing me into a strange dance without music. I try to speak. The words grow thick in my mouth. Trapped. A guttural noise replaces them.

'He's having a fit,' someone says.

'Maybe he's an epileptic.'

'Don't let him swallow his tongue.'

'He's frothing at the mouth.'

'Rabies! Don't touch him.'

Sick and trembling, I try with every ounce of willpower to stop myself moving, but my body won't obey me. Leaning against the bus shelter, I manage to hold myself upright, as sirens draw nearer. Relax, I tell myself. Inhale. Exhale. My eyes are on fire.

'What's your name, sir?' asks a new voice. I see a police constable through my fractured tears. I try to speak, but the words are garbled.

'I'm just going to look for identification, is that all right, sir?'

His hands go to my pockets of my trousers, finding no wallet, no money, no phone, no pills.

'Water!' I moan.

'Get him some water,' says the constable.

A bottle is thrust into my hands. I tilt my head back and try to flush out my eyes, but my hand jerks so much that water runs down my shirt. I try again, scrubbing at my face.

'Let me help you,' says the constable. He takes the bottle and pours the water over my eyes.

'Thank you,' I say thickly.

I can hear the woman who pepper-sprayed me telling another officer that I tried to steal her phone. I want to defend myself, but I'm past caring.

The officer with the water bottle asks me if I've taken any drugs. I try to explain, saying I live up the road. Another patrol car has pulled up. More officers. One of them crouches next to me.

'I'll take it from here,' she says. 'We've been looking for him.'

'What's his problem?' the constable asks.

'He has Parkinson's.' She touches my arm. I recognise her. It's the detective I met at the police station; the one with the freckles on her nose and braces on her teeth. DS Hawthorn. She wouldn't tell me her first name.

'Can you hear me, Professor?'

I nod.

'The man with the knife – where did he go?'

I shake my head. 'His name is Ewan. He's Olivia Blackmore's son. Please don't hurt him.'

The woman who attacked me is demanding that I be arrested. Detective Hawthorn tells her that pepper spray is a prohibited weapon and that she risks being charged with assault.

'I was defending myself,' she says angrily. 'He tried to steal my phone.'

'I asked to borrow it,' I say, trying to reconstruct my dignity, knowing it's too late.

Detective Hawthorn leads me to a patrol car and lets me sit in the back seat with my legs in the gutter, head between

125

my knees. She finds more water to flush out my eyes. Dozens of bystanders are watching from the footpath.

'I'm sorry,' I say.

'Don't apologise.' She pulls out her phone. 'I'm going to take you to the hospital – as a precaution. Is there someone I can call?'

'Vincent Ruiz.'

17

'What were you thinking?' asks Ruiz, as he paces the kitchen, making it look small. 'He had a knife!'

'He needed help.'

'Really? A psychotic hearing voices from God.'

'He's not crazy.'

'No, you are!'

I'm showered and medicated and wearing fresh clothes, but my eyes still feel like open wounds. Emma has gone to sleep in Charlie's room, but not before checking and rechecking the window latches, deadlocks and security chain. Whenever she is frightened she falls back on to the same obsessive-compulsive routines.

Charlie tiptoes from her bedroom, gently closing the door behind her. Seeing Ruiz, she skips across the floor and throws her arms around his chest. He lifts her off the ground. 'You're heavy. Must be that enormous brain.'

'What's your excuse?' she asks, patting his stomach.

Ruiz sucks it in. 'That is solid muscle.'

'Self-delusion,' Charlie says. 'I'm learning all about that.'

Ruiz looks at me. 'Are you going to let her talk to me like that?'

'You're a big boy.'

'My point exactly,' says Charlie, who dances away, grabbing an apple from a bowl and taking a bite. Every time I see her, a hook snags in my heart because she looks so much like Julianne. University life has added experience to her dark, uncomplicated beauty, separating her from childhood and her younger sister. I can still see the little girl inside her because I know what to look for, but she's grown up in every other way.

'What did the police say?' Ruiz asks.

'They're looking for him.'

'Could he be my uncle?' asks Charlie. 'I mean, if he's your half-brother . . .'

I can't answer her. Ewan knew so much about me. He knew where Emma went to school and where we lived, yet his existence came as a complete shock to me.

'There's only one way to be sure,' I say, grabbing my coat, checking the pockets twice for my phone and pills.

'You can't go out now,' Charlie says. 'What if he comes back?'

'Vincent is going to stay the night.'

I glance at Ruiz, hoping for confirmation.

He nods. 'I'll sleep on the sofa.'

'No, you take Emma's room,' insists Charlie. 'She can share with me.'

I kiss her forehead. Ruiz walks me to the door. 'Are you sure about this? DI Macdermid told you to stay away from Olivia Blackmore.'

'That's before I knew about Ewan.'

Gripping my hand, Ruiz pulls me closer. His breath smells of hops and cheese-and-onion crisps.

'One of the things I've always admired about you, Professor, is that you don't jump to conclusions, or spout wild theories. You look for the evidence before you condemn someone.'

'I only want to talk to her,' I say, aware that I'm trying to reassure myself. 'I won't be long.'

It's almost eleven when a taxi drops me outside the house in Chiswick. The lower floor is dark, but windows glow upstairs. I ring the doorbell. Wait. A light triggers. A shape appears beyond the leaded glass, fractured and drawing together as it moves closer. The door opens on a security chain. Olivia is wearing a dressing gown cinched at the waist.

'Can I come in?'

'What's wrong? Is it William?'

'No.'

She glances over her shoulder, along the hallway, as though she has company.

'It's late. I'm tired. Come back tomorrow.'

'Why didn't you tell me about Ewan?'

Olivia doesn't react. Her coolness is remarkable.

'He forced his way into my home tonight. He held my daughters at knifepoint.'

Olivia's eyes widen. 'He wouldn't hurt anyone. He's not dangerous.' She notices my face. 'What happened to your eyes?'

'I tried to follow him. It didn't end well.'

Something shifts in her thinking and she unlatches the chain, opening the door fully. I push past her, moving along the hallway to the kitchen.

'Are the girls OK? I didn't think he knew your address.' She steps from foot to foot as though standing on hot sand. 'I was going to tell you about Ewan.'

'When?'

'It was too much. First you learn about me, then you discover . . . I didn't think . . . expect . . .'

'You kept him a secret.'

'No.'

'Where are the photographs? Are they in separate journals? Do you have a special room for them?'

She doesn't answer.

'Who is Ewan's father?'

'What did *he* tell you?'

'I want to hear it from you.'

Olivia is breathing faster, as though my questions are using up all the oxygen in the room.

'He's not William's son, if that's what you're worried about.'

'Who is the father?'

She drops her voice. 'I was pregnant when Todd died. The baby survived the accident. I sometimes wonder if that's why Ewan . . .' She doesn't finish the statement.

130

'What's wrong with him?'

'He's bipolar.'

'No, it's more than that. He's hearing voices and quoting from the Bible.'

Olivia takes a seat, tucking the dressing gown around her thighs. I pull out a chair and keep the table between us. Although we're on the same level, eye to eye, I have the curious feeling that she's somehow set above me, looking down. She has done something to her hair, tied it back, or brushed it in a different away, exposing her ears, which glow pinkly when lit from behind.

'Ewan was born six weeks prematurely and spent a month in hospital. I was seeing William by then, but we hadn't you know . . . fallen in love. It's a courageous thing – to bring up another man's baby. Selfless. William didn't hesitate. And not once, in all the time we've been together, has he ever said he regretted being here with Ewan and me.'

Olivia plays with the belt of her dressing gown, as if waiting for some acknowledgement that I believe her. I say nothing. She carries on, constructing sentences as though reading from a teleprompter.

'Ewan was such a bright, bubbly little boy, who charmed everyone with his cheeky sense of humour and his hugs. I wish you could have met him then . . . he brought us so much joy. It was only when he turned fourteen that he began to struggle, becoming withdrawn and socially awkward. He didn't laugh at the same things as his friends. It was easy to put it down to puberty – something he'd grow out of – but other things began to bother me. I'd go to wake him for school and discover him staring at the

131

wall, barely blinking. At other times, I'd hear him talking to himself, having animated conversations. I asked him who he was talking to, but he said I wouldn't understand.

'At sixteen he went away to Europe on a school trip. Something happened. Ewan suffered a breakdown and was taken to a psych hospital in France. William suspected it might be drugs, but had no proof. We flew him home and took him to different specialists, but Ewan became even more silent, retreating from the world. He rarely left his room. Some nights I'd hear him through the wall, arguing with himself, or saying things over and over.

'Eventually, he told me about the voices. "What do they say?" I asked. "They tell me I'm no good." "Why?" "Because I'm not."'

Olivia wipes her eyes with the back of her hand.

'We kept going to different doctors, but none of them found anything wrong with Ewan. They didn't realise how clever he could be. He could act normal during the interviews and psych tests. He came across as bright and engaging, just like his old self, but it wasn't really him. The voices were telling him what to say.

'When he began his A-level studies we discovered that he'd been skipping classes and spending his days in the park or at the local library. He said his teachers were "imposters" and couldn't teach him anything. He had lost interest in school and food and family. It was like watching him slowly disappear, his body being hollowed out and subsumed by something else.'

'Was he ever hospitalised?'

'Twice.'

'What happened?'

'A month after his eighteenth birthday he suffered another breakdown. He tore up his room, smashing furniture and pulling up the carpets looking for listening devices and hidden cameras. William called an ambulance. Ewan spent five weeks in a psych ward and was diagnosed with schizophrenia. They put him on medication and kept him in the hospital until the dosages were right.'

'What about the second time?'

'He and William had an argument. Ewan had stopped taking his pills. We found them stockpiled in his room.'

'Was it a physical altercation?'

'No!'

'He's never attacked him?'

'No.'

Her eyes tell me she's lying; a tiny micro-expression that she blinks away like a speck of dust.

'Where does Ewan live?'

She hesitates. 'He moved out of home fourteen months ago.'

'Why?'

There is a long silence. Olivia sighs. 'Things began to go missing. Valuables. William found a glass pipe in Ewan's room and accused him of taking drugs. Methamphetamines. He threatened to have him sectioned again, but Ewan ran away.' Olivia's voice cracks. She clears her throat. 'I thought we'd lost him . . . I thought . . .' She starts again. 'Two weeks later we had a call from the Salvation Army. Ewan had turned up at a homeless shelter in Birmingham. William brought him home. He ran away again at Easter. The police found him naked on Hampstead Heath. Someone had beaten and robbed him. It went on like that for months – him disappearing and turning up bashed, or penniless, or high on drugs. William was beside himself. We both were.

'We had him sectioned, but Ewan went to court and fought the order. He hired his own lawyer and made a statement, accusing William of sexually abusing him as a child. It was a terrible lie, but Ewan got what he wanted.'

'What did he want?'

'Freedom.'

'When was this?'

'August. That's why there aren't any photographs of Ewan in the house. William made me take them down. He swore that if Ewan ever set foot in here, he'd call the police. He made me promise to do the same.'

'But you didn't.'

Olivia looks at her hands. 'I couldn't. He's my son.'

'Is that why you have a gun? You're frightened of him.'

'No. He would never . . .'

Her shoulders shudder and she drops her head. Her left wrist is exposed and I notice four small bruises. Fingermarks. Someone has gripped her there, squeezing hard.

'Did he do that to you?'

Olivia pulls down her sleeve.

'My father had old bruises on his body. Someone gave him a beating.'

'It wasn't Ewan.'

'Who then?'

Olivia shakes her head. Tears are shining in her eyes like drops of glycerine.

'Please let me see William.'

'No.'

'Why?'

'Because I can't trust you.'

As I utter the words, I hear a sound upstairs. Olivia's eyes flick to the ceiling and down again, betraying her.

'Is Ewan here?'

'No.'

'You're hiding him!'

My eyes sweep across the room. There are two cups on the draining rack. Two plates in the sink. I head towards the hallway. Olivia intercepts me, bracing herself across the stairs.

'I want you to leave.'

'You're protecting him.'

'Get out!'

I brush her aside and climb. Olivia pulls at my arm, trying to drag me back, screaming at me to get out.

The main bedroom is empty, the bedclothes pulled back. I try the next room. The door is locked. Kneeling on the floor, I see light coming from underneath. I rattle the handle.

'Ewan? Are you in there? I want to talk, that's all.'

'Get out of my house!' says Olivia, her voice laced with threat. I turn and see the shotgun. She's holding it in both hands, aiming it at my chest. From this angle, the twin barrels look like enormous black holes.

'I can help him.'

'Get out!'

Her finger tightens on the trigger. She has not flinched.

'This isn't over,' I say, walking backwards down the stairs. 'Ewan is going to hurt someone, or harm himself.'

'He's not here.'

'You lied to the police and you're lying to me.'

'My whole life has been a lie,' she mutters, still holding the gun, which is dipping towards the floor as it grows heavy. She lifts it again. Anger fills her frame and I see a woman capable of doing violence . . . of pulling the trigger . . . of crushing a man's skull.

The front door slams behind me. The lock turns. The chain slides into place.

Standing outside the house, I turn twice in circles, trying to decide what to do. She's hiding Ewan. I should call the police, but Macdermid told me to stay away. Olivia won't forgive me. If I turn this into a feud, nobody wins, least of all my father.

I shouldn't even consider Dad, but I can't bring myself to give up on him yet. Instead I want to march into the ICU and yell at him to wake up. I want to know if he was a better father to Ewan than he was to me. Did they do things together? Did they discover books and films, or follow sports? All my life I've wanted a father who engaged with me and was part of my life, but he was always indisposed, or busy, or somewhere else. Perhaps it wasn't his career that kept him away from home, or made him such a distant figure. Maybe it was me.

Day Four

18

My dreams hum with images of streaming eyes and burning skin; the flames robbed of their heat, yet I claw at the air, fighting for each breath. Daylight comes as a relief and I take comfort from the ordinary: getting Emma ready for school, unpacking the dishwasher and taking out the rubbish.

Lucy phones me from the hospital.

'I've called all of Mum's friends. Nobody has heard from her.'

'Maybe she went back to Wales.'

'She wouldn't leave Daddy.'

Patricia's husband Simon drove down from Cardiff last night. He's a criminal barrister, working mainly for the Crown, which means he understands how police put cases together.

After dropping Emma at school, I visit a florist shop and

buy flowers for Olivia, writing an apology on the card. I went too far last night. She lied to me, but that's no excuse to frighten a woman in a place she should feel safe. If she's protecting Ewan, the police will find out soon enough and she'll lose any chance of being accepted by my family, let alone tolerated.

The salesgirl helps me choose a bouquet. 'Where would you like them to be delivered?'

'I'll take them with me,' I say, watching her skilfully trim and arrange the carnations and gerbera.

Nobody answers the doorbell at Olivia's house. I ring again, holding my finger on the bell. The curtains are drawn. Lights are off. I prop the bouquet against the door and retrace my steps along the path.

'Lovely morning,' says a voice. It belongs to an elderly man dressed in pristine white running shoes and a tracksuit. His Labrador sniffs at my trouser cuffs.

'Nobody home?' he asks.

'No.'

He pulls the dog away. 'Are you a friend or family?'

'Family.'

'Who's side? William or Olivia's?'

'William's.'

'How is dear William? I heard he had a fall. I hope he's all right.' He spies the flowers on the doorstep. 'Please tell me that he's not . . .'

'He's in a coma.'

'Right. Good. I mean not good. Terrible. Horrid news.'

'Do you live around here?' I ask.

He points to a house across the road. 'That's me: Number

138

72. Lived here for thirty years.' He holds out his hand. 'George Hartigan. Call me George.' He shakes my hand. 'Olivia is a very nice lady. We used to walk our dogs together before Sally died.'

'Is Sally your wife?'

'Heaven's no,' he laughs. 'Sally is a Jack Russell. Olivia loved that dog. Terrible business. Someone poisoned her – threw a bait into their back garden.'

'Why would someone poison her dog?'

'Exactly. I've been extra careful ever since.' He crouches and scratches his Labrador's head. 'People can be so cruel.'

I change the subject. 'Do you know Ewan?'

'Of course. Nice lad. Delivered my paper for a while, before he got sick.'

'Sick?'

'Mental problems. Bipolar or some such thing.'

'When did you last see him?'

George scratches his cheek. 'Few days ago. Maybe a week. He moved out. They all do. I have three kids, two grandchildren. Don't see enough of them.' He drags his Labrador away from my crotch. 'How are you related to William?'

'I'm his son.'

'Right, of course. I'm telling you the bleeding obvious. I do that. My wife says I could have a conversation with a wall.'

'Did you see Ewan on Sunday?'

'I don't think so. There were loads of paramedics. I knew it must have been serious. Was it the stairs?'

'William was bashed.'

139

George's eyes widen and he scans the street, as if the attacker might be lying in wait. 'Well, that explains a lot.'

'Pardon?'

'I had a constable knock on my door and ask if I saw anyone suspicious hanging around the house. I told him about the courier.'

'What courier?'

'He drove up and down the street on a motorcycle, looking for the address. I thought it was odd delivering so late on a Sunday.'

'What makes you think he was a courier?'

'Looked like one – leathers, helmet, gloves. His bike had saddlebags.'

'What time was this?'

George scratches the same cheek. 'Before the woman, I think.'

'The woman?'

'Didn't I mention her?'

'No.'

'I told the constable. I couldn't give him a description. I didn't see her face. She arrived in a cab. Didn't stay long. I don't think anyone was home.'

'Were there lights on inside the house?'

'Yes, come to think of it. I don't know how I remember that.'

'Does Olivia have many friends?'

'What do you mean?'

'People who visit.'

'One chap comes around quite a bit. I waved to him once. He didn't wave back.'

'What does he look like?'

'Your height. Younger. Wears expensive clothes and drives a BMW – very nice, top of the range.'

'Does he ever stay the night?'

George stiffens at the suggestion. 'I hope you're not . . . because if you are . . . I mean, you're here standing outside Olivia's house, I don't jump to conclusions. I'm not one to pry. None of my business. Live and let live, that's my motto.'

'Absolutely,' I say. 'You're a good neighbour.'

'Come on, Toby,' he says. 'Let's get home.'

19

The café has steam condensing inside the front window and a kitchen full of shuddering pots and pans. Seated alone, DI Macdermid is tucking into a late breakfast of Cumberland sausages, smothered in brown sauce, that look like turds in a toilet bowl. Triangles of toast are buttered on a side plate and a mug of tea rests near his gnarled right fist. It's almost midday. Only one of us is eating.

'I told you to leave Mrs Blackmore alone,' he says, cutting a fried egg into quarters with a knife that he's forced between his clawed fingers.

'She lied about having a son.'

'Ewan Blackmore was never a secret.'

'You knew?'

'Of course.'

'Why didn't you tell me?'

'Do I look like a family counsellor?'

His sarcasm annoys me, which seems to amuse him even more.

'What you keep failing to understand, Professor, is that you're not part of this investigation and I'm under no obligation to share details with you. Right from the outset, I told you to keep your nose out of this, but you couldn't help yourself.'

'Ewan Blackmore forced his way into my flat with a knife.'

'And you've chosen not to make a statement. Why is that?' He doesn't wait for me to answer. 'Don't tell me — brotherly love?'

'He's *not* my brother. I wanted to talk to Olivia first . . . to be sure.'

'You went to her house and threatened her.'

'No.'

'She has bruises on her wrist.'

'That wasn't me.'

Macdermid wipes his lips with a serviette and tries to dislodge sausage gristle from between his teeth with his tongue. A ruby jewel of a shaving cut glistens on his neck.

'I asked some of my colleagues about you, Professor. They said some good things. They called you insightful and brilliant, but frankly, I don't see it. I think you're a glory hound, who can't stay out of the spotlight.'

'You're wrong. Did Ewan attack my father?'

'He has an alibi.'

'Who?'

'Mrs Blackmore says she visited Ewan after she left the theatre.'

The missing hour in her timeline.

'They're alibiing each other!'

Macdermid pushes his plate away, no longer hungry. 'Stay out of this, Professor.'

'She's playing you.'

'Enough!' He jabs a butter knife at me. 'You went to Mrs Blackmore's house last night and forced your way inside. You assaulted her.'

'That's a lie.'

'I've seen the bruises.'

'She threatened me with a gun.'

'She was defending herself.'

'With an illegal firearm.'

'Licensed to your father.'

'Improperly stored.'

'And now confiscated.'

'Why are you taking her side on this?'

'I don't take sides, Professor. I look at the facts. According to Olivia, your father brought the shotgun into the house against her wishes because he was frightened of his stepson. Olivia wanted nothing to do with it. She might be lying. She might be telling the truth. Regardless, it has nothing to do with you. This is *not* your investigation.'

Macdermid looks at me smugly, like a poker player with a winning hand. Satisfied that he's won the argument, he raises a mug of tea to his lips, swallowing noisily and wiping his mouth with the back of his hand.

'Has your mother showed up?'

'No.'

'You have until five o'clock this afternoon to find her, or I'm issuing a warrant for her arrest.'

He signals a waitress, asking for the bill.

'How did you know about the shotgun?' I ask.

'Mrs Blackmore gave us a full account this morning when she surrendered the weapon and made a formal complaint against you. She also applied for a restraining order, which prevents you going anywhere near her or Ewan. To make matters worse, she has briefed a lawyer, which means we can't talk to her without having some pin-striped Rumpole whispering in her ear, telling her not to answer. I blame you for that.'

The detective takes out his wallet and removes several bills, tossing them on the table.

'I wish we could swap jobs for a day, Professor. It must be so easy, dealing with people's fantasies and delusions instead of living in the real world. I have a victim who may or may not wake up, two wives who both lied about their whereabouts on the night of the attack; and two sons – one who hears voices from God and the other who thinks he's God's gift.' Macdermid belches to punctuate the statement. 'But I will give you one heads-up. Olivia Blackmore is applying to the Court of Protection to be appointed as a deputy to William O'Loughlin.'

'What's that?'

'Your father didn't grant lasting power of attorney over his affairs should he become ill or incapacitated. Mrs Blackmore is applying for the role. If she becomes a deputy, she'll make all future decisions about his welfare and his finances.'

'She can't do that. We're his family.'

'So is she — and right now she's pissed off.' He picks up his jacket from the back of his chair and slips his arms through the sleeves. 'Having met most of your family — I don't blame her.'

20

'Joe, is everything OK?' asks David Passage, answering his mobile. He's somewhere busy with a hubbub of voices in the background.

'I need to see you.'

'I'm at an art auction – bidding for a friend. I can meet you afterwards.'

'Where?'

'Come to Sotheby's.'

The auction rooms are in New Bond Street, flanked by high-end fashion boutiques and jewellery designers. A pretty young woman greets me at the door and directs me to an air-conditioned room with about forty people seated on chairs.

'Would you like a paddle?' she asks.

'I won't be bidding.'

'Take one anyway,' she says, giving me a smile. A large screen displays images of an antique barometer. The auctioneer is wearing a salmon-coloured shirt and dashing necktie. He peers over half-glasses, pointing to new bids in the room and acknowledging those on the phone. His pulse never seems to miss a beat, or eyes fail to pick out a paddle. I have never been to an auction, but I feel myself growing nervous for others, as the bidding climbs to £30,000 and the hammer falls.

I'm seated near the back and can't see David. The next lot is a carriage clock circa 1870, silver mounted with an engraved plaque. The auctioneer details the provenance, mentioning King George V and his wedding presents. The bidding begins at £4,000. A woman near the front row raises a paddle, adding a thousand. Others appear. The auctioneer acknowledges each with a nod of his head. The bids begin to slow at £7,000. The woman smiles confidently.

Then I see David's raised hand. The woman looks surprised at a new player. She hesitates. Counterbids. David calmly comes back, causing a frown on her powdered countenance. I imagine her cursing under her breath.

'The bid is against you, madam,' says the auctioneer. 'I'm selling it on this side of the room.'

She shakes her head.

He scans the floor. 'Are we done? Finished? Going once, twice . . . Sold! Congratulations, sir.'

There is a smattering of applause. David stands and moves down the centre aisle. The woman seems to be glaring at him. David waves to me, looking pleased with himself.

'I'll be right with you,' he says.

I wait in the foyer while he signs the paperwork and arranges payment.

'You bought a clock,' I say, stating the obvious. 'Why that one?'

'I have a client who collects them.'

We're outside on the footpath. 'Let's get a coffee. You can tell me why you're here.'

'Olivia Blackmore is applying to take control of my father's affairs.'

'I know.'

'What?'

'She called me this morning and asked me to represent her.'

'You can't.'

'I know. I recommended a friend of mine.'

I look at him incredulously. 'Why did you do that?'

'She's not the enemy. She regards herself as William's wife – common law or otherwise. That doesn't give her the same rights as your mother under English law, but she can still make things dificult.'

'She wants to control his money and his treatment?' I say.

'I wouldn't let that happen.'

David makes it sound so simple. 'I'm not playing sides here, Joe. I am doing my job. Clearly, the best outcome is for your family to sit down with Olivia and come to an agreement. I can help negotiate a truce – for want of a better word. Nobody wants this to finish up in court.'

'Except the lawyers,' I say.

David blinks at me sadly, like a puppy told to get off the couch.

'Let me talk to Olivia.' he says. 'In the meantime, try not to antagonise her.'

'Did you know about Ewan Blackmore?' I ask.

David falters again.

'Has my father made provisions for him in his will?'

'I can't discuss that, Joe.'

My eyes drop to his feet. He's wearing the same runners as before.

'Ewan is not Dad's son,' I say. 'Olivia said she was pregnant before they met.'

'William's name is on Ewan's birth certificate.'

'We could do a DNA test.'

'Why? You have no legal right to deny William's wishes, or to have Ewan written out of his will. Your father accepted Ewan as his son. It doesn't matter if the relationship was biological, or adoptive or common law.'

I want to argue, but my urgings sound small-minded and jealous, even before I voice them. This isn't about money, or paternity, or who inherits the family silver. Ewan followed Emma home from school and held my daughters at knife-point. He stole from my father and accused him of sexually abusing him.

When I was at Sunday School, I hated the parable of the Prodigal Son; the idea that one child could piss away his entire inheritance on whores and partying, yet be welcomed home by the father, who gives him new clothes and shoes and kills a fatted calf for a feast. Meanwhile the elder son, the one who was prudent and pious and respectful, the one who stayed home and looked after the family, comes in from the fields and hears music and feasting and partying.

He sees his brother being treated like a returning hero and refuses to enter the house because he's angry at his brother being forgiven so easily. His father comes out to him and says, 'This brother of yours was dead and is alive again; he was lost and is found.'

The story is supposed to be about redemption and absolution, but I can't see any moral lesson because the outcome is so unfair. There's no benefit to being the 'good son'; no equity, or grace or justice.

21

Mum has shown up. She walked into the ICU just before midday and sat next to Dad as though she'd never been away.

Lucy is on the phone, telling me the news.

'She spent last night in a hotel near Paddington station because she needed time to think.'

'About what?'

'Olivia Blackmore, I assume, although she won't mention the woman's name.'

'Has she talked to the police?'

'Not yet. Simon spoke to the detective in charge and promised to take her to the station in the morning.'

'Where is she now?'

'In the chapel. She looks exhausted and I don't think she's eaten.'

I can picture Mum praying, holding rosary beads between her thumb and forefinger, murmuring each Hail Mary and Our Father. She has always been a devout Catholic. She took us all to Sunday Mass until I was fourteen and the girls were older. Since then she's gone more often – two or three times a week – no doubt praying for her sinful husband and godless children.

'Where did I go wrong?' she once asked me. 'None of you go to church.'

'You gave us a faith to embrace or reject,' I replied.

'And you rejected it.'

'I'm an agnostic, not an atheist.'

'A fence-sitter.' She made it sound worse.

'I prefer to think I'm keeping an open mind.'

'You're hedging your bets.'

Lucy is still on the phone. I ask her to call a family meeting. 'I need everyone there.'

'Why?'

'Olivia Blackmore is applying to get control of Dad's affairs.'

I hear her sharp intake of breath. 'Can she do that?'

'She's hired a lawyer. Make sure Simon is at the meeting. He'll know what to do.'

'What do I tell, Mummy?'

'Nothing. Not yet.'

The hospital chapel is cool and quiet, with low-wattage bulbs glowing at floor-level along the aisles. Dipping a finger into holy water, I make a sign of the cross and move forward, feeling the silence on my skin. I can understand why people spend time in churches. There is a calm about them; a sense that the world has stopped turning for a moment. This doesn't require faith in a creator, merely an ability to still the mind and reflect. Breathe. Relax.

My mother is sitting two rows back from the altar. She's alone in the chapel, wearing the same dress and cardigan as yesterday, with a knotted silk scarf around her neck. She's kneeling in prayer. The pew creaks under my weight. She doesn't turn her head or acknowledge my presence.

'What are you doing?' I ask.

'Praying.'

'And last night?'

'The same.'

Her rosary beads are made of jade and polished wood. They were a present from my grandmother on Mum's First Holy Communion. I got into trouble as a child when I dressed up as a hippy and used the rosary beads as part of my costume.

'I talked to DI Macdermid this morning. He's going to have you arrested if you don't cooperate.'

'I haven't done anything wrong.'

'Why did you follow Dad to London?'

She turns to look at me. Her eyes are bruised with tiredness and her skin as thin and creased as parchment. 'I was worried about him. Frightened.' She traces her forefinger over the crucifix on her beads. 'He's been acting out of sorts for weeks, spending hours in his study, locking the door, barely coming out to eat and sleep. I demanded to know what was wrong and he told me not to worry. Of course, I was going to worry. We've been married for more than sixty years. I know his moods. I know his breathing and the rhythm of his heart. I know when he's fixated on something.'

Reaching into her handbag she takes a tissue from a pack but doesn't blow her nose. Instead she folds it in half and half again, before polishing the rosary beads.

'William forgot our wedding anniversary. He's never done that. I thought he might be sick; that he had cancer or some other terrible disease. His father died of liver and bowel cancer. I thought he was keeping it from me, because he didn't want to be a burden. I asked him. He made fun of me.'

I can imagine him doing that.

'Then I thought he might be leaving me. After all these years, he'd made a choice – chosen her over me.'

'He wouldn't do that,' I say, trying to sound genuine.

Mum tries and fails to summon a smile. 'What do I have to offer him? I was never his equal in intellect or ambition. He met someone younger, prettier, healthier. Isn't that what men are programmed to do? It's in your genes.'

'It doesn't work like that.'

Ahead of us, above the altar, a stained-glass window portrays Jesus on the cross with Apostles at his feet and angels around his head. All the characters look white and western, with similar features, but look bored rather than adoring.

My mother puts her rosary beads in a velvet pouch. 'I asked William if he wanted a divorce. He was shocked. We argued. He accused me of being melodramatic. He called me hysterical. I hate that word. Why are women crazy if they

155

disagree with a man, or fight for what they believe?' There's a note of defiance, or perhaps pride, in the question. 'I know when something is wrong. That's why I came down to London. I wanted to know why William had changed from an easy-going, happy, retired doctor into a short-tempered, brittle man whose heart was wrapped in barbed wire.'

'Who were you going to ask?'

She hesitates, looking at her hands. 'Her.'

'Olivia Blackmore?'

She nods.

'Have you spoken to her before?'

'No. Not really.' Her chest fills and she exhales. 'Sometimes I'd call William's mobile and a woman answered. I assumed it was her.'

'Did you say anything?'

'It had gone on too long. Years. And I don't like confrontation.'

I want to scream at her passivity; demand that she stand up for herself and stop being so stoic and stiff-upper-lip, so bloody English!

'Did you know that Olivia has a son – Ewan?'

'Yes.'

'And you knew where to find her?'

Another nod. 'I wanted to know what was wrong with William . . . why he was acting so strangely.'

'You rang the doorbell?'

'Nobody answered.'

'And then what?'

'I went home.'

'You came all the way to London and simply walked away?'

'Yes.'

'Why didn't you tell the police any of this?'

Mum looks at me plaintively. 'I was scared. I thought they might blame me for what happened.'

'They do now. You've made yourself a suspect.'

She's shaking her head. 'I would never hurt him.'

'What time did you arrive at the house?'

'I'm not sure. Eleven thirty.'

'Were the lights on?'

'Yes. Downstairs.'

'Are you sure?'

She nods.

'How long were you outside?'

'Ten or fifteen minutes. It took me a while to pluck up the courage. Eventually I rang the doorbell, but nobody answered. I knew William was inside.'

'How?'

'I heard someone moving around.'

'Olivia Blackmore said the house was in darkness when she arrived home at midnight.'

My mother blinks at me, unsure of what I'm trying to say. Then the truth dawns on her. A hand goes to her mouth. 'I could have saved him. I could have called an ambulance sooner.'

'You weren't to know.'

'He was lying at the bottom of the stairs. If I'd known . . . If I'd . . .'

Nothing I say is going to console her now. She's convinced that she's to blame. Taking her hands in mine, I squeeze them tightly and make her focus on me.

'I found old bruises on Dad's body. He was beaten up more than a week ago. He must have been in pain. Did you notice anything?'

Mum shakes her head, shocked.

'Did anyone ever come looking for money – debt collectors, or bailiffs?' I ask.

'We're not that sort of family.'

We're not poor, is what she means.

'Maybe she beat him up . . . that woman.' She means Olivia. 'You've spoken to her. Did she do this?'

'I don't think so.'

Mum keeps talking. 'What's she like? Is she . . . Can you see why William would want to be . . . ?' She doesn't finish either question. 'She's young, isn't she? I've seen photographs. She's very sporty. William loves his tennis. I should have taken more interest . . . made more of an effort.'

'This is not your fault.'

'I wasn't enough. I couldn't keep him happy.'

'No! He cheated on you. He gave everything to other people and left nothing for us. He's selfish and self-centred and narcissistic . . .'

She reacts as though I've slapped her. 'How dare you call him those things! He's a wonderful man.'

'Oh, come on—'

'No, you listen to me. I love your father. Always have. Always will. You think he's a monster. You think he abandoned us. You're wrong. He didn't just look after us, he saved hundreds of lives. People survived because of William. Families were whole.' Her eyes are shining. 'I remember one day he came home from hospital and found me asleep

158

on the sofa. You were lying on my stomach, having fallen off the breast while feeding. William told me I looked beautiful. I knew that I looked an absolute fright – with red-rimmed eyes, greasy hair and old clothes. "Am I doing something beautiful?" I asked him. "Yes," he said. "Everything."

'I love you, Joseph. I love Lucy and Patricia and Rebecca, but I love your father more. With a child, you get what comes along, but I *chose* William.'

'And he chose someone else.'

'I will *never* believe that until I hear it from his lips.'

Something seems to break inside of me. Perhaps it is several things, tolerance, balance and decency, all of them unravelling and transforming into one thing. Rage. I want Mum to be angry. I want her to feel like I do. Betrayed. Humiliated. Abandoned.

I once saw a famous stage play called *Gas Light* set in 1930s about a husband who drives his wife crazy by dimming the gas lights in their house and denying there has been any change when she notices. It's where the term gas-lighting comes from – manipulating someone into doubting his or her sanity. That's what my father has done to my mother. Instead of dimming the lights, he has withheld his love, eroding her confidence in hundreds of small ways, until she questions her own reality, or blames herself for what he's done.

That's what I can't forgive.

22

'Here, Joe, take these.'

Lucy hands me napkins, knives and forks. I carry them to the sitting room where the family has gathered on sofas, dining chairs and cushions from the sunroom. Lucy and Eric live beneath the flight path to Heathrow and every few minutes a jet passes overhead, just audible through the triple-glazed windows.

Everyone is here except my mother – who has stayed at the hospital, refusing to leave my father's side.

Lucy and Patricia have prepared supper – quiche, boiled new potatoes and a green salad, washed down with wine, a bottle of red and one of white, provided by Simon, who married into the family but feels like a brother. A big man, with a fleshy face, I've always found it hard to imagine him in a wig and gown, cross-examining defence witnesses. It must be like being accosted by a panda bear.

Holding a bottle between his thighs, he pulls the cork and offers it around.

'Is that appropriate?' asks Patricia. 'Drinking, I mean.'

'Well, I'm definitely having one,' says Rebecca, holding out her glass. My youngest sister arrived from Khartoum, via Geneva, this afternoon, sporting an African suntan and a new hairstyle. The auburn tresses that I remember her brushing every night have been replaced by a chin-skimming bob that sweeps over her cheekbones.

The food is served. Eaten. My sisters fall into set roles when they're together: Sensible, Bossy and the Diplomat – parts that have become more apposite as they age. Lucy is the mother-hen figure, Patricia is the bossy second child and Rebecca the peacemaker.

'This is the first time we've been together since Julianne died,' Patricia says. Realising what she's said, she apologises: 'I shouldn't have said that.'

'It's fine,' I reply, aware that my sisters are looking at me.

Simon pours more wine. 'I hear you had a meeting with David Passage yesterday.'

'Is that the same David who used to come on holidays with us?' asks Rebecca.

'He and his brother,' answers Lucy. 'We used to babysit them. They were sweet boys.'

'Mmm,' says Rebecca, sounding doubtful.

'What's that look for?'

'David once tried to kiss me.'

'How old was he?'

'All of six.'

'Cheeky sod,' says Lucy. 'Didn't he elope with the head-master's daughter at your school?' She looks at me.

'I don't think they eloped, but they did get married. Two kids. Divorced. He's a lawyer now. He took over from Kenneth.'

I recount my meetings with father and son, revealing details of the two trusts and the life insurance policies, and the deed-of-trust.

'That's so typical of Daddy,' jokes Rebecca. 'Two wives, two houses, two of everything. He could have built an Ark.'

Patricia isn't in the mood for humour. 'Olivia Blackmore gets half of everything. Is that funny too?'

'I don't care about money,' says Rebecca, looking hurt.

'What about her son – Ewan?' asks Patricia. 'He'll have his hand out.'

'You don't know that,' says Rebecca.

'As far as I know, there is no special provision for Ewan,' I say.

'Have you seen the will?' asks Patricia.

'No, it's sealed.'

'Exactly! He could get it all.'

I'm desperate to change the subject. I glance at Rebecca. 'Olivia says she met you once, years ago.'

'Me!'

'It was outside a restaurant near Sloane Square. You bumped into Dad and a former patient.'

'I remember,' says Rebecca, her eyes lighting up. 'He said

they played mixed doubles together. She was very pretty
. . . and young. Far too young for Daddy.'

'Clearly, not,' says Lucy. 'And now we have a half-brother.'

'Is that what he is?' asks Patricia, unsure of the precise
genealogy.

I correct her. 'I think he's our stepbrother.'

'I want to meet him,' says Rebecca, shocking Patricia.

'He's a paranoid schizophrenic!'

'So?'

'Look what he did to Emma and Charlie – held them
at knifepoint.'

'We can't pretend he doesn't exist,' I say.

'Why not? Last week he didn't exist.'

'He's *always* existed.'

Patricia folds her arms across her chest as though the
subject is closed. 'Well, he's not coming anywhere near me.'

The disagreement threatens to derail the meeting. I
change the focus and reveal Olivia's application for Lasting
Power of Attorney over Dad's affairs.

Simon takes over. 'Power of attorney normally resides
with a lawyer like David Passage,' he explains, 'but this isn't
valid when someone loses his or her mental capacity. Unless
William set up a Lasting Power of Attorney, the Court of
Protection can be asked to designate someone.'

'Shouldn't that be a member of the family?' Lucy asks.

'Yes, normally,' replies Simon, 'but Mrs Blackmore may
try to argue that she is family.'

Patricia makes a *hmmmfff* sound. 'How do we know she
married him? Has anyone seen the marriage certificate?'

Simon ignores the question and continues. 'English law

163

doesn't recognise common-law husbands and wives, which means that Mary would have a greater claim to being William's deputy, because her marriage came first and was never annulled. That being said, Olivia is quite within her rights to make an application. If we don't make a counter-claim, she gains control over William's accounts, investments and property. More importantly, she would make decisions about his medical treatment.'

'Surely that's up to the doctors,' Lucy says.

'Right now, yes, but there may come a time when it ceases to be a medical decision.' Simon looks uncomfortable. 'If William were deemed to be brain-dead, or more particularly if he's on life support with no likelihood of recovery, a deputy could decide to refuse consent for life-sustaining treatment.'

'She could turn off the machines!' Lucy splutters.

Simon nods. 'At the very least, she could have William transferred to another hospital, or to a palliative care hospice, or take him home.'

'Why would she do any of that?' Rebecca asks.

'Isn't it obvious?' replies Patricia. 'She wants him out of the way.'

'You don't know that,' I say.

'She's a suspect. What if Daddy is the only witness? She gets rid of him and she's home free. She gets the house . . . the money.'

The discussion is getting away from me.

'I think this is my fault,' I say, surprising them. 'Olivia asked if she could come to the hospital and I told her she wasn't welcome.'

164

'She's not,' Patricia says.

'I forced her hand. I denied her access and now she's applied to control everything.'

Rebecca understands. 'I think Joe is right. Regardless of whether we trust Olivia or not, she's been our father's mistress for a long time. That has to count for something.'

'Not if she attacked him,' Lucy says.

'We don't know that,' I say.

'Well, I'm not going to welcome her,' Patricia says. 'And I don't want anything to do with her schizophrenic son.'

'Daddy's son,' Rebecca says.

'Allegedly,' Lucy adds.

Patricia turns to Simon. 'Surely there's no judge in the land who'd give them control over Daddy's affairs?'

Simon clears his throat. 'My advice would be to talk to Olivia and to find common ground. Avoid turning this into a legal battle.'

'I'm happy to meet her,' says Rebecca, looking at me. 'What's she like, Joe? You're good at reading people.'

Where do I start? Charming. Articulate. Secretive. Cunning.

'I haven't managed to get a fix on her yet,' I say, unwilling to share my thoughts.

Simon opens his briefcase and takes out a form.

'In the meantime, we should prepare our own application for lasting power of attorney.'

He takes a fountain pen from his pocket and begins filling out the questions, taking down full names and dates of birth.

'How long will the application take?' Lucy asks.

'Any court hearing could be months away.'

165

'What do we do until then?' Patricia asks.

'I think we should let Olivia see Daddy,' says Rebecca. 'I think it's only fair.'

'Fairness has nothing to do with it,' scoffs Patricia. 'What if she smothers him with a pillow?'

'She won't be alone,' I say. 'One of us will be there.'

Simon agrees with me. 'It could reflect badly on our chances if this goes to court and we haven't given Olivia access.'

'Mummy isn't going to like it,' Lucy says.

'We can try to keep them apart,' I say.

A vote is taken. Rebecca and I say yes. Simon abstains. Patricia has begun collecting plates, pretending to ignore us. All eyes go to Lucy. Reluctantly, she raises her hand.

Day Five

23

The single-column story on page four of *The Times* reports the attack in Chiswick, calling it a home invasion. Dad is described as a 'pioneering surgeon' and 'medical philanthropist'. The accompanying photograph, plucked from the archives, shows him shaking hands with Prince Philip at the opening of a new research centre. There's no mention of Olivia Blackmore or what he was doing in London. Not yet.

I'm standing in a café, waiting for coffee beans to be ground, pressed and run through with hot water. The barista has a waxed moustache, bushy beard and stovepipe jeans, as though he's undecided what era to embrace.

'You got to pay for that?' he says, motioning to the paper.

I put a pound into the plastic box and carry the newspaper home.

Ruiz is sitting on the front steps, with his collar turned up, blowing on his hands.

He motions to the coffee. 'Where's mine?'

'I didn't know you were coming.'

I unlock the front door and Ruiz makes a show of wiping his feet like a lethargic bull who can't be arsed to charge at a matador.

He glances at the stairs, not relishing the climb. 'Fancy a trip up to Alperton?'

'Where?'

'I've been looking into your wicked stepmother.'

'She's not my stepmother.'

Ruiz grins, enjoying my reaction. He hands me a sheet of paper, which is numbered and dated. It's a partial transcript from a coronial inquest.

Summary of Judgement:

Todd Bryan Blackmore, 50, died from blunt force head trauma sustained while a passenger in a Jeep Cherokee four-wheel-drive that collided with a concrete pillar on Robin Hood Way, Kingston upon Thames, Surrey, at 12:58 a.m. on Saturday, 18 January 1997. Despite rain earlier in the evening, road conditions were essentially dry.

The driver of the vehicle, Olivia Blackmore, 31, told police she was driving northward in the middle lane of three when her vehicle was overtaken by a white van travelling at high speed, which veered sharply into her path while trying to take the exit into Beverley Way. Taking evasive action, Mrs Blackmore said she lost control of the

Jeep Cherokee, which collided with a pillar at a speed estimated at 70 mph – 20 mph above the designated speed limit.

Todd Blackmore, in the front passenger seat, died instantly, while Mrs Blackmore sustained serious leg injuries and had to be cut from the wreckage. When later tested, her blood alcohol level was zero.

Examination of CCTV cameras stationed along the route and a search for witnesses has not enabled police to identify any other vehicle travelling at high speed along Robin Hood Way in the minutes before or after the crash.

I attach a brief of evidence prepared by the Road Death Investigation Unit and recommend the Crown Prosecution Service review this brief and consider whether charges should be laid.

I glance at Ruiz. 'What's in Alperton?'
'The Road Death Investigation Unit.'

Ruiz has new wheels – a black Mercedes E-class that looks like it belongs in a presidential motorcade and should be permanently flanked by secret service agents and motorcycle outriders.

'It once belonged to the Saudi ambassador,' he says, pressing the fob and unlocking the doors and giving me a tour. 'Heated leather seats, mahogany trim, surround sound . . . Did I mention the bullet-proof glass and reinforced doors?'

'Are you expecting trouble?'
'Not today.'

The passenger seat is more comfortable than my mattress. Ruiz eases into the traffic, driving with his wrist draped over the top of the wheel.

'I also looked at the tennis academy – which is solvent, but losing money.'

'How did you get access to the accounts?'

'I'm a corporate fraud investigator, remember?'

'What about Ewan?'

'There's evidence of big medical bills. Private psychiatric clinics and therapists. She's also paying rent on a bedsit in Kilburn. Three months upfront. The police were searching the place yesterday. Ewan hasn't been home for four days.'

'Does he have a criminal record?'

'Nothing as an adult. He was charged as a juvenile for assaulting a teacher, and given a good behaviour bond.'

'What about the guy he was with the other night?'

'I came up empty on him. One of the neighbours told me someone has been sharing the place, but couldn't be more specific. Most of the residents don't answer their doors. I sensed a distinct lack of community spirit, although I'm sure they gratefully cash their dole cheques.'

'Your politics are showing again.'

'Sorry. Old habits.'

Alperton Traffic Garage takes up a corner block on an industrial estate where most of the nearby businesses are panel-beaters, spray shops and tyre-fitters. It looks like an ordinary factory, apart from the CCTV cameras, swipe-card entries and razor wire coiled along the edge of the rooftop.

A woman answers the buzzer, sounding bored. 'Can I help you?'

'We're here to see Detective Sergeant Angus Froome,' says Ruiz.

'Does he know you're coming?'

'Tell him it's Vincent Ruiz.'

She bursts out laughing. Ruiz glances up at the camera, annoyed. 'What's so funny?'

'It's the way you said it, love, like you're someone important.'

'Maybe I am.'

'OK, sugar, I'll remember to curtsy.'

The door unlocks and she meets us inside; a full-bodied woman in a figure-hugging dress and high heels.

'Walk this way,' she says, sashaying down across the garage.

Ruiz visibly straightens and tries not to limp as he follows her through the reception area.

'If you suck your gut in any harder your belly button will fall out your arse,' I whisper.

'Fuck off!'

The workshop looks like any other garage, with hoists, grease traps and racks of tools, but these vehicles are being autopsied not repaired. Mechanics in overalls are taking measurements and inspecting tyres, brake pads, speedometers and cables, trying to piece together the last moments before each crash.

The woman stops at a silver Porsche that has been sheared in half by the force of an impact. The two halves sit ten feet apart, twisted into obscene shapes like monstrous sculptures, splattered with blood.

'Visitors, Angus.'

A man slides out from beneath the wreckage. Dressed in

blue overalls and rubber-soled boots, he has sloping shoulders, silver hair and protruding pale eyes.

The woman points to Ruiz, her eyes twinkling. 'May I present the one and only Vincent Ruiz.'

'Well, I'll be damned,' he replies. 'DCI Ruiz.'

'Call me Vincent.'

The woman looks surprised. 'Why didn't you say you were police?'

'I'm retired,' says Ruiz.

She motions to his left hand. 'You're missing a finger. What happened?'

'I didn't like being married.'

'Couldn't you just take the ring off?'

'I never thought of that.'

She laughs.

'My wife used to work with Vincent,' explains Froome, wiping his hands on an oily rag.

'How is Laura?' asks Ruiz.

'Good. Great. She had breast cancer a few years back, but survived the chemo. Full remission. She's a grandmother now. Little boy.'

'Congratulations,' says Ruiz. 'She still working?'

'Retired. She wants me to do the same, but I wouldn't know what to do with myself.'

'Tell her I say hello.'

'I will. She'll be thrilled.'

The receptionist seems reluctant to leave.

'Thank you, Geraldine,' says Froome. 'I'll take it from here.'

She turns and leaves. Ruiz and Froome follow her progress.

'There are a few perks to this job,' says the mechanic, 'but don't tell Laura I said that.' He shakes my hand. 'What brings you to the car morgue?'

'We're looking at a fatal crash from 1997 in South London,' says Ruiz. 'The passenger died. The driver survived with serious leg injuries.'

'Olivia Szabo.'

'You remember her?'

'Hard to forget.'

'It's been almost twenty years.'

'You're making me feel old.'

Froome reaches up to turn off a recording device suspended above the wreck.

'Why remember this one?' I ask.

He rubs at a spot of grease on his forearm and seems to collect his thoughts.

'I was young – new to the job. It was my first experience giving evidence at a coronial inquest. Olivia Szabo – Mrs Blackmore – had a slick barrister who picked apart everything I said – my findings, my experience and methodology.'

'He ripped you a new arsehole,' says Ruiz.

'I finished up doubting my own name.'

'Why did she have a barrister for an inquest?' I ask.

'She knew how the evidence stacked up.'

'Meaning?'

Froome rocks his head from side to side, stretching the muscles in his neck.

'I'll tell you what I told the Coroner. Olivia Szabo claimed a mystery van swerved in front of her and she took evasive action, but lost control. I photographed that crash scene. I measured every angle and skid mark. We did computer simulations using all the known facts and only one of them mirrored what happened.'

'I don't understand,' I say.

'Evasive action usually means stomping on the brakes, or swerving, but she didn't fishtail or slow down. The vehicle actually accelerated, hitting the concrete at seventy clicks.'

'Maybe she fell asleep at the wheel,' Ruiz says.

'That's not possible.'

'Why?'

Froome tucks the rag into the back pocket of his overalls. 'Let me show you something.'

He takes us up a set of stairs to an office overlooking the workshop. Turning on a computer, he calls up Google Earth. The planet appears on screen, spinning in space. Froome types in the name of a road and cross-street. The camera seems to fall from space, zooming downwards, creating a giddying effect.

We're looking at Kingston upon Thames. Froome points out the road and the overpass. Taking us to street level, he shows us the view Olivia would have had as she approached the overpass in the Jeep Cherokee.

'That's the support pillar,' he says, pointing to the screen. Pulling back, he shows us a series of concrete bollards that are staggered diagonally across a walkway, protecting pedestrians from traffic.

'Were they there in 1997?' Ruiz asks.

Froome nods.

I still don't understand.

'The concrete bollards are between the road and the pillar,' says the sergeant. 'Somehow Olivia Szabo managed to weave between them and hit the pillar doing seventy miles per hour. Nobody does that if they're asleep at the wheel.'

'Did Olivia give evidence?' I ask.

'She refused.'

Ruiz glances at me and we're both aware of the implications.

'You're suggesting she did it on purpose.'

'I'm just telling you the facts. She wasn't drunk. She didn't fall asleep. And we found no trace of another vehicle forcing her off the road.'

'But she was seriously injured.'

'That's what's so weird,' says Froome, leaning back in his chair. 'At first I thought it could be some sort of murder–suicide, you know, but at the last second, she changed her mind and steered away, saving herself, but killing her husband. Then I thought maybe she set out to kill him and took a risk that she'd survive any crash, but she was pregnant and could have lost her baby. All I know for certain is that her story made no sense, which is why the coroner recommended she be charged with careless driving, or unlawful killing.'

'Did that happen?'

Froome grunts in disgust. 'The CPS didn't prosecute. Todd Blackmore's family weren't very impressed. His ex-wife came to court every day of the inquest, sitting in the public gallery. This one time, during a lunch adjournment, I saw the two women pass each other in the corridor. If looks could kill.'

Froome picks at grease beneath his fingernails. 'So why the sudden interest after all these years?'

'Olivia Blackmore married my father,' I say, watching his grey eyebrows arch in unison. 'Someone almost beat him to death last Sunday night. He's in a coma in hospital.'

Froome looks from face to face, as though waiting for the punchline.

'Is she a suspect?'

I nod.

He whistles through his teeth. 'Some wives should come with a health warning.'

Sitting in the passenger seat of Ruiz's car, I go over the details of Todd Blackmore's death. Olivia hired a barrister and refused to give evidence at the inquest, which is not an admission of guilt, but the implications are clear. She didn't want to be cross-examined and to have her actions questioned.

Every time I concentrate on this woman, I struggle to bring her into focus psychologically. One day she's fashioned of forged steel and the next she's as fragile as blown glass. Either that or she's like a mirror that reflects her surroundings, revealing nothing of herself.

Pushed hard enough, in the right circumstances, we're all capable of taking a life, but it takes a special kind of fortitude to steer a car into a concrete pillar, never touching the brake or flinching at the wheel. It takes a similar amount of toughness to crush a man's skull while he's lying at your feet.

Olivia 'married' again – choosing my father, or did he

choose her? The younger woman—older man paradigm is more ancient than time itself and has always fascinated evolutionary psychologists and gossip columnists. Everyone has a 'mate value' that makes us attractive as a partner. In caveman days, it might have been the ability to hunt woolly mammoths, or having a womb that wouldn't quit. Today it comes from money, status and power if you're a man; and youth and physical beauty if you're a woman. This is the simplified version. Of course, other factors come into play. People are attracted by intelligence and humour and kindness. They are also drawn to those who are like themselves, or what they aspire to be. I have no idea what Olivia saw in my father, but I know that research shows women are more biologically selective than men. They tend to mate with the one they love, whereas men mate with the one they can get. Usually. Not always.

These are the thoughts that churn through my mind as Ruiz drives through North London, manoeuvring the Mercedes like it's a much smaller car.

'Even if she did kill Todd Blackmore – it doesn't automatically mean that she bashed your father,' he says.

'I know.'

Ruiz glances at me, as though trying to read my thoughts. 'She's not exactly burning through husbands.'

'Meaning?'

'The Black Widow scenario. Women who marry rich men and bump them off.'

'Todd Blackmore wasn't rich.'

'Exactly. And she's been with your dad for what – twenty years?'

We drive in silence. Minutes pass. Ruiz drums his fingers on the steering wheel.

'You're not going to let this go, are you?'

'Probably not.'

'Nobody is going to care about a fatal car accident in the late nineties. It doesn't establish a pattern of behaviour.'

'I want to talk to Blackmore's ex-wife.'

'What can she tell you?'

'She sat through the inquest. She must have an opinion.'

'Mmm,' Ruiz says doubtfully. 'In my experience, ex-wives tend not to speak highly of The Upgrade.'

'In your experience?'

'Miranda once explained it to me.' (Ruiz's ex-wife – number three.) 'She promised never to judge me by my ex-wives, but rather on the good taste I showed when I married her. She said it proved I was capable of self-improvement.'

'What does she say now?'

'I'm not going to ask.'

24

Crossing an asphalt playground of Emma's school, I hear a choir singing in an assembly hall and children rote-learning chemistry tables in one of the classrooms. A young girl in a tartan dress dashes past me, her pigtails bouncing on her back. She's carrying an envelope to the office or back again. I can't remember ever being so enthusiastic about an errand or being allowed to run between classes.

My secondary schooling was a sombre, strait-laced endurance test that saw me sent away to boarding school at the age of twelve, handed over to men in gowns and mortarboard hats who were tasked with turning the boy into the man – an Englishman, of course, reserved, apologetic, uptight.

Brighton College contacted me a few years ago and asked permission to put my name on an honour roll in the auditorium, alongside other old boys who had died in battle, or risen to prominence in their chosen profession. *Over my dead body*, I replied. They haven't been in touch again.

Entering a Gothic-looking building, I follow signs to the school office. Turning a final corner, I see Emma sitting on a chair, hunched over a notebook, madly scribbling. Curls shield her face.

'Hey, Squeak,' I say, taking the seat next to her.

She snaps the book closed, holding it to her chest.

'What are you writing?'

'Nothing.'

'Are you planning your escape? I could help.'

'Would you?'

'Depends. Are we tunnelling out or going over the fence? I'm not fond of tunnels.'

'And you don't like heights.'

'True.'

A door opens and a woman appears. 'Oh, you're both here,' she says. 'You should have knocked.'

The headmistress is younger than I expect, in her late thirties with short dark hair that almost covers the diamond studs that sparkle in her earlobes.

'I'm Christine Houten. It's a pleasure to finally meet you, Professor O'Loughlin.'

'Please call me Joe.'

She smiles at Emma. 'How are you?'

'Fine.'

'I hope you haven't been writing any more letters.'

'What letters?' I ask.

'Emma wrote a complaint to the Board of Governors. If memory serves, she likened me to Josef Mengele and accused me of carrying out experiments on children. I was impressed with her knowledge of the Third Reich. We don't study Nazi Germany until Year 10.'

Emma is staring at the floor.

Dr Houten has a teacher's smile. 'We've sorted things out since then, haven't we?'

Emma nods.

We follow the headmistress into her office, which is dominated by a large desk and arched window with lead-lined glass panels. Seats are offered and taken. A file is opened. Paperwork. Never a good sign.

'Here at North Bridge House we encourage our students to be creative and use their imaginations,' says Dr Houten. 'We love hearing their stories. We also value their opinions. Unfortunately, some of Emma's ideas have upset other students.'

'What ideas?'

'Although we are not a faith-based school, we teach tolerance and respect for religious beliefs and do not discriminate against anyone on the basis of his or her faith.'

'What did Emma say?'

'She told a group of students that God didn't exist and that the Bible was a book of fairy stories.'

'I see.'

'She called Jesus an imaginary sky-pilot, or maybe it was a space wizard.'

I look at Emma, who is staring at the floor.

'Emma has a wonderful imagination. She told her English teacher that her mother died on board the Malaysian Airways flight shot down over the Ukraine; while her geography teacher was told that Mrs O'Loughlin was in witness protection due to give evidence against a Colombian drug czar.'

'Why would you tell people that?' I ask Emma.

She doesn't answer.

'I'm not telling you these things to embarrass Emma,' says Dr Houten. 'I empathise with any child who has lost a parent. I also love Emma's sense of spirit and enquiring mind. Unfortunately, matters have since escalated.'

'Escalated?'

'I've written to you three times. You haven't responded to my letters.'

I feel Emma flinch beside me. The skin around her mouth is taut and her jaw locked tightly.

'Yes, the letters, of course. I'm sorry. I've been very busy. If you could remind me of the issues . . .'

'I've arranged for our school counsellor, Mr Carmine, to talk to you. He's waiting in the conference room. Emma can stay with me.'

She points to a room along the hall. I knock and enter. Mr Carmine rises to greet me. In his forties with a sunbed tan and shaved scalp. He's overweight, dressed in neatly ironed business shirt and trousers that are a size too small for him. A tweed jacket hangs on the back of his chair and a leather satchel is propped open beside polished brogues. Inside, I glimpse a bottle of vitamin pills and a Tupperware container full of carrot sticks and salad.

'Please, call me Terry,' he says, offering me a damp handshake.

I sit opposite him. He has a notepad between his elbows and three coloured pens arranged side by side.

'I really appreciate you coming to see me, Professor. I've taken a keen interest in Emma's welfare since she joined us in January, particularly in the light of her losing her mother. My condolences, by the way.'

'Thank you. What exactly has Emma done?'

'Before we get to that, would you mind answering a few questions?'

'Fire away.'

He consults his notes.

'Is Emma on any medication?'

'No.'

'Was she born prematurely?'

'No.'

He makes twin marks on the page, as if ticking boxes.

'Do you regard yourself as being a strict parent?'

'Firm but fair.'

'Do you employ any form of discipline at home?'

'Of course.'

'What does it entail?'

'Emma is sometimes sent to her room, or has her pocket money deducted, or loses her TV privileges.'

'What about corporal punishment?'

'No.'

'Do you encourage open communication?'

'Yes.'

'Is there any history of anti-social behaviour in your family?'

'No.'

'What about mental illness?'

'Can you just tell me what this is about?'

183

'Pardon?'

'You're asking me all these questions – I want to know why.'

'I'm learning more about Emma.'

'For what reason?'

'Because of the incident.'

'What incident? What is Emma supposed to have done?'

The counsellor's right eyebrow lifts as though tugged by a hook. 'I assumed you were made aware of the details.'

'No.'

'Emma assaulted one of her classmates.'

'When you say "assaulted" . . . ?'

'She pushed her down the stairs. The student suffered a broken arm. She'll have to wear a cast for six weeks.'

'Did Emma say why?'

'She wouldn't discuss the circumstances. We were hoping she might have talked to you.'

I shake my head. 'This is the first I've heard about it.'

'What about the letters that were sent?'

'I've been away,' I explain, not wanting to blame Emma. Mr Carmine continues. 'Obviously, the school takes these matters very seriously. Given Emma's behaviour, I wanted to investigate whether she was having any problems at home.'

'No!' The answer is too blunt.

'How has Emma coped with the loss of her mother?'

'She misses her.'

'Has she been acting out, or showing aggression?'

'No.'

I can feel my throat tightening and my voice changing timbre.

Mr Carmine consults his notes. 'Emma is a gifted child. Her IQ scores are exceptional, but she does have certain behavioural quirks.'

'Quirks?'

'According to her teachers, she doesn't work particularly well with groups and can become quite restless.'

'Boredom will do that.'

'She doesn't make friends easily.'

'She's self-contained.'

Mr Carmine seems to debate whether to ask his next question.

'Has Emma ever been assessed by a psychiatrist, or a psychotherapist?'

'I'm a psychologist.'

'Someone independent, I mean. It has been suggested that she might be – how can I put this? – "on the spectrum".' He makes inverted commas with his fingers. 'Low down, of course. Which is why I feel she could benefit from seeing someone who can make us aware of her deficits.'

Did he just say that?

'Emma doesn't have any deficits.'

'That was the wrong choice of words. I mean challenges.'

'There's nothing wrong with Emma.'

'She pushed a girl down the stairs.'

'Do you know why?'

'She couldn't give a reason.'

'Couldn't or wouldn't?'

'Either way, we cannot put other students in harm's way. We require an independent assessment before Emma will be guaranteed a place at the school next term.'

185

Something breaks inside me like a small dry twig snapping under my heel. Speaking slowly and clearly, I ask how much time the counsellor has spent with Emma.

'I've quizzed her.'

'How long?'

'Forty minutes.'

I repeat the number for effect. 'I've spent twelve years raising Emma. Let me tell you what she's like. She's bright, inquisitive and deeply thoughtful. She can also be single-minded and occasionally wilful, but there isn't a mean bone in her body. Yes, she avoids eye contact and struggles to make friends. Occasionally, she takes things too literally and questions consensus, but that's what I love about her. When Emma was three years old she went to a birthday party but instead of playing pin the tail on the donkey, or bashing the piñata, she spent two hours with a slinky toy, setting up more and more elaborate experiments as she rolled it downstairs. Does that make her odd? Maybe. Different? Yes. But it doesn't make her autistic or disruptive or difficult to teach.'

Mr Carmine sighs and closes his folder. 'Sometimes parents are the last people to realise—'

'Stop!'

He looks up, surprised.

'You don't have children, do you?'

'That has no relevance—'

'I don't think you even *like* children. You chose to become a counsellor because it means spending less face-to-face time in a classroom, talking to children, understanding them.'

'You know nothing about me.'

'I know enough. You're wearing a wedding ring. Your

wife is most likely younger than you, which is why you're so worried about going bald and choose to shave your head every morning. You're also self-conscious about your weight, bringing salads to school and wearing trousers that are a size too small. The gym membership has proved a waste of money, but you use the sunbed because you think it makes you look younger.'

Mr Carmine glances at his leather satchel, closing the flap. His keys are on the table with a gym membership fob attached.

'Your wife works full-time,' I say. 'I suspect she earns more money than you do, which is why your shirts are professionally laundered and pressed, but they put too much starch in your collars, which is why they chafe your neck.

'She wants children, but you're not so keen. You take the zinc supplements to boost your sperm count, but you won't be too upset if it doesn't happen. You see enough children every day and think they're the bane of your life. Why can't they be more like adults, you think. Why can't they grow up?'

Mr Carmine blinks at me, lost for words.

'Did Emma apologise to the girl whose arm was broken?' I ask.

He nods.

'If you provide me with the name and address of her parents, I will personally visit them and offer to pay for any medical and out-of-pocket expenses.'

Getting my feet, I leave the conference room and walk directly to Dr Houten's office. Emma is sitting in the corner, writing in her journal.

The headmistress looks up, surprised to see me so soon.

'Is my daughter being expelled?'

'She's on probation. A decision will be made at the end of term.'

'Well, make it quickly. In the meantime, I'm taking her home.'

Emma follows me into the corridor. I put my arm around her shoulders as we walk out the swinging doors and across the playground.

'You pushed a girl down the stairs.'

'Petra Temple.'

'Why?'

Emma lowers her head. Her fringe falls over her eyes.

'She said Mummy killed herself because I'm so weird.'

'Mummy didn't kill herself,' I say.

'I know.'

'And you're not weird.'

'OK.'

We walk in silence out the gates and as far as the main road, where I search for a cab. Emma has been quiet.

'What you did was wrong,' I say.

Emma nods. 'I didn't mean for her to fall down the stairs. She tripped over her schoolbag.'

'Do you want to stay at that school?'

'I do,' she whispers.

'You sure?'

She nods again. 'Daddy?'

'Yes.'

'I am a little bit weird.'

Day Six

25

The summer before I started medical school I worked as a deckhand on a fishing trawler out of Colwyn Bay and saved enough to buy my first car. I saw a Morris Marina advertised in the local paper and paid four hundred quid to a used-car dealer called Tony Smith, who seemed pleased to get the car off the lot.

'How much did you pay?' my father asked.

I told him it was three hundred.

'You were ripped off.'

'It's only done seventy thousand miles.'

'They wound back the clock.'

'The what?'

'The odometer.'

'It has a reconditioned engine.'

'It's burning oil. Show me the sales docket.'

'It's my money.'

'Show me.'

Dad made me follow him as we drove back to Tony's Auto-Village in Wirral. He purposely parked across the driveway and went through the office door. Tony Smith had prison tattoos and a reputation as a local hard man. I'd heard stories of how he put two guys in hospital when he caught them stealing number plates.

Tony was sitting behind a desk, eating a hamburger from a box. He didn't get up.

'My name is William O'Loughlin. You took advantage of my son,' Dad said. I stood by the door, ready to run.

Smith put down his burger and wrapped it in a sheet of waxed paper, as though saving it for later.

'Says who?'

'Me. You engaged in misleading conduct.'

'Fuck off.'

'Please don't swear in front of my son.'

Smith slowly rose to his feet. He had a strange energy in his eyes, as though a shitty day had suddenly improved.

'You calling me a liar?'

'You misrepresented the condition of the car – in particular the engine and the mileage.'

'Buyer beware.'

They were standing chest to chest. I was begging Dad to leave. I told him I'd pay for the repairs. I said I didn't care about the engine.

'Be quiet, Joseph,' he said. 'Leave this to me.' He eyeballed Smith, speaking calmly: 'The Consumer Rights Act states that a second-hand car must be of a satisfactory quality, fit for purpose and as described. None of this applies to the car you sold my son.'

'Sue me.'

'I hope it won't come to that. Here is the list of repairs. You either refund his money, or you replace the engine and the tyres at your expense.'

Smith laughed. 'That won't be happening.'

Dad took an envelope from his pocket.

'My son's rights have been breached. This is a letter from my solicitor, triggering legal proceedings against you. I am also making a complaint to the Office of Fair Trading and the Motor Ombudsman.'

The dealer's eyes were bulging and his neck had turned red. He shoved my father hard in the chest, jabbing him again and again, trying to force him out the door. It must have hurt like hell, but Dad didn't flinch or pull away. The harder Smith jabbed, the more Dad leaned into each blow.

Slowly, the atmosphere changed. Uncertainty clouded the dealer's face. He couldn't understand why my father didn't back off. Why wasn't he scared? Smith reached into his office drawer. I was sure he was going to pull out a gun, or a blade. Instead he produced a wad of cash. Peeling off the notes, he tossed them on the floor. I began picking them up.

'No, Joseph. Stay where you are,' said Dad. 'Mr Smith is going to hand you the money, and you will give him the keys. Then you will shake his hand because our business will be over.'

Nobody moved. Seconds ticked by. Surely, Smith wouldn't humble himself and kneel before my father. But that's exactly what happened. He crouched and scooped up the cash and gave it to me.

'Count it,' my father said.

'I'm sure it's fine.'

'Count it.'

I did as he asked.

'Give Mr Smith the keys . . . now shake his hand.'

I reached out. I expected Tony to crush my fingers. Instead I felt the sweat on his palm. He was beaten. Bettered. Done.

Every family has its good versus evil stories, moments of triumph and surprise, but this one has stayed with me my entire life. I don't know if my father was frightened or foolishly brave or brilliantly deliberate. Regardless, I was in awe of him that day. Not love. Awe.

Having washed and disinfected my hands, I move between beds in the ICU. For the past few days I've avoided coming to the hospital, making excuses and leaving it to others. The place, not the person is to blame. I have too many memories of hospital rooms, blinking machines and hours of waiting and hoping for a miracle.

Something comes loose in my head whenever I think about Julianne's death. It's like a broken piece of machinery rattling inside a spinning drum. Everything reminds me of her. It could be a song on the radio, or a story in a magazine, or some silly video on YouTube that I know would have made her laugh. 'I'll have to show her,' I say to myself and then I remember that she's not here and my heart hurts all over again.

Moving between beds in the ICU, I recognise some of the regular visitors. Mrs Walsh is at her daughter's bedside. Kimberley, an only child, still in her teens, collapsed into the arms of her boyfriend at a music festival after taking a tablet she thought was Ecstasy. The contents of the pill are unknown. The damage to her brain similarly indeterminate. I haven't seen the boyfriend, but Mr Walsh will be in later when he finishes work. I've heard him crying at night when he thinks nobody is listening.

Nearing my father's bed, I see a figure leaning over him. At first I think it's a male nurse, but he's not wearing a uniform. My next thought is Ewan, but this man is bigger. Older. Instinctively I know he's going to run. I yell for him to stop but he keeps going.

I grab his arm. He feints left and then right, before dropping his shoulder into my chest, sending me backwards into a metal stand.

I'm on the floor, caught up in tubes. A machine beeps in alarm. Untangling myself, I give chase, yelling at him to stop. He's halfway along the corridor, heading towards the exit. A nurse steps out. He charges into her as though she's a figment of his imagination. She goes down. I reach her in a dozen strides, crouching next to her.

'Are you all right?'

She nods. Winded. Gasping.

'Call security!' I say. 'And the police.'

Both lifts are on the lower floors. He must have taken the stairs. I follow, letting gravity pitch me downwards, swinging off the railings. I can hear him below me and occasionally catch a glimpse as he makes each turn, getting further away. We're on the ninth floor. I lose count on the way down, but hear him opening a door. Emerging from the stairwell, I'm in a wide, brightly lit corridor with offices on either side.

A woman appears from an office.

'Did he come this way?' I yell.

She steps back, alarmed by the question, shaking her head.

I choose the opposite direction, hearing his steps, growing fainter. Turning left, then right, I reach a dead end. He can't have come this far. I listen. Silence. There are doors down either side. Offices. Storerooms. Clinics.

Retracing my steps, I try to hear sounds above my heartbeat and the blood coursing in my ears. Something *thunks* to the floor. A storeroom door is ajar. I nudge it further open and see metal shelves, stacked with paint cans, turpentine, floor polish and disinfectant. A broom has fallen from a cleaner's trolley.

Reaching out, I search for the light switch, running my fingers down the wall. I touch a hand. It grabs my wrist and jerks me inside, twisting my arm behind my back and wrapping a forearm across my neck, crushing my larynx.

A male voice: 'Are you his son?'

I claw at his forearm, desperate for air.

'Are you his son?'

He eases the pressure.

'Who?'

'The surgeon.'

'I don't know what you're talking about.'

'Is he going to die?'

He tightens the chokehold, keeping me off balance. I can't get any purchase with my heels.

'He's in a coma,' I croak.

'But the brain tumour – it's killing him, right?'

'What?'

'The tumour.'

What is he talking about?

My eyes are adjusting to the ambient light. I can see the man's distorted reflection in the curved metal surface of a paint can. He is taller and heavier than I am. Stronger and quicker.

'I called the police,' I say. 'They're on their way.'

He hesitates, as though unsure of what to do next.

'Did you come here to kill him?' I ask.

'What?'

'My father.'

'If I wanted him dead, he'd be dead.'

'What's that mean?'

I feel his grip loosen. In the same instant, he kicks at my calves, making me kneel. His forearm releases me and I try to turn as he pulls a shelf down on top me. Tins, paint cans and bottles bounce off my head, back and shoulders. Shielding my head, I expect to be crushed, but the cleaner's trolley stops the shelf from toppling completely.

Crawling out from underneath, I reach the door and drag myself on to my feet. At the end of the corridor is a T-junction. Nothing. Where did he go?

Nearby is a fire door. I shoulder it open, blinded by the brightness, looking left and right. An ambulance ramp spirals down to the main road. Sprinting down the driveway, I reach the street. Where are the police . . . the guards? Moments later a red motorcycle roars past me, weaving between cars. The rider throttles hard, lifting the front wheel from the asphalt where it hovers for several seconds, defying gravity, before he accelerates away.

An overweight security guard lumbers into view, holding a radio in one fist and a baton in the other.

'Hands against the wall,' he says.

'It's not me you want.'

He raises the baton. 'Hands on the wall.'

I splay my hands against the brickwork as he pats me down. A police car pulls up. I recognise the driver – DS Hawthorn.

'He's gone,' I say, pointing along the road. 'He's on a motorbike.'

'Did you get a number?'

'No.'

She reaches out and touches my scalp. 'You've cut your head.'

I see my reflection in her sunglasses. One side of my face is covered in blood. I can smell the scent of her body-wash and shampoo.

'You seem to find trouble, Professor,' she says.

'And you seem to find me, DS Hawthorn.'

The wound is cleaned, disinfected and stitched just above my right ear. It doesn't look so bad, apart from a bald spot where my hair was shaved. The doctor holds open my eyelids and studies the pupils with a small penlight.

'How many fingers can you see?'

'Two.'

'Any blurred vision?'

'No.'

'Headache?'

'A big one.'

'I'll give you something for that.'

Detective Hawthorn is leaning against the wall with her shoulders back and her hands tucked into the pockets of her dress jeans, beneath a white fitted blouse that flares over her belt.

'You can take him now,' says the doctor, snapping off his latex gloves. 'Sadly, I can't save that shirt.'

DS Hawthorn hands me my jacket and holds open the door. As I pass her, she whispers something.

'Pardon?'

'Kate. You asked me my name the other day.'

'Is it short for anything?'

'I was named after Katherine Hepburn.'

'A great beauty.'

She flicks hair from her eyes. 'Are you flirting with me?'

'Is that allowed?'

'I'm on duty.'

'Does that mean I can try later?'

Her half smile shows the braces on her teeth.

DI Macdermid has arrived. Unshaven and careworn, he looks annoyed rather than concerned for my welfare. The hospital director is with him, a middle-aged woman with mahogany-coloured hair lacquered into a helmet and a face like an axe-blade.

'You should have called security immediately,' she says, accusingly.

'He ran the moment he saw me.'

'You accessed an area of the hospital that is off-limits to visitors.'

'I chased him.'

'Which is not your responsibility.'

The director seems more worried about public liability than someone having breached her security.

'Did you get a good look at him?' Macdermid asks.

'Forties. Six-foot. Heavy-set. Dark hair. He might be a soldier.'

'What makes you say that?'

'He had a tattoo on his forearm, some sort of insignia or badge.'

'Would you recognise it again?'

'Yes.'

We're in the security office looking at the CCTV footage. Time-coded images show a man entering the main doors at 2.47 p.m. and speaking to a receptionist at the information desk.

'That's him,' I say, pointing to the screen. His face is hidden. The image changes to a different camera. The new angle provides a clearer picture.

'Ever seen him before?' Macdermid asks.

'No.'

'He said he was family,' says the hospital director, who shows us the visitor's log where the name *O'Loughlin* has been typed into the relevant field.

'Did he show any identification?'

'A driver's licence, but it wasn't checked properly. The staff member has been disciplined.'

More CCTV footage is put on screen. The intruder is shown arriving on the ninth floor, where he pauses and asks for directions. A nurse raises her arm, pointing him along the corridor.

'Are there cameras in the ICU?' Macdermid asks.

'No.'

'What was he doing there?' I ask.

The hospital director is quick to answer. 'There's no evidence that he tampered with equipment or administered any substances. An ICU nurse was present at all times.'

'He must have done something,' says Macdermid.

'According to the nurse, he was whispering to the patient. She only heard a few words. He said he was sorry.'

'Sorry for what?' I ask.

The director shrugs, her arms tightly folded across her chest.

Macdermid turns his attention to me. 'Did he say anything to you?'

'He asked if my father was dying. I said he was in a coma. He seemed to think that Dad had a brain tumour and was dying anyway.'

'Why would he think that?'

'No idea. I asked him if he'd come to finish him off. He said, "If I wanted him dead, he'd be dead."'

The footage on screen has changed again. This time it shows the road outside the hospital. A motorcycle roars past me and I seem to raise my hand as though waving farewell.

'We'll have the images enhanced and run them through

our facial recognition software,' says Macdermid, getting ready to leave.

'What about my father?'

'I'll post a guard outside the ICU.'

I sense there are things he's not telling me. I follow him outside, asking about the motorcyclist. 'What if it's the same guy who showed up at the house on the night of the attack?'

Macdermid ignores me. He's striding across the foyer, past the café, through the sliding glass doors. A police car is waiting. Engine running. The driver holds open a door. The DI tosses his coat into the car and slides into the passenger seat.

'What about Ewan Blackmore?'

Macdermid scratches the stubble on his jaw, as though deciding how much to say. 'We found bloodstained clothes in the garden behind his bedsit. Someone tried to burn them in a drum.'

'My father's blood?'

'The DNA tests will confirm it. In the meantime, I've issued an arrest warrant.'

The door shuts and the car pulls away. Kate Hawthorn appears at my shoulder.

'Did you know?' I ask.

She nods. 'We've upgraded the case to attempted murder.'

Day Seven

26

It's been a November of storms. Another breaks over London, with sporadic bursts of lightning and accompanying thunder. Trees are thrashing at the air and raindrops sound like fists of gravel being thrown against the windows. The buzzer sounds. It's late for visitors.

Answering the intercom, I glance at the display screen and see Olivia Blackmore on the doorstep. She raises her face to the camera. Hair is plastered to her scalp and her neck.

'I'm sorry. I know it's late,' she says. 'I wanted . . . hoped . . . we might talk?'

'With or without our lawyers being present?'

She lowers her gaze, pulling her collar higher, although it's useless against the driving rain. 'It's about Ewan.'

'Do you know where he is?'

'No.'

Olivia looks up at the camera again, moving a lock of wet hair from her cheek. Her eyes plead her case. I can't tell if she's been crying.

Pressing a button, I unlock the front door and direct her to the top of the stairs. Lights trigger in the stairwell. I wait on the landing and take her wet coat, fetching a towel for her hair. Her grey dress clings to her, pushing flesh into curves.

'What happened to your head?' she asks, pointing to the bandage on my scalp.

'It's nothing.'

Her eyes search mine, aware that we're not friends who are going swap pleasantries or show concern. I point her towards the sitting room. She takes a seat in an armchair, keeping her knees together and hands on her lap as though being interviewed for a job.

'The police think Ewan attacked William, but they're wrong.'

'Why are you telling me?'

'I want you to understand. He would never hurt William. Never.'

'Then you have nothing to worry about.'

A bruised helplessness enters her eyes. 'I've looked everywhere for him. He hasn't been to his bedsit for days and this morning he missed an appointment with his psychiatrist.'

'He's not taking his medication.'

She doesn't answer.

'Why are you here, Olivia?'

'I'm frightened. If the police find Ewan first he's likely to panic and do something stupid.'

'Like force his way into someone's home and threaten their children with a knife.'

Olivia flinches and looks even more miserable.

'How am I supposed to help?' I ask.

'You could talk to the police – tell them it wasn't Ewan.'

'Based on what – your word? You've been lying all along. Where were you the night Dad was attacked?'

'At the theatre.'

'The show ended at ten thirty. There's an hour missing in your timeline.'

'I went to see Ewan.'

'No.'

Pinkness colours her throat. 'I had a drink with a friend. He's married and having an affair. He's worried that his wife might suspect something. He wanted my advice.'

I want to laugh at the irony, but press ahead. 'Where did you meet him?'

'A bar in Covent Garden.'

'Does the bar have a name?'

'I can't remember.'

'Why was your mobile phone switched off?'

'I turned it off during the show. I forgot to turn it on again.'

'I don't believe you.'

She lifts her chin defiantly. 'Haven't you ever forgotten something, Joe? Haven't you ever made a mistake?'

'Is that your defence?'

'I don't *need* a defence.'

'You've hired lawyers and taken out court orders, trying to get control of my father's affairs.'

'Because you won't let me see him.'

We both pause, glaring at each other. Olivia cracks first, dropping her head. A tear collects and hovers at the outside edge of her left eye, before rolling down her cheek. I wonder if she can cry on demand.

Taking a box of tissues from the mantelpiece, I put them next to her. She blows her nose. Sniffles.

'I wish William were here. He'd tell you to stop being so cruel to me.'

'He's not here.'

Olivia steels herself again, looking me squarely in the eyes, challenging me to analyse her feelings, to read her mind.

'What is it that you do, Joseph? What's your job?'

'I'm a clinical psychologist – you know that.'

'What does that mean?'

'I treat people who are suffering from mental health disorders like anxiety or depression or substance abuse; or those struggling with relationships, or phobias.'

'You fix them?'

'I help them cope.'

'I think you're the one who is damaged.'

'Me?'

'You blame William for being a terrible father, but what is a father's job? To protect. To nurture. To provide. To love. William did these things, but you think he didn't hug you enough, or praise you enough. You think he ignored you.'

'He did.'

'He taught you how to survive, to be a warrior.'

'I didn't *want* to be a warrior.'

'He made you strong. Independent. Resilient.'

'I am those things despite him, not because of him.'

'Have you told him that?'

'What?'

'Have you told William how you feel?'

'It doesn't matter any more.'

'If it doesn't matter — why are you taking it out on me?'

I can't answer her. At the same time, I refuse to take relationship advice from my father's mistress.

'If you're so convinced that Ewan didn't hurt my father, who did?'

Olivia pauses, chewing at her bottom lip. Uncertain. Deciding.

'There's someone Ewan met in hospital. Another patient. His name is Micah Beauchamp. He's a drug addict, who's been sponging off Ewan for months, taking his money, asking him to steal.'

My mind goes back to the attack at the bus stop. 'What does Micah look like?'

'A monster. He has bleached hair and missing front teeth. When Ewan first came home from the hospital, he brought Micah with him. Initially, I thought he was a good influence — even though he looked scary. He managed to get Ewan to talk and to go outdoors. Then I began noticing that things were missing. Cash. Jewellery. William's watch. William confronted Ewan. They argued. It was horrible. Ewan left.' Olivia glances sideways at me, as though glimpsing herself in a mirror. 'The next day Micah came to the house and threatened us. William immediately had the locks changed and upgraded the alarm.'

'That's why you have a gun?'

She nods.

'Did you tell the police?'

'No. We didn't want to get Ewan into trouble. William hoped that he might see sense and ditch Micah. In the meantime, he wasn't allowed back into the house.'

'You cut him adrift?'

'William said it was for his own good.'

'You couldn't do it – could you? You were secretly giving him money. You rented him the bedsit.'

'I looked after my son.'

'Does Ewan have a key to the house in Chiswick?'

Olivia shakes her head, less certain than before.

'Did he ever come to the house when William was in Wales?'

This time she nods, looking miserable. 'He stole from us again. A digital camera. My credit card.'

'Did you tell the police?'

'No.'

'My father?'

'No.'

Olivia starts to say something else, but looks at her hands, rubbing at the palms as though removing dirt. Silence is a language she seems to have perfected.

'There were old bruises on my father's back and beneath his ribs. Was that Micah?'

'Yes.'

'What happened?'

'William kept up his medical practising certificate after he retired. He did part-time work for a clinic treating migrants and refugees. A few weeks ago he discovered that his prescription pad was missing. He went to the bedsit and confronted Ewan. Micah was there. They argued. Fought. I didn't realise – not until I saw the bruises. William wanted to call the police. I begged him not to – because of Ewan. I was wrong. I'm so sorry. If I could take it back . . .'

'You've known this all along and didn't say anything.'

Olivia screws up her face, not wanting to be reminded. She's like my mother, waiting for the world to apologise for all the nameless wrongs she believes have been done to her.

'Do the police know about Micah?' I ask.

'I gave them a new statement today.'

'What did DI Macdermid say?'

'He wouldn't talk to me.'

'Police have found bloody clothes in Ewan's garden. He tried to burn them.'

'He didn't attack William. He wouldn't.' She rocks her head from side to side.

I let the silence drag out. Olivia grows flustered, avoiding my gaze. She glances around the room, looking for a distraction.

'Where are your daughters?'

'Emma is at my sister's house and Charlie has gone to hospital to visit her grandfather.'

'How is William?'

'The same.'

'Can I visit him?'

'I'm not sure any more.'

'Let me talk to your mother.'

'No.'

'What did she say about me?'

I don't answer.

'She's known all along, hasn't she? She confronted me once. Years ago. I had a phone call. She asked me outright if I was sleeping with William. I remember because she used my maiden name. Hardly anyone does that.'

'What did you say?'

'I denied it.'

'You lied.'

'I wanted to protect William.'

'That's another lie.'

'OK, I wanted to protect what we had. William, me, Ewan, we're a family.'

Her steel has returned. What am I to do about this woman in her sodden dress and ruined shoes, who is dripping water on my newly upholstered sofa? I hate what she represents yet she feels like the only clue to finally understanding my father. Why is it that men's lives so often turn around a single woman, the one whom all other women are judged against?

I ask her again why she came here.

'I need you to believe me . . . to help Ewan.'

'I think you're frightened that he's responsible and that you let it happen. Your life is falling apart and you want me to pick up the pieces.'

Olivia swallows as though a bubble of air is trapped in her throat. She is staring straight ahead, her gaze boring into the floorboards. She stands and walks to the door.

'Can I call you a cab?'

'I have my car.' She puts on her coat and turns suddenly, her face close to mine. 'Can I ask you for something?'

'That depends.'

'Hold me?'

'What?'

She speaks quickly. Nervously. 'I had a massage today. Not because I was stiff, or my muscles were sore, but because I craved the touch of another human being. She could have held my hand, or brushed my hair, or stroked my cheek and I would have been happy. Will you hold me?'

There is a beat of silence before I put my arms around her and she presses herself so tightly against me that I can feel the underwire of her bra. The crown of her head is at the level of my shoulders and her entire body sways.

Letting go, Olivia turns quickly, murmuring something before descending the stairs. I can still feel the pressure and warmth of her body like an impression left in a bed after someone has spent the night.

She is my father's mistress. Vulnerable. Beautiful. Dangerous.

Day Eight

27

Should Vincent Ruiz ever be invited to appear on *Mastermind* his specialist subject would most likely be: 'London pubs that haven't been ponced up or gentrified'. He would answer questions on real ale, Scotch eggs and pork pies; while railing against the gastro-pub malaise that has turned a toasted cheese and ham sandwich into a croque-monsieur.

The Cumberland Arms falls into the 'old school' variety. Just off Mile End Road in Stepney Green, the pub squats in the shadows of a concrete tower block that rises like a lone finger in a clenched fist passing judgement on the richer boroughs to the west.

Mid-morning and a half-dozen regulars are slouching on stools, bellies settled over belts, squinting whenever a door opens letting in daylight. Ruiz is at the end of the bar, nursing an empty pint glass.

'Couldn't you find a more depressing place?' I ask.

'It's full of character.'

'Which one?

He signals the barman. 'What are you drinking?'

'Lime and soda.'

'You can be really embarrassing. What happened to your head?'

'Shaving cut.'

'Funny.'

Our drinks arrive and we carry them as far as possible from a series of lurid fruit machines that clatter and whoosh, enticing players to lose their money.

Ruiz downs two-thirds of his pint in four huge swallows.

'I have a question about modern etiquette,' he says, wiping foam from his top lip. 'I'm in the supermarket this morning, waiting at the checkout, and there are two young women behind me. I'm not in a hurry, so I say, "Would you ladies like to go ahead of me?" The shit hits the fan. "How dare you call us ladies," they said. "We're not someone's property. Nobody owns us." What was that all about?'

'Some women find the word "lady" offensive.'

'Since when?'

'Everything is contextual.'

'I have no idea what that means.'

'It means you're getting old.'

Ruiz takes a battered notebook from his jacket pocket and unhooks a rubber band that is holding the pages together. It falls open and he licks his thumb, turning several pages that are covered with his spidery scrawl.

'I found Todd Blackmore's first wife, Trudy Waring. She works for a car hire company at Heathrow. Shift-work. Won some money on the National Lottery a few years back. Paid off her house.'

'Which is where?'

'Around the corner. That's why we're here.'

'Did she and Todd Blackmore stay in touch?'

'No idea. She reverted to her maiden name when they divorced. There were two children by the marriage – a boy and a girl – both grown up now. The boy, Cameron Blackmore, played tennis for a while, junior leagues, but didn't progress past the satellite tour. He works in sports management. I couldn't find anything about the daughter.'

Ruiz puts the notebook away and we finish our drinks before walking to the next street, turning right past a row of terraced houses and soot-stained factories.

Trudy Waring doesn't answer her buzzer. I try again. A neighbour pokes his head from the adjoining house, holding back a dog on a leash, who launches a bid for freedom, only to be yanked back with a strangled croak.

'Nobody home?' he asks, apparently stating the obvious.

This time I knock. A woman yells from inside: 'I'm coming. I'm coming. Keep your shirt on.'

The door opens. Trudy Waring is in her sixties with dye-darkened hair, damp eyes and a scowling countenance. She's wearing a floral blouse and a black skirt, half-zipped and under pressure on her hips.

'What do you want?'

'I'm Joseph O'Loughlin. This is Vincent Ruiz. We're investigating the death of your ex-husband, Todd Blackmore.'

'You don't look like coppers.' She glances at Ruiz and seems to reconsider. 'Maybe he does.'

'I'm a former Scotland Yard detective,' says Ruiz, bowing slightly. 'Joe is a clinical psychologist.'

The neighbour is contorting his body, trying to listen to the conversation.

'Can I help you, Derek?' asks Ms Waring, giving him the eye. He slinks away, dragging the dog.

Ms Waring studies us, as though trying to decide whether she wants the aggravation.

'Well, you'd best come inside,' she sighs, turning on her heel. We follow her along a darkened hallway to a kitchen that smells of Demerol with overtones of chop fat.

She's wearing slippers, but her black leather boots are set out on a sheet of newspaper next to a tin of polish, a brush and several rags. Sitting heavily, she puts her hand inside one of boots and picks up a rag.

Ruiz takes it from her. 'Let me do that.'

'You don't have to.'

'I like polishing boots. I had a lot of practice at police college. The trick to getting a great shine is to clean off any dirt with a damp rag and let the boots dry for a few minutes. Then you apply the polish.'

Ms Waring touches her throat absently and glances at a clock on the wall. 'I have to leave soon. Best tell me what you want.'

'How well do you know Olivia Blackmore?' I ask.

Her lips turn to tight lines. 'Don't use that name in this house. Call her Olivia Szabo or "that slut" or the "foreign bitch" but don't use Todd's name.'

213

'They were married.'

'Until she killed him.'

'What makes you say that?'

Her eyes glitter like broken shards of glass. 'It's what the Coroner said. He recommended she be charged with dangerous driving, but nothing ever happened. She got away with murder.'

'Olivia was seriously injured,' says Ruiz, who unscrews the lid of polish.

'OK, but she survived, didn't she? And she collected Todd's life insurance and shacked up with the surgeon who saved her.'

'What life insurance?'

'See! Now you're getting the picture. Todd had a policy made out to the kids. He might have been a shitty husband, but he tried to do right by Cameron and Lesley.'

Ms Waring stops in mid-sentence. 'Why are you so interested?'

Ruiz glances at me, wondering how much I'm willing to reveal.

'My father is the surgeon who married Olivia after Todd's death.'

'More fool him.'

'He's in a coma,' I say. 'Someone attacked him.'

'Bitch,' she mutters under her breath. 'I warned people about her. I warned him.'

'My father?'

'I wrote him a letter and told him all about her.'

'Did he write back to you?'

'I didn't want a pen friend,' she says, shaking her head at my stupidity.

'How long were you and Todd married?' I ask.

'Fifteen years. Two kids.' She glances at the clock. 'Cameron is coming to take me to the doctor.'

'Nothing serious, I hope.'

'Everything is serious at my age.'

Ruiz puts one boot down. She hands him the other.

'How did Todd meet Olivia?' I ask.

'He brought her home from a training camp in Romania. Told everyone she was the next Navratilova. Lots of coaches had started looking in Eastern Europe for tennis stars. Olivia was a proper little madam even then. Thirteen going on eighteen. Know what I'm saying?'

Not really, but I let her go on.

'We took her into our home – made her part of my family. Olivia and Cameron were the same age. Lesley a few years younger. The girls shared a bedroom.'

'Did Olivia go to school?'

'Yeah, until she got expelled for stealing money from a staffroom. After that Todd told people she was being home-schooled, but Olivia wasn't one for books or learning. Too lazy. Todd wouldn't hear a word against her. Treated her like a princess, giving her special meals and vitamin supplements. He said that science was going to help make her a champion, but that girl was all show and no go.'

'What happened?' asks Ruiz.

Ms Waring makes a *Pfff* sound. 'It started with tendonitis in her right wrist. Then it was a problem with her ankle. She had to have an operation, which put her off the court for five months. Cost us a fortune in physio sessions. Todd kept saying that it was only a matter of time, but I knew

Olivia was never going to be a champion. She didn't have it here, you know.' Ms Waring taps the centre of her chest.

'What did Todd say?'

'He had a blind spot when it came to Olivia.'

'What sort of blind spot?' asks Ruiz.

We're edging closer to the question we both want answered. Ms Waring knows it's coming.

'Let's just say that by the time Olivia had her operation, she was more interested in playing my husband than playing tennis.' She waits for our reaction. 'Do I have to spell it out? Olivia's career was tanking. She was scared that Todd might send her back to Romania, so she began flirting with him. You should have seen her – jumping on his lap in her short tennis skirts, flashing her knickers at every opportunity, calling him Daddy. She had this whole Lolita act going. I swear, she had him wrapped around her little finger. Men and their dicks, am I right?'

I don't react. Ruiz seems to polish harder on her boot.

'When did they start sleeping together?' I ask.

'I don't want to know.'

'Was she under the age of consent?'

'That girl was born old enough.'

Ms Waring stands and straightens her blouse, touching her hair as she looks in the mirror. 'Don't get me wrong – I blamed Todd as well. I hated that man for a long time, but he was the father of my children.'

'He was Olivia's guardian. If he began sleeping with her, he was breaking the law.'

'Yeah, well, if it's good enough for Woody Allen.'

Her passive aggressiveness irritates me, but I don't let it

show. Ms Waring takes the boots from Ruiz and slips her feet inside.

'Make all the excuses you want, but that little madam destroyed this family. She stole my husband and then she killed him.'

The last statement is like something caught in her teeth that has to be spat out.

'How do you know she killed him?' asks Ruiz.

'I was at the inquest.'

'She was never charged.'

Ms Waring makes the same *Pfff* sound. She takes a lipstick from her handbag and leans towards the mirror, painting her lips, making them look larger than they really are.

'Why would she want to kill Todd?' I ask.

'You're the psychologist – you should know all about people like her – psychopaths and narcissists.'

'She doesn't strike me as either of those things.'

'That makes you another man who she's twisted around her little finger.'

Ms Waring purses her lips and separates them like a zipper opening.

'Let me tell you about Olivia. Right from the beginning, Todd bragged about how cut-throat she was. You could see it on court during matches – the way she stared down opponents at the change-of-ends, or eyeballed them before each serve. If looks could kill, you know . . . She was ruthless on court. Clinical. Brutal. This one time I watched her play a junior tournament final and the little girl over the net was vomiting because of some stomach bug. She asked to take a five-minute break, but Olivia lodged a protest with the chair umpire, saying it wasn't allowed under the rules. The tournament referee came on. Olivia kept arguing. She made the girl forfeit the match.'

'That hardly makes her a killer,' says Ruiz.

'It shows she'd do anything to win,' Trudy Waring snaps back. 'How about this. She once put laxatives into the drink bottle of an opponent to guarantee herself a forfeit. Todd was furious. He threatened to send her back to Romania, but she took the ranking points and carried on. When the injuries started, Olivia wanted to take steroids to quicken the healing process. Todd told her it wasn't worth the risk. She didn't care. Like I said – she's a psychopath.'

Ms Waring juts out her chin, challenging me to dispute the diagnosis.

'Why are you asking me these questions? You should be talking to her. Ask her why she refused to give evidence at the inquest. And why she brought her own barrister along.'

'Why do you think?' Ruiz asks.

'Obvious, isn't it? She was guilty as sin. Maybe she got bored with marriage, or she wanted the insurance money.'

'How much did you give her?'

'Half. She threatened to sue. My lawyers told me to settle rather than risking a drawn-out legal battle.'

'Did you see her again?'

'No.'

'What about the kids?'

'They were grown by the time Todd married Olivia. Cameron was eighteen. Lesley was sixteen. Cameron took it hardest. It was like his sister had suddenly become his stepmother. He had a soft spot for Olivia.'

The front doorbell sounds, echoing along the hallway.

'That'll be him now.'

Ms Waring picks up her handbag and checks that she has her purse and keys. We follow her to the front door and out the gate, on to the footpath. A dark-coloured Audi, engine idling, is double-parked. A man gets out of the driver's side.

'Is everything all right, Mum?'

She waves him away, annoyed at the question.

Cameron has his father's blondness and athletic frame. He looks at me as though recognising someone familiar, before opening the passenger door for his mother. I'm a pace behind her. Cameron body-checks me before I reach the car.

'It's all right,' says Ms Waring, putting her hand on his fore-arm.

'How big was the life insurance policy?' I ask.

'Four hundred thousand pounds. Like I said, Todd was a shitty husband but a good provider.'

The door closes and the Audi accelerates away. Through the tinted windows, I can see Cameron gesticulating, demanding answers.

Ruiz is sucking on a boiled sweet. 'Hell hath no fury like a wife dumped for a younger woman.'

'Are you misquoting the Bard?'

'It's out of copyright.'

28

Samuel Rhodes works for a boutique accounting firm in the City of London with offices on the thirtieth floor of a thuggish comedy villain of a building known as the Walkie-talkie, which has concave walls of glass that are famous for melting cars and causing wind gusts that can knock pedestrians off their feet.

'I think it suits the banking district,' says Ruiz, as we wait in the foyer.

'How so?'

'It gets fatter as it rises.'

We're collected by an intern with designer stubble on his jaw, whose tight-fitting trousers are so short they show his bare ankles above his shoes.

'Don't people wear socks any more?' whispers Ruiz. 'What do they get for birthdays or Christmas?'

Samuel Rhodes stands as we enter. A slackly handsome man in his forties with oiled chestnut hair, he greets us with a flourish. 'Please call me Samuel. Can I call you Joe? I was shocked to hear about William. It's scarcely believable, attacked in his home. How is he?'

'No better or worse,' I reply.

'Please, accept my condolences. If there's anything I can do . . .'

'Thank you.'

Ruiz has gone to the floor-to-ceiling window, which offers a clear view in both directions along the Thames. To the east I can see City Airport and the grey waters of Albert Dock and beyond the immense obelisk of Canary Wharf. To the west are the Houses of Parliament, Big Ben and the London Eye. Everything old and everything new is beneath us, divided by elevated concrete ribbons or railway tracks, or the ageless river.

'On a clear day, you can see more than thirty miles,' says Samuel, who has a slight American accent. He's wearing a lavender shirt with a white collar and rolled white cuffs. Half-glasses hang on a string around his neck, resting on a red necktie.

Ruiz takes a chair beside me, spreading his knees wide.

'How did you hear about the attack?' I ask.

'William and I were due to meet on Monday. When he didn't show up, I called his mobile. A police officer answered.'

'What was the meeting about?'

'I took over as treasurer of the O'Loughlin Foundation in June. Being new to the board, I conducted a forensic audit to make myself fully cognisant of the foundation's holdings and investments. That's when I discovered certain discrepancies.'

'What discrepancies?'

'I'm not really at liberty to discuss the audit – not without permission from the board.' He hesitates. 'These matters are commercial in confidence.'

'We're talking about a charitable trust, not a listed company.'

'Even so, there are legal implications. William expressly told me not to reveal the details of the audit until we'd spoken.'

'Why?'

'He was seeking advice or considering his position.'

'You make it sound as though he's done something wrong.'

Samuel doesn't answer.

'My father was attacked and left for dead. I'm trying to understand why.'

Samuel looks surprised. 'The newspaper said it was a home invasion. A robbery gone wrong.'

'It's now attempted murder.'

The accountant looks from face to face, as though seeking confirmation. Pushing back from his desk, he opens the drawer of a filing cabinet and hands me a folder.

'This is what I sent to William. I was due to deliver the same report to the trustees at the AGM on Wednesday, but it has been postponed out of respect for William.'

There are twelve pages in the report, detailing the accounts. I turn immediately to the summation, a list of assets and values, earnings and expenses. The O'Loughlin

Foundation is worth about £65 million, having distributed £6 million in medical research grants in the previous twelve months.

'What am I looking at?' I ask.

Samuel directs me to the third page, where the fourth paragraph is in bold type under the heading: *Untraced Funds*.

'Eight years ago, the O'Loughlin Foundation sold a property in Denmark Street, London, to Westminster Council, which was looking to redevelop the land. The sale realised twelve million pounds and that money was placed with a number of managed funds and investment vehicles.

'The lion's share, nine million pounds, was given to a company called Faraday Financial Management, a reputable investment house, with a solid track record and forty years of history. That's what we thought,' says Samuel. 'In reality, the money was sent to a shelf company in the British Virgin Islands called Faraday Fiscal Management – almost the same name, but not the same company. It's a fake entity. Faraday Fiscal Management has no office-bearers, no staff, no payroll records, no tax liabilities. It exists merely as a private mailbox.'

'You're saying the money was stolen,' says Ruiz.

'It appears so.'

'By whom?' I ask.

Samuel opens his hands. 'I have no idea. Organised crime. The Mafia. The Russians . . .'

My mind rattles through the possibilities. 'Was it unusual to give one investment company such a large sum to invest?' I ask.

'In my experience, yes.'

'Who approved the strategy?'

'The board.'

'OK, but someone must have suggested they use this company and failed to see the switch to the new name.'

Samuel stands and walks to the window. Like many tall men, his shoulders are slightly rounded.

'Six years ago, the O'Loughlin Foundation didn't have a designated investment advisor. Your father did most of the research and due diligence. I've studied the minutes of past meetings and his recommendations were usually rubber-stamped with very little discussion or debate. It's different now. The board has an investment manager: Sydney Phillips, who came to us from Citibank. Good egg. Very thorough.'

'You're saying the board was duped.'

'Yes.'

'Why didn't anyone realise it until now?'

'That's the other interesting thing,' says Samuel. 'Whoever took the money very cleverly provided regular updates, writing quarterly reports and producing dividend statements that showed solid returns. It's like how Bernie Madoff created his Ponzi scheme, fooling investors into thinking they were making money, but the balance sheets were forgeries.'

'Why not just steal the money and disappear?' asks Ruiz.

'That puzzled me too,' says the accountant, who rubs his hands together persistently, producing a slippery, rasping sound. 'Perhaps whoever stole the money needed time to cover their tracks.'

'Six years is a long time,' says Ruiz.

'Who else knew you were conducting an audit?' I ask.

'Everybody on the board – but only William received

the final report. I sent it directly to him and we spoke on the phone.'

'When was that?'

'Ten days ago, although I did flag my concerns in September when I sent William a list of questions.'

'How did he react?'

'Surprised. Shocked. I stressed the seriousness of the situation. As a charitable foundation, there are strict regulations regarding paperwork and tax. The penalties are severe and the trustees are liable.'

'You're talking about fines,' Ruiz says.

'Or prison. That's why I recommended to William that we go straight to the police, but he wanted to call a board meeting first.'

'Could the previous accountant have stolen the money?' Ruiz asks.

'That's highly unlikely. He recommended me for the job.'

'Who then?'

Samuel shakes his head. 'All I know for certain is that funds are missing and I'm obliged to report the matter to the police. That's exactly what I plan to do once I've presented the audit to the board.'

'When is the meeting?'

'It's been rescheduled for next Tuesday.'

As the lift hums towards the lobby, a warning note is sounding in my mind. Nine million pounds is enough to pay for a second family and paper over a lot of cracks. It's also enough motive to silence someone.

The O'Loughlin Foundation was set up in 1949 by my

great-grandfather to fund medical research and ground-breaking surgical techniques. My father has been chairman for forty years, filling the board with friends, family and prominent medical figures. I was asked, but declined. Lucy and Patricia have both taken turns.

My family's wealth is something that I used to take for granted like electricity and running water. Growing up, I didn't regard myself as being privileged because most of my school friends lived in nice houses and went on similar holidays. It was only later as a teenager that I began to appreciate the gap between my life and the vast majority of people. For a while I felt embarrassed; I even pretended to be working class, dropping my 'h's and middle 't's, saying 'muvar' and 'nuffing', letting people think I had clawed my way out of the soot-blackened tenements of a Welsh mining village. The same guilt made me rail against capitalism and champion issues like homelessness, inequality, and Third World debt. It embarrasses me now – not because I'm uncaring, or less passionate about social justice, but because I acted like a celebrity who adopts an African baby, or an aristocrat driving a beaten-up car, telling myself I was 'keeping it real'.

Mercifully, I long ago dropped any pretence of having working-class roots and instead convinced myself that I overcame a greater burden than poverty or deprivation – my father's expectations.

Ruiz is with me. We're by the river, walking towards his car. He takes his tin of boiled sweets from his pocket and offers me one.

'You ever see *All the President's Men*?' I ask.

'Nixon. Watergate. What about it?'

'When the journalist Bob Woodward met up with Deep Throat in the underground garage, he grew frustrated because he couldn't see the whole story and the whistle-blower refused to spell it out. Deep Throat gave him one piece of advice.'

'What was that?'

'Follow the money.'

29

Charlie has taken Emma to see a movie and I'm alone, staring at the contents of the fridge, trying to summon the enthusiasm to cook. Other chores have been completed – linen changed, washing folded and school blouses ironed – mundane domestic rituals that prove I can be a single parent.

I am listening to my old vinyl: Pink Floyd's *Dark Side of the Moon*. The girls don't like my 'Dad music'. I was the same at their age. Every Sunday morning after Mass, my father would make my sisters and I kneel beside his leather armchair while he lovingly wiped dust from a classical music LP and lifted the needle into the groove. He would sit back, close his eyes and silently conduct the orchestra with floating hands.

Telling a school-age child to sit still for an hour on a Sunday morning is a form of torture. At times, we tried to sneak out when we thought Dad had fallen asleep, but that usually led to an extended sentence. The result? To this day, I can identify almost any piece of classical music; naming the interpretations, orchestras, conductors and soloists. At the same time, I break out in a cold sweat when I hear a TV commercial backed by Mozart, or Beethoven, or Handel. It doesn't matter if it's for toilet paper, or beer, or margarine, my response is always the same – I'm transported back to those Sunday mornings, feeling trapped and bored shitless.

Closing the fridge door, I pick up my mobile and look up a number. Kate Hawthorn answers on the second ring.

'Kate?'

'Who's this?'

'Joe O'Loughlin. I hope you don't mind me calling.'

'Is there a problem?'

'Have you eaten?'

'Why?'

'There's a little French place in Soho. Shabby chic. Great food. Good wine list. You'll feel like you're in Paris.'

'Are you asking me out?'

'If you don't want dinner, we could have a drink.'

'I think we should keep this purely professional.'

'That doesn't mean we can't eat . . . or drink.'

The line hums with silence. 'Maybe another time,' she says.

Kate hangs up and I wonder what else I could have said. I'm standing in the kitchen, looking across the rooftops. Wisps of smoke emanate from various pipes and funnels and chimneys. My mobile begins vibrating on the bench.

'It's not a date,' Kate says.

'Definitely not.'

'And you can't ask me about the case.'

'OK.'

'What time?'

'How about now?'

'Give me forty minutes. I'll text you my address.'

I give a little fist-pump, happy and amazed and maybe a little anxious because I don't know what I'm doing. Actors often ask directors, 'What does my character want in this scene?' I couldn't answer that question. Maybe I have no expectations, or I'm too nervous to give them any thought.

Having showered and shaved, I choose something casual to wear – an open-neck shirt and blue blazer. Black shoes with yellow stitching on the seams. I check my medication. I don't want to fall apart mid-meal.

Quietly pleased with the results, I catch a cab to Abbey Road in St John's Wood, not far from the pedestrian crossing made famous by John, George, Paul and Ringo. *More Dad music.*

Kate is waiting outside a mansion block. She's wearing different shades and textures of black. Jeans. Ankle boots. A tight sweater. A leather jacket. Her earrings have blue stones that match the colour of her eyes. Glimpsing her, I feel a quickening of my pulse. It's a meal, I tell myself. Nothing more.

As I open the cab door, she looks along the street as though expecting someone to be watching. She does the same thing when she's sitting next to me.

'Are you having second thoughts?'

'No.'

'You're allowed to have a private life.'

'I don't think my boss would agree.'

'I'm not a suspect – am I?'

'You promised not to talk about the case.'

'Sorry.'

The cab passes Lord's Cricket Ground and skirts Regent's Park before heading down Bloomsbury Street past elegant squares and Georgian terraces. We chat about what Londoners usually do: the weather, property prices and traffic woes.

'I bought my flat after the divorce,' Kate says. 'It's the only good thing that came out of the marriage.' She sneaks a glance at me, to see if I'm surprised.

'How long were you together?'

'Eight years. Married for two. It's the age-old story – we thought marriage might save a terminal relationship.'

'Any kids?'

'No. How about you?'

'Daughters. Charlie is twenty and Emma is twelve. My wife died sixteen months ago.'

'What happened?'

My voice thickens. 'Medical complications. A blood clot after surgery.'

'You must hate hospitals.'

'Yes.'

The cab does a U-turn and stops outside Bistro Boulevard, a small restaurant wedged between a café and clothing boutique. The streets throng with theatre-goers and early diners. Many of the shops have Christmas window displays and coloured lights, along with the ubiquitous SALE signs. Is there ever *not* a sale? That would deserve a sign.

The restaurant is crowded and noisy, but smells wonderful. I wish it were quieter. Kate removes her jacket and scarf. Guardedly, I sneak a look at her figure – a male curiosity – and go back to the warm symmetry of her face.

We chat easily. Kate is self-conscious about her braces and covers her mouth when she laughs.

'You don't have to do that. You hardly notice them,' I say.

'You're a terrible liar, Joseph O'Loughlin.'

I like the way she says my full name – as if it amuses her in some way.

'I couldn't afford to have my teeth fixed when I was younger,' she explains. 'It's embarrassing at my age.'

We order. Kate has a glass of wine. I stick to sparkling water and give her a potted history – the short version – born and raised in Wales, university in London, three years of medicine, then psychology, marriage, two girls, estrangement, widowhood . . .

Kate's soft face is propped on her hand. She hasn't said much about herself or her life. Even when she does, her voice is tinged with puzzlement, as if it happened to someone else.

'Why did you become a police officer?' I ask.

'I met someone who convinced me that I could turn my life around. Make a difference . . . be a better person.'

'Who was that?'

'Someone I heard speak.' She changes the subject. 'I was a tearaway as a kid; trouble with a capital T. I'm lucky the neighbours didn't have me arrested.'

'Where was home?'

'A council house in Watford.'

'Do your parents still live there?'

'My mother does. I never knew my father. He was a parole officer at a prison. That's how my mother met him.'

'She worked for the prison service.'

Kate shakes her head. 'She was an inmate. She majored in shoplifting and ran out of second chances.'

There is a touch of roughness to her vowels, or a sense of untamed energy, held in check.

I lean closer. 'Are you sure we haven't met before?'

She looks away. 'No.'

'You look so familiar.'

'I'm not.'

The statement is tinged with sadness. Maybe that's why I'm drawn to Kate. It is not her beauty, or her curls or the spray of pale freckles on her nose, or her crooked teeth, or her decency and courage. In addition to all of this she seems to carry a secret burden, a sadness that she won't share easily.

Self-consciously, she reaches for her red wine and knocks over her glass, spilling it across the tablecloth. She apologises, admonishing herself. A waiter arrives with extra serviettes, increasing her embarrassment, which makes her talk too quickly. I'm fascinated by her top lip, which is shaped like a stylised bird in a child's drawing. I wonder what it might be like to kiss that lip.

'You're staring at me,' she says, covering her mouth self-consciously.

'I'm sorry. I do that sometimes.'

'It's very unnerving.'

I notice a ring on her right hand. I tell her it's pretty. 'It was a present to myself,' she says. 'After the divorce. I gave him back my engagement ring.'

'Why?'

'It belonged to his grandmother. I thought it only right.'

'Would you like another glass of wine?'

'No.'

'Dessert?'

'Only if you share. A true gentleman has to take some of the guilt.'

She chooses the 'Death by Chocolate' and coffee.

It's nice to banter and flirt with a pretty woman. Julianne and I used to be like this, teasing each other, making observations, righting the wrongs of the world.

'Why did you decide to become a psychologist?' she asks.

'My Aunt Gracie was agoraphobic. She died in a house fire because she refused to leave.'

'That's horrible. Were you close to her?'

'Very.'

'Where do you work now?'

'I have a private practice. Part-time. Referrals from doctors. Cases that other psychologists have put in the too hard basket.'

'You like a challenge?'

'Nobody should be given-up on.'

She smiles and I feel my earlobes grow warm.

'I know I promised not to talk about the case, but I have one question.'

'Which I won't be answering.'

'Does the name Micah Beauchamp mean anything to you?'

Kate shakes her head.

'According to Olivia, he's been sponging off Ewan for months – getting him to steal things.'

'Did she tell Macdermid?'

'She's given a new statement. Micah might be the guy who attacked me at the bus stop . . .'

'I can't comment.'

'Have you identified the intruder at the hospital?'

Kate's eyes flash. 'I asked you to leave this alone.' She turns and takes her coat from the back of her chair.

'Please don't go.'

'This was a mistake.'

'What about dessert?'

'I'd like to go home.'

Kate insists on splitting the bill. Moments later we're standing on the footpath outside being jostled by the crowds. Kate shivers and wraps the scarf around her neck, pulling her jacket tighter about her chest.

'Let me take you home.'

'I can make my own way.'

'Forgive me, Kate. It's been a while since I've done this.'

Her features soften and she looks sorry for me. It's absurd, almost embarrassing, but I could spend hours staring at her face.

A cab pulls up. Kate takes a half step and leans against

me, kissing me quickly. Before I can react, she pirouettes away and slips into the back. The door closes. The cab pulls out, disappearing into the glare of headlights before Kate's name can form on my lips.

Day Nine

30

This is how I wake, sliding out of sleep as though I've spent the night sheltering in a cave. Opening my eyes, unsure of where I am, I recognise the window, the wardrobe, my bedroom. It's not dark or light outside. The city has a dim grainy glow.

A breath catches in my throat and I'm convinced that Ewan has broken into the flat. He's after Emma and Charlie. My arm sweeps down, searching for a weapon, knocking over a bottle of pills, sending them bouncing and scattering across the wooden floor. Grunting at my stupidity, I lean out of bed, scrabbling for the pills. I find one and swallow it dry. Settling back. Relaxing.

My bladder is full. Swinging my legs out of bed, I go to the bathroom, feeling the cold of the tiles on my bare feet. I catch a glimpse of myself in the mirror and feel a sudden rush of self-pity, unfocused and pure. In that same instant, I hear Julianne's voice, telling me not to be so melodramatic. She wraps her arms around me and whispers.

'They're good girls.'

'I know.'

'Look after them.'

'I will.'

In the months after she died, Julianne would often visit me. The past would leak into my present, creating cognitive slips and optical illusions. The smallest of details could bring her to me – a pattern of shade; a white car like the one we first owned; a woman walking in the street with the same gait; an earlobe, a laugh, a fragrance. What I have never found again is Julianne's smell, which has faded from her clothes and her pillow (which I still have). I would pay a fortune to anyone who could recreate that scent for me.

In that instant I feel a cold draught, as though someone has opened a door to the outside. Following the temperature change, I walk along the hallway and see pale curtains billowing above the kitchen sink. That's strange. During the summer, we sometimes leave the window open to catch a breeze, or to access the small flat rooftop outside. It's a good vantage point to view the sunset, or watch fireworks on the Thames on New Year's Eve.

Leaning over the sink, I grip the lower frame to pull the sash-window down. In the same instant, I see Emma standing on the edge of the roof, looking at the street below. She's wearing a long nightdress, which is blown hard around her thin body. Her arms are outstretched as though she's holding herself against the wind, or preparing to jump.

My heart squeals on metal wheels. Climbing on to the sink, I call to her. She doesn't answer. I clamber through the window, barking my shins on the tap as I crawl across the bitumen roof.

Emma hasn't acknowledged me. If I frighten her, she could fall, or leap instinctively. Edging closer, I whisper her name. Her eyes are closed. Her arms spread wide.

Reaching out, I grip the edge of her nightdress, bunching it in my fist. I pull her back towards me, encircling her waist, holding her tightly on my lap. She utters a small cry and her heart flutters against mine. I say her name over and over. She is curled up, her head buried into my neck, her teeth chattering.

Carefully, picking her up, I carry her to the window and watch her crawl inside. Back in my bedroom, I wrap a duvet around her shoulders, holding her between my arms and legs.

'What were you doing?' I ask.

She shakes her head.

'Did you have a dream?'

'I don't remember.'

Later, when she's warm, she rests her head on my lap like a little girl with an earache.

'I miss Mummy,' she whispers.

'Me too,' I say, gently stroking her hair. 'Is that why you were outside?'

'I don't think so. I don't know.'

Since Julianne's funeral, Emma has barely mentioned her mother. Each time her name comes up, I almost see Emma flinch and squeeze her eyes shut, mentally closing down. Is it healthy? Not always, but there are many different methods of coping with grief or trauma. Some people pack and re-pack their feelings like a beach holiday suitcase. That's not Emma. She travels light.

Her breathing slows and softens as she falls asleep. Floorboards creak. Charlie appears.

'What happened?'

'Emma was outside.'

'Where?'

'On the roof. I think she was sleepwalking.'

'Can someone do that – open a window when they're asleep?'

'She did.'

Charlie sits on the edge of the bed. 'She could have . . .'

'Don't say it.'

My left hand is twitching again.

'Do you need a pill?'

'No, I'm fine. Help me get Emma to bed.'

'She can sleep with me,' says Charlie. 'I'll wake if she gets up.'

I carry Emma to Charlie's room and pull the duvet beneath her chin. She mumbles something and rolls on her side.

Charlie follows me to the door and puts her arms around me.

'Am I a good father?' I ask.

'Of course you are.'

'Sometimes I wonder . . .'

'Is this about Granddad?'

'Possibly.'

'You always taught me that people have hidden lives. You said everyone had at least one secret and they all lied. That's one of the reasons I chose to study psychology.'

'Understanding human behaviour doesn't make life any easier.'

'I know, but it makes it less mysterious.'

'Goodnight, Charlie.'

Once she's gone, I find my toolbox in the cupboard below the fuse box. Searching through the sad assortment of screwdrivers, spanners and wrenches, I find what I need. Using an electric drill, I put two holes in the window frame and affix wooden blocks to stop it opening more than a few inches.

Julianne talks to me as I work.

'She needs a mother.'

'I can handle this.'

'We promised each other that if something happened to either of us—'

'I know what we promised.'

'You need someone. Nobody should be alone.'

'I'm not alone. I still have you.'

31

David Passage lives in a large mock-Tudor semi in the shadows of St Thomas the Apostle Church in Hanwell, West London. Two children, rugged up against the cold, are racing their scooters up and down the footpath. The eldest is a girl, aged about six, in a bright pink parka and woollen hat with matching ear muffs that flap as she picks up speed. Her companion is a younger boy who keeps telling her to slow down.

'Not fair! Not fair! You said I could win.'

'I gave you a head start,' she replies, her cheeks red with the cold.

I step around them and open the front gate.

'That's our house,' says the boy, wiping his nose on his sleeve.

A Scottish Terrier darts from beneath a bush and charges

across the lawn, yapping furiously and bouncing from side to side, keeping a safe distance.

'That's Buster,' says the boy. 'He's all bark and no bite.'

'He bit Granddad that time,' says his sister.

'Only because he stepped on Buster.'

'Is your daddy home?' I ask.

'I'll get him,' says the boy, dropping his scooter and running down the path, bursting through the unlocked front door and yelling.

A woman appears, wiping her hands on the back of her jeans. She's in her late thirties, two pregnancies past her optimum weight, with similar features to her children.

'Can I help you?'

'I'm looking for David Passage.'

'Of course, just one moment.' The boy is clinging to her leg. 'Tell Daddy we have company.'

'Can't Valerie go?'

'Do as you're told. He's in the shed.'

The boy disappears again, dashing down the hallway and gliding on tiny wheels in the heels of sneakers.

The woman smooths down her blouse and touches her hair self-consciously.

'I'm Joe O'Loughlin,' I explain.

'Oh, right. David's old school friend.' She relaxes and smiles. 'I'm Madeleine. Please call me Maddie. Everybody does.'

Her outstretched hand is cool and damp.

'How was the other night?' she asks.

'Pardon?'

'Your dinner with David.'

'Right. Yes. Dinner.'

'David didn't get home until three. I almost locked him out.'

What is she talking about?

'Let me take your coat,' she says, hanging it on a rack near the front door that is already bulging with anoraks and parkas. 'I was sorry to hear about your father. How is he?'

'We haven't given up hope.'

'Quite right.'

David appears in the kitchen. He's wearing jogging bottoms and a Harlequins rugby jumper.

'Look who's here,' says Maddie, touching her hair again. 'We weren't expecting anyone . . .'

David looks perplexed.

'Your office said you were working from home today,' I say. 'I should have called ahead.'

'No, it's perfectly OK. Come in. Come in. You've met Maddie and the rug rats. This is Hugo and that's Valerie outside.' He ruffles the boy's hair. 'How about a coffee? Unless you prefer tea.'

'Tea would be nice. Can we speak privately?'

'Right. Yes.' He looks at Maddie. 'We'll be upstairs in the study.'

'I'll bring the tea up,' she replies. 'You should ask Joe what happened to your coat,' says Maddie. 'He might remember where you left it.'

David laughs nervously. 'Joe's not interested in my wardrobe. Go on up. First door on the left. Mind the toys.'

The study is a cramped fourth bedroom with just enough

244

room for a desk, filing cabinets and two wooden chairs. Taking one of them, I wait for David to join me. The window overlooks the back garden, which is a soggy rectangle with a Wendy house and a swing set.

David turns side-on, sucks in his stomach and squeezes past me to reach his seat. He rescues a Thomas the Tank Engine from under his buttocks and puts it on the desk.

'Apparently, we had dinner the other night,' I say.

'Sorry about that. Slight misunderstanding.'

'Not on my part.'

He sighs and smiles sheepishly. 'A white lie. I didn't expect—'

'You're having an affair.'

'Good heavens! No!' He looks offended. 'It's nothing like that. Sometimes I blow off a little steam – I have a few drinks, or go and see some really slow foreign movie, where I fall asleep in the back row.'

'You're unhappy?'

'No. I love them all to bits, but I'm exhausted.'

'And I'm complicit.'

'Won't happen again. Scout's honour.' He gives a three-fingered salute, before tilting his chair back and clasping his hands behind his head. 'What brings you to my humble abode?'

'Is it humble?'

'It's hardly a palace. Positively poky when you have four of us, cooped up together like battery hens. I've never liked living in the suburbs. The lawnmowers, traffic fumes and barking dogs.'

'Why not move?'

'Can't afford it – not until the old man pops off. Not that I'm hoping. I love the old bugger.'

'Where would you move?'

'Gloucestershire most likely. That's where Maddie comes from. I'd stay in London during the week, come home weekends.'

'Like my father.'

'Yes. Well.' David falls silent.

'I talked to Samuel Rhodes. I know about the missing money.'

'What missing money?'

'The nine million pounds stolen from the O'Loughlin Foundation.'

David blinks at me. 'What on earth are you talking about?'

'You don't know?'

'I haven't a fucking clue.'

I tell him what I've learned and watch his eyes widen and brow furrow. He quizzes me for the exact details.

'And this dodgy investment deal cost us nine million quid?'

'It wasn't lost – it was stolen.'

'Christ!' David runs his fingers through his hair. 'How?'

'Faraday Fiscal Management only exists on paper. Its head office is a postbox in some dusty village in the British Virgin Islands. Whoever took the money has been providing fake investment reports and dividend statements to cover their tracks.'

'Jesus! I need to talk to the board.'

'When did you join?'

'Ten, maybe eleven years ago. William asked me. He knew

Dad was retiring and he wanted another lawyer to replace him. Cheap legal advice.'

'Do you remember the investment?'

David squints. 'Vaguely. I remember we sold a property in Denmark Street in Soho.'

'It was twelve million pounds.'

'It was eight years ago. I was getting remarried. I hope you're not suggesting that I acted improperly. I was doing William a favour joining the board. None of the directors are paid. We show up to meetings, we review proposals, we hand out money for research projects . . .'

'Who made this decision?'

'I have no idea. Nowadays we have a financial advisor on the board, but back then William did most of the work, or we all made suggestions.'

'Samuel Rhodes wants to involve the police.'

David reacts instantly. 'We should get a second opinion.'

'Don't you trust him?'

'It's not that.'

There's a knock on the door. Maddie appears, carrying a tray with two mugs and a plate of biscuits that are shaped like teddy bears.

'It's all we have,' she explains apologetically.

She's still holding the tray. David helps clear a space. Maddie smiles in thanks, before pausing at the door. 'Are you still talking business?'

'Yes,' David says, curtly.

'Right. OK. I thought we should invite Joe to my birthday party.'

'He won't know anyone.'

'He'll know us.' She looks at me. 'I'm having my fortieth next week. You don't have to come. I'll leave an invitation downstairs.'

The door closes and David apologises for the interruption.

'She's nice,' I say.

'Yes, she is,' he replies unconvincingly. He notices my reaction. 'Don't get me wrong. I love her to bits, but doing this all again – starting a second family at my age – it's a tough gig. Maddie used to be so much fun. God, she could make me laugh. Still does, when she's not exhausted or pre-menstrual, which is twenty-eight days a month.'

He's looking for a sympathetic ear, someone who understands the burden of being middle-aged, male, successful, white and married to an attractive wife. For a moment, we lock eyes and he realises that I'm not the right person and decides to let it go. He picks up his mug of tea and dunks a biscuit.

Getting back to the missing money, he says, 'I would advise against involving the police until we can talk to William. He should be given an opportunity to explain what happened to the funds.'

'You're not suggesting *he* stole it!'

David is surprised at my reaction. 'It's one conclusion.'

'He could have been duped or the victim of a fraud.'

'Yes, but you said there were regular updates and dividend statements. That suggests whoever took the money was on the inside. Why else would they keep up such a subterfuge for six years, instead of taking the money and disappearing?'

He's right. The ongoing smokescreen points to someone

close to the O'Loughlin Foundation. The lawyer dunks another biscuit and proceeds cautiously. 'There are some issues I should perhaps have mentioned earlier, regarding your father's finances.'

'What issues?'

'William lost half of his net worth during the Global Financial Crisis. He cashed out his shares near the bottom of the market and didn't buy back in until the correction was over. Properties had to be sold. Expenses trimmed. Having two families didn't help. There were also medical bills. Ewan had several stints in private hospitals that were costing £500 a day. There were psychiatrists and therapists. I warned William that his finances were becoming depleted, but he said it wasn't my problem.'

'When?'

'Post-GFC.' David gets to his feet and stretches, exposing a hairy stomach over the waistband of his sweatpants. 'William was nearly bankrupt, but two years later his finances were restored.'

'How?'

'Exactly.'

I struggle to keep my voice even. 'That's not evidence.'

'Whether it's true or not, implications can be more damaging than facts,' says David, 'which is why William should be given the chance to explain. If we take this to the police, every trustee will come under suspicion. It will damage all of us.'

The pragmatism of lawyers infuriates me, but everything he says makes sense. When I do speak again, I sound less defensive.

'These debts that my father accrued – how do I learn more about them?'

'I can send you his bank statements and tax returns. It's probably breaking confidences, but given the circumstances . . .'

David's mug is empty. My tea is untouched. Standing by the door, he signals wordlessly that it's time for me to leave.

'There's a lot we don't know about our fathers,' he says pensively, as we reach the top of the stairs. 'My old man almost went to prison.'

'Kenneth?'

'They struck him off the roll of solicitors for altering a witness statement. It took him years to get his practising certificate back. William had his ladies and Kenneth had his humiliations.'

'What do you mean: "ladies"?'

'Olivia Blackmore, of course.'

'Were there more?'

David hesitates, but continues. 'When he wakes up, you should ask him about Bethany D'Marco.'

'Who?'

'Every year he sends £40,000 to an address in East London. No message, just the money. The firm draws the cheque and has it couriered to a house.'

'And you don't know why.'

'No idea and it's none of my business. She could be a mistress, or a love child, but he's been paying her for the best part of forty years.'

'What address?'

'Hoxteth Gardens in Newham.'

32

The row of terraced houses backs on to the North Circular where traffic hurtles forward like a stampede of maddened animals. Some of the houses are being renovated, the facades covered in scaffolding and plastic sheets. Building skips, bulging with broken plasterboard and shattered tiles, take up parking spaces on the street.

Counting down the numbers, I stand in front of a house with yellowing net curtains and a weed-choked front yard dotted with discarded rubbish. The gate creaks and I step on to concrete pavers. A motorbike is parked beneath a plastic rain cover. It snags something in my memory.

Crouching beside the bike, I lift the cover high enough to see the polished red of the fuel tank.

'What the fuck are you doing?' says a man, who has stepped from the doorway and is standing over me. The sun is directly behind his head. I raise a hand to shield my eyes. He's my age, maybe younger, dressed in oil-stained jeans and a checked shirt.

I get to my feet and step away from the motorbike, taking note of his wide-set eyes, broad upper lip and flat forehead. Recognition comes in a rush.

'You were at the hospital.'

'What?'

'The hospital.' I point to my head, showing the stitches. 'You pulled a shelf down on top of me.'

'Fuck off!'

He turns to go back inside. I lunge forward and jam my foot in the door.

'What did you say to my father?'

'Move or lose it,' he says, kicking at my foot.

'Every September William O'Loughlin sends a cheque to this address – the same amount, on the same day – I want to know why.'

'Guilt.'

'What?'

'You heard me. Now fuck off!'

I push back against the door, but he's fitter and heavier than I am. It slams shut.

'The next knock you hear will be the police,' I yell. 'I'm calling them now.'

I punch out Macdermid's number and listen to it ringing. Meanwhile, the door edges open.

'I had nothing to do with what happened,' he mutters.

'How do you know my father?'

'I've never met him.'

He's lying. 'You knew he was in hospital.'

'I read a story in the paper. I wanted to see if it was true.'

'You didn't believe the newspaper?'

'I wanted to be sure.'

'Why?'

The man looks behind him down a hallway. 'Please leave us alone. I had nothing to do with what happened. That's what I tried to explain to him.'

'He couldn't hear you – talk to me instead.'

The door is closing again. I brace my hand against it. 'Who is Bethany D'Marco?'

'Fuck off!'

I raise the phone to my ear. 'Is that DI Macdermid? This is Joe O'Loughlin.' I'm talking to dead air, but the man in the doorway doesn't know that.

He steps back, letting it swing open. I pocket my phone and follow him into a cluttered sitting room that reeks of cigarette smoke and Chinese takeaway. Light filters through a dirty net curtain, giving everything a jaundiced look, like newspapers left too long in the sun. There are photographs on the mantelpiece in tarnished frames: a mother holding a baby, a father with a son on his shoulders, children feeding ducks at a pond. A football match is playing on the TV with the sound turned down.

'Is Bethany here?'

He doesn't answer.

'Can I speak to her?'

'Beth is indisposed.'

I notice a pile of letters. Unpaid bills in torn envelopes. 'Overdue' stamps. A name above the address: Ray D'Marco.

'Are you Bethany's husband?'

'Her brother.'

I look again at the photographs, recognising the man in the boy.

'You live here with your sister?'

He nods.

'And your parents?'

'Mum died ten years ago. Dad went a year later. Your father killed them.'

D'Marco watches for my reaction. 'You think I'm lying. He killed them sure as I'm standing here. He wore them down, bit by bit. I watched them disappear.'

Lighting a cigarette, he drags at it aggressively as though trying to fill his entire body with smoke.

A bell rings from somewhere above us. His eyes roll upwards and his head suddenly drops. Examining the half-finished cigarette, he carefully stubs it out in the over-flowing ashtray and tucks the butt behind his left ear.

'Is that Bethany?'

Silence. D'Marco walks to the kitchen and opens the fridge, taking out a loaf of white bread, butter, cheese, pickles and a juice box, arranging them on the bench beside a corroded stovetop. Bread is buttered and smeared with pickles, topped with a slice of cheese, before he removes the crust and cuts the sandwich into triangles.

The bell rings again.

'I'm coming,' he mutters, adding a packet of crisps to the tray. He acknowledges me. 'You want to see where your father's money goes?'

I nod.

'Come and meet the Queen.'

Picking up the tray, he leads me along the hallway and up the stairs to the first floor. Pausing outside a locked door, he slides a deadbolt to the left and nudges it open with his foot, revealing a little girl's room decorated in bright primary colours with a canopy bed covered in soft toys. I see a rocking horse, bookcase and a large doll's house with a gabled roof and miniature furniture. Dozens of figurines of owls are lined up along a shelf. The heating is turned up and the air is thick with the stench of faecal matter and musk perfume.

I step further inside and see a wheelchair. The occupant looks neither male or female. Child-sized with huge brown eyes. A mouth opens, pink and wet. A tongue lolls out. A hand goes to the mouth. Fingers creep inside.

Not a child. A woman. Crippled. Disabled. Underweight. Middle-aged. She's wearing a padded leather helmet like I've seen worn by rugby players. Tufts of tangled grey hair poke through the holes between the padding.

D'Marco crosses the room and puts the tray on a table in front of the window.

'We have a visitor, Beth,' he says, holding the straw to her lips. She takes a drink from the juice box. Her body twists from side to side, but her cheek appears to be almost glued to her shoulder. She raises her arms, which are covered in scratch marks.

'She wants a hug,' D'Marco says.

He's testing me. I move closer and embrace Bethany, smelling her stale breath and the urine that stains her dress. Her arms lock around my neck and squeeze too tightly, as

255

though trying to stop me leaving. I recall the photographs on the mantelpiece. She was the baby. What happened to her?

'Let him go, Beth. Eat your sandwich,' says D'Marco.

Reluctantly she releases me and puts a triangle of bread and cheese into her mouth, chewing noisily with her mouth open. Masticated food falls into her lap. I crouch beside her chair, resting my hands on the wheel.

'My name is Joe.'

Bethany picks up an old-style mobile phone, which is tucked next to her hip. Flipping it open, she says, 'Hello, Joe, how are you?'

'I'm fine.'

Bethany shakes her head.

'You have to talk on the phone,' D'Marco explains.

I take out my mobile. 'Hello, is that Bethany?'

'Yes, it's me. I'm having my lunch.'

'What are you eating?'

'A sandwich and some juice.'

She talks as though I'm not in the room.

'I went to the zoo today,' she announces.

'What did you see?'

'The elephants and camels and monkeys.'

'Did you see a kangaroo?'

'Three of them.'

I glance at her brother, who gives me a small shake of the head.

'We don't get out so much,' he explains. 'Occasional day trips. The council helps.'

'You look after her alone?'

'A physio comes in three times a week. Health services send someone to help me shop and clean.' He collects toys and puts them on the bed. Books are closed and put on a shelf. 'When people think of intellectual disability they always go to the Forrest Gump example, but Forrest didn't have an IQ of 32 or have seizures every few hours.'

'Seizures?'

'Severe epilepsy.'

'What happened to her?'

'Ask your father.'

'I can't do that.'

D'Marco cajoles Bethany into finishing her sandwich before sweeping the soggy crumbs from her lap and wiping down her mobile phone. He puts it within easy reach.

'Does she call anyone?'

'It's not charged. And who would she call?'

Bethany is humming a nursery rhyme, rocking her head from side to side. Her brother puts on a DVD and man-oeuvres the wheelchair in front of the TV. She leans her head against his hand like a cat being stroked. He takes the cigarette from behind his ear and lights up. Bethany looks at him and says, 'Me too. Me too.' He holds the cigarette to her lips and she inhales. Exhales. He takes it away.

'More. More.'

'That's enough.'

D'Marco raises the sash window and flicks the ash outside.

'What happened?' I ask.

He leans on the sill. 'Mum was seven months pregnant, coming home from work, when a lorry ran a red light and slammed into the side of the bus. Six people died. Her

257

chest was crushed; her lungs filled with blood. They rushed her straight into surgery, but there were no signs of a foetal heartbeat. Your father ordered an emergency caesarean. Bethany came out blue. Lifeless. They all ignored her. Eventually a nurse noticed that her lips had changed colour and they resuscitated her but by then it was too late. She'd suffered brain damage. Cerebral palsy. Epilepsy. They said she wouldn't live past the age of three. She's forty-seven.'

'What about your mother?'

'Mum lived. They told her she couldn't have any more children because of her injuries, but I came along. On good days I think I was compensation. On bad days I wonder if I was born to look after Bethany once they'd gone.'

'I'm sure that's not true.'

'How would you know what's true?' His anger is palpable. Bethany looks away from the TV and studies him for a moment, as though concerned she's done something wrong.

'Was there an investigation?'

'You mean a cover-up.' He stubs out the cigarette against the brickwork, tossing it outside. 'The hospital closed ranks. Sang off the same hymn sheet. They said Bethany's injuries were caused by the accident, not their negligence.'

'Maybe they were right.'

'Bollocks! My parents were sent a letter from an eyewitness – someone who was at the hospital when it happened. This person saw William O'Loughlin snorting lines of cocaine at a party less than two hours before he operated on my mother.'

'My father doesn't take drugs.'

'You would say that – wouldn't you?'

'I'm serious. The idea is ridiculous.'

D'Marco grunts dismissively. 'I was six years in the army and my bullshit-meter works just fine. Let me show you something.'

He picks up the tray and we go downstairs, first to the kitchen and then the sitting room, where I watch him retrieve a scarred wooden box from a cupboard below the TV. Opening the hinged lid, he produces a single sheet of folded paper, yellowing with age.

Unfurling it gently, he places it on the coffee table in front of me. Handwritten in blue ink, it reads:

Dear Mrs D'Marco,

Your baby did not deserve to die. Unforgivable mistakes were made — delays in treatment and poor decisions. The surgeon who performed the emergency caesarean was under the influence of alcohol and drugs. He didn't expect to be working that night, but should have recused himself. Bethany deserved more. You deserved more.

Please forgive my cowardice for not signing this letter. I cannot risk becoming involved. It would cost me my career because no hospital will employ a whistle-blower.

Yours sincerely,

A friend

D'Marco reaches into the same wooden box and produces a photograph with curling corners and bleached colours.

The image shows a crowded room where furniture has been pushed back and rearranged against the walls. A dozen people are dancing, but the framing doesn't show their faces. Instead the camera is focused on a couple who are locked in a kiss on the sofa. The man's face is obscured by the woman who has one leg draped over his lap and her arms around his neck. She's wearing a light blue nurse's tunic that has ridden up her thighs, revealing the white crotch of her panties. She doesn't seem concerned by the exposure.

In the foreground, the glass-topped coffee table is dotted with wine glasses and a heavy glass ashtray overflowing with crumpled fag-ends. In the centre of the table, a space has been cleared for a mirror which is intersected by two parallel lines of white powder an inch apart. Two similar lines, now smudges, lie beneath a rolled banknote.

The back of the photograph has a handwritten date: *24 September 1971.*

D'Marco points to the man on the sofa. 'That's your father.'

'How can you tell?'

'It came with the letter.'

'That doesn't prove anything.'

D'Marco snatches the photograph away from me. 'You're like all the others – protecting him.'

'No, please, let me look.'

I study the image again, taking in every detail, feeling my certainty waver. It could be my father. His left hand is resting on the woman's thigh, just below the hem of her dress. Fingers spread. He's wearing a distinctive wristwatch. I recognise the brand, Baume & Mercier. My father was given it on his graduation from medical school.

Instinctively, I begin calculating the dates and making connections. Dad would have been in his early thirties, finishing his surgical training in Cardiff. Married with four children. The woman on the sofa is not my mother.

At the same time my mind is screaming: Cocaine! Ridiculous!

D'Marco takes another cigarette from a crushed packet and leans on the mantelpiece as he smokes, watching to see my reaction. I consider the letter again. It's unsigned. Undated. Without an author or corroboration, it's useless as evidence.

'What did your parents do?' I ask.

'They tried to sue for negligence, but your father had a brace of clever lawyers and the hospital had deep pockets. The court case bankrupted them. They lost the house, the car, their furniture – the bailiffs came knocking. Dad had to borrow money from his brother to get started again and his brother never let him forget.'

'When did the cheques start arriving?'

'Before I was born.'

'How did you discover who sent them?'

'My old man didn't care where the money came from. I mean, he suspected it was guilt money, but he didn't ask questions. After my parents died, the cheques kept coming. Always on the same date – Bethany's birthday – September 24. This one time I bribed the courier, who gave me the name of a legal firm in Chancery Lane.'

'Passage and Moore.'

'Yeah, that's the one. I did some more digging and discovered the link with your father.'

'Did you approach him?'

'No.'

'I don't believe you.'

'Suit yourself.'

'The police are going to find out. They'll trace your calls.'

D'Marco contemplates this, rolling it over his tongue, not liking the taste.

'Yeah, well, maybe I talked to him.'

'When?'

'A few weeks ago.'

'Why?'

'I figured he could pay more. I called it a cost-of-living increase.'

'You threatened him?'

'No!'

'He refused to pay, so you attacked him.'

'Fuck off!'

D'Marco flicks the burning cigarette into the fireplace where it sparks off the blackened bricks. 'It's time you left.'

'A nurse overheard you telling my father you were sorry.'

'I am. If he dies, the money dries up.'

As if on cue, the bell rings from upstairs. D'Marco glances at the ceiling and his face seems to collapse in on itself.

'Don't look at me like that,' he says.

'Like what?'

'You pity me.'

'I admire you.'

'I don't want your admiration, or your sympathy. Are you going to guarantee the cheques keep coming?'

'My father isn't dead.'

'No, but he's dying.'

We eyeball each other wordlessly and I see the possibility that everything he has told me is true. His gaze compels me to believe, to accept his dark vision of my father, and it creates a feeling close to panic. I hate this wretched house, which is stuffy and cold at the same time.

'Can I borrow this photograph?' I ask.

'Why?'

'I want to make sure.'

'I keep copies,' he says, still wary of my motives.

The bell rings again. D'Marco leads me down the hallway to the front door. It closes behind me before I can say goodbye. Drawing fresh air into my lungs, I try to rid myself of the smell and sadness and wasted years in that upstairs room; and the damaged woman, whose luminous eyes continue to stare at me even now.

Walking without any real purpose, I pass buildings, cars, shops, billboards and houses that blur into a smeared grey tableau of urban existence. My father – a man incapable of admitting a mistake – was accused of medical negligence. Did he ask others to lie for him and conceal evidence? None of this fits with the man I know, but why else would he keep paying the money and keep Bethany D'Marco a secret?

I wish I didn't care, but I do. I've seen a ghost and that ghost is my father; an oversized man with a heart of stone who once occupied a pedestal, but whose legacy is as fouled and be-shitted as a London statue.

Day Ten

33

After midnight, unable to sleep, I open my laptop and begin searching for details of a medical negligence case that unfolded in the age before the Internet. I type my father's name and then narrow the search using 'Bethany 'D'Marco' as a filter. It throws up a date and a listing number in the High Court of Justice Queen's Bench Division on 17 February 1975. The Honourable Mrs Justice Fontaine presided. I can't find her judgement.

Closing the laptop, I doze until woken by daylight and the rumblings of a rubbish truck in the street outside. At nine o'clock I call the court directly and talk to an archivist who sounds like he's locked in a basement and doesn't want to be disturbed or rescued.

'The records are only accessible with a written application,' he says, clicking his tongue in annoyance.

'How long would that take?'

'Six to eight weeks.'

'What if I came to the court?'

'Are you a member of the legal fraternity?'

'No.'

'Is it for a pending case?'

'No.'

'Then that's not possible.'

'There must be some way I can read the judgement.'

'You could try the Inner Temple Library,' he says, giving me the phone number.

The next librarian is more helpful. I make an appointment for midday and catch a cab to Fleet Street, alighting opposite the Cheshire Cheese, a famous watering hole from the days when printing presses rumbled in basements and liveried trucks carried newspapers all around London and beyond.

The library is housed in a Gothic-looking building with arched doorways and lead-light windows. A plaque commemorates the reconstruction after fire raged through Inner Temple in 1941, triggered by a German air-raid. The main reading room is a cavernous space, lined with leather-bound volumes of law reports and legal tomes that seem to be holding up the roof.

The librarian has fire-engine red hair and a tattoo of a fox that peeks from the folded sleeve of her sweater. Her name is Yael and she reminds me of Kate – not her looks, but her youth and vitality.

'If it was an important case, or went to appeal, the judgement should be here,' she says, nudging the mouse and clicking through screens. 'A full transcript may be harder to find.' She stops scrolling. 'This looks promising.'

She runs her finger down a list and has me jot down dates and case numbers.

'I'll order these for you. It shouldn't be long.'

Half an hour later I'm looking through a bound volume of a law report from 1975.

Bethany June D'Marco versus Cardiff Royal Infirmary and William O'Loughlin

My father was represented by a Queen's Counsel instructed by a solicitor, Kenneth Passage.

The claimant, Bethany D'Marco, is a four-year-old girl with complex mental and physical disabilities. As currently pleaded, the action is for damages arising from alleged breaches of duty to provide appropriate care during her delivery and in the immediate aftermath.

There are two distinct grounds for negligence. One is that the resident surgeon did not act quickly enough to perform a caesarean and protect Bethany. The second breach involves the management of her postnatal care.

Mrs Justice Fontaine outlined the facts of the case, which match what Ray D'Marco had told me. His mother was seven months pregnant when the bus she was a passenger in was struck side-on by a lorry that had run a red light. She suffered extensive chest injuries and internal bleeding.

Having been treated by paramedics at the scene, she was taken to Cardiff Royal Infirmary. A foetal heart test was performed in which no foetal movement or heartbeat was detected. The resident surgeon, William O'Loughlin, performed an emergency caesarean at 1.24 a.m.

The baby, a girl, failed to breathe spontaneously and did not respond to attempts at resuscitation. Believing they had lost the baby, the surgical team focused its attention on the mother, Louise D'Marco.

A disputed yet significant period of time elapsed before a nurse noticed the baby convulsing. Further attempts were made at resuscitation, involving the clearing of air passages and intubation.

I try to picture the chaotic scenes: the blood, the shouting; my father's desperate bid to save two lives. He delivered a baby he thought was stillborn. He saved the mother against the odds.

Judge Fontaine made her ruling:

I have reviewed the conflicting accounts of what happened in the operating theatre and tried to find common ground. What is not in dispute is that Bethany D'Marco endured a period of near-total acute hypoxic ischaemia while still in the womb or post-delivery. As a result, Bethany, now aged four, suffered significant brain damage that caused developmental retardation, cerebral palsy and epilepsy. She will require full-time care for the rest of her life.

It is not possible to conclude with any certainty that the paramedics or surgical team could have lessened or alleviated Bethany's condition had they acted earlier, or if different decisions had been made. It is, however, clear that the surgeon failed the hospital's own guidelines, particularly in failing to run the CTG for sufficient time, or to immediately intubate and ventilate Bethany D'Marco.

The plaintiff has argued that if this had been done within nine minutes of the birth, rather than seventeen, Bethany may not have suffered such devastating injuries. It is equally possible, as the defendants have countered, that Bethany suffered irrevocable damage before she reached the hospital.

On the evidence presented, I am unable to decide on the balance of probabilities what proportion of the plaintiff's injuries were caused by the accident, or the failure of medical staff to adequately resuscitate and ventilate Bethany post-delivery. On that basis, I rule in favour of the defendants in this matter.

The judgement makes no mention of an anonymous letter or photograph; or allegations of my father being affected by drugs. There is, however, a transcript of comments made by Justice Fontaine after she had ruled on the case.

Regrettably, evidence was presented during these proceedings that points to witness statements having been altered and pages removed from vital submissions. This was compounded by the disappearance of medical notes from the surgical unit. I strongly suspect this was a blatant attempt to pervert the course of justice.

It is not within my remit to investigate or punish such actions, but I will be writing to the Solicitor's Regulation Authority asking for a full inquiry into the role played by legal officers. You may have won this case, gentlemen, but you have no right to celebrate.

My shoes squeak on the marble tiles as I leave the library and follow a cobbled laneway to Fleet Street. Hailing a black cab, I climb inside and ask the driver for St Mary's Hospital in Paddington.

'Busy day?' he asks, trying to start a conversation.

'Not particularly,' I reply, trying to close it down.

Outside, shoals of pedestrians are ebbing and flowing across intersections like fish attracted to the changing lights. Enough already, I want to shout. Enough questions! Enough revelations! Ray D'Marco was right. The hospital orchestrated a cover-up. Someone tried to expose their corruption, but they won the case anyway, bankrupting a family, but saving my father's career.

I look again at the photograph from the party. The woman in my father's arms is wearing a nurse's uniform and looks barely out of her teens. Who would know her name?

34

The neurologist in charge of my father's case is so softly spoken that everyone leans forward, hanging on his every word. Dressed in pale chinos and an open-necked shirt, buttoned to his chin, Dr Lorimore fusses over my mother, making sure that she's comfortable. Patricia and Lucy sit on either side of her; while Rebecca shares a couch with me. Olivia is slightly removed, seated with her handbag on her lap. I haven't seen or spoken to her since the night she came to my flat during the storm.

My mother hasn't acknowledged her presence. They're like two palace guards, staring straight ahead from their sentry boxes, ready to defend my father from each other.

'It's good to see that William has so much support,' says Lorimore, in a tone somewhere between a newsreader's gravity and a sports broadcaster's zeal. 'I'm pleased to report that William's cranial bruising has settled down and we are no longer using drugs to keep him in a coma.'

'When will he wake up?' asks Lucy.

'That's difficult to say. This morning, I repeated the Glasgow Coma Scale test and William scored a five. I measured his eye movements and checked for temperature changes in the inner ear, as well as brain stem function. His responses were minimal. Although his pupils are reactive to light, the swelling and haematoma has produced incipient herniation, which indicates that there are more haemorrhages than previously thought.'

'But you can fix them?' asks Rebecca.

'Further surgery may cause greater problems.'

'So you're telling us to wait.'

Dr Lorimore grimaces slightly and focuses on a point above our heads as though he's rehearsed this speech and wants to remember it exactly. 'The latest scans indicate that the primary damage is in those areas of his brain that control speech and consciousness. Even when he does wake up, William is likely to have little awareness of his surroundings. His eyes will be open. He will have sleep cycles. He will respond to stimuli such as light or pain, but that doesn't mean he's conscious or aware of what's happening around him. The messages are reaching his central nervous system, but not his brain.'

'Are you saying the damage is permanent?' I ask.

'I'm afraid so.'

My mother makes a whimpering sound.

'How long could he live like that?' Lucy asks.

'Weeks. Months. Years.'

271

'With no improvement.'

'That's correct.'

My voice sounds hoarse. 'There must be some chance – one per cent? Two per cent?'

'One in ten thousand.'

A weight seems to crush my chest. Everybody in the room finds somewhere else to look, at the walls, or the floor, or out the window.

'We can keep William comfortable,' says the neurologist. 'But we can't make him better.'

'I want a second opinion,' Patricia says.

'By all means. Bring in whoever you wish,' replies Dr Lorimore, who seems to be ready for the reaction.

'What happens next?' I ask.

'Once the prognosis has been agreed and William has been stabilised, I recommend he be moved to a nursing home, or a palliative care ward.'

'He'd rather be dead,' says Olivia, looking at her hands.

The statement seems to charge the room.

'You shouldn't say that,' Lucy says.

Olivia doesn't back down. 'You know I'm right. William would hate the idea of living like . . . like a vegetable.'

My mother's whole body stiffens and her face creases in fury. 'Be quiet.'

'Pardon me?'

'I said be quiet.'

Olivia's neck turns a blotchy red colour. 'I have every right to express an opinion.'

'Don't you dare speak for my husband.'

'He's my husband too.'

Dr Lorimore looks from face to face, suddenly lost. He raises his hands. 'Please, please. There's no need to make any decision now.'

Lucy interrupts him. 'Who decides?'

'You do – the family – unless your father gave some sort of advanced direction. Did he make an advance care plan?'

'No,' says my mother.

'Yes,' counters Olivia. 'He wrote a living will.'

Olivia opens her handbag and produces a letter, which she hands to the neurologist.

'That's William's signature,' she says. 'He makes it clear that he doesn't want to be kept alive should he suffer permanent brain damage.'

My mother starts to protest. Lucy and Patricia join her. Dr Lorimore reads the letter and passes it to me.

I, William Joseph O'Loughlin, being of sound mind would like to make the following wishes known. I refuse ALL medical procedures or interventions aimed at prolonging or artificially sustaining my life if in the opinion of two appropriately qualified doctors the following occur:

1. I have an imminently life-threatening physical illness or condition from which there is little or no prospect of recovery.

2. I suffer serious impairment of the mind or brain with little or no prospect of recovery together with a physical need for life-sustaining treatment.

3. I have been diagnosed as being in a persistent vegetative state or minimally conscious state and have been

so for at least twelve weeks with no prospect of recovery.

I know that at any time I can change my mind about these conditions by tearing up this form and writing a new one.

The signature was witnessed by David Passage and signed seven months ago.

I hand the letter to my mother. Lucy helps her find her reading glasses. I watch as the blood drains from her face.

Dr Lorimore continues: 'William nominated twelve weeks, so there's still plenty of time for you to consider his wishes. In the interim, we can keep him comfortable, pain-free and monitor his progress. If anything changes, I'll let you know.'

We all stand and make our way outside. Olivia leaves quickly, avoiding any interaction. She's still waiting for the lifts when we emerge from the office. All of us shuffle inside, descending in uncomfortable silence.

Somewhere between floors, my mother speaks: 'If you love him, you won't do this.'

I barely recognise her voice. Olivia doesn't respond.

Mum tries again. 'You might love his money, but not the man.'

'Be quiet, Mum,' I say.

She ignores me, fixing her gaze on Olivia. 'Give him back to us if you don't care. Walk away. Let us decide.'

Olivia has closed her eyes, as though wishing it might block out the words.

'You want him dead,' Mum says.

'That's enough,' I say, grabbing her arm. She knocks it away.

'She wants him dead,' she repeats.

'He's already dead,' whispers Olivia.

'Both of you, please be quiet,' I plead. My mobile is vibrating. I cancel the call without looking.

'I'm thinking of William,' says Olivia.

'You're thinking of yourself,' replies my mother.

Olivia looks at her sadly. 'There is no dignity in living when he has no ability to love or laugh or feel joy. He's an empty shell. I wouldn't wish that upon my worst enemy, let alone my family.'

'We're his family – not you!'

Olivia glances at me, hoping for support. I don't react. The lift doors open and she walks quickly across the foyer towards the entrance. My mother shouts after her. 'I'm his wife and I'm not giving up. William will come back to me.'

Olivia stops. Turns. Something ice-cold fills her eyes.

'He left you twenty years ago – there's no coming back from that.'

Leaving my mother with Lucy, I chase Olivia, hoping to catch up and to apologise. She's hailing a cab, closing the door. I knock on the glass. Her eyes meet mine. Disappointed. Angry.

'Don't go,' I say. 'Talk to me.'

She says something to the driver who pulls away.

Cursing under my breath, I feel my mobile vibrating again. I look at the screen. Answer.

'It's me,' says Kate.

'Oh!' I reply, sounding distracted.

'Did you hang up on me earlier?'

'I was busy.'

'Are you still busy?'

'No.'

'I want to apologise for the other night.'

'No, it was my fault. I shouldn't have talked about the case.'

She pauses, trying to find the words. 'Can we meet somewhere . . . for coffee?'

'When?'

'I start work at four.'

'We could do it now.'

Kate chooses a tea house near Ravenscourt Park where we sit at a table outside, overlooking a muddy expanse of grass where grey squirrels are foraging among the fallen leaves. Toddlers and dogs periodically give chase.

Kate's hair is different again – pulled back and pinned high off her neck. Her lips are pink, not red, and she's wearing a baggy sweater, jeans and a suede jacket.

'Is this too cold?'

'No, I'm fine.'

'How is your head?'

'Better.'

She toys with the handle of her teacup.

'You asked me about Micah Beauchamp. I searched the database. He's twenty-three, with a history of drug use and priors for burglary, carjacking and malicious wounding. He grew up in North London, raised by his older sister. I don't know about his mum. There's a note on his file referring to a juvenile sentence. When he was thirteen, he set fire to a neighbour's house – a guy called Marcus Swinburne, a convicted paedophile. Turns out he'd been abusing Micah since he turned six.'

'What happened to Swinburne?'

'Third-degree burns. Lost fingers on both hands. Micah spent three months in juvie and went back to his sister's. Trouble followed him after that.'

'Ewan met Micah in a psych hospital,' I say.

'Court-sanctioned. Micah was diagnosed with a border-line personality disorder, but not everybody agreed. The police thought he was using the mental health system to stay out of prison.' She pauses, picking flecks of polish from her fingernails. 'I talked to Micah's sister. She hasn't seen him for three weeks.'

'He's been living with Ewan.'

'How do you know?'

'Ruiz talked to the neighbours.'

Kate frowns. 'Don't let Macdermid catch you investigating this on your own. He's not your biggest fan.' I try to shrug it off, but she looks at me sternly. 'I'm not joking, Joe. Be careful of Macdermid.'

'Why?'

'He cuts corners.'

'What does that mean?'

'Just be careful.'

Kate's not going to elaborate. She has turned her gaze into the park where small children are feeding ducks at the pond.

'There's something else – Micah's fingerprints were found at the house in Chiswick.'

'What about the bloodstained clothing?'

'The DNA results are due back on Friday.'

'Why are you doing this?'

Kate pauses, biting her bottom lip. 'I had a brother. He committed suicide when I was sixteen. It changed my mum . . . me.'

'I'm sorry.'

'Let's make a deal. I won't feel sorry for you about losing your wife, if you don't feel sorry for me.'

'Deal.'

35

My mother continues her vigil in the ICU. I wonder how long it's been since she had a proper night's sleep, or ate a decent meal. Her figure has diminished with age and the skin on her face sags and buckles. I suggest a walk. The fresh air. She doesn't want to leave Dad alone.

I take a seat beside her and we watch his chest rise and fall beneath a white sheet that glows pink under the light from the machines. His cheeks are hollow and his lips bloodless yet he looks surprisingly serene.

'I have something to ask you,' I say, unsure of how to continue. 'Do you remember Dad being sued for medical negligence?'

'Which time?'

'It happened more than once?'

279

'He was a surgeon for nearly fifty years, even the best make mistakes.' She makes it sound so matter-of-fact.

'Was Bethany D'Marco a mistake?'

Mum frowns. 'I don't think I remember.'

'A newborn left profoundly disabled after an emergency caesarean.'

A memory registers on her face. 'In Cardiff. A bus and lorry accident. The mother was pregnant. William saved her life.'

'The family sued the hospital for medical negligence.'

'They lost.'

'Did Dad ever talk about the case?'

'No more than any other.'

'Are you sure?'

'A surgeon can't afford to fixate on the patients he couldn't save. He is paid to make life-and-death decisions, not to doubt his abilities.'

I can hear my father's voice in the speech and wonder how often she's heard him deliver the same words.

'You accept that he made mistakes?'

'Of course.'

'What about in this case?'

'He was cleared of any wrongdoing.'

'Would it surprise you to learn that he's been sending money to Bethany D'Marco?'

'He's a generous man.'

'Forty thousand pounds, on her birthday since 1975.'

Mum straightens in her chair.

'That family should be grateful. William saved the mother's life. She had other children.'

'How do you know that?'

My mother looks at me blankly. 'What?'

'How do you know she had another child?'

Flustered, she waves her hands dismissively. I take the photograph from my jacket pocket and put it on the bed in front of her. She looks at the image and just as quickly looks away, staring at the far wall.

'Have you seen this before?'

Mum doesn't answer.

'The man on the sofa, you know who it is.'

'No.'

'Look at his wristwatch.'

Her mouth tightens. 'Leave this alone, Joseph. William is a good man. He deserves respect.'

'You've seen this photograph before, haven't you?'

Her shoulders are stunted wings, rising and falling beneath her blouse.

'When?'

'Someone sent it to me years ago.'

'Why?'

She shrugs again. 'They were trying to cause trouble.'

'What's the nurse's name?'

'It doesn't matter.'

'It does to me. Who is she?'

'A figment of his imagination . . . a fantasy.'

'Did she work with him? Is that where they met? Where were you?'

Mum's mood changes from one of mild annoyance to anger. 'She played with fire and she got burned. It happens to girls with loose morals.'

'Now you're being pompous.'

'It's true. She was a trainee nurse who enjoyed seducing married men.'

'Why?'

'Because she could – and the men were weak.'

'What happened to her?'

'She tricked someone into marrying her and moved away.'

'Did Dad stay in touch with her?'

Mum hesitates and shakes her head.

'Could the nurse have sent this photograph?'

'No!'

'Maybe she wanted to blackmail him.'

'Rosie doesn't need money.'

'You called her Rosie.'

'No! Please, Joseph, leave this alone.'

I know that name. I look at the photograph again. The nurse's legs are crossed and her uniform has ridden up. Two buttons are undone on her blouse.

'Is that Rosie Passage?' I ask.

My mother doesn't react.

I say the name again, stunned by the revelation. Kenneth's wife. David's mother. Images come back to me of those holidays in Cornwall, the surfing and sailing and beach cricket. Often I shared a room with David and Francis. Rosie would come to kiss her boys goodnight.

'I suppose you're too old for a kiss,' she'd say, sitting on the edge of my bed.

'Yes, I am,' I'd reply defiantly, when the opposite was true. I wanted a kiss more than anything in the world.

A decade later, watching *The Graduate*, I pictured Rosie

as my Mrs Robinson and I wore out the spindle hole on the album as it became the soundtrack to my adolescence.

'Did Kenneth know?' I ask, ignoring my mother's discomfort.

'Water under the bridge.'

'And you're certain?'

'Yes, I'm certain,' she says tersely, hating the subject.

'You were friends with them. They came on holidays with us. Why?'

'It's called forgiveness, Joseph. You should try it some time.' She glances at my father. 'You expect too much of him.'

'He expected too much of me.'

'Then you're both to blame.'

36

The sink is ringed with purple dye where Emma has vandalised her hair. Charlie is standing in the doorway. 'I'm really sorry. I thought she was having a shower.'

'How bad is it?'

'It's only a streak.'

'Purple?'

'Uh-huh.'

'Where did she get the dye?'

'It belonged to Andie.'

Emma is sleeping now. Rather than wake her, I creep into her room and take stock of the damage. Her lovely light brown hair has a two-inch wide purple stripe running from back to front, above her left ear. It's not even straight.

'Maybe we can dye it a different colour tomorrow,' whispers Charlie.

'We'll go and see a hairdresser.'

'I'm sorry.'

'Don't keep saying that.'

Charlie helps me clean up the bathroom, disposing of the evidence. I don't think the towel that Emma used can be saved. Afterwards, I take a long bath, soaking away the aches and pains.

Before I go to bed, I check on Emma again. She's sleeping on her side, with one hand closed into a fist beneath her chin, surrounded by a menagerie of stuffed toys that I've been waiting for her to out-grow. Next to her head is a small tattered blue blanket, which she has treasured since she was a baby. Almost intuitively children choose a particular toy, or piece of fabric, which they infuse with special meaning, or a unique essence or life force, something that will comfort or protect them. Emma hasn't *needed* her 'blankie' since she was about seven, but it has never been relegated to a box, or a cupboard. Every night it is folded beside her head where she can reach out and touch the fabric, or hold it against her nose, as though reminding herself that she still exists.

I'm about to leave when I notice a book peeking out from beneath her pillow. Gently pulling it free, I recognise the notebook that Emma was scribbling in when I met her school headmistress. It's some sort of diary or journal, full of notes and drawings. Holding it up to the night light, I see an image I recognise – a scarecrow with a patchwork hessian head and black holes for eyes and a grinning mouth. Emma has drawn the arms like skeletal bones draped over the horizontal spar of a crucifix, the claw-like fingers growing towards the ground.

I know who it is: the Raggedy Man, a creature of Emma's nightmares. Ever since she was little, she's been terrified of scarecrows in the same way that other people are frightened by clowns, or bridges, or of falling asleep. There's even a name for it: *Formidophobia – a fear of scarecrows*. When we lived in Wellow, Emma would want me to check the fields before we went on Sunday walks, or to fly her kite, or fishing in the river. I thought she'd forgotten the Raggedy Man, particularly now that we're in London, but the notebook is full of drawings. Sometimes she has pressed so hard on the page to create the eyes that the paper has torn and left ragged holes. One image shows the scarecrow sitting in a chair holding a knife. My heart flips over. How did I miss this? I've been so busy worrying about my dad that I've failed to recognise trauma in my own child.

Emma had her first period a few months ago and I had to rely on Charlie to explain to her what she should do. That's a mother's job. Now it's *my* job. I should have been ready, but I was so wrapped up in my own grief that I've neglected Emma, leaving her to fend for herself.

Charlie has coped with losing her mother, but Emma is still fighting against the tide. She didn't want to move to London, or for Charlie to go to university. She wanted us to stay in Wellow, living in the cottage, pretending that nothing had changed, despite everything changing. She's sleepwalking, hiding letters from me, having nightmares and drawing pictures of the Raggedy Man. She's struggling to make friends and growing more isolated.

Victoria Naparstek once called me a 'pathological mourner' who can't discuss my loss. I argued with her.

Overcoming grief isn't about reliving the events, putting them all in place, before packing them away in the attic like summer clothes. I rail against this. Why should I pack them away? I know I've lost Julianne, but I refuse to forget her. Nobody can tell me that their grief is the same as mine, because no loss is ever the same. Unless they were standing in the same pub in Trafalgar Square when I met Julianne, or were there when I kissed her for the first time, or put a ring on her finger, or held her hand through two births, or unless they were a party to the countless special moments between us. I don't need to review the circumstances of Julianne's death. *I was there.* I don't have to 'process the news'. *I was there.* I don't have to 'come to terms with it'. *I was there.*

I can't force Emma to confront her grief, or to share emotions she's not ready to explore. Nor can I make assumptions or jump to conclusions. She will decide when she's ready to talk and I have to be there when that happens, willing and able, totally on board.

Lying awake, staring at the ceiling, I feel myself growing irrationally angry, wanting to lash out or to scream at the top of my lungs into the deepest of wells. Nobody is to blame: not me, or Emma, or Julianne, or Ewan, or my father, or God, or fate, or the Raggedy Man. Life isn't fair or unfair. It is what it is.

Day Eleven

37

Kenneth and Rosie Passage live in Berkshire less than a mile from Windsor Castle as the crow flies. The turrets and spires of the royal palace appear and disappear between the trees as I near the village.

Turning off the narrow lane, I pull through pillared gates with a brass plaque announcing Aslan House (the great lion from the *Chronicles of Narnia*). The drive curves along an avenue of oak trees, past a summer house, pond and a croquet lawn. Parking beside an old stable block converted into a garage, I climb the main steps and press my thumb against a doorbell the size of a small dinner plate. A shape moves behind the frosted glass. Rosie answers.

Now in her sixties, she's still striking, with white-grey hair, high cheekbones and a fine figure. Dressed in a tweed

288

skirt and silk blouse, with the barest hint of make-up, she looks ready for a photo shoot for *Country Life*.

'Can I help you?' she asks, before emitting a squeak. 'Joseph!' She hugs me and thrusts me away, holding me at arm's length. 'Look at you! What a surprise!'

'Hello, Mrs Passage.'

'Christ! Call me Rosie.' She hugs me again. 'Poor William. How is he?'

'Unchanged.'

'I've been praying for him.'

'I didn't know you were religious.'

She laughs. 'I'm getting old and hedging my bets.'

'You'll never be old.'

She laughs again and hooks her arm through mine, as though I'm escorting her into a ballroom.

'Let me take your coat. How are you? And the girls? Are they coping? I haven't seen you since the funeral, and we didn't talk then.'

'They're fine. We all are,' I say, only half lying.

'That's the way with children, isn't it? They muddle through. We're a nation of muddlers, shopkeepers and tea-drinkers.'

Rosie takes me across the entrance hall to a sitting room with a large bay window and Chesterfield sofas. There are photographs on the mantelpiece of David and Francis. A glass box contains a folded British flag. Another displays his military medals. Rosie touches them as though paying her respects.

'You remember Francis, don't you?'

'Of course.'

'When we lost him, I didn't think I could go on, but we find ways,' she says, running her fingers along the glass. 'I still miss him. They say you should love all of your children equally and they're each special in different ways, but Francis was my baby.'

She brushes tears from her eyes, acting annoyed with herself. 'This room is positively freezing. Let's go to the kitchen. Have you come to see Kenneth? He's having a physio session, but shouldn't be long.'

I follow her to a spacious kitchen, warmed by an electric Aga stove, with pots and pans hanging from a rack above the island bench. Through the window, I see a quad bike being ridden across the frosty field. Two large black and tan dogs with cropped ears and docked tails lope after the bike. Dobermann pinschers.

'That's Eugene,' explains Rosie. 'He's digging a pond because Kenneth wants a trout-fishing lake.'

'Is that possible?'

'Who knows,' laughs Rosie. 'They're like big kids with too much time on their hands.'

I watch as Eugene parks the quad bike beside a mechanical digger. He wrestles with the dogs, making them bark and jump, before he climbs into the digger and starts the engine. His thick forearms vibrate on the controls.

There are shouts from a sunroom, which is visible through double doors. Kenneth is on a massage table. His legs are being straightened and stretched by a woman in a blue uniform.

'He's such a baby,' says Rosie, ignoring his cries. 'She's the third physiotherapist in a month.'

'Is he getting better?'

'Incrementally,' she says, filling a kettle.

The weather is discussed. Biscuits are put on a plate. The tea cosy is a knitted turtle.

'Do you remember our holidays together?' Rosie asks.

'Of course.'

'You were very good with David and Francis, looking after them.'

'My sisters did most of that. Why did you stop coming to Cornwall?'

'The boys grew up and we discovered Tuscany.'

'Is that the only reason?'

'I think so.'

I take the photograph from my jacket pocket and put it on the table. Rosie gives it a cursory glance and goes back to pouring the tea.

'That's you,' I say.

'Yes.'

'You're kissing my father.'

'No, *he's* kissing me.'

She gives the photograph a proper look, gazing at it wistfully. 'William was so handsome.'

'And married.'

'It was a long time ago – before I married Kenneth. I was eighteen. Young. Foolish.' She waves her hand in the air dismissively.

'A few hours after that picture was taken my father operated on a pregnant woman and her baby suffered terrible injuries.'

'He saved that mother's life.'

'You remember.'

'Yes.'

'Was he drug-affected?'

'No.'

'I've seen a letter written by someone who was there – either at the party or in the emergency room. Was it you?'

She looks surprised. 'Why would I want to hurt William?'

'But you've seen this photograph before?'

Rosie nods. 'There are things you don't know.'

'Explain them to me.'

Rosie's hand slips and she spills tea into a saucer. She mops it up with a paper towel. The silence of the kitchen seems to amplify every sound.

'I did my nurse's training in Cardiff. That's where I met William. He was a young hotshot surgeon, working ridiculous hours, scrubbing in to whatever surgeries he could for the experience.

'William had done back-to-back shifts, but I convinced him to come to a party at a house I shared with other nurses. At ten o'clock that night a lorry ran a red light and hit a city bus. People were dead. Dying. We were called back to the hospital. I was still a trainee, but I went to help.'

'Were you high?'

'Forget the drugs,' she snaps. 'They're not important.'

'How long had you been sleeping with him?'

'Who told you we were lovers?'

'It seems pretty obvious.'

'That's only a kiss. I married Kenneth.'

As if summoned by the mention of his name, the old

lawyer appears in the kitchen, limping on a polished wooden walking stick. He's wearing a tracksuit that rides up to reveal his skinny white ankles that look like chicken bones picked clean and sticking from a pair of tartan slippers.

'Did you hire that sadist?' he says to Rosie, not noticing me at first. 'I swear she wants to kill me. Maybe that's your plan. Get rid of me and marry someone younger.'

'There's an idea,' laughs Rose, rolling her eyes for my benefit.

'It bloody hurts.'

'And I had two children. Don't start telling me about pain.'

Kenneth opens the door of the fridge and pours himself a glass of water. Drinks. His wrists are spotted and threaded with veins. He wipes his mouth and notices me.

'Joseph!' He looks at Rosie. 'Why didn't you say he was here?'

'He just arrived.'

'You're looking much better, sir.'

'Rubbish! I'm falling apart.' He swaps the walking stick to his left hand and we shake. 'I didn't know you were coming?' He looks at Rosie. She shakes her head.

'I would have called ahead, but I don't have your home number.'

'That sounds ominous,' he chuckles. 'Have you had some tea?'

'Yes.'

'Good. Right. Perhaps we should talk in the library. Rosie, can you bring us some ice.'

'You're not allowed any Scotch.'

Kenneth sighs. 'I might not live longer, but it's going to feel that way.'

I'm taken into a book-lined room with a large window overlooking the garden. A fat white cat is sleeping on the windowsill. It yawns and stretches and settles again.

Kenneth stands at the window and waves to Eugene, who is clearing mud from the wheels of the digger. The dogs are chasing rabbits in the distance.

'He's a good lad. Served in the army with Francis. I gave him a job when he came out. Least I could do. Now he's part of the family.'

I take a seat in an armchair that smells of leather polish.

'How is William?' he asks.

'No better.'

Kenneth unlocks a filing cabinet and sets out two glasses and pulls out a bottle of Scotch, cracking the lid. He looks past me. 'Don't tell Rosie.'

'None for me,' I say.

Having poured himself a drink, he tucks the glass between his thighs.

'What brings you here, Joseph?'

'Nine million pounds was stolen from the O'Loughlin Foundation.'

Kenneth reaches for an oversize fountain pen and twirls it across his knuckles.

'You knew,' I say.

'Yes.'

'How?'

'William called me. He wanted legal advice. I told him to stop the audit. Bury the details.'

'You're talking about a cover-up.'

'Oh, don't be so obtuse, Joseph.'

Nobody has ever called me obtuse.

Kenneth takes a sip of Scotch and hides the glass again. 'I simply suggested that William delay the process. The foundation has adequate funds. Nobody need know. Let it come out years from now.'

'When he's dead?'

'Why not?'

'Did he tell you who took the money?'

Kenneth's tone changes, growing softer and kinder.

'He made certain admissions.'

'Are you saying he confessed?'

'I don't know what to tell you, Joseph. William had two families to support. He made some bad investments. The global financial meltdown took its toll. I rebuked him for not telling me earlier – when I could have done something.' He pauses and lets the information sink in. 'If it makes it any easier, Joseph, your father was determined to repay the money.'

'How?'

'He had a plan, although he wouldn't tell me the details. He didn't want me involved.'

'Have you told the police any of this?'

'It's privileged information.'

'You're impeding an investigation.'

'William is my client. I am his lawyer.'

Kenneth unfurls his hands outward and after several moments drops them again, as though they're too heavy to hold.

Glancing around his library of legal texts and popular fiction, I notice an assortment of family photographs, mainly children and grandchildren. I recognise Francis and David as boys. One image shows Kenneth waist-deep amid the waves, sunlight glistening on his body as he throws a young boy in the air. On a higher shelf is a wedding photograph. Rosie looks young enough to be the flower-girl. She's wearing a white mini-dress and a wide-brimmed hat. Very sixties. Bohemian. Looking closer, I notice the tell-tale swell of a pregnancy. Second trimester. Starting to show.

My sisters were the bridesmaids. My father is the best man. The camera has caught Rosie, looking past Kenneth, her eyes on William, smiling widely.

'What do you know about Bethany D'Marco?' I ask.

Kenneth's head jerks up and he shows me an entirely different face. His gaze drifts to the bookcases and he seems unsure for a moment, as though looking for a title.

'Your father sends a cheque to her every year.'

'Was he negligent?'

'He was cleared of any blame.'

'I've read the judgement. His lawyers were accused of removing and doctoring crucial evidence. Was that you?'

Puckering his lips, Kenneth's mouth disappears into wrinkles. 'That's ancient history.'

'You broke the law.'

'I saved William's career.'

'You risked prison for him.'

'Because he's my friend. Because he would have done the same for me. It's what I do, Joseph. I watch his back and he watches mine.'

Kenneth's voice is as strident as my own. There's a knock on the door. Rosie appears. Kenneth checks that his glass is hidden.

'Don't forget you have a doctor's appointment at two,' she says.

'Yes, yes,' he replies, sighing, his anger having evaporated. Rosie looks at me apologetically and leaves the door open.

'You should have talked to me after Julianne died,' Kenneth says. 'I would have sued the hospital for you.'

'You're retired.'

'David would have taken the brief.'

'It was an accident.'

'No. An accident is when somebody spills red wine, or stubs a toe, not when they take a life.'

'It wouldn't have brought Julianne back.'

'True, but you'd have felt better.'

He's wrong, but I know his heart is in the right place.

Kenneth reaches for his walking stick and rises slowly, our conversation over. Rosie walks me to my car, slipping her arm through mine as we cross the gravel turning circle.

The dogs spy Rosie and come bounding across the field, racing each other with ears pinned back and paws blurring with speed. Skidding to a halt, they leap around her. Rosie laughs and tells them to quieten down. The dogs sniff at my shoes and trouser cuffs.

'Eugene wants to breed them. Not these two. They're brother and sister,' says Rosie, rubbing behind their ears.

From across the field comes a high-pitched whistle. The dogs stop and turn, frozen like statues, watching Eugene. A second whistle and they take off, tearing across the field towards the mechanical digger.

'Thank you for not saying anything about the photograph to Kenneth,' says Rosie.

'How long did it last – the affair with my father?'

'It was hardly an affair – more a schoolgirl crush.'

'Did Kenneth know?'

'Of course, but I don't want to remind him.' She gives me a melancholy smile. 'I've been happy with Kenneth. He's a good husband and father. We've experienced tragedy, but life is like that. Without darkness, you can't appreciate the light.'

She kisses my cheek and I catch a whiff of her perfume. In a heartbeat, I'm transported back to Cornwall, to a windy August afternoon when dozens of kites floated over the beach. I remember running back to the cottage to get mine, crawling beneath my parents' bed, reaching for the big suitcase. In that instant, the door opened and I heard my father's voice, hushing and whispering, stumbling in an awkward dance with an unseen partner.

They giggled, they kissed, they pressed their bodies together. I lay beneath the bed and discarded clothes fell on either side of me: a bra, knickers, a torn foil wrapper . . . My father's trousers were around his ankles. The mattress sagged. I turn my face to one side to avoid the plunging bedsprings. She uttered God's name, but it wasn't my mother's voice. I know that now. Perhaps I knew it then.

38

Emma emerges from the school with her bag looped over both shoulders and her straw hat angled low over her eyes. Other children swarm into groups, laughing and jostling and saying goodbye to each other. Emma shuffles past them, speaking to nobody. 'Youth doesn't need friends – it only needs crowds,' Zelda Fitzgerald said. Emma has neither.

I take her schoolbag from her and she falls into step beside me, lengthening her strides to match mine.

'Let's go out for dinner,' I say. 'Just you and me.'

'What about Charlie?'

'She's at the hospital, visiting Granddad.'

'Where will we go?'

'You choose.'

'Anywhere I want?'

'As long as it doesn't bankrupt me.'

When we get home, Emma does her schoolwork and then gets ready, putting on a denim skirt, leggings and ankle boots, turning twelve into sixteen. She does a twirl for me. Is that make-up? Although not as beautiful as Charlie – not yet – Emma has an interesting face that photographers often comment upon because her eyes are so expressive and her lips are bowed and turned down at the edges.

'It's my resting bitch face,' she once told me. 'I look like I'm either disappointed or sad.'

'You don't.'

'Trust me, Dad. I know.'

She chooses the restaurant – an American-style burger bar called Shake Shack in Leicester Square, which is crowded with teenagers and tourists. We order cheeseburgers, milkshakes and crinkle-cut fries. The purple streak in her hair glows under the neon lights. Three boys are sitting at a nearby table. They glance at Emma, nudging each other. 'She's twelve,' I want to say, but they're not much older. When I was their age I had acne, braces and terrible clothes, but these boys have clear skin, invisible braces and product in their hair.

Emma notices. Smiles. Why is she encouraging them?

Instinctively, I want to protect her from the very things she desires or soon will. Adventure. Admiration. Love. Excitement. Within a few years, the boys at the other table will have *everything* in common with Emma and I'll have precious little.

'Will you see someone for me?' I ask, wanting to distract

her. 'A nice lady called Victoria. She's a friend of mine – a therapist.'

'You've asked me that already.'

'I know, but I think it's important.'

'I don't need to talk about Mummy.'

'You never mention her.'

'Does that matter? She's dead. People keep telling me that I can keep Mummy alive in my memory, but that's not true. She's not a ghost. She's not in Heaven. When you're dead, you're dead.'

When did my daughter become so cynical?

'Are you angry with her?'

'Yes.'

'Why?'

'She's gone. We're here.'

'She didn't have a choice.'

'I'm angry at you too.'

'Me?'

'You pretend nothing has happened. You go off to work. I go off to school. Charlie goes off to university. We accept things.'

'What else can we do?'

Emma sighs helplessly. 'It should hurt more.'

Could it hurt any more than this?

'I understand how you feel,' I say. 'I miss her too. I miss being able to ask her things.'

'Like what?'

'I'd ask her about you.'

'You mean girl stuff? Charlie can handle that.'

'Other things. She was very wise, your mother. She had

301

a way of looking at the worst of people and seeing good things in them.'

Emma is toying with her straw, stirring lumps of ice cream at the bottom of her milkshake.

'You can't be a mum and a dad.'

'Why not?'

'It's too much work.'

'I can try. If Mum were here now, is there anything you'd want to ask her?'

Emma frowns in concentration. 'I'd ask her if she minds that I haven't visited her grave, or that I can't stand looking at photographs of her.'

'She doesn't mind.'

'Are you sure? I mean, we're hanging out here, eating burgers, drinking milkshakes, as though nothing has happened.'

'We're talking about her. She'd like that.'

'I want to know if she gets cold.'

'What do you mean?'

'Lying in the ground like that. I know you're not supposed to feel anything when you're dead, but I keep seeing her in there, wearing her dress – the one we gave them. It wasn't very warm.'

She's talking about the frock that Julianne was buried in. The lump in my throat makes it hard for me to answer.

'Why did it happen to her?' asks Emma.

'She was unlucky.'

'Did someone else get her good luck?'

'I don't think luck works that way. Anything else you'd like to ask her?'

Emma shakes her head, before her face brightens.

'You should ask her how she makes her roast potatoes so crunchy. No offence, Daddy, but yours are rubbish.'

39

Kate has trapped my bottom lip between her teeth and is running her tongue over my teeth. I've not kissed that way before. It's strange. Sexy. Car horns are sounding. People whoop and clap. A driver yells, 'Get a room!' Kate blushes but kisses me again. Now her tongue is deep in my mouth.

My mobile is ringing. Ignoring it, I put my arms around her waist, pulling her close, and taste my pillow. Flustered and a little ashamed, I look at the clock. Red digits glow: 03.10.

My phone rings again.

'Joseph, is that you?'

'Olivia?'

'I'm sorry, I didn't know who else . . . it couldn't wait . . . I need . . . will you . . .' She's speaking in a rush.

'Are you at the hospital?'

'Yes, but it's not William.' She takes a breath, composing

herself. 'I've found Ewan. He left a note under the wiper blades of my car. It looked like a flyer. I almost threw it away. It's an address in Brixton.'

'Call the police.'

'No!'

'He has a warrant out for his arrest.'

'We can take him to the police. It'll be safer that way. He won't panic, or hurt himself.' She's speaking too quickly again.

'Ewan isn't the problem. Where's Micah Beauchamp?'

'He's gone.'

'How do you know?'

'That's why Ewan left me the note. He's on his own. He's scared. You understand schizophrenia. You can help him.'

I want to argue with her, but Olivia won't budge and she isn't going to tell me the address until I agree to help. I hang up and begin getting dressed, struggling with buttons and laces, everyday rituals that have become more difficult with each year.

I knock on Charlie's door. She rubs her eyes. 'What's wrong?'

'I have to go out.'

'Now?'

'I won't be long.' I kiss her forehead. 'If I'm not home in two hours, I want you to call Vincent and give him this address.'

'I don't like this.' Charlie reads the slip of paper. 'Let me come.'

'I'll be fine. I need you here to look after Emma.'

★ ★ ★

305

The streets are shiny with rain and almost empty of traffic. At each red light, I question what I'm doing. I should call Kate, give her the address. At the same time, I know what a terrible record the police have in dealing with the mentally ill. Two of my patients have been victims. David Gibbs, battling depression, was shot five times by police in the hallway of his home. Gary Wright, a paranoid schizophrenic, was arrested for shouting obscenities in a park, and put in a chokehold by police before he collapsed and died. Pointless. Unnecessary.

Ewan is known to be armed, which means the police won't take chances. They'll come in force, wearing body armour, with weapons drawn. What then?

It takes me twenty minutes to reach Brixton and to find the street. Slowly passing the address I see a factory or workshop that looks derelict or abandoned, surrounded by a chain-link fence. A faded sign advertises a smash repair shop, but the contact number has been painted over. The rusting roller door is scrawled with graffiti and the boarded-up windows look like black holes.

Olivia's car is parked opposite. The bonnet is still warm. I call her mobile, but get her voicemail.

'Where are you?' I ask. 'I'm outside.'

Five minutes pass with no reply. Crossing the road, I rattle the padlocked gate and follow the fence until I discover a metal post where the wire has been cut away and pulled back to form an opening. I crawl through and cross the pitted asphalt forecourt, which is clumped with weeds and glittering with broken glass.

The roller door is locked at either end. I check the windows and follow a passage down one side of the factory, using my phone as a torch. I come to an open door. The darkness inside smells of sewer gas and something feral. Swinging the torch from side to side, it falls upon piles of broken plasterboard, twisted cables and empty drums. Rusting machinery throws shadows against the walls that move as I move. Steel walkways form a grid across the ceiling above my head and beyond I see gaping holes in the roof. Edging further inside, I step over swollen bags of rubbish and food scraps, some broken and scattered. Ahead, I hear a sound and turn off my torch. Faint lights glow from an opening at the rear of the building.

Warily, I edge closer, looking around the edge of a door. Olivia Blackmore is sitting on the floor with her back against a wall and her knees to her chest. Her hands are hidden. Ewan is pacing back and forth in front of a kerosene lantern, muttering to himself, hitting his forehead.

I step through the doorway. Olivia notices me first. Her eyes go wide and she shakes her head, wanting to me to leave. Ewan spins around. He has a knife.

He looks at his mother.

'You told! You told!' he cries accusingly.

'No,' she says.

'You promised!'

'Hello, Ewan,' I say, trying to distract him. 'How have you been?'

He doesn't answer. Olivia's hands are holding her stomach. She's bleeding.

'What happened?' I ask.

'It was an accident,' she says. 'He thought I was someone else.'

I show Ewan my phone. 'I'm going to call an ambulance.'

'No!'

'She needs a doctor.'

'The police will come.'

'No. Just an ambulance.'

'Liar!'

He hits his forehead with his fist. The handle of the knife leaves a mark. He's still pacing.

'Let me look at her,' I say.

He doesn't react. I move closer and crouch beside Olivia. She lifts her hands, which are slick with blood. Shining. Her blouse and the top of her jeans are soaked. My medical training, brief as it was, comes into play.

'I need a bandage.'

Ewan ignores me.

I shout, 'Listen to me! Find me a shirt, or towel.'

The order registers in his mind and he kicks aside a sleeping bag and picks up a filthy shirt.

'Tear it into strips. The sleeves first.'

He uses the knife and slices through the fabric. I collect the pieces, balling the cotton in my fist and pressing it hard into Olivia's abdomen. She groans in pain.

'Hold it there,' I say. 'Apply pressure.'

Ewan has gone back to muttering. His eyes look haunted. Hollow.

'Your mother needs a doctor.'

'No doctors.'

'She could die.'

'No. I am the final prophet; the one who comes before.'

'She doesn't need a prophet.'

'They say the devil knows his own name.'

308

'What name is that?'

He glares at me accusingly. 'That's a stupid question! Everybody knows his name. I won't answer stupid questions.'

'The devil has many names,' I say. 'Satan. Beelzebub. Lucifer. Spoiler. Tempter.'

'He knows his name,' says Ewan. 'He doesn't care what you say.'

I notice two mattresses. Two sleeping bags. Micah Beauchamp has been here.

'It takes only one sperm to make a baby,' says Ewan, as though he's preaching a sermon. 'Two contact points. When they fuse it's like nuclear fusion, but it's human fusion. One sperm. One egg. Boom! One explosion forms the mind. Another forms the soul. A chain reaction . . .' He's pacing as he talks, waving the knife.

Olivia has gone quiet. I feel her pulse. Her eyes open.

'I want you to stay awake. Can you do that?'

She nods.

Ewan is still talking gibberish.

'Let me call an ambulance,' I say, trying to break into his thought loop.

'No.'

'I'll take her out of here. We won't tell anyone where you are.'

'She lied to me. She promised.'

Ewan is rocking from side to side, unable to decide. Suddenly, his eyes go wide and he steps back. I turn and see Micah in the doorway. Dressed in a hooded coat, he looks more spectral than human with skin like a latex glove stretched over his skull.

Ewan shrinks away. 'I'm sorry. I'm sorry.'

'What have you done?' Micah asks, stepping into the light. 'I leave you for a few days and you go running back to Mummy.'

'I thought you'd gone. I thought . . . I didn't think . . .' Ewan is blubbering. Shaking.

Micah motions him closer. Ewan approaches. Micah runs his fingers through Ewan's hair, cupping his neck, pulling their heads together. Their foreheads touch.

'It's OK. I'm here now.'

Micah straightens and pushes back the hood of his overcoat, revealing his shorn bleached-white hair and pockmarked cheeks. He points to Olivia. 'Is she alive?'

'It was an accident,' Ewan tries to explain. 'I thought it was them.'

'She needs an ambulance,' I say.

'Nobody leaves,' Micah says.

He tears the filter tip from a cigarette and cups his hands round a flame, blinking away the smoke. I turn back to Olivia, pressing my hand against the cloth, which is saturated with her blood.

'Ewan stabbed her. He'll be blamed,' I say. 'I could take them both with me.'

'Ewan stays here. We're a team.'

'He needs his medication.'

'That's all the doctors do – dope him up. You're drug pushers, not healers. They want to take away his voices, but they're his friends, his mentors, his gods.'

'They're not gods.'

'How do you know?'

'I'm a psychologist.'

'Just my fucking luck – another talking head.' Micah picks a strand of tobacco from his tongue with his thumb and forefinger. 'How many psychologists does it take to change a lightbulb?'

'I've heard the joke,' I say.

'Not the way I tell it,' brays Micah. 'Because this lightbulb doesn't want to change. Instead it gets passed from one psychologist to the next until they all call it unstable and decide to lock it away in a mental hospital.'

'Is that what happened to you?' I ask.

'There's nothing wrong with me.'

'You set fire to a house with a man inside it.'

'He deserved it.'

Ewan has stopped pacing and is listening to us.

I keep talking. 'You were six years old. A child. Marcus Swinburne was a paedophile. A predator.'

'Did he touch you?' ask Ewan.

'No!' says Micah, growing more agitated.

'Your sister let Marcus babysit you because he seemed such a nice man. She should have protected you. Did you blame her?'

Micah doesn't answer.

'No, you blamed yourself. How long did it go on for? Three years? Four?'

'Congratulations, you can read a file.'

'Oh, I don't need a file to understand you, Micah. I think you befriended Ewan because he's more damaged than you are. He listens to you. He looks up to you. Nobody has ever done that. You want to stay together, but you need money for drugs. The craving is keeping you awake. It's like having a swarm of bees inside your head. Always buzzing. I bet it gets so bad you think you could put a gun to your temple if you weren't so scared of the blackness.'

Micah runs his hand over his shorn pate, making a rasping sound. Peeling back one corner of a sleeping bag, he picks up a two-foot length of metal pipe with one end wrapped in masking tape to form a handle.

'Don't let the drugs define you. You can beat this,' I say.

Olivia's head has fallen sideways on to her shoulder. She's losing consciousness.

Ewan shakes her, but she doesn't respond. 'Micah, I think she's really sick.'

'Shut up!'

'But—'

'I said shut up!'

Micah hasn't taken his eyes off me. 'I'm gonna crush your skull and scoop out your brain with my bare hands.'

He drags the pipe along the brick wall, making it bounce over the mortar joints.

'The police know we're here,' I say.

Micah laughs. 'If they knew, they'd be here.'

I push myself off the floor and stand with my back against the wall. 'Take my wallet. I'll give you the PIN to my accounts.'

'I don't want your money.'

'Don't hurt him,' says Ewan.

'I told you to shut up.'

Something moves in the shadows behind Micah. A fleeting figure crosses the doorway and disappears. A head appears. Ruiz. His eyes meet mine. He holds a finger to his lips. A half brick weighs down his other hand.

He slips inside the room, still five yards from Micah, edging closer. Ewan hasn't seen him. Micah taps the metal bar against the wall, the sound getting louder as he nears. His other hand is deep inside his baggy jeans, cupping his scrotum. This excites him – my fear, his violence . . .

'Nobody has to get hurt,' I say.

'Really?'

I nod to Ruiz. Doubt flickers in Micah's eyes. For a split second, he contemplates looking behind him, but dismisses the notion. He raises the pipe.

In the same heartbeat, Ruiz smashes the brick against the back of his head. The pipe rattles as it hits the floor. Micah staggers and drops to his knees, then on to his side, holding his head.

'Call an ambulance.'

'It's coming,' Ruiz says, crouching next to Olivia.

'How did you find me?'

'Charlie called.'

'I told her to wait.'

'She's cleverer than you are.'

Olivia's pulse is steady. She's not bleeding out.

Ruiz gets a sleeping bag to wrap around her shoulders. There are sirens in the distance, drawing nearer. Ewan is sitting on the back of his heels, holding his knees, rocking slightly.

Something is wrong. I can't see Micah. He's not on the floor. In the same instant, I see the pipe swinging towards Ruiz's head. He ducks. The pipe glances off his shoulder, sparking where it hits the wall. He swings again. Ruiz is warding off the blows.

Ewan throws himself forward, the knife flashing in his hand. I hear a popping sound like a tyre blowing out and see blood blooming beneath Micah's ribs. Micah looks down, surprised to see a knife sticking out of his chest. His eyes open wider. His ribs let go of the blade and it slides across the concrete floor.

Ewan backs away as Micah drops to his knees, his lungs bubbling and blood leaking from his mouth. He coughs, twitches, stares and topples forward, no longer blinking.

The next twenty minutes are a blur of police and paramedics, bright lights and bottles of plasma. Olivia is strapped to a stretcher and wheeled outside, across the pitted asphalt to the open doors of an ambulance.

She reaches for my arm. 'Ewan?'

'He's fine.'

The stretcher is lifted and slid inside. A medic climbs after it, hooking a bottle of plasma to a stand.

'You can ride along,' she says.

A police officer interrupts. 'We need a statement.'

'You know where to find me.'

The ambulance doors are closing. Looking up, I see Ruiz leaning against his Mercedes, sucking on a boiled sweet.

I mouth the words, 'Thank you.'

He nods back.

Day Thirteen

40

When I was fifteen, home for the summer, I pedalled my bike to Colwyn Bay so I could watch teenage girls sunbathing on the beach or promenading on the pier. They had sunburnt shoulders and blond tints in their hair and laughed with such confidence that I was too nervous to talk to them.

I knew one of the girls, Ginny Moore, who was a year older than me and lived on a working farm not far from ours. She and her friends were eating fish and chips from paper cones. Further along the pier, I saw four youths approaching: skinheads from Liverpool with shaved heads, tight T-shirts and jeans rolled above their Dr Marten boots. They were drinking cans of lager and jostling each other.

'Can I have a chip?' one of them asked Ginny, leaning

close and sniffing her hair. She recoiled and told him to get lost.

'C'mon, darling, just the one. It's a chip not a poke.'

'Don't be disgusting.'

He snatched the newspaper cone from her hands and held it out of her reach. She tried to take it back. Jumping higher. Her breasts jiggled in her bikini. The boys laughed.

'Give me a kiss,' the ringleader said, putting a chip between his lips.

The other girls had fled, leaving Ginny on her own.

She told him to fuck off. He tipped up the cone, spilling her chips on to the splintery wood, saying, 'Oops!'

'Hi, Ginny, anything wrong?' I asked.

The ringleader spun round, sizing me up. 'Fuck off, faggot!'

'What makes you think I'm a faggot?'

'Are you deaf or something?'

'What's the something?'

I don't know where the words came from. It was as though the path between my brain and my mouth had been temporarily disengaged.

He screwed up the chip wrapper and bounced it off my forehead. 'I'll kick your fucking teeth in.'

'Why?'

'Because you're a faggot.'

'You seem very sure that I'm queer. I mean, we don't know each other. We've never spoken, but you claim that I'm a homosexual. It's like you have a gift – a sixth sense – a "gaydar". Maybe it's your superpower.'

One of his mates laughed. The ringleader gave him a

death stare. Ginny had managed to slip away and I caught sight of her running along the pier, not looking back.

I didn't have a crush on her. I mean, she was nice and I'd thought about kissing her, but that applied to a lot of teenage girls. I could fall in love walking along the street.

The world seemed to slow down. I smelled the salt and the seaweed. A gust of wind blew the greasy ball of newspaper against my flip-flops. The skinhead grabbed my shirt in his fists and pushed his face close to mine. He had vinegar and beer on his breath.

I ducked the first punch, which glanced off the side of my head. The second found my stomach, taking my breath away. I swung my own punches, but few of them landed, before I fell. Curled in a ball, I shielded my face from the boots.

'Hold his head against the bench,' the ringleader yelled. 'I'm going to break his fucking jaw.'

One of them gripped my hair in his fists and pushed the side of my face against the metal footings of a bench seat. I knew my jaw would shatter, or my teeth, or my skull.

The ringleader took two steps back to get a run-up. He rocked forward, swinging his steel-capped boot. At the last moment, I managed to twist my head just far enough for the metal-cap to miss my cheek and hit the hand holding my head. Bones were broken. Not mine. There were curses. Recriminations.

I heard shouting and people running on the boardwalk. The youths scattered like seagulls as two policemen arrived.

I don't remember getting to the hospital. I woke to find my father sitting next to the bed. My eyes could barely open, but I recognised his outline and the sound of his voice.

'What did you say to them?' he asked.

'Nothing.'

'Why did they bash you?'

'They were bullying three girls.'

'And you came to their rescue.'

He didn't say it sarcastically. He sighed and nodded, but didn't sound disappointed in me.

'Some men are fighters, Joseph, and some are thinkers, and sometimes we meet our fate on the road we take to avoid it.'

I didn't know what he meant – not then. It took me years to understand that fate is what happens despite our plans.

Near the end of those holidays, I saw Ginny. She stepped out of the sea, squeezing water from her hair, squaring her shoulders, trying to walk across the sand like it was a catwalk. She smiled at me. I should have said something. She could have been my beginner romance, the one every adolescent boy needs. It could have made my summer magical before the loneliness of boarding school.

Another hospital. A different bedside. Olivia is out of surgery. The knife missed her major organs and she's going to be fine. The nurses think I'm her partner or husband, which is why they've let me stay. I haven't corrected them, but I wonder if there's someone I should call, friends or family.

I've heard it said that you can discover how you feel about someone when you watch them sleeping. You see

318

things you don't look for at other times. The elegance of an open mouth, the absence of anxiety, the vulnerability of each breath, a small vein pulsing beneath her pale skin. How do I feel? Conflicted. I wish she was someone else's mistress or wife.

As if reading my thoughts, Olivia's eyes open. She takes in her surroundings before focusing on me. Her dry lips part. 'Ewan?'

'The police have him. He's safe.'

'He needs a lawyer.'

'I called David Passage.'

Olivia relaxes and glances at the drip in her arm. She grimaces.

'Are you in pain? I can call the nurse.'

'No. It's fine.'

'The police are waiting to talk to you.'

'He didn't mean to stab me. It was an accident.'

'Tell them that.'

Olivia closes her eyes. 'What time is it?'

'Midday.'

'What day?'

'Saturday.'

'Have you been here all that time?'

'I had nowhere else to be.'

'What about your daughters?'

'Charlie is looking after Emma.'

'You're very lucky to have them.'

'I know.'

Her eyes film over. 'How is William?'

'The same.'

'I'm sorry for what I said to your mother the other day. It was cruel. Please tell her that.'

'You can tell her yourself.'

'I don't think she'll listen.'

Olivia asks for a sip of water. I hold the cup and put the straw in her mouth. She sucks. Swallows.

'Is there someone I can call? Family. A friend?'

'My mother lives in Donetsk. My father died ten years ago. Emphysema.'

'What about brothers or sisters?'

'They're living in Romania. Married with grown-up children.'

'Do you ever visit them?'

'I barely remember them. I was thirteen when I came to England.'

'How did you meet Todd Blackmore?'

Olivia doesn't seem surprised that I know about her past.

'He saw me playing in a junior event and talked my parents into letting me come to London. They were farmers. We were poor. It offered me a way out. Money. Sponsorship. Equipment deals.'

'You must have missed them?'

'Yes, but it wasn't so bad; Todd had two children who were about my age. It wasn't the same as having my own brothers and sisters around me, though. I saw my parents twice a year. The rest of the time it was tournaments and practice and more practice.'

Olivia stares past me at a spot on the wall as though watching scenes from her childhood being projected on the plain white surface.

'You see all these young athletes striving to succeed, all of them blessed with athleticism and great reflexes and hand–eye coordination, but one serious injury – a roll of an ankle, a twist of a knee, or genetic weakness – and the dream shatters.'

'Is that what happened to you?'

'My body wasn't strong enough. Or maybe I wasn't good enough.'

'You married Todd Blackmore.'

'I know what you're thinking.'

'Really.'

'You think he groomed me. You think he took advantage of a child and began a sexual relationship.'

'Did he?'

She rocks her head. 'I don't know any more. Maybe he raped me. Maybe I seduced him.'

'How old were you?'

'Old enough to know what I was doing.'

'Did you love him?'

'Yes.'

She has a look on her face that I cannot read. Some people carry their failure around with them, bent at the shoulders, weighed down. Others are untouched by sadness or displacement or suffering. Olivia is caught between the two – sometimes strong and sometimes vulnerable.

'I know how he died,' I say. 'I've read the coroner's report and talked to the accident investigator. Both doubted your version of events.'

'They weren't there.'

'Todd's ex-wife thinks you killed him.'

'She's always hated me.'

'You stole her husband.'

'He stole my childhood.'

'What does that mean?'

Olivia shakes her head, biting her bottom lip.

'Here's where I have a problem, Olivia. You keep telling me you're a good person; that my father loves you, but you won't level with me. You say you didn't attack him, but evidence points to you killing your first husband.'

'I don't care if you believe me,' she says defiantly.

For a long while we listen to the hum of the air conditioning and the rattle of trolleys in the corridor outside. Olivia's lips part, she moistens them. Her voice has grown small.

'I was fourteen. It began with hugs and touches. He called them "special cuddles". He would brush and plait my hair before tournaments, saying I was "crazy beautiful". One weekend we were sharing a hotel room during a junior tournament in Blackpool. We often did that to save money. I made the final on Sunday. The night before he woke me and said I'd been crying in my sleep. "It must have been a nightmare," he said, lifting the covers and sliding into bed next to me. At first he just held me, but I knew what he wanted. I told myself it wasn't rape. I loved him. I was homesick.'

Her voice grows more certain.

'Todd left his wife when I was seventeen and we moved in together. It caused a scandal. The British Coaches Association suspended his membership. The LTA withdrew his funding. It was horrible. Things settled down when we got married. I was playing the satellite circuit, trying to earn ranking points, but there were injuries, operations, comebacks and setbacks. My ranking fell. I lost my sponsorship deals. Money was tight. Todd drank too much.

'Eventually, we borrowed money and set up a coaching school, starting small, teaching kids and school groups. I quit the circuit and helped. We grew the business and slowly Todd was accepted back into the tennis world. We bought a house and I talked about starting a family.'

Unexpectedly, tears come to her eyes. 'I should have recognised the signs – the excuses he made, the way he interacted with some of the girls. One of them complained that Todd had touched her inappropriately. Her father threatened to go to the police. Todd paid him off. He promised me it was a misunderstanding. I wanted to believe him.

'We'd been married fourteen years when I fell pregnant with Ewan. It was perfect timing. I told myself that anyway.' Her eyes are shining. 'Todd was so excited. We decorated a nursery and began buying baby clothes. One afternoon in the summer, I packed a picnic basket and walked to the tennis centre. I thought I'd surprise Todd and we'd have dinner on Wimbledon Common. He wasn't in the pro-shop or the change rooms. I saw him sitting in his car, staring straight ahead. I tapped on the window. That's when she lifted her head from his lap. She was thirteen. Our budding champion.'

The words are coming in short gasps. 'I knew then that he'd never stop. He'd keep going . . . until one day he'd get caught and my whole life would come crashing down with him. I wouldn't be a victim. I'd be his enabler – the woman who looked the other way while children were groomed and abused.'

Olivia wipes her eyes with the edge of the sheet. I offer her a drink of water. She waves the cup away.

'You asked me what happened on the night of the accident. Was I speeding? Yes. Had we argued? Yes. Did someone force me off the road? No. Could I have stopped? Yes. Did I want to stop?' She hesitates and lowers her gaze. 'I can't answer that.'

'Can't or won't?'

'Both.'

Day Fourteen

41

'Do we have to do this?'

'Yes.'

'Can't I just write her an email?'

'No.'

'What about a Facebook message . . . with an emoji?'

'No.'

Emma drags her feet as we walk along a street in West Hampstead, looking at house numbers. She's carrying a large bunch of flowers wrapped in coloured cellophane.

'This is what normal people do when they make a mistake,' I say. 'They apologise.'

'Donald Trump doesn't apologise.'

'He's not a normal person.'

'He's a malignant narcissist.'

'Who told you that?'

'Charlie. She should know. She's going to be a psychologist.'

What do they say about a little knowledge . . . ?

The Temple family live in a white stuccoed house with neatly trimmed hedges and a bespoke weather vane on the roof that looks like a camel, but could be a whale. The man who opens the door has a round fleshy face and pear-shaped body encased in Lycra cycling shorts and a brightly coloured singlet.

'Mr Temple?'

'Yes.'

'I'm sorry to bother you. I'm Joe O'Loughlin. This is Emma. I was hoping we might have a word with you and your wife. And Petra, if she's home.'

He blinks at me suspiciously, but it might be the sweat running into his eyes.

'Right. Yes. Um. Come in. Wait here.'

He leaves us in the hallway. I hear him arguing with a woman in the next room.

'What do they want?'

'I don't know.'

'Should we call the police?'

'They've brought flowers.'

'Flowers?'

'Yes.'

Emma takes hold of my hand and looks up at me hopefully.

Husband and wife appear and we're ushered into a front room. Mrs Temple is wearing jeans and a long-sleeved top. She's the same size as her husband but top-heavy instead of hippy. She shouts up the stairs. 'Petra!'

'What?'

'Come down here.'

'I'm missing my show.'

'Do as you're told.'

Petra complains all the way down to the sitting room where she does a double-take at the sight of Emma. She's wearing a plastic cast on her left arm.

Emma steps forward reluctantly. 'I'm really sorry for what happened, Petra. Please forgive me. These are for you.'

She holds out the flowers. Petra doesn't move. Mrs Temple takes the bouquet.

'How's the arm?' I ask Petra.

Her top lip curls. 'Broken.'

'Does it hurt?'

'Some.'

I turn to her parents. 'I want to reassure you that I'll cover any expenses. Doctors. X-rays . . .'

'I missed four days of work,' Mrs Temple says.

'I'll cover that as well. Let me know the amount.'

'Made of money, are we?' Mr Temple says.

'No, but it's the least I can do.'

Mrs Temple addresses Emma. 'You've caused a lot of trouble, little madam, pushing people downstairs.'

'Emma knows,' I say. 'She's very sorry.'

'Sorry doesn't fix a broken arm. Petra could have been paralysed.'

'It was a misunderstanding.'

'It was a vicious unprovoked attack.'

'Emma reacted inappropriately to something Petra said.'

'I didn't say anything,' Petra squawks.

327

'What did she say?' Mr Temple asks.

'It doesn't matter. We're here to apologise.'

'I'd like to know what she said.'

'I said nothing,' Petra whines. 'She's making it up.'

I have my hand on Emma's shoulder. I squeeze it, sending her a message to be quiet.

She ignores me. 'Petra said Mummy committed suicide because I'm so weird.'

The statement seems to dim the lights.

'She's lying!' Petra says, her eyes wide with innocence. 'I would never say such a hurtful thing.'

'So that's why you're here,' says Mrs Temple, with a face like the north end of a southbound cow. 'You give us flowers and you make accusations.'

'No, I'm doing the opposite.'

'You think Petra is a bully and your daughter is a saint.'

'No.'

'Maybe Emma has the problem. Maybe she does weird things and doesn't have any friends.'

'Please don't talk about her like that.'

'I bet you're one of those fathers who panders to his little princess, letting her get away with pushing other girls down the stairs. You should be ashamed of yourself, coming here, making Petra feel bad. She's not the problem. Your daughter is.'

Emma steps back, trying to hide behind me.

I can feel my jaw clenching hard as my peripheral vision blurs. No longer listening, I seem to focus on the woman's red gash of a mouth being twisted out of shape as she talks. I want to turn the other cheek. I want to stay quiet. That's what Julianne would do. She'd smile, say goodbye and walk away, but it gets cold on the moral high ground.

Emma tugs at my hand. 'It's all right, Daddy. Let's go home.'

'In a minute,' I say, touching her cheek. 'Mr and Mrs Temple, I want to thank you. I've been a psychologist for nearly thirty years and I've never met the perfect parents of a perfect child. I've met some pretenders, of course, those who drone on about how smart, athletic, gifted and talented their children are, but I've never actually encountered the real deal. You should be proud of Petra. She's obviously pretty with clear skin and white teeth and lovely hair. I hope that one day, what's on the inside will match the outside.'

We leave without saying another word, walking in silence along the path and out the gate, turning left towards where I parked the car. Emma skips every so often to keep up with me. Taking hold of my hand, which refuses to swing, she says chirpily, 'Well, I think that went well.'

Day Fifteen

42

The day is bright and cloudless with near-alpine clearness and a low sun catching shop windows and reflecting from car windscreens outside Westminster Magistrate's Court.

David Passage greets me warmly, looking relieved to see a friendly face. He's dressed in a charcoal grey suit, white shirt and MCC tie. The foyer is full of lawyers, dressed in similar clothes, all of them murmuring to each other as though at a funeral. Elsewhere groups of family and friends mill around, here to support or to squire petty thieves, drunk drivers, delinquents and traffic violators awaiting their day in court. Periodically a door opens and a case number is called.

'Have you seen Olivia?' asks David. 'Is she coming? I left her a message.'

'She only came out of hospital last night.'

'Ewan is more likely to get bail if she's here.'

A thought occurs, left unvoiced. I don't want Ewan to be released – not until he's properly assessed and medicated. Until then he's like a hand grenade with a loose pin.

The automatic doors open and Olivia appears, pale from her ordeal and wincing as she walks.

'Am I late? Have you seen Ewan? I brought these.' She has a plastic bag with a clean shirt, trousers, socks and shoes. 'Can I give them to him?'

'I'll see what I can do,' says David.

He talks to a court officer. Phone calls are made. Forms completed. Access is restricted to legal counsel, but David describes me as a psychologist assessing Ewan's mental state before his court appearance.

Approval won, we take a lift downstairs where we surrender our mobile phones and keys before passing through a metal detector and a series of doors that are unlocked remotely by a controller sitting in a glass booth. A uniformed guard escorts us along a corridor with cell doors on either side.

The guard stops. Yells. 'Hands on the back wall.'

The deadbolts slide open. Ewan is dressed in prison overalls, braced against the painted bricks, his arms and legs spread wide. He turns at the sound of Olivia's voice. They embrace. She tries not to cry.

Ewan looks more centred and self-aware than in our previous encounters. Rested. Clear-eyed. Present. His voices have been quieted for the moment, or have softened to background noise.

'I've brought you some clean clothes,' says Olivia, helping Ewan get changed. His shirt is buttoned and shoelaces are tied. Afterwards they sit next to each other on a bench seat that is bolted to the wall and covered with a thin stained mattress.

I crouch at eye level with Ewan, asking him if he remembers me.

He nods. 'Can I go home now?'

'Not yet.'

'Where is Micah?' he asks.

'Micah is dead.'

Ewan shakes his head. 'No, no, no. Micah is fine . . . just like the girl.'

'What girl?'

'She fell.'

I look at Olivia, who shakes her head.

'Tell me about the girl.'

Ewan's eyes linger on mine. 'I'm not supposed to say.'

'Why not?'

'Micah made me promise.'

'You don't have to keep that promise now.'

Ewan is blinking rapidly. I can almost see him trying to reach inside his own mind, debating how much he should say.

I start again. 'You said she fell.'

'It was an accident. Micah didn't mean to scare her.'

'Where did she fall?'

'Wembley.'

Ewan grabs at his shirt, bunching it in his fists as though trying to pull the words from his stomach. Knuckles rap on the door. Ewan looks up in fright. His case has been called. David issues last-minute instructions.

'Stand up straight. Put your hands behind your back, not in your pockets. Don't say anything unless you're asked a question.'

'What if I don't know the answer?'

'They won't be hard questions.'

'Can I go home after that?'

'I'm going to ask the judge – but there's a chance you won't get bail. If that happens, you'll go to a remand prison.'

'But I want to go home. It was an accident. You said I could go home . . . you said.'

Olivia grips his hand, making shushing sounds. 'I'll see you upstairs. I love you.'

From the public gallery, I glimpse Macdermid and Kate Hawthorn in the well of the court. The DI is talking to the prosecutor, nodding and laughing like they're old golfing buddies.

There are no wigs or gowns or gavels. The judge, a stout woman with an ash-blond perm, is reading a brief of evidence. Above her head is a royal coat of arms that seems to be swimming in dust motes from a shaft of sunlight angling through a window. Ewan appears in the dock, flanked by two guards. The clerk of the court reads the charges – one count of murder and another of malicious wounding. Olivia flinches beside me. Her fingers find mine, locking together.

'Does the defendant wish to enter a plea?' asks the judge.

'My client reserves that right,' says David, 'but I wish to make an application for bail.'

Beside him at the bar table, the prosecutor snorts in derision.

'Is that an interjection or indigestion, Mr Pyne?' asks the judge.

'I'm sorry, Your Honour. I'm surprised that my learned friend would seek this defendant's release into the community. A young man is dead, a woman stabbed. According to the police, further charges are likely. The defendant's father was savagely beaten two weeks ago and sustained serious brain injuries. In the circumstances, the Crown strongly advises that he be remanded in custody for his own safety and that of the wider community.'

The judge motions for Mr Pyne to resume his seat. 'I'll hear the application.'

David has stayed on his feet. 'Your Honour, Ewan Blackmore is twenty-one years old with no felony arrests on his adult record. He has a loving mother who is in court today. She is committed to taking him home with her and ensuring that he turns up in court to defend these charges.'

'He stabbed his mother,' says Mr Pyne.

'That was accidental.'

'Oh, I see, so she ran into the knife.'

'Details of the stabbing are in dispute. My client also denies attacking his father and will argue self-defence in the death of Micah Beauchamp.'

Quietly, yet passionately, David pushes back against the weight of evidence, respecting the story that Ewan has told him. There are no verbal fireworks or debating flourishes as he lays out the details of Ewan's history of mental health issues.

'He has been prescribed Olanzapine 20mg twice a day and Quetiapine 200mg twice a day, along with a sedative, Diazepam.'

Mr Pyne interrupts: 'Anti-psychotic medication! All the more reason for him to remain in custody.'

'Prison is no place for him to receive the specialist psychiatric care he needs,' says David. 'His mother can make sure he takes his medication and attends his appointments with medical staff and this court.'

'Bloodstained clothing was found in a garden incinerator outside his bedsit,' says Mr Pyne.

'Those clothes haven't been linked to any crime.'

'DNA tests are pending.'

The judge interrupts, telling both men that she's heard enough. She addresses Ewan. 'Given the circumstances, I'm reluctant to allow bail. Instead, I am remanding you to a secure psychiatric hospital where you will receive the required care. Do you understand?'

'I want to go home,' says Ewan, looking from face to face.

'Your defence can make another application for bail if the facts of the case change.'

A court officer taps Ewan on the shoulder. His voice grows louder. He pleads with Olivia. 'You said I could go home.'

Crossing the well of the court, I stand in front of Ewan, wanting him to focus on me. He's hyperventilating.

'Breathe slowly, Ewan.' I do it with him. 'Inhale. Exhale. Everything is going to be OK. They'll take you to hospital and you'll see your mum soon.'

Ewan wipes his nose on his sleeve. The handcuffs rattle. He's led away, muttering, 'I must let go. I must let go.'

★ ★ ★

DI Macdermid is taking questions from reporters outside the court. Dressed in a sheepskin coat and a tweed cap, he looks more like a bookie than a detective. I hear snippets of his answers: '. . . victim known to police . . . history of violence . . . the investigation is ongoing . . . further charges are likely . . .'

The questioning ends and the circus moves on. Macdermid notices me and comes closer, taking a stick of gum from his pocket and folding it on to his tongue.

'Tell me again, Professor: whose side are you on?'

'Are there sides?'

'Two weeks ago, you were convinced your wicked step-mother had tried to kill your father. Now you're comforting her in a courtroom.'

'She's not my stepmother.'

Macdermid smiles, aware that his words are needling me.

'I'm not convinced that Ewan attacked my father,' I say.

The DI shrugs dismissively. 'It may have been Micah Beauchamp. Perhaps we'll never know. Either way, they were thick as thieves, a two-man crime spree – one a pill-popper and the other a schizo.'

'And the motive?'

'Money or drugs.'

'Nothing was taken.'

'Maybe Ewan wanted to get rid of the old man so he could collect the inheritance.'

'Ewan gets nothing.'

'His mother does. Being a shrink, you should know all about the Oedipus complex. Father and son fighting over the mother's affections. Very Freudian.'

336

'Ewan is a schizophrenic.'

'Exactly. He doesn't need a motive.'

'Which is why he'll never stand trial.'

'Not my decision. I just catch them.'

I want to wipe the smug look from his face, but a part of what Macdermid says is right. The system has failed Ewan, nobody else.

'He told me that he didn't hurt the girl,' I say.

'What girl?'

'Exactly.'

Macdermid frowns. 'What are you trying to pull?'

'I'm telling you what he said.'

'No, you're shitting in my pool.'

Macdermid swaps the gum from one cheek to the other and looks at the sky, where pristine blue is being invaded by ugly grey clouds.

'Since we're confiding, Professor, I will tell you this for nothing. Ewan might be crazy, but he isn't stupid. He knows how to lie – just like his mother. They both made sworn confessions, alibiing each other.' He pauses, wanting me to react. 'That's the thing with lies – they're like landmines. They get planted early and covered up, forgotten by everyone, until somewhere down the track, someone unwittingly steps on the pressure plate and *boom!*'

An unmarked police car pulls up to the kerb. Kate Hawthorn is behind the wheel. She gets out and opens the passenger door, waiting for her boss. Macdermid doesn't say goodbye. He slips into the car and waits for Kate to close the door. She looks up at me, giving me a half smile.

I hope I'm smiling back. I can't always tell when I'm wearing my game face or a Parkinson's mask.

Watching the police car pull away, I wonder if Macdermid could be right. Motive, method and behaviour all point to Ewan and Micah's guilt, yet the act and the clean-up tell me otherwise. Hitting someone over the skull requires proximity and brute force. It is up close. Hands-on. Personal. Bones will break and the blow will reverberate through arm and body. Blood sprays on skin. Stickiness covers hands. Bowel and bladder evacuate. Whoever attacked my father did so with anger and pent-up rage, rather than panic or fear of exposure. Micah was a sadist, more likely to torture his victims. Ewan is trapped between reality and the voices he hears. Both are capable, yet neither fits the empty picture-frame that I mentally carry with me whenever I profile a crime.

Glancing up, I see Olivia emerging from the courthouse. David Passage shields her from waiting reporters, ignoring their questions. He hails a cab. Opens the door. Olivia kisses his cheek and I notice his hand sweep down her back and rest momentarily on the swell of her buttocks. It's an intimate gesture, jarring because it's so unexpected. What have I missed?

In the same breath, I tell myself not to jump to conclusions. Olivia could have known David for years. He's my father's lawyer. She will have signed papers and witnessed signatures. Yet small, incidental details like this are what I pick up on – the patterns that others fail to see; the anomalies and capricious acts that form the outliers and define the frontiers of human behaviour. Impulsive. Volatile. Violent.

Surprising. We all seek safety in the normal, but I'm like a medieval cartographer mapping the known and identifying the unknown areas of the globe, drawing illustrations of mythological creatures and sea monsters in the blank spaces, as a warning to the unwary that 'here be dragons'.

Day Sixteen

43

Morning. Birdsong early. I watch from the sitting-room window as a street-sweeping machine weaves between parked cars sending stray leaves spinning from the bushes.

The intercom buzzes. I check the screen. Kate Hawthorn waits on the front the steps, shaking her limbs to stay warm. She's been running.

'Is it too early?' she asks.

'No. Come on up.'

She hesitates before pushing open the door. I greet her at the top of the stairs. Barely out of breath, she's dressed in a woollen hat, exercise leggings and a tight top that hugs her curves in a pleasing way.

'The girls are still in bed,' I say.

'I don't want to interrupt.'

'You're not. I have coffee and croissants.'

'Water is fine.'

'I've seen you running before,' I admit.

'Where?'

'Regent's Park. I walk most mornings around the Outer Circle. You glide past and disappear.'

Kate leans on the sink, sipping from a glass. 'The DNA tests are back on the clothes. The blood doesn't belong to your father.'

'Who then?'

'It doesn't match Ewan or Micah Beauchamp.'

The beat of silence is full of unspoken questions. Without DNA evidence, there's little to link Ewan and Micah to the attack on my father.

'Ewan mentioned a girl,' I say. 'He said she was hurt.'

'What girl?'

'I don't know.'

'Unless he gives us the details . . .' Kate doesn't finish. 'It hasn't changed anything. Macdermid is still convinced that Ewan and Micah are responsible.'

'He doesn't have enough.'

'Their fingerprints are in the house.'

'They could be old prints.'

'I shouldn't be telling you any of this . . .' Kate hesitates and seems to debate how much to say. 'The boss wants to put someone undercover in the psych hospital, posing as a patient. He thinks he can get Ewan to confess or incriminate himself.'

'That's entrapment.'

Kate becomes defensive. 'Macdermid isn't a bad copper. He's under pressure. Too many cases, not enough resources. Occasionally he cuts corners. We all do.'

'No, not all of you. I think you're telling me because you don't agree with him and you want to find some way to stop it.'

Kate doesn't respond.

Charlie arrives in the kitchen with tousled hair and pillow marks on her cheeks. Introductions are made. Kate asks about Oxford and Charlie answers politely, unsure why a detective is visiting so early in the morning.

Emma shows up moments later, still wearing her pyjamas.

'I like your hair,' Kate says. 'I used to have a purple streak like that.'

'Really?' Emma asks, beaming.

'She's being facetious,' I say.

'No, I'm not. I was making a statement. It was the mid-nineties and I did the full palette of hair colourings, as well as navel piercings, pink leggings, tank tops and short shorts.'

'What did your parents say?' asks Charlie.

'They were thankful it wasn't sex or drugs.'

Emma screws up her face in disgust. 'Ew!'

The girls chat to Kate about clothes and music. She accepts a coffee and shares a croissant. It feels nice having her here. Comfortable and captivating. Different in a good way. Afterwards, I walk her downstairs to the front door. Kate pulls the woollen hat on to her head and zips up her tight-fitting top, covering her neck.

'There's something else I haven't told you,' she says, hesitating. Still unsure. 'The cryptic note we found on the floor in Chiswick.'

I nod.

'It had traces of DNA. The lab ran it through the data-base and came up with a match – a guy called Ray D'Marco, a former soldier.'

'I've met him,' I say, taking Kate by surprise. 'He's the guy who ran from me at the hospital.'

'What does D'Marco have to do with William O'Loughlin?'

'His sister is severely disabled. He blames my father for her injuries.'

'Does Macdermid know any of this?'

I look at her blankly.

'Christ, Joe, he's a possible suspect. He spent a year in prison for assaulting a senior officer.'

'I didn't know any of that.'

'And he pulled a shelf down on your head.'

I try to explain, telling her about the botched birth of Bethany D'Marco and how my father sent her money every year.

Kate is still angry. 'Why did Ray D'Marco go to the hospital?'

'He said he was worried the cheques might stop coming.'

Kate wavers, as though still not convinced. 'Everything I've told you is classified. You understand?'

I nod and lean to kiss her cheek. At the last moment, Kate turns her head and our lips touch. My arms fold around her and my fingers spread against the small of her back. I taste the coffee on her tongue and feel the heat of her body against mine.

'You've got nice lips,' she says.

'Can I kiss you again?'

'Maybe later.'

She gently pushes me away and jogs down the steps, turning along the footpath, showing the orange soles of her trainers with each stride.

44

Dad has been moved to a private room on the sixth floor with a window facing north towards the towers of Wembley Stadium. It's a view that's wasted on someone who has barely blinked in the past three hours.

Now out of his medical coma, he is waking and sleeping in cycles. His IV bag empties. His catheter bag fills. His whiskers grow, along with his fingernails and hair. He's alive in almost every way except the most important one — consciousness. The rest of us move in a bright pool of perception, but Dad remains trapped in a silent land, no more sentient than a houseplant.

We do the crossword. I read him letters from *The Times*. Nothing registers. A person's face should allow others to access their private selves. It should signal feelings and intent, otherwise it's a subterfuge, or an empty vessel.

Can he hear me? I have no idea. There isn't enough oxygen in the room to say what needs to be said, but what needs to be said has become vaporous and pointless. Olivia is right. I've left it too late.

Many years ago, in my teens, I woke in the middle of the night and saw the bathroom light was on; the door half open. I found Dad sitting on the edge of the bathtub, reading a letter. Crying.

'Are you OK?' I asked.

He wiped his eyes. 'I'm fine.'

'Can't you sleep?'

'My snoring was keeping your mother awake.' The letter was balled in his fist. 'I'm going to give her a chance to fall asleep and go back in.'

'Right. OK. I'll see you in the morning.'

I should have said something or tried to comfort him, but I feared embarrassing him even more. Instead I went back to bed, pleased to have avoided a moment of intimacy, yet haunted by his pain. I still don't know what made him cry.

A nurse knocks on the door. She's due to massage Dad's muscles to prevent bedsores and infections.

'I'll be a little while,' she says, suggesting I get a cup of tea.

Pulling on my overcoat, I go downstairs and head out of the main doors, turning left into a bitter wind. Walking aimlessly, I cross over the Grand Union Canal into Little Venice, pausing to watch a canal boat negotiating a lock. Children, rugged up like Michelin men, are throwing sticks into the sluggish current.

My phone is vibrating.

'What are you doing?' asks Ruiz.

'Thinking.'

'You must be sick of that.'

'Yes.'

He gets to the point: 'I've been looking at Faraday Fiscal Management – asking my bank contacts if the missing money can be traced. It's a shelf company, set up in 2009. The address is a postbox in Road Town in the Virgin Islands. A local shopkeeper, who owns a chain of laundrettes, rented the box. He's a dummy director for more than forty companies with the same address. He gets paid to sign the papers.

'On 16 February 2010, the O'Loughlin Foundation transferred nine million pounds to Faraday Fiscal Management using an account at the CBIC First Caribbean bank in the Virgin Islands.'

'Who set up the account?'

'There's no way of knowing. That's the advantage of tax havens – the owners' identities don't have to be registered. Twelve hours later it left again as an unsecured loan to a construction company called Havenbrook Continental, based in Geneva. The deal was arranged through Mossack Fonseca, the Panamanian law firm that hit the headlines a few years ago for money-laundering. Havenbrook was supposedly building a luxury ski resort outside of St Petersburg, but construction has been delayed for years. In 2010, the company made three loans worth £8.2 million to Dilan Holdings, an affiliate of a Cypriot maritime insurer. That money was transferred to various trading accounts in Switzerland as compensation for cancelled share deals, then nothing, the trail goes cold. We'd have more chance of finding Elvis.'

Squeezing my eyes shut, I open them again and feel dizzy, as though I've been spinning in circles and suddenly stopped. The ground tilts and I clutch a railing.

'Are you all right?' asks Ruiz.

'Fine. Could you do one more thing for me?'

'Name it.'

'Investigate my father's finances. Look for any red flags – real estate holdings, lavish purchases, large amounts being transferred . . .'

'You think he stole the money?'

'I'm not sure of anything.'

Still unsettled, I turn back, retracing my steps, across the canal and beneath the concrete pillars of the Marylebone Flyover. Drops of rain are creating circles on the pavement that begin to merge as the downpour grows heavier. Holding my coat over my head I run the final hundred yards to St Mary's.

The door of my father's room is ajar and the curtains are drawn around his bed. The window throws shadows against the fabric showing a figure leaning over the bed. For a moment, I'm convinced that Dad has woken and managed to stand. I utter his name and pull back the curtains to find Rosie Passage standing over him, holding a pillow across her chest.

'What are you doing?' I ask, challenging her.

'I'm helping William sit up,' she says, as though it should be obvious. 'He'll find it easier to breathe this way. I was a nurse, remember?'

Rosie pulls him forward and tucks the pillow behind his head. Her platinum white hair is cut short in a chin-level bob revealing large silver earrings that sway back and forth against her neck. 'Kenneth would have come, but he hates the way I drive and I gave Eugene the day off,' she says.

Rosie takes a seat next to the bed and opens a brown paper bag, offering me a grape.

'You brought him grapes?'

'I brought them for you.'

She pops one in her mouth. 'Do you think he can hear us?'

'I don't know.'

'He looks quite perky – apart from the bandages, I mean. If I didn't know better, I'd expect him to sit up at any moment and ask for a gin and tonic. Is he improving?'

'No.'

'What do the doctors say?'

'He's beyond repair.'

A shiver travels across Rosie's skin, raising goosebumps on her forearms.

'Do you know about Olivia Blackmore?' I ask.

'Yes.'

'Were you friends with her?'

'That's a good question. I'm not sure how to answer it. We didn't socialise, if that's what you mean. I think I was jealous of her youth.'

'She's not much younger than you are.'

Rosie smiles. 'That's very sweet.' She takes another grape. 'Men always imagine that women are bonded by ideas of sisterhood and solidarity, but we pick our fights and our friends. I wouldn't interfere in your mother's marriage, any more than she'd interfere with mine.'

'But you *did* interfere – you had an affair with my father.'

'That was different.'

'How?'

'I was young. Careless. Carefree. It was the seventies . . .'

'Were you in love with him?'

'Once, perhaps. He saved me.'

'How?'

'I fell pregnant. I went to William, hoping he might help me.'

'With an abortion?'

'Oh, heavens no! Please don't laugh at me, but I'm a Catholic. I was seeing Kenneth by then. I didn't think he'd marry me – not because he didn't love me, but because of his family. They wanted a debutante for a daughter-in-law, or someone from a good family. Instead they got an Irish Catholic from County Wicklow.'

'Who was the father?'

'Kenneth, of course. I was a party girl, but not a slut.' Rosie plucks another grape from the stem. 'We married. David was born. Kenneth struggled at first with fatherhood, but fell madly in love. Then we had Francis . . . my baby.' Her eyes have clouded over. 'He should never have joined the army. I blame William for that.'

'Why?'

'When Francis finished school he had no idea what he wanted to do with his life. He took a gap year and travelled to Australia, but he came back just as uncertain. He went to William for advice – they were always close. Together

350

they chose Sandhurst, without consulting us. I was furious. "It's officer training," William said. "It's not as if he's going to war." But there's always a war, isn't there? Northern Ireland. The Gulf. Bosnia. Afghanistan. Iraq. Always some reason for us to send young people into danger. I thought I'd go mad after Francis died. Maybe I did for a while. It was like an endless night.'

Rosie touches her cheek as though expecting to find tears.

'I know it sounds selfish, but I remember wishing that someone else had died, not Francis.' She picks up my copy of *The Times*. 'Do you ever read the death notices?'

'No.'

'I do. Every day. I'm not interested in the old people who die. I read about the young ones – those who are taken early, with their whole lives ahead of them. It's as though I want confirmation that I'm not alone . . . that other parents suffer as I've done.'

'You're not alone,' I say.

'I know.'

Rosie glances inside the brown paper bag. The grapes have gone. She shrugs guiltily. 'Waste not, want not.'

Getting to her feet, she leans over the bed and kisses my father on the forehead, speaking to him directly.

'You were never much of a conversationalist, William, but do try a little harder next time.'

After she's gone, I sit in her chair, gazing out the window at construction cranes etched against the fading day. A passenger jet descends towards Heathrow, its red light blinking. Another follows on the same flight path. Below, in the distance, long chains of trains move with deliberate slowness. Feeling nostalgic, I search the sky for a star, but the glow of the city has veiled them.

Lucy is coming at midnight. In the meantime, I recount stories from my childhood, remembering pets, holidays and Christmases past. Dad always seemed to love the festive season. For most of the year he was withdrawn, distant, verbally combative and selfish, but come Christmas all of that changed and he fussed over the tree and the lights and made his secret recipe for mulled wine.

Having talked for two hours, I grow tired of the one-sided conversation, and lapse into silence, dozing dreamlessly, disturbed periodically by the rattle of trolleys or conversation in the corridor outside.

Jerked awake, I look around me. I'm alone in the softly lit room. Night-time London is beyond the glass. I must have imagined his voice. Leaning over the bed, I look at Dad. His chest rises and falls. His nostrils dilate.

'It's me, Joe,' I say. 'Can you hear me?'

His eyelids open, looking past me.

I squeeze his hand. 'Can you feel that?'

His lips part and a thread of spit stretches and breaks. He's making sounds, trying to speak. I lean over him, putting my ear next to his lips.

'Say it again.'

I feel his breath, but can't make out the words.

'Take your time. Slowly.'

The heart monitor emits a warning beep. He groans. The alarm gets louder.

'What is it? I'm here.'

352

Dad's right hand grips my forearm with surprising strength as though he's clinging to this moment of consciousness. His mouth opens. Each word is wet and slurred.

'Let . . . me . . . die!'

Day Seventeen

45

'I don't doubt what you're telling me,' says Dr Lorimore, 'but none of our tests support the possibility that your father is aware of his surroundings.'

The neurologist is wearing jeans and trainers and a black leather jacket, having been summoned to the hospital on his day off.

'Clearly this is a heartbreaking situation for any family, but let me explain again what's happening. In the second stage of coma, patients often open their eyes, or make sounds, or violent movement. These are known as automatisms, but it doesn't mean they are conscious. William cannot follow commands, or speak, or interact. He's in a vegetative state, with little evidence of brain activity.'

'I know what I heard.'

We're talking in Dr Lorimore's office, while my mother

and sisters wait outside. He dips his head. 'How much sleep did you get last night?'

'I wasn't asleep. I mean, I was dozing, but I woke when I heard him.'

'You're sure.'

'Yes.'

Dr Lorimore's lead-grey eyes seem to doubt me. 'Have you told your mother, or your sisters?'

'I wanted to speak to you first.'

'Of course.'

'They have a right to know.'

'Yes.'

'Why do you say it like that?'

'Like what?'

'Like you think it's a mistake.'

'It's just . . .' The neurologist steeples his fingers. 'I have a philosophy on matters of truth,' he says. 'I prefer not to know how much my wife spends on shoes, so she tells me that each new pair costs fifty quid, bought on sale. I'm happy that way. I'm also happier not knowing how many calories there are in a piece of chocolate cake; or what's inside a hotdog, or if there's a spider living in our broom cupboard; or where my teenage children are when they say they're sleeping over at a friend's house. We live in a world where people think that being informed is important or that knowledge is power, but you and I both know that isn't always true.'

'You're saying ignorance is bliss.'

'No. Not ignorance. It's choosing what to learn and what to leave alone. If I could tell you, beyond doubt, the exact details of when and how you are going to die, without any possibility of changing the outcome, would you want the knowledge?'

'No.'

'You'd prefer not to know.'

'Yes.'

'That's why I'm asking you to hold off from saying anything to your family until I've run the tests again. If you're right, I'll be celebrating with you.'

It's a reasonable request, yet I feel like a kid whose party balloon has blown out of my hand and is drifting over the rooftops, never to be seen again.

My mother and sisters are seated in a row in the corridor. They look up in unison, their eyes asking the same question.

'He turned his head,' I say. 'I thought he might have reacted to something I said.'

'Did he recognise you?' asks Lucy.

'I don't know.'

'Did he say anything?'

'He made some sounds. Dr Lorimore is looking into it.'

Lucy takes hold of my mother's hand. 'It's a good sign,' she says. Rebecca and Patricia nod in agreement. Their faith in doctors and surgeons seems absolute, never doubting that modern medicine will triumph, which is strange considering that Dad always stressed that medical science could only do so much: 'We're physicians, not miracle workers.'

At the far end of the corridor, Ruiz emerges from a lift, walking along the corridor with his distinctive gait, like a pirate on the deck of a ship. People automatically turn their heads, following his progress.

My mother doesn't want me to leave. She thinks my father will show improvement to me and nobody else. I promise her that I'll come back soon.

Ruiz is double-parked outside the hospital. A handwritten 'POLICE' sign is displayed on the dashboard.

'Impersonating a police officer is a criminal offence,' I remind him.

He tosses the sign on to the back seat. 'I spent forty-three years as a copper and, in my experience, most of my bosses were impersonating cops. Where do you want to go?'

'I need a coffee.'

'Done.'

Soon we're sitting in a café that smells of boiled milk, waffles and grease. Ruiz bites into a bacon roll, sending brown sauce dripping down his wrist.

'You're not hungry?' he asks, chewing noisily.

'My arteries are hardening from here.'

'Haven't you heard – fat isn't the killer any more. Now I can eat more pork than Kermit.'

'That's an image I won't get out of my head.'

Ruiz takes another mouthful. 'You really think the old man spoke to you?'

'Yes.'

'That's positive news. At least he's not brain-dead . . . of sound mind and all that. What did he say?'

'He wants to die.'

'Oh.'

I change the subject. 'I think David Passage and Olivia

357

Blackmore may know each other better than they're letting on.'

'Are we talking adult sleepovers?'

'The night that Ewan broke into the flat and I went to see Olivia, I heard someone else in the house.'

'You thought it was Ewan.'

'Now I'm not so sure.'

'Evidence?'

'I talked to a neighbour who said Olivia had a regular visitor when my father was out of town – someone who drove a dark BMW.'

'What does Passage drive?'

'Can you find out?'

Ruiz sighs. 'You're drawing a long bow, Professor.'

'Maybe, but David Passage knew about the insurance policies and the contents of my father's will. He was also on the board of the foundation when the money went missing.'

'Why would he bash your old man?'

'Money. Sex. Jealousy.'

'You want me to pick one?'

'It could be all three.' I stare into the dregs of my tea, struck by the flaws in my theory. David Passage has been open with me from the outset – telling me about Bethany D'Marco and the forensic audit and Dad's financial problems.

Ruiz wipes his mouth on a paper serviette. 'Macdermid wants to close the book on this one. It's only a matter of time before he charges Ewan.'

'Even if he's right, it doesn't explain the missing money.'

'You could be conflating two different crimes.'

He's right, but I want to keep digging, hoping that each new layer will reveal a different history.

'What are you going to do?' asks Ruiz.

'Talk to Ewan.'

'He's in a high-security psychiatric wing.'

'And I'm a psychologist.'

46

From a distance, Twin Rivers Lodge looks like a leisure centre or a junior school painted in primary colours, with a basketball court and five-a-side football pitch. Only as we get nearer do I notice the razor wire and security camera guarding the fences.

'You missed our coffee appointment on Monday,' says Victoria Naparstek, who is waiting in the visitor's centre. 'That was two in a row.'

'I'm sorry. My father . . .'

'How is he?'

'No change.'

'You're tired of saying those words.'

'Yes.'

I introduce her to Ruiz, who has been hovering in the background.

'The professor has kept you a secret,' he says, holding her hand like he's meeting a princess.

'Oh, really?' replies Victoria. 'You're exactly as described.'

Ruiz frowns, looking uncomfortable. 'What's he said?'

'I can't divulge that.'

He looks at me. 'What have you been saying?'

'Nothing.'

'But she said—'

'She's joking.'

Victoria gives him a cheeky smile. Ruiz whispers to me, 'I don't like her any more.'

'I can only get one visitor into the unit,' she says, collecting paperwork from the front desk.

'I'm happy to stay here,' Ruiz says. 'I can catch up on my trashy reading.' He points to a stack of gossip magazines with celebrities on the covers.

'Vincent doesn't like psych wards,' I explain.

'Any personal experience?'

'No,' says Ruiz, a little too quickly.

A buzzer sounds. A door unlocks. Each new section of the unit has added cameras and extra staff. The high-security unit wing has gender-specific wards with communal areas, games rooms and lounges. Each patient has a single room, which is locked at night and monitored.

'Ewan has agreed to see you,' explains Victoria, 'but he can stop the interview at any time.'

'How has he been?'

'He's out of observation, but it could take weeks to balance his medication.'

We follow a covered walkway flanked by flowerbeds to

361

a greenhouse made from Perspex panels that are pieced together to form a pale pyramid. Once inside, the air is humid and dense with greenery. Condensation clings to the walls, dripping in rivulets that run into channels and irrigate rows of flowers and vegetables.

Ewan is transplanting seedlings from a tray into individual pots, lifting each one carefully so as not to damage the roots. A staff member is supervising, but now slips into the background, watching from a distance.

'What are you growing?' I ask.

'Tomatoes, I think,' says Ewan, as he presses his fingers into the dark soil around each seedling.

'How are you feeling?'

'OK. They take away my blankets to get me out of bed. And they say I have to eat, even when I'm not hungry.'

'You should eat.'

'I can't taste anything. And the food is rubbish.' His mind jumps. 'They gave me a needle. I hate needles.'

'It's a routine blood test,' explains Victoria, who has positioned herself on a stool near the door. I notice an emergency alarm button near her right hand.

Ewan makes eye contact with me and whispers, 'I shouldn't be here. This place is full of crazies. They scream at night. I complained to the head nurse about the noise, but she threatened to have me sedated. Can she do that?'

'Yes.'

Ewan shakes his head as though surprised at what the world has come to.

'Do you remember my name?' I ask.

'Joe.'

'How do you know me?'

'You're my half-brother.'

The answer jars. 'What day is it today?'

'Friday.'

'What is the date?'

'The fourth.'

'What month?'

'July.'

'What makes you say that?'

'It's hot.'

'We're in a greenhouse, Ewan. It's cold outside.'

He shrugs dismissively.

'It's November. A Wednesday,' I say.

'They won't let me have a phone,' he replies, as though explaining his mistake.

'You didn't always like phones — you said they were spying on you.'

He doesn't answer.

'When you were growing up, Ewan, did you ever have an imaginary friend?'

'No.'

'But you heard voices.'

'Yes.'

'Why do you think they chose you?'

'I'm special.'

'In what way?'

'Nobody else can hear them. I've been chosen.'

'Do you have any control over them?' I ask.

'Sometimes. When I'm medicated I can't hear them any

more, but I hate the drugs – how they make me feel. Slow and stupid, like I'm half asleep.'

'Do you trust the voices?'

'Not when they tell me to do bad things.'

'What would happen if you stopped listening to them and trusted someone like me?'

'You'd want to make me like everyone else, not special any more.'

'I know about the girl,' I say, taking a tray of seedlings and working alongside him. 'Did the blood frighten you?'

Ewan doesn't answer.

'Is that why you burned your clothes?' I ask.

'Micah told me to.'

'Were they his clothes or yours?'

'Mine.' Ewan chews on the inside of his cheek. 'It was an accident. Micah said he'd call an ambulance. He said she was going to be all right.'

'I can check for you. What's her name?'

'I don't know. She looked like Jenny?'

'Who's Jenny?'

'I met her at Ticehurst Hospital. Jenny used to barricade herself in the bathroom and throw up her food.'

'You said the girl lived in Wembley. Did you visit her?'

'She didn't know we were coming.'

'Where does she live?'

'I don't remember the address. It's a house. Micah's cousin lives there. He owes Micah money. That's why we went to see him, but he wasn't home. His girlfriend wouldn't let us inside. She looked like Jenny.' He starts telling me the same story again. I draw him back to the house in Wembley.

'She yelled at Micah. I wanted to go home, but Micah wouldn't leave without his money. He got angry and kicked down the door. The girl ran upstairs. Micah was chasing her.'

'Where were you?'

'Outside. Keeping watch.'

'And the girl?'

'I heard a window open. She crawled on to the roof, but kept slipping on the tiles. I wanted her to go back inside.' Ewan stares at his hands, trying to wipe the mud off his fingers. 'She didn't scream or anything. The spike went right through her stomach and was sticking out of her back.'

'What spike?'

'She landed on the fence. I tried to lift her off, but she was too heavy. Micah said we had to go because we'd be blamed. I told him we had to get help. He said he would.'

'You left her on the fence?'

'Micah said the ambulance was coming.'

Ewan is wiping his hands on the front of his jeans. His eyes have glazed over. 'Is Jenny all right? She's bulimic. She's my friend.'

He's dissociating now, letting the past merge with the present. He hits his forehead. 'I must let go. I must let go.'

Victoria calls time on the interview and takes Ewan back in his room. Afterwards, she accuses me of pushing him too hard.

'He knew more.'

'You're a psychologist, not a bully.'

'You're right. I'm sorry.'

Victoria calms down by the time we reach the main entrance and collect our possessions. She holds out a thin gold chain. 'Can you help me?' My hands tremble as I fumble with the clasp.

'You're going out tonight,' I say. 'Is he someone new?'

'How do you know,'

'Your dress. Your boots. Your make-up.'

'I've worn make-up before.'

'You've taken extra care. You must like this guy.'

Victoria averts her eyes. 'I wish you wouldn't do that. It feels like you're spying on me.'

'I'm sorry.'

'Are you seeing anyone?'

I think for a moment about Kate and tell her no.

'You should. It's time.'

Victoria stays behind. Ruiz and I walk across the near-empty parking area. The doors of the Mercedes unlock with a dull *thunk* and a flash of lights.

'You think he was telling the truth?' he asks.

'It explains the blood on his clothes.'

'They could still have bashed your old man.'

'Yes.'

'So, we're back to square one.'

If only there were squares, I want to say, and this was a game with a referee or a rulebook or a stopwatch or, better still, a mercy rule.

Day Eighteen

47

Nobody answers the doorbell. Stepping back on to the footpath, I glance up and see Bethany D'Marco's face at the first-floor window. Tufts of hair stick from her leather helmet. She raises a mobile phone to her ear and speaks. I lift my phone and pretend I can hear her.

'That's Bethany,' I say.

'Would she be home alone?' asks Ruiz.

'I doubt it.'

He motions over his shoulder. 'Let's try around back.'

At the end of the terrace, we find a narrow walkway between houses leading to a laneway built for the old night-soil carts that collected waste from this part of London. I count down the houses and push open a gate, entering a small yard. Ray D'Marco is crouched beside his motorbike, tightening a wheel nut.

'I rang the doorbell,' I explain.

'I thought you were Mormons,' he replies, not bothering to look up.

'This is Vincent Ruiz.'

D'Marco straightens and appraises Ruiz like a fighter weighing up his chances. Ruiz is used to that. It's why he never stands with his back to a door, or with his hands in his pockets; and he instinctively notices if someone favours his left or right hand.

'You a copper?' D'Marco asks him.

'Used to be.'

'And now you're Miss Marple.'

He takes a fresh pack of cigarettes from his overalls, unwrapping the plastic and tapping out a smoke. He cups his hands around the flame, looking at me. 'How come you never smile?'

'I have Parkinson's.'

'Bummer. I thought maybe you were Sicilian. My grand-father came from Palermo. He once told me that Sicilians only smile just before they pull the trigger.'

He grins at the joke and cocks his head to one side. 'When you tell people that you have Parkinson's, do they feel sorry for you?'

'Mostly.'

'Do they ever tell you that God doesn't give us anything that we can't handle?'

'Yes.'

'Comments like that truly shit me. People never say, "I'm coming over to help you clean shit off the sheets, or to give Bethany a bath." Never that.'

He holds one nostril and blows snot into a clump of weeds in a garden bed.

'You know what my father did for a living? He worked as a sewer flusher for Thames Water. He cleaned blockages in the old Victorian-era sewers: nappies, face wipes, congealed fat, dead rats . . . He shovelled other people's shit for nearly thirty years. Can you imagine that? He used to shower before he came home. He scrubbed himself clean and kept his fingernails cut short, but he was so paranoid about the smell that he'd douse himself in cologne until he stank like a rum distillery full of dead flowers. He was a strong man – had to be – but even he crumbled under the burden of looking after Bethany. It wasn't the daily grind. It was the unfairness that ate away at him. The lorry driver went to prison for two years, your father got off scot-free. But my parents had to suffer every day for the rest of their lives.'

'Is that why you attacked him?'

D'Marco bristles with anger. 'I didn't touch him.'

'Why did you ask if he had a brain tumour?'

'I heard a rumour.'

Another lie.

'You told me that you'd never met him, but you knew about his house in Chiswick. Your motorbike was seen on the night he was attacked.'

'Lots of bikes look like mine.'

D'Marco drops the cigarette from his fingers and turns his back, reaching into the toolbox.

'The police found a note inside the door. Your DNA was on it. You left a message saying you couldn't do something. What did you mean?'

His shoulders arch and his muscles ripple as if something is slowly uncoiling beneath his skin. When he turns, he's holding a wrench in his right fist. His knuckles are white.

'Get out!' he rumbles.

Ruiz picks up the lid of a metal rubbish bin, holding it like a shield. 'Time to leave, Professor.'

'Is that what you attacked him with?' I ask. 'How many times did you hit him?'

'Fuck off!'

'An old man. Defenceless. Alone. Some soldier you are.'

D'Marco swings the wrench. Metal hits metal. Ruiz parries the blow. The two men are circling each other and the yard has shrunk to the size of a boxing ring. He swings again. The bin lid clangs.

I look for a weapon . . . something to help. The movement distracts D'Marco and Ruiz seizes the moment, driving his fist beneath D'Marco's ribs, doubling him over and dropping him to the ground where he gasps for breath. The wrench clatters to the concrete.

'Don't get up,' says Ruiz. 'We'll show ourselves out.'

48

Less than a block from the house, two unmarked police cars overtake at speed and swing in front of the Mercedes. Ruiz stamps on the brake. The car groans and sways. I'm thrown forward against the seat belt before ricocheting back into the seat, smelling the burning rubber.

Doors open in unison.

'Keep your hands on the wheel,' says a bull-necked officer with a shaved head and a weight-room physique. Another detective pulls me out and pushes me to the ground, putting a knee in the small of my back. Ruiz is getting similar treatment.

He raises his head from the pavement. 'Don't resist.'

'What have we done?'

'Both of you shut up,' says the bull-necked detective, who has pulled Ruiz's arms behind his back.

Cuffs snap around my wrists, tightened an extra notch. I'm pushed on to the rear seat of the police car. Ruiz is put into a separate vehicle. People are watching from the footpath and nearby doorways. Taking photographs. Within minutes we'll be uploaded on to Instagram, Facebook or Twitter as updates for their friends or news for their feeds or content for their followers.

The cars pull away.

'Where are you taking us?'

No answer.

'You can't arrest us for no reason.'

Still nothing.

I notice a camera with a long lens between the front seats. Take-away coffee cups. Fast-food wrappers. They've been watching someone. Ray D'Marco. Shit!

We drive in silence into central London, through the Limehouse Link Tunnel, past Tobacco Dock, Tower Bridge and along Victoria Embankment where the tourist coaches are lined up like uncoupled train carriages. Turning left into Richmond Terrace, we pass through iron gates and swing down a ramp into a secure car park beneath New Scotland Yard. I'm escorted upstairs to an interview room.

'My daughter is due home from school,' I say. The bull-necked detective ignores me. The door bangs shut.

'I want a lawyer,' I shout.

Nobody answers. I'm alone in a small cell-like room with a table, three chairs and a CCTV camera angled from the ceiling. This is Macdermid's doing. Punishment. Deserved.

He arrives an hour later, shrugging off his sheepskin coat and hanging it on the back of a chair. He doesn't bother sitting down. He has a small muscle in his otherwise puffy cheek that twitches when he gets angry.

'I expressly told you to stay away from this investigation.' I watch the muscle pulsing in and out.

'I had no idea you were watching the house. If I'd known . . . if you'd told me.'

'Why would I tell you anything? You're not involved.' His right hand looks even more claw-like, bent at the wrist and turned in on itself. 'How did you know about D'Marco?'

'My father has been sending cheques to Bethany D'Marco for years. I wanted to know why.'

'So you went and knocked on the door?'

'Yes.'

'You recognised Ray D'Marco – the man who assaulted you at the hospital – but you didn't think to inform the police.'

'I felt sorry for him.'

'Bullshit!' Macdermid's nostrils are dilated and pale. His cheek still twitches. 'We've had D'Marco under surveillance since we traced his motorbike from CCTV footage taken outside St Mary's. Now, thanks to your little stunt, we've had to arrest him before we have sufficient evidence. I've spent the past hour asking him questions, but he's lawyered up, saying nothing. It's like talking to a wall.'

Macdermid braces his fists on the table in front of me.

'But a strange thing happened, Professor. Somehow D'Marco's lawyer knew about DNA we found on a note in the hallway in Chiswick. That's information we'd withheld for operational reasons. Any idea how he'd know a detail like that?'

The question triggers a warning bell and I realise the magnitude of my mistake.

Macdermid looks at me with loathing. 'You know the worst thing, Professor. It's not that you've compromised my investigation, or cost me time and money. To be honest, I don't give a damn about budgets and clean-up statistics. The worst thing is that you've destroyed the career of a good detective.'

'No! Please! It's not her fault.'

'DS Hawthorn has been suspended pending a disciplinary hearing.'

'This is my fault.'

'She allowed a civilian access to privileged information. If she's lucky, she'll be busted back to uniform. Personally, I'd save time and kick her out completely.'

'It wasn't Kate.'

'You're a lousy liar.' Macdermid's knuckles rap on the door. 'You're free to leave, Professor. I'll skip shaking hands. Everything you touch turns to shit.' A uniformed constable appears. 'Get him out of here.'

The DI leaves before me, his wide shoulders bumping people aside as he strides down the corridor. I follow him, trying to think of all the clever things I should have said – the comebacks and one-liners; the passionate defence of Kate. I come up with nothing.

Instead I feel exhausted and strangely frightened, as if I've woken up in a circle of hell and I'm slipping deeper inside. From somewhere nearby, I hear a voice full of pain and longing, shouting through a closed door.

'Bethany needs me. Who's going to look after her?'

Ray D'Marco is growing hoarse, bashing against the door. 'Please. Let me go. She won't eat for anyone else.'

I look at the constable. 'What's happened to his sister?'

'She was taken into care.'

'Where?'

'That's up to the Local Health Authority.'

49

I lift the brass knocker again, dropping it against a worn metal plate. The sound echoes along a hallway. At the same time, I call Kate's number. She's not answering.

'I don't think she wants to talk to you,' says Ruiz, who is leaning on a lamppost.

Ignoring him, I drop the knocker again and again. The door opens suddenly. Kate's eyes are red-rimmed and swimming with frustration and bitterness.

'Leave me alone.'

'Let me explain.'

'You fitted me up.'

'I didn't mean . . . It was a mistake. I'll fix this.'

'How?' she asks scornfully. She's wearing old jeans and a checked shirt. 'Macdermid wants me fired. At the very least I'll be transferred out of CID.'

'There must be something I can do.'

'Yes. Leave me alone.'

She glances up and spots Ruiz, instinctively dropping her gaze, as though embarrassed. The door is closing. The lock turns. A chain is slipped into place. I feel like weeping. Macdermid is right – everything I touch turns to shit.

I walk in silence back to Ruiz's car. We sit and stare out of the windscreen.

'You like her, don't you?' he says.

'Yes.'

'She's changed a lot.'

'What do you mean?'

'Don't you recognise her?'

'No. I mean, she looks familiar, but Kate says we've never met.'

'That's understandable.'

Ruiz is waiting for me to catch up to him. That's the thing about Vincent. He never forgets. Nothing is vague or hazy, or frayed at the edges when it comes to the past. Names, dates, places, witnesses, perpetrators, victims, Ruiz can remember them all. I used to think this was a curse – having total recall, being unable to forget, but Ruiz doesn't dwell on his mistakes or let the past define him.

'Has she ever talked about her old life?' he asks.

'No.'

'And you haven't asked?'

I shake my head. Ruiz makes a clicking sound with his tongue. 'Maybe it's best that way.'

'Why?'

'I should stay out of this.'

'No. Tell me.'

He scratches at his unshaven cheek, making a rasping sound. 'Langton Hall in Clerkenwell in 2004. You gave a talk to sex workers – telling them how to stay safe on the streets.'

'It's where I met you,' I say, picturing the near-empty hall and a group of perhaps forty women, rugged up against the cold, ranging in age from their late teens to mid-forties. Some had come straight from work and wore overcoats over fishnet tights and leather miniskirts. Others had dressed down, or scrubbed off their make-up. They were prostitutes and call girls, some drug-addicted, or on Methadone, or single mothers, or college girls paying their way through university. I didn't have to tell them about the dangers they faced. Sex workers make up the biggest sub-group of victims of violent crimes – of rapes, robberies and murders. I gave them advice and taught them survival skills. How to operate a buddy system and take down number plates and to warn each other about suspicious clients.

I met Ruiz for the first time that night. He came to Langton Hall with a photograph of an unidentified murder victim, hoping one of the women at the meeting might recognise her.

How does any of this relate to Kate? In the same breath, I picture a pale-skinned girl in the front row, whose buckteeth pushed out her top lip creating an over-bite. She stood out. I don't know why. Her freckles. Her age. Her teeth. She looked nervous. Lost. New to the game.

'You don't often see something like that,' says Ruiz. 'A prostitute becoming a copper. A detective sergeant, no less.

The Met won't take recruits with a criminal record and they certainly don't fast-track them into major crimes.'

I think back to the French bistro when I asked Kate if we'd met before. She was adamant. Angry. Now I understand her secrecy and vulnerability. She turned her life around, getting recruited and promoted, overcoming the sexism and boys' club mentality of a police force that has been slow to change.

'How do I fix what I've done?'

'Stay out of it,' says Ruiz.

'It was my mistake.'

'No, it was hers.'

The engine rumbles. Gears engage automatically.

I want to argue, but I have no defence. I have damaged someone who tried to help me. Anger, self-pity and frustration jostle for ascendancy, until a newer sharper feeling overwhelms me – utter despair.

Day Nineteen

50

My mother has arranged for a Mass to be said for my father. More than a hundred people have showed up at St James's Church in Sussex Gardens – a mixture of family, friends, former patients, neighbours and ex-colleagues. Lucy and Patricia have come with their husbands and children. Rebecca is alone. She might have a boyfriend or partner in Geneva, but she doesn't reveal much about herself. Charlie and Emma sit alongside my mother, passing her tissues as needed. I stoop beneath the brim of her black hat to kiss her cheek, her skin disconcertingly cool.

I recognise Samuel Rhodes and some of the other board members, as well as hospital staff, including the lovely Jamaican nurse who looked after Dad in the ICU. Rosie and Kenneth Passage arrive late, delaying the start while the wheelchair is manoeuvred into place. Kenneth makes a point of talking to Mum and each of my sisters as well as our children. That's one of the things I remember about him – his memory for birthdays, christenings, graduations and anniversaries. I once asked him how he kept track of all those dates. He confessed to being pedantic and having 'damn good secretaries'.

The priest interrupts, wanting to begin. He must have an early train to catch because he rifles through the introductory rites, barely waiting for people to settle.

'Lord, grant your healing grace to all who are sick, injured or disabled, that they may be made whole,' he says.

The congregation replies, 'Lord, have mercy.'

'We ask that you look after William O'Loughlin, a much-loved father, husband and friend. Give him strength. Help him heal.'

'Christ, have mercy.'

Hymns are sung, readings read and the Eucharist is blessed. I notice Ruiz sitting near the back, with his head bowed.

'Are you praying?' I ask, slipping on to the seat next to him.

He doesn't open his eyes. 'If I wanted to talk to a bearded man with delusions of grandeur, I'd ask my barista how his band is doing.'

He produces an envelope from his inner pocket. Inside is a newspaper clipping with the headline:

WOMAN IMPALED WEMBLEY

Fire crews used specialist cutting equipment to free a woman impaled on a railing fence after falling from a roof in Talbot Road.

Neighbours were alerted by the woman's screams late on Sunday evening and found her hanging from the fence on a spike that had entered her lower back and exited through the left side of her abdomen.

Cutting equipment was used to slice through the railing and paramedics transported the woman, 22, to Northwick Park Hospital where she underwent emergency surgery.

'She checked herself out of hospital three days ago,' says Ruiz. 'I talked to a mate in the northern crime squad. The house is a suspected drug den that's been raided twice in the past six months.'

'Did she give a statement?'

'Claimed she fell off the roof trying to rescue her cat. The neighbours reported seeing two men running from the scene. No descriptions.'

'Ewan and Micah.'

'I checked the times. There's no way they were in Chiswick at midnight on that Sunday.'

A door opens behind us. DI Macdermid slips inside, holding his hat in both hands. He moves along the side of the church, not bothering to take a seat. The Mass is ending and the priest leads a procession out the main entrance. He takes up a post near the doors, shaking hands and offering words of comfort like an unctuous undertaker. My mother gets extra support and is told that God has my father's back, as though they're in a foxhole together, under fire.

Macdermid waits until Mum is with Lucy before approaching.

'Mrs O'Loughlin, I'm sorry to interrupt. I wanted to let

you know that we've arrested someone for the attack on your husband.'

'You mean Ewan?'

'No, ma'am. A man called Ray D'Marco.'

Mum looks at Lucy and then at me. 'Do we know him? Why would he hurt William?'

'The medical negligence case,' I say. 'The newborn baby.'

'But that was years ago.'

'We believe D'Marco was hired to kill your husband,' says Macdermid.

'By whom?' I ask.

'I'm not at liberty to say.'

Mum seems lost. I know how she feels.

'Does that mean you're looking for someone else?' I ask.

'The investigation is ongoing. That's all I can tell you. I'm sorry.'

Macdermid dons his hat and turns on his heel, pushing past me. His shoes echo on the flagstone path as he walks to a waiting police car. Kate Hawthorn isn't waiting. I feel a pang of guilt.

Ruiz joins me. 'What did he want?'

'They've charged D'Marco.'

'Shit! I didn't see that coming.'

I'm already moving away from the church, walking towards Ruiz's car.

'Where are we going?' he asks.

A road trip.'

'Anywhere nice?'

'Wales.'

51

We take the M40 out of London, heading west to the outskirts of Birmingham before veering north through Staffordshire and Cheshire. For the first few hours, Ruiz drives hunched over as if competing with every other vehicle on the road, but once we're off the motorway, he relaxes, draping his wrist over the wheel and humming along to Sinatra on the stereo.

I stare out the window, watching farmland and forest wash past in a blur of brown and green. We pass through Stoke-on-Trent and Wrexham and dozens of small villages that blend into the landscape. None of this makes sense. Why would Ray D'Marco jeopardise Bethany's welfare? My father had been paying him £40,000 every year – surely that should have guaranteed his safety?

'What are you thinking?' asks Ruiz.

'D'Marco said something to me at the hospital. When I

accused him of attacking my father, he told me, "If I wanted him dead, he'd be dead."'

'Maybe he botched the job on purpose.'

'No. Whoever attacked my father didn't hold back. They thought they'd killed him. And why leave that note inside the door: *I can't do it. Find someone else.*'

'He had second thoughts, but went through with it anyway.'

We're deep in the countryside, lurching down narrow lanes between hedges and rolling fields, dotted with hay wheels and sheep that look like balls of wool blown on to green baize.

At the farmhouse, I find a letterbox stuffed with mail and leaves blown up against the steps.

'Mind your head,' I tell Ruiz, as I duck under the door frame. The kitchen ceiling is criss-crossed by beams that are bowed with age and painted black against the whitewashed spaces in between.

'This place was made for Hobbits,' says Ruiz.

'I thought you grew up on a farm.'

'I was shorter back then.'

Going through the house, I draw back curtains and throw open windows, airing out the rooms. Plants need watering and fruit flies are hovering around the bowl.

My father's study is at the back of the house with a view over a meadow. An antique desk dominates the room, along with his collection of classical music, which fills most of the shelves and is arranged alphabetically. The old-style turntable rests on a low table with twin speakers that are big enough to fill the fireplace.

'What are we looking for?' asks Ruiz.

'Financial records. Minutes of board meetings. Bank statements. Correspondence. Anything dating from eight years ago.'

Taking a seat behind the desk, I press the keyboard. The screen lights up and requests a password. I try the obvious ones – birthdays, middle names, pets and grandchildren. Nothing.

Leaning back in the swivel chair, I look around the room, aware that my father is not the sort of man to respect the vulnerabilities of personal computers. His desk blotter is scrawled with doodles and calculations. Lifting one corner, I find a Post-it note with a handwritten name: *meddyg*. It's the Welsh word for doctor.

When I type it into the password field, the screen unlocks and I'm looking at a list of his most recent documents. There are thank you notes, RSVPs and appointments; ideas for a speech, agenda items and a complaint letter to the local council. Scanning the list, I find the minutes of a board meeting of the O'Loughlin Foundation on Monday, 8 February 2010. The meeting began at 1.30 p.m. and ended at 3.24 p.m. My father ran proceedings. Those present were David Passage, Peter Woodville (the previous accountant), Eric Sanderson (a long-time friend of my father's) and Daniel Fraser, a medical research scientist. Apologies were offered by Kenneth Passage and my sister Lucy.

The Foundation had sold a property in Denmark Street, London, realising £12 million. The decision to sell had been unanimous and a range of possible investments were agreed, including Faraday Financial Management. The company's glossy prospectus was included in the minutes. The board signed off on a strategy and within a week of the sale being completed, £9 million was sent to the British Virgin Islands to an account in the name of Faraday Fiscal Management.

Ruiz had been reading over my shoulder. 'Who did the bank transfer?'

'My father.'

Continuing through the recent documents, I find dividend statements and investment reports – two every year – provided by the fake company. I'm surprised at the level of detail, which includes sector allocations, breakdowns by country, top exposures and fund returns after fees. These are fictions that make the missing funds seem more like an elaborate hoax than a brazen robbery.

I open my father's email account and skim his messages, most of them dull beyond reckoning. Once more I begin to despair that unless he wakes up we'll never find the answers.

He was corresponding with Samuel Rhodes about the forensic audit. They'd arranged to meet on Monday.

Rhodes wrote: *I will insist that any meeting is recorded. I hope you understand that this doesn't mean I disbelieve you, or have lost trust in your chairmanship. I simply wish to protect myself.*

My father replied: *I'm not asking you to lie, or alter your report. I simply want more time to investigate what happened. Ultimately, this is my responsibility.*

The two men agreed a time and place. On the day in question, Samuel sent my father a message: *Where are you,*

William? It's after ten. Are you running late? Twenty minutes later he tried again: *I have another appointment at 11 a.m. I hope everything is OK.*

'There are more boxes in the attic,' I tell Ruiz. 'You keep reading the messages. We'll compare notes later.'

As I climb to the first landing, I hear the tell-tale creak of a floorboard. I pause and step on it again. As teenagers we grew accustomed to that sound. Late home from the village pub, the step would creak and Dad would say, 'Goodnight, Lucy', or 'Goodnight, Patricia', or 'Goodnight, Joseph.'

'Goodnight, Daddy,' we'd reply.

Boyfriends or girlfriends weren't allowed upstairs and sex before marriage was definitely not condoned. Lucy was nineteen and engaged to Eric when she discovered how to beat the system. One Saturday night they came home from the pub and didn't want to sleep in separate beds. The step creaked just the once.

'Goodnight, Lucy,' said Dad.

'Goodnight, Daddy,' she replied, as Eric carried her in his arms. Problem solved.

The girls were on the first floor, while I slept in an attic room beneath roof beams and sloping slate roof. Now a storeroom, I squeeze past tea chests and cardboard boxes to find my single bed, tucked into the corner. Sitting on the mattress, I pull boxes closer, looking for financial records or bank statements. Instead I find old school books, award certificates and debating trophies – souvenirs of my childhood.

I come across a programme for the Brighton College

musical in 1976. I played Bottom in *A Midsummer Night's Dream,* a performance made more memorable because I kissed Cassie Egan at the cast party and tasted champagne for the first time. A photograph flutters from inside. It shows a curtain call, taken from the wings. The principal cast are holding hands and bowing to the audience, who are on their feet, applauding wildly. In the front row, Dad has his hands above his head, clapping and grinning. Why don't I remember him being there?

Closing the last box, I lie on the bed like a child sent to my room. I see at a collection of dog-eared Polaroids stuck to the ceiling; snapshots from my teenage years.

Hours later, my eyes open. It's dark outside. Why didn't Ruiz wake me? I hear pots and pans downstairs; and the burble of a TV.

'Are you hungry?' he asks. 'I found some eggs.'

'I fell asleep.'

'You needed it.'

He divides the omelette in two and slides it on to twin plates. We eat and talk, half-listening to headlines on the evening news. Afterwards, he washes the dishes and I dry. I notice an old-fashioned answering machine in the corner, behind a potted plant that needs watering. The message light is flashing full.

Pressing play, I listen to friends and neighbours sending get well wishes, or wanting news of Dad. The messages go backwards in time getting closer to the attack. The next voice is one I recognise.

'Are you there, William? Pick up the phone. I've just been told about the audit. I don't think we should involve the police – not

until the board has been consulted. This sort of thing could do terrible
damage to the Foundation . . . to all of us. Please call me . . .'

My heart sinks. I glance at Ruiz.

'What's wrong?' he asks.

'David Passage told me he had no idea money had gone
missing from the Foundation.'

'His pants are on fire.'

'Let's go tip a bucket on him.'

52

The two-storey house is lit up from every window and burning Tiki torches are spaced along the front path to a marquee that juts into the garden. A catering truck has parked in the driveway with its doors open and boxes of dinnerware and glasses are stacked inside.

I pass through an arch of fairy lights and ring the doorbell. A breathless child answers. I recognise her from my previous visit.

'Coats go in the dining room. Birthday presents on the table,' she says, indicating in each direction. A silver balloon bounces on the end of her wrist. 'Oh, you don't have a present.'

'I'd like to speak to your daddy.'

Rosie Passage appears behind her. She's wearing a sparkling dress and a miniature top hat at a jaunty angle.

'Joseph! I didn't know you were coming.'

'I need to see David.'

'Is it William? Has he woken? Come inside.'

'No. I'd rather stay out here.'

She frowns. 'I hope you're not going to ruin Maddie's party.'

As if on cue, Maddie appears. She's slightly tipsy and wearing a cocktail dress with an oversized badge announcing: *40 and Fabulous*.

'You came! How wonderful!'

The same conversation is repeated, but I don't offer an explanation. Soon I'm waiting alone on the steps, listening to the music and laughter. Ruiz is standing in the shadows on the far side of the road.

David emerges, closing the door behind him. He's dressed like he's having drinks at a yacht club, in a navy blazer and open-neck shirt.

'This had better be good.'

'You lied to me about seeing the forensic audit. You knew about the missing money.'

'Is that why you're here?'

'Answer the question and I'll leave.'

'Christ, Joe, relax. Come in. Have a drink.'

'I'm serious.'

David is playing for time, trying to formulate a response. First, he'll bluster. Then he'll accuse, or become aggressive.

'I don't know what you're talking about,' he says.

'I heard the message you left for William.'

'Is that all? I suspected something. I didn't know the details.'

'That's a lie.'

His face grows hard. 'I'm not going to be insulted or interrogated by you – not in my own home. You want to see me – make an appointment.'

He's turning away, reaching for the door.

'How long have you been fucking Olivia Blackmore?'

David's head snaps around. His eyes wide. He glances at the house to make sure nobody has heard me. Then he grabs my arm and drags me further away from the house.

'Are you fucking insane,' he mutters, trying to compose himself. 'Whatever you've heard is wrong.'

'Do you drive a blue BMW?'

'What difference does that make?'

'According to a neighbour, you're a regular visitor at Olivia's house.'

'Don't drag me into this.'

'Oh, you're in way over your head. Sleeping with the wife of the victim . . . representing her. That makes you a suspect.'

'Don't be ridiculous.'

'Are they billable hours?'

'What?'

'When you fuck her?'

David lunges at me, grabbing my shirt. Buttons pop and disappear into the turf. I have him by the lapels of his blazer and he tries to put me in a headlock. We push and pull, as though unsure of what to do next. Almost as quickly the anger dissipates as we both realise how ridiculous we must look, grown men wrestling like schoolboys, both lacking the conviction to throw a punch.

Ruiz appears, ready to intervene. I tell him it's OK and he retreats as far as the front gate. David wipes his hands on his torn shirtfront and sits on the low brick wall.

'I know what you think, Joe, but I wouldn't do anything to hurt William.'

'Were you with Olivia on the night William was attacked?'

'We met after the theatre. Olivia was worried about Ewan. She wanted my advice.'

'You had time to get to Chiswick.'

'Don't be ridiculous.'

'The evening that Ewan broke into my flat, I went to see Olivia, demanding answers. It was you who was skulking upstairs.'

'I don't skulk.'

'Hiding in a woman's house after midnight – I'd call that skulking.'

David shakes his head, looking exasperated. 'Everything I've done has been to protect William and the Foundation.'

'By covering up a crime.'

David sighs tiredly. 'What are you looking for, Joe? Vengeance? Justice? You want to believe that William is innocent, but I think he stole that money. He made the pitch. He organised the transfer—'

'He wouldn't steal from his own trust.'

'He was facing bankruptcy.'

'Not good enough.'

'Why can't his motives be base and avaricious? William's not a saint. He's not even very nice.'

'Someone tried to kill him.'

'Yes. Maybe he ripped off some middleman or got into

bed with gangsters. None of us are perfect, Joe, but if it makes you feel any better, I think he planned to pay the money back.'

'How?'

'He came to see me a few weeks before the attack and asked about his life insurance policies. He made some crack about being worth more dead than alive. I told him not to be so morbid and he said: "Life is only precious because it ends."'

'Are you saying he knew he was in danger?'

'I don't know – maybe he was joking – but he did ask me about increasing his insurance coverage. I told him it wasn't worth the added premiums. He's eighty years old.'

David turns at the sound of his name. Maddie is standing on the porch. 'Will you be long?' she asks. 'They want to cut the cake.'

'I'm coming now.'

David glances back at me. 'Are you going to the police with this?'

'I have no choice.'

He exhales and sighs. 'My mother did warn me.'

'Warn you about what?'

'That your family would always bring us trouble.'

I give him a puzzled look.

'Ask William, if he ever wakes up.'

David turns and walks back to the house. Moments later, I hear champagne corks popping and people singing 'Happy Birthday'. The cheers grow fainter as I walk away. Ruiz is standing beneath a streetlamp, sucking on a boiled sweet.

'What did he say?'

'He knew about the audit, but swears he was trying to protect the Foundation.'

'Do you believe him?'

I stop suddenly, as though my feet have locked in place. Ruiz is used to my sudden pauses, but this has nothing to do with Parkinson's.

'My father asked about his life insurance two weeks before he was attacked.'

'You think he knew?'

'I don't know, but Ray D'Marco left him a note saying: *I can't do it, find someone else.* What does that sound like?'

'A job?'

'Exactly.'

Day Twenty

53

The visitors' centre at Wormwood Scrubs is housed in a set of temporary buildings that look incongruous beside the Victorian prison façade of red-brown brick, Portland stone and octagonal towers.

I step through a metal detector and let a drug dog sniff at my shoes and pockets. Most of the other visitors are women. Wives and girlfriends, some with children tugging at their hands, already bored. After filling out a form and proving my identity, I wait for my application to be approved or denied. Numbers are limited and I have no appointment, which means waiting until everyone else has gone in before they confirm that I have a place. In the meantime, I study the list of prohibited items for visitors: no metal hair accessories, no pins, no steel-capped shoes, no sunglasses, no heavy metal jewellery, no low-cut tops, no miniskirts or hot pants or sheer blouses.

Eventually, I'm given a number and get herded through several checkpoints, where the guards seem to enjoy issuing orders and confiscating cash. Visitors are allowed to carry a maximum of twenty pounds – coins only – for the dispensing machines.

Entering a long glass-walled room, I put my docket into the letterbox at the far end and take a designated seat, while Ray D'Marco is brought from his cell. He arrives through a different door, looking past me, as though hoping I might have brought someone else. When he realises I'm alone, his shoulders slump beneath prison overalls that look two sizes too large.

'What do you want?' he asks, challenging me with his stare.

'Help.'

'Why should I help you?'

'I didn't put you in here.'

D'Marco drops his gaze to the scarred wooden table where his clenched fists are braced apart.

'Where's Bethany?'

'She's in a residential care home.'

'Is she eating?'

'They wouldn't tell me.'

He falls silent, pinching the skin on his forearm where a tattoo has faded into a blue-black Rorschach blot. A part of me feels sorry for him. Another part sees an ex-soldier with a hair-trigger temper and a life-long loathing for my father.

'I was in prison when my parents died,' he says. 'The council put Bethany in a care home. Nobody could get her to eat. She lost sixty pounds and got sick. I pleaded with them to let me talk to her. Finally they agreed and I would call Bethany twice a day and make her eat while I was on the phone, telling her I was coming home soon.'

'How long were you in prison?'

'Served a year.'

'I can try to talk to her carers,' I say.

D'Marco nods mutely and in that moment I get a glimpse of the child he must have been — the boy who grew up in the shadow of a severely disabled sister, never at the centre of his parents' thoughts. There were no family holidays, or trips to the seaside, or picnics by the river. When Bethany did go out in public she drew stares and pity from adults and children. Was he jealous of Bethany, or resentful that his freedom was restricted? Did he rebel? Did he bully other children who were weaker — the fat kids and asthmatics and the effeminate — because it gave him a sense of control that he had nowhere else? He struggled academically; fell into truancy and petty crime, until the military saved him — at least for a while.

'Why were you in prison?' I ask.

'I tried to kill my commanding officer,' he says bluntly.

'Why?'

'Do you own a dog?'

'I used to.'

'I had one for a while. She wasn't any particular breed; a mongrel I guess, all skin and bone and sinew. I found her scavenging through the bins at the camp in Helmand —

399

that's in Afghanistan. She followed me back to my tent and the next morning she was still there, waiting for me. I went to the latrine and the mess. She followed. It's not like I fed her or patted her or encouraged her at all. She chose me, not the other way around. Pretty soon she'd become part of the troop. I started training her to sniff out IEDs. She was good, a quick learner. She could go places that we couldn't because of her size and her weight, but the Ruperts weren't happy.'

'Who?'

'Our CO kept banging on about rabies and fleas, threatening to get rid of her, but like I said, I didn't choose her, she chose me. There were five of us in the bomb disposal unit. Nobody told us about the sheer number of IEDs we'd have to disarm or destroy. The bombs were the easy bit. The Taliban had snipers who'd wait for us to arrive, picking us off as we crawled forward. Either that or they'd watch us and work out to how to plant the bombs differently next time.

'I did fifteen one day. It was so hot that I couldn't wear a bomb suit and see through the sweat. I came back to camp, exhausted and went looking for my dog, but I couldn't find her anywhere. One of the kitchen staff told me what had happened. The CO had put a bullet through her head and tossed her on the rubbish tip.' D'Marco takes a shuddering breath. I can smell the sweat coming off him, as well as something metallic and faintly medicinal.

'You lost your temper,' I say.

'I wanted to kill him.'

'You were lucky you failed.'

'He was luckier.'

'Have you ever met my father?' I ask.

D'Marco hesitates. 'No.'

'But you've spoken to him.'

He nods.

'Did he tell you he had a tumour?'

'He said he was dying.'

'When?'

Tilting back his chair, D'Marco stares at the strip lights along the ceiling. 'I told the police what happened. All I did was incriminate myself.'

'Tell me.'

He studies my face. 'On one condition.'

'What's that?'

'If something happens to me – will you promise to look after Bethany?'

I nod.

'I have your word?'

'Yes.'

D'Marco bites at his thumbnail. 'Your old man told me he had six months to live and didn't want the pain. He called it an act of mercy, which made me laugh. Since when did he deserve mercy?'

'What did he want you to do?'

'Isn't it obvious?'

'Start at the beginning. Tell me exactly what happened.'

'I had a phone call in early October.'

'From my father?'

D'Marco nods. 'I'd never spoken to him before. He'd never acknowledged my existence, but suddenly he wanted to meet. He named the time and place – a café below the escalators at Paddington station. Eleven o'clock. I waited. He didn't show. I was about to leave when a courier turned up and gave me a padded envelope. Inside was a mobile phone. Cheap. Disposable. I turned it on. The phone rang. Your father apologised and said that we shouldn't be seen together. He said he'd explain everything, but first I had to collect a bag from the left luggage room. I told him I wasn't going to play his games, but he said if I walked away, Bethany would get nothing else. No cheques. No money . . .'

D'Marco lowers his voice to a rasping whisper. 'I picked up the bag. Inside was twenty grand in cash and a set of keys. He rang me again. "The money is yours," he said, "but I want something in return." That's when he told me he was dying. "I've made provisions for Bethany," he said. "She'll be looked after by the insurance money, but only if you do this for me.'

My mouth has gone dry. 'Do what?'

'Do I have to spell it out? He wanted to die. I said he was crazy and hung up. He rang back. He apologised about Bethany and what he did to my parents; how he lied to the judge and avoided the blame. He said he wanted to make amends and do the right thing.

'"You've made amends," I said. "Just keep sending the cheques."

'"You don't understand – I'm dying."

'"I'm not a killer," I told him.

'"Neither am I," he said, "but we often meet our fate on the road we take to avoid it."'

That's my father's line.

'He used that phrase?'

'Yes.'

'You agreed to do it?'

'No. I hung up again, but he kept ringing back. He said, "You can decide where and how. I don't want to know, just make it quick and painless." He gave me two addresses – one in Chiswick, one in Wales – along with the keys.'

'You took his money.'

'Yes, but I didn't do it.' D'Marco's face flexes. 'OK, for a while I considered the possibility, but then I realised what would happen if I got caught. I tried to call him on the mobile, but he didn't answer. I left messages. I went to his lawyer's office and to the house in Chiswick.'

'Did you see him that night?'

'No.'

'You rang the doorbell.'

'Yes. I had the money with me. I was going to give it back. Nobody answered.'

'You're lying.'

'I don't give a shit what you think.'

His voice is raised. Heads turn. A guard steps closer.

I back down, softening my tone, studying him more closely.

'Why didn't you tell the police any of this?' I ask.

'I did, but my DNA is on that note. I was hired to kill him and now he's in a coma. Makes no difference what I say.'

'Why risk going to the hospital?'

'I heard what happened. I thought he must have hired

someone else. Either that or he threw himself down the stairs.'

'You told him you were sorry.'

'I am. He wanted to die and somebody fucked it up. I also thought he had a brain tumour. Nobody lies about something like that.'

'He did.'

D'Marco shrugs, unable to explain.

A buzzer sounds. Visiting hours are over. I'm not ready to leave. There are too many details that don't make sense. Burner phones. Secret meetings. Notes left on doormats.

D'Marco is already on his feet, joining the line of prisoners being escorted back to their cells.

I call out to him. 'Your dog . . . in Afghanistan . . . did she have a name?'

'Lucky.'

Charlie is sitting on the window seat, gazing down at the street. She takes my overcoat and hangs it behind the door. Then she holds both my hands, facing the palms down, watching to see if my left hand is shaking.

'Where were you?' she asks.

'At the hospital. Did something happen?'

I notice family photo albums lying open on the coffee table.

'I took them out,' explains Charlie. 'I thought Emma might like . . .' She pauses and starts again. 'She wouldn't look at the photographs of Mummy. She told me to burn them.'

'It's how she copes.'

'That's denying, not coping.'

I settle into an armchair. Charlie prefers the floor, where she sits with her legs drawn up to her chest and her pale arms clasped around her shins.

'Everybody is different when it comes to grief,' I say. 'For some people, memories are like snapshots. You can line them up in a different order, but to make another story. Emma is trying to arrange those pieces into something she can live with.'

'How long will it take?'

'I don't know. The only real cure for sorrow is motion – we have to keep moving forward.'

Charlie tilts her head. 'Are you moving forward?'

'I'm trying.'

'The detective who came around – the one with braces – she seemed nice.'

'Yes.'

'Are you going to see her again?'

'I don't think so.'

'Why not?'

'I messed up.'

Charlie frowns and rests her head on my knee. 'You'll work it out. You always do.'

I appreciate her vote of confidence, but I don't feel very clever or wise.

'When are you going back to Oxford?' I ask.

'I thought I might defer for a semester. Stay home. Help you with Emma.'

'She's not your responsibility.'

'She's my sister.'

405

'And you're not her keeper.'

Charlie has marshalled her arguments, but I stop her.

'We're fine. Go back to Oxford.'

'What about Granddad?'

'There's nothing you can do.'

Charlie nods and yawns. 'I'll wait until Andie gets back from Australia.'

She kisses me goodnight and I make my way along the hallway, stopping at Emma's room. She's sleeping with one hand tucked under her pillow and the other beneath her chin. I straighten her duvet. Emma murmurs and settles.

Moving soft toys, I sit for a moment in an armchair by the window where I can watch her sleeping. Exhaustion washes over me. Hours later, I wake in the same chair. Stiff. Cold. Groggy. Emma's bed is empty. Gripped by panic, I stumble through the flat, checking the doors and windows. Peering into Charlie's bedroom, I expect to see both girls in the bed, but Charlie is alone.

Going back to Emma's room, I search under her bed and open her wardrobe. I almost miss seeing her beneath the hanging dresses and coats. She is lying on her side, curled up among the shoes, clutching her 'blankie' to her chest.

'Emma . . . Wake up.'

She stirs. I pull her up, carrying her back to her bed, where I pull the duvet over her, rubbing her sides to get her warm. I look at her green-grey eyes, her lashes, her eyebrows. She looks right back at me.

'Did you have a nightmare?'

'I saw him.'

'Who?'
'The Raggedy Man.'
'You know he's not real.'
'Yes.'
'Then why are you shaking?'
'Somebody always dies when I see him.'

Day Twenty-One

54

Sunday morning and I'm ankle deep in mud beside a rugby field, recalling the sporting humiliations of my childhood. I played Second XV for the school; exiled to the wing where I was more in danger of hypothermia than making a tackle or handling the ball.

DI Macdermid is eating a sausage and onion roll beside a food caravan with a shuttered roof. His son's team are playing next. Fifteen boys in pristine jumpers are jogging back and forth along the sideline, tossing a ball to one another. Father and son are both lumpy and squat, but Macdermid has less hair and more lumps.

'How did you find me?' he asks, masticating food.

'I spoke to your mother.'

'Which means you have my home number. I should have Ruiz arrested.'

'He's a good man.'

'Who should take up golf.'

'Then we'd all be in trouble.'

I put my hands deep in my pockets, trying to warm my fingers. My overcoat flaps against my knees.

'I'm not convinced that my father arranged his own death.'

'Make an appointment, Professor. It's my day off.'

'He didn't have a brain tumour.'

'No, he had money problems – nine million of them. I know about the audit. Samuel Rhodes gave us a statement.'

'There's no evidence my father stole that money.'

'He signed the documents. He organised the transfer.'

'He could have been duped.'

'In which case, he should have gone straight to the police. Instead he doctored up dividend statements and kept it hidden.' Macdermid bins his half-eaten roll and wipes his hands on his scarf. 'Families,' he says, blowing out a derisory breath. 'Your father must have known this day was coming. That audit report was like pulling a pin on a grenade. He tried to put the pin back in, but couldn't, so he threw himself on top of it.'

'I don't believe that.'

'Which bit? That he'd manufacture a tornado to blow out a match; or that he'd keep a secret wife for nineteen years? Look at it from your father's point of view: if he succeeded, the investigation would have fizzled out. The insurance companies would have paid out. The Foundation is secure; his wives are looked after; his reputation is dented, but his legacy survives. Everybody wins, relatively speaking.'

'Except he'd be dead.'

'OK, that's one downside.'

A referee blows his whistle. The ball is placed and kicked. Forwards collide in the first ruck, their breaths condensing to form a cloud. Macdermid moves along the sideline, following the play. I keep pace.

'What happened to the nine million pounds?' I ask.

The detective grunts ambivalently. 'Who knows? I think he spent it on keeping his two families; or maybe he gave it away to his children. That place of yours must have cost a pretty penny.'

'I didn't need his money.'

Macdermid smiles at my reaction.

'You're a strange one, Professor. First you blamed Olivia Blackmore, then Ewan, then Micah Beauchamp. I had a call from David Passage this morning saying you crashed his wife's birthday party and threatened him.'

'He's having an affair with Olivia Blackmore.'

Macdermid laughs. 'You're like a piñata – whack you hard enough and everything spills out.'

'I'm being serious.'

The detective sighs tiredly. 'Let me lay it out for you, Professor. Your mother and Mrs Blackmore both provided statements saying your father had grown increasingly moody, depressed and anxious in recent weeks. Twelve days before he was attacked, he purchased two burner phones from a shop in Hammersmith. We found the shop receipt in his bedside table in Chiswick. Both of those phones were turned on and used at Paddington station on 20 October when he called Ray D'Marco and took out a contract on his own life. We've triangulated the signals and can place each mobile within the vicinity of a café. We also know your father caught a train from Wales that day and can put him at Paddington at the relevant time.

'Subsequently, we found twenty thousand in cash at D'Marco's house, which he collected from a luggage locker at Paddington station. We have also confirmed that he took at least one trip to Wales and drove past the house in Chiswick, scoping out both locations.'

'He denies going ahead with the plan.'

'He would, wouldn't he?'

'Why leave a note?'

'It was a mistake.'

'He's not that stupid.'

'He was court-martialled for attacking his commanding officer in front of a dozen witnesses.'

Macdermid makes it seem so obvious. My father organised a hit on his own life to conceal the theft of nine million pounds and to avoid the consequences. Insurance would look after his two 'wives' and at least partially repay the medical foundation.

Arranged in the right order, the facts fit this story almost perfectly. Almost. Why did D'Marco risk going to the hospital and drawing attention to himself? Why would he jeopardise Bethany's future? Yes, he's angry at historic slights and prey to secret hungers, but he loves his sister.

If I've learned anything over my career it's that human behaviour is only predictable up to a point. Two hundred years of empirical data has set up norms and revealed patterns, but not every act can be plotted on a bell curve or listed on a table. People make mistakes and do stupid things. They fuck up in big and small ways.

How did my father get away with taking nine million pounds? Trust explains most things. Trust is the oil that greases the machine of banking and investment. Nobody questions someone like William O'Loughlin. He's like the pilot who flies us on holiday, or the engineer who services the aircraft. We accept. We trust.

Macdermid's son has bulldozed his way into a ruck, mud already streaking his face. The whistle blows. A penalty.

'Oh, come on! It's not netball!' yells the detective, drawing a glare from the referee.

'What about DS Hawthorn?' I ask.

'They'll bust her back to uniform.'

'That's not fair.'

'If life were fair I'd arrest my wife's divorce lawyer and I wouldn't be living with my mother.'

On the field the fly-half has lined up a penalty kick. He steps back, crouches and holds his hands together as if praying. Looking at the posts, he rocks forward, takes four steps and launches the ball, watching it curl between the posts. Macdermid curses under his breath.

Turning away, I head past the food caravan and the crowds, finding Ruiz in the warmth of his car.

'So that's it,' he says, staring out the windscreen.

'I expected more of him.'

'Macdermid?'

'My father.'

'All parents disappoint us eventually.'

I know he's right. We start out idolising our parents,

loving them unconditionally, believing them to be infallible, until one day we catch them lying, or cheating, or showing their prejudices; and our gods plummet to earth.

For the past three weeks – ever since the assault – I've been trying to rebuild a relationship with my father by piecing together memories or stories related by others, but he will never be as bright and shiny again. At the same time, I think I'm closer to him now because his flaws make him more human and he's easier to like, if not to love.

As we near St Mary's Hospital I ask Ruiz to pull over.

'We're almost there,' he says.

'I want to walk.'

He drops me on the next corner and I cross the road to Paddington station and enter the cathedral-like concourse below the famous arched roof.

I take a seat in the café below the escalators and watch the tide of people being sucked to and from the underground.

Someone has spilled a scoop of ice cream, which has melted into a sticky puddle. If commuters see it early enough, they step around the mess. Others track it on their shoes or their walking frames or the wheels of their luggage, spreading the stain.

I try to picture my father arriving here to set up his own death. In the weeks beforehand, he had checked on his life insurance and rewritten his will. Nearer the time, he bought two 'burner' phones, withdrew twenty thousand pounds and arranged to meet Ray D'Marco at a busy railway station, amid hundreds of people with hundreds of phones. He chose somewhere public where he could disappear quickly

413

into the crowd. He never intended to meet D'Marco in person. Perhaps he feared that a physical connection would make it harder for someone to carry out the contract.

I look for the CCTV cameras. They are spaced apart, set high above the concourse. Where was he standing? At the top of the escalators? On the mezzanine floor? Dad didn't like mobile phones. He couldn't see the point of them. People without phones are careful not to be late, he said.

Not everything makes sense to me now. I still don't know what happened to the Foundation's money, but I'm closer to understanding why my father finished up in hospital.

Getting to my feet, I weave between shoulders and jostle down escalators, anonymous in the crowd. I glance at my reflection, fascinated and frightened by the stooped man I see in the café window. In that instant, an uneasiness washes over me and I see a different version of the truth.

55

'You're selling the house.'

Olivia turns at the sound of my voice. She's balancing a handbag on her raised knee, searching the dark interior for her keys. She looks past me at the 'For Sale' sign staked in the garden.

'I can't afford to keep this place.'

'What about the tennis school?'

'It's been losing money for years, but William kept indulging me.' Her keys are found. The door opens. 'Ironic, isn't it? He thought he'd look after everyone by arranging his own death, but he voided the insurance policies. There won't be any payouts, only medical bills and legal fees.' Olivia bends to pick up mail from the doormat.

'I know about you and David Passage,' I say.

Olivia doesn't react. Perhaps she's tired of lying, or there's nothing left to fight over.

'Did my father know?' I ask.

Olivia shakes her head, less certain than before. 'Maybe he suspected. William always said that one day he'd grow too old for me or I'd go looking for someone younger, but he began leaving me long before I ever thought of leaving him.'

'I don't understand.'

'In the past few years William has spent more time in Wales and less time in London. He hated the travelling, he said, but then I began noticing that his favourite things were disappearing – certain books and pictures. I blamed Ewan at first, but it was William. He was making a choice, going back to your mother. You should tell her that. It might bring her some comfort.'

'Let me see his journals.'

'The police took them.'

'Only the latest one. I'm interested in eight years ago, when the money went missing.'

Olivia hesitates, as though trying to decide. She steps back and lets me enter the house. I walk into the hallway, glancing at the bottom of the stairs. She has placed a patterned rug on the stained floorboards.

I follow her into the sitting room where she unlocks a bureau and pulls back the concertina doors, revealing two shelves of books arranged with their spines facing out. My father wrote in Moleskine-bound journals, dated on each page. He recorded his life not just in words, but mementos, theatre tickets, postcards and bookmarks.

'Each one covers a six-month period,' Olivia explains. 'Some days he only wrote a few paragraphs. Other days, he'd write pages.'

'I'm looking for early 2010.'

Olivia is on her knees, searching through the journals. She runs her finger back and forth along the spines.

'It's not here.'

'Did the police take it?'

'No. I have an evidence receipt.'

'And that's the only one missing?'

'I think so.'

I kneel and search through the journals again, just to be sure.

'The police found a shopping receipt in his bedside table for two pay-as-you-go phones. They think he used the phones to secretly communicate with Ray D'Marco.'

Olivia frowns. 'Why keep the receipt if the phones are meant to be secret?'

She's right.

I need to go back to the beginning and retrace my father's steps on the night of the attack. He arrived at Paddington station and caught a taxi. He let himself into the house. Olivia had left a light on in the hallway. I look at the front door. There was no sign of forced entry, or a struggle.

'You said he was wearing slippers,' I say to Olivia.

'He didn't like wearing shoes in the house.'

'Where did he keep them?'

'Upstairs in his wardrobe.'

Dad must have gone upstairs when he got home. Whoever attacked him could have been waiting in the darkness. Either that or he let them inside and they followed him while he changed out of his shoes and hung up his jacket in the bedroom.

Struck from behind on the landing, he tumbled headfirst down the stairs. His attacker followed, hitting him again and again. Each time the weapon fell, blood sprayed across the wall.

My eyes follow him down, imagining his shock and fear; his arms raised, unable to stop the blows. Was my mother outside? Could she have prevented this? I look along the hallway and picture myself scrubbing at the floorboards, the water turning pink. The larger pool of blood lay beneath his head. There were two blood spots closer to the door. Circular. Spaced out. I think of the spilled ice cream at Paddington station and the tracks left behind.

'What about his overnight bag?' I ask.

'It's in the wardrobe.'

'Can I see it?'

Olivia leads me to the bedroom and retrieves an old-fashioned leather doctor's bag that opens out to reveal dozens of compartments. Once it would have been full of medical instruments and bandages, but now it holds an old newspaper, pens, train tickets, a timetable and a manila folder containing the forensic audit prepared by Samuel Rhodes.

Turning the pages, I recognise my father's handwritten notes in the margins. He has underlined certain dates and transactions. A circular tea-stain transects a corner of the page, where he must have rested a cup during the journey. He has circled a name more than once in red pen, pressing so hard the page has almost torn: Dilan Holdings.

My mind jumps across the gap like a spark firing on a plug. When Ruiz tried to trace the money, he came across some of the same names as the audit – shelf companies, foreign banks and law firms. One of them was Dilan Holdings.

Taking out my phone, I do an internet search, looking up the name Dilan Holdings. Scrolling down the screen, I find a reference to a company registered in Cyprus.

'Do you know what the name Dilan means?' I ask.

Olivia shakes her head.

'It's Irish. It means "like a lion".'

56

When I reach the Passage estate, the sky has opened and rain sweeps across the road in waves that turn silver in the high beam. A brass plaque announces Aslan House as I pull through the pillared gates and along an avenue of trees that lead towards the manor.

As I circle the fountain, I see a quad bike is parked at the open doors of the garage, engine running and headlights shining across open ground to where a fire is burning beneath the bare branches of trees that must shade the pond in the summer. I check my phone. I've left Ruiz a message but he hasn't answered. I know what he'll say, 'Call the police,' but Macdermid won't listen to another one of my theories. I'm like the boy who cried wolf once too often.

Lightning flashes on the horizon, creating long shadows that appear and disappear in the flutter of an eyelash. I pull the collar of my overcoat around my neck as I run to the house, mounting the stairs and pressing the doorbell. The rain is so heavy, I don't hear it ringing inside. I hammer my fists on the door. Nobody answers.

Muffled popping sounds emanate from the fire and a grey column of smoke rises above the garage as though fighting against the rain. Retracing my steps, I move over the gravel, still holding my coat over my head, heading towards the fire. Peering around the corner of the building, I see a cloaked figure tipping a box of papers into the flames. I smell accelerant and notice a plastic drum of fuel that glows orange in the firelight.

A second, larger figure emerges from the back of the house, carrying a desktop computer, which is thrown into the flames, sending sparks exploding into the air. The plastic drum is opened. More fuel added. Consumed in a whooshing sound.

The bonfire throws shadows against the trees, making the figures look like participants in a pagan ritual. Kenneth Passage is the smaller one, leaning on a walking stick. That's what gave him away – the bloodstains in the hallway. When someone uses a walking stick, they hold it in the hand closest to their damaged leg. It rocks forward at the same time as their good leg, touching the ground every second stride. That's why the circles of blood in the hallway were spaced so evenly. That was the weapon he used.

More files are feeding the flames. They're getting rid of the evidence. Destroying the past. I reach for my phone. It's not in my pocket. I must have left it in the car.

I hear a voice behind me.

'Joseph. What are you doing out here?' asks Rosie.

My mouth opens as a clap of thunder shakes the air. I glimpse a movement in the corner of my eye. My head turns as something swings towards it and lands with a flash of white pain. My knees buckle. The ground tilts.

Darkness . . .

This is how I wake, curled in an embryonic ball, bound at the wrists with garden twine. I recognise the room, the fireplace, the photographs. A youngest son's medals are on display, along with the flag that once covered his coffin, now folded neatly beneath glass.

Kenneth Passage is seated in an armchair with his eyes closed. His grey hair drips with rain and a puddle has formed on the floorboards beneath his Wellingtons.

Groaning, I manage to roll over, drawing my knees up under my chin and twisting my body into a sitting position with my back against the wall. There is no sound except for the rain.

Kenneth's eyes open and he blinks at me with a watery paleness. He looks different. Fitter. Leaner. Less feeble. A shotgun rests across his lap.

'The police will be here soon,' he says, with an undercurrent of fatal consequence. 'We'll tell them we had an intruder and I armed myself. That's what happens when you break into someone's house.'

'I didn't break in.'

'The evidence will prove otherwise.'

'Where's Rosie?'

'She's upstairs, getting ready for bed.'

I close my eyes, waiting for the nausea to pass. The bindings are so tight, I'm losing feeling in my hands. I flex my fingers, using the pain to help me focus. The details are almost complete. Subconsciously, I seem to have known them for a long time, but the rational part of my brain has taken longer to catch up. Kenneth was a board member of the O'Loughlin Foundation when the nine million pounds went missing. He didn't attend the critical board meeting, but could easily have recommended the investment. When the forensic audit revealed the truth, my father told Samuel Rhodes that he needed legal advice. He phoned Kenneth, not David. They argued about whether to involve the police, but not for the reasons the old lawyer gave me.

Ray D'Marco never met my father face-to-face. They communicated by phone and text message. Kenneth Passage set up the contact. He withdrew the twenty thousand pounds from my father's account. He bought the mobile phones and put the receipt in the bedside drawer. He also took the journal from the cabinet so the original investment decision could never be linked back to him.

'Why?' I ask.

Kenneth's nostrils swell with air. 'I was owed.'

'You're his friend.'

'Don't talk to me about friendship,' he says savagely, his jaw flexing. 'It has to work both ways. A friend forgives. A friend sacrifices. William used to tease me about how my accent had changed since university. "You should be proud of your roots," he'd say in his best Geordie accent. "You're not even a champagne socialist, you're a sell-out, a hypocrite."'

'I'm sure he was joking.'

'Mocking me, you mean. I risked everything for William. He should have been struck off for what he did to Bethany D'Marco, but I changed statements and doctored evidence. I saved his career and it cost me mine. The judge wanted to send me to prison, but they took away my practising certificate instead. It took me twelve years to get it back. From then on I was shunned by other lawyers, barristers and judges. I was a bent solicitor. A pariah.'

'I'm sure my father was grateful.'

'Fuck him! Fuck all of them!' Kenneth spits the words, gripping the shotgun with both hands. His swept-back mane of iron-grey hair is plastered to his scalp.

'William was going to ruin me again. I asked him to stop the audit, but he wouldn't listen. I offered to pay the money back. I pleaded with him. He didn't care. William takes what he wants. Always has. Always will.'

'Are you talking about Rosie?'

His eyes film over. 'She was beautiful. Barely out of school. I loved her from the moment I set eyes on her. I saw her in a pub in Cardiff when I was visiting William. He knew I was smitten, but didn't care. It didn't matter that he was married with four children, or that we were friends. He took her because he could.

'For months I went back and forth to Cardiff every weekend, hoping to see Rosie, but she only had eyes for William. It didn't matter that treated her like a whore, never taking her to parties or restaurants, never buying her flowers or saying he loved her. Yet whenever he came knocking, Rosie would always open her door and her legs for him.'

Kenneth's left knee jiggles up and down, moving the shotgun on his lap. I shift my weight, trying to work my wrists to stretch the twine. 'I begged William to stay away from her. I even threatened to tell Mary. He laughed at me. It was a game to him, a competition, and he had to put me in my place.'

Kenneth doesn't try to hide his bitterness. 'When he grew bored with Rosie, he pushed her into my arms, expecting me to be grateful. I thanked him. Can you imagine that?'

I don't answer.

'Rosie fell pregnant. She swore blind that the baby was mine. I did the honourable thing and married her. David was born, then Francis. Rosie and I were happy. We were a family. I forgave William.'

Kenneth gets to his feet and crosses the room to the mantelpiece. He looks at the medals and the flag that once decorated a coffin. The focus changes in his eyes, as though he's watching the past being replayed on the inner surface of his lids.

'Then he took Francis from us.'

'You can't blame him for that.'

'Why not? If William hadn't suggested to Francis that he join the army, if he hadn't encouraged him, he would never have been in Northern Ireland. He would never have been on that patrol when the bomb went off. He died in Eugene's arms. He cradled my son's head. Do you know his last words?'

I don't answer.

'My brave son was crying for his mother.'

In the silence that follows, a clock sounds in the hallway and rain rattles against the windows.

'Why involve Ray D'Marco?' I ask.

Kenneth's face creases in disappointment. 'I've watched him over the years, seen him growing up, losing his parents, looking after his sister . . . I thought he'd jump at the chance to take his revenge, but he proved to be a coward.'

'He's hardly a coward.'

'He tried to renege on our deal.'

'It was never *his* deal. You pretended to be my father.'

Kenneth waves his hand dismissively. I won't let him get away with that.

'Dad knew you'd stolen the money. He put the pieces together.'

'William told me to pay the money back or he'd call the police. It would have meant losing everything.'

'He offered you a way out.'

'Bankruptcy. Ruin. After the 2008 crash, how do you think William got back on his feet? I guaranteed his loans. I paid his debts. I gave him seed capital.'

'With money you'd stolen!'

'Who cares! I saved him, yet he was going to ruin me all over again.'

Eugene appears. His jacket is dripping and his steel-wool hair is beaded with rain. A Glock pistol is tucked in a holster beneath his left arm.

'Did you burn everything?' Kenneth asks.

He nods.

'Once the fire dies down, I'll call the police. Remember the story. We'd all gone to bed. I heard noises downstairs

426

and thought it might be a burglar. You went to investigate and confronted an intruder. There was a struggle. The shotgun went off.'

'Nobody will believe you,' I say.

Eugene puts a finger to his lips, urging me to be quiet. His face is like a Halloween mask, his lips twisted in a rictus, halfway between a snarl and a smile.

'Why are you doing this?'

Kenneth answers. 'Eugene doesn't say much, but he's very loyal. He loved Francis as much as we did.'

'This isn't about Francis. This is about the money you stole.'

The old lawyer is about to answer when something outside attracts his attention. Through the window he sees a pair of yellow headlights wobbling in the rain and flickering between the trees as a car approaches the house.

Eugene turns off the table lamp, plunging the room into darkness. The headlights swing around the circular drive, casting brightness across the walls of the sitting room, illuminating medals on the mantelpiece and the neatly folded flag.

Ruiz's Mercedes pulls up behind my car. I can just make out his silhouette behind the brightness of the lights. He's holding his mobile, trying to call me.

Kenneth nods to Eugene and gives him the shotgun. 'Don't be afraid to use it.'

'It's the police,' I say.

'Shut up!'

Kenneth takes the Glock from Eugene and points the pistol to the ceiling in a theatrical way, like a magician about to perform a new trick. He slides the barrel back to show me a bullet in the chamber.

Moments later, I hear the front door open and close. I need to warn Ruiz. Kenneth reads my thoughts, pressing the pistol into the side of my head above my left ear.

Outside, Eugene appears behind the Mercedes, keeping in Ruiz's blind spot. He approaches the driver's side window, raising the shotgun, tapping it against the glass. Ruiz turns to look at him. My mouth opens, yelling a warning, but the sound is drowned out by twin blasts fired at close range. Pale circles appear in the glass. Ruiz crumples sideways.

Reacting instinctively, I drop my shoulder and charge at Kenneth, collecting him in the midriff and carrying him through the front window, shattering glass and splintering wood. We're falling through the air, landing in shrubbery. His body breaks my fall, air escaping. Bones breaking. I push myself up. Kenneth's eyes are open. Liquid bubbles in his mouth. A jagged triangle of glass sticks out of his neck, glistening in the headlights. I pick up another shard, holding it my palm as I scramble to my feet and run, past the fountain and into the darkness.

It's difficult to move quickly with my hands behind my back. Zig-zagging, half crouched, I head for the darker shadows of the treeline, expecting to hear a shotgun being cracked open and reloaded.

Stumbling headfirst into a ditch, I inhale muddy water, fetid with dung and grass clippings. Coughing and spluttering, I roll on to my back, using the broken glass to cut at my bindings, sawing at the doubled twine until it shreds and breaks.

Pressing myself to the ground, I peer over the top of the mound. The headlights of the Mercedes are still blazing. I slide sideways and move along the ditch, water parting and closing around me. Weed and wrack are draped over my head and shoulders. There are walls around the estate. I might be able to climb over them, or reach the front gate. What will Eugene do? He can't let me leave.

The muffled noise of an engine reaches me through the rain. The quad bike. It roars from the garage, bucking and rearing over the uneven ground. The headlights flare in my eyes and I duck down until it swings away. The bike churns past, carving tracks in the muddy ground, searching for me. I hear another sound. Barking. The dogs are loose.

Glancing at the line of trees, I know I can't make them. I'm outpaced. Outgunned. Outnumbered.

I once had a patient – a former marine, suffering from PTSD – who told me the only thing that differentiates prey from predator is the ability to think. Humans sit at the top of the food chain because we're cleverer than other creatures. We're not as fast, we can't fly and we can barely swim or climb, but we can adapt and improvise. I'm closer to sixty than fifty. I have Parkinson's. What chance do I have?

The dogs have followed me to the edge of the ditch where the water has masked my scent. Eugene whistles again. They're running along the bank, hunting me. I lower my face to the mud, trying not to breathe. I hear them. They're close. Panting. Sniffing.

One of them growls. I'm found. Finding my feet, I start to run. The dogs bound across the ditch and give chase.

Light flares in my eyes and the ground turns to silver. I'm zig-zagging left and right, feinting, diving and tumbling. Something slams into my back, sending me down. A dog is on top of me. Jaws open. Snarling. I punch it hard in the face and spin up, stumbling to my feet.

Ahead I see the mechanical digger and the line of trees beyond, silhouetted against the sky. The second dog has grabbed my forearm, trying to rip it off, but the wool is thick enough to protect my skin. I swing it around and kick hard, feeling my shoe sink into soft organs. The dog yelps and tumbles away. I've reached the digger. A shovel is sticking from a mound of earth. Gripping it with both hands, I swing it back and forth. The dogs are leaping and snarling. Retreating and attacking. The blade of the shovel connects. Bones break. A dog whimpers and retreats. Its sibling hangs back, suddenly uncertain.

The quad bike is bogged in the ditch. I hear Eugene cursing and revving the engine, rocking it back and forth, trying to get it unstuck. He abandons the bike and walks towards me. Silhouetted against the lights, I see the shotgun in his right fist.

I start to run, heading towards the house. One foot follows another, each caked in mud, slowing me down. Eugene whistles. Only one dog responds. He doesn't have to outrun me. The dog will do that.

I'm sixty yards from the garage, my shadow shortening in front of me. Fifty yards . . . forty yards . . . Sweat stings my eyes, making the buildings blur like I've smeared Vaseline on my pupils.

Ruiz says the First Law of Policing is to protect yourself.

430

The Second Law is that inaction is a form of defence so long as it doesn't conflict with the First Law. There is a Third Law. What is it? Something about surprise.

Veering to my right, I head towards the fire with the dog close behind. Blood roars in my ears and a hot poker seems to skewer my chest like a bayonet. Is this a heart attack?

I hurl myself into the flames, hearing the whoosh of sparks and the sizzle of my wet clothes. Rolling over and over, covering my face with my coat, I reach out blindly with my remaining hand, searching for a weapon. My fingers close around a branch. Flesh sizzles.

The dog skirts the fire, appearing from the smoke like a hound released from Hell, its mouth like a gaping wound. I'm on my knees, eye to eye. The dog lunges. I swing the branch, which arcs through the air like a spluttering firework, smashing into the dog's neck, showering it with sparks. Yelping in pain, it tumbles away, blinded, with glowing embers sticking to its wet fur.

My chest heaves, sucking in air. Eugene is watching me from the far side of the fire. He pushes back the hood of his raincoat and I recognise someone whose world has turned to a red and purple melt of rage.

In the same heaving breath, another sound reaches me – a warlike bellow. Glancing to my right, I see Vincent Ruiz charging from the darkness. He looks like a man who doesn't care, a man angry beyond reason, a man with bullet-proof glass in his Mercedes which everybody laughed at, including me.

Angling his run, he cuts down the distance and throws

431

his body at Eugene, diving at full length in a rugby-style tackle that knocks Eugene backwards, taking the air from his lungs.

Ruiz straddles him, holding Eugene's head with one hand, punching with the other. Eugene's head flops sideways time and again. Blood leaks from his mouth and nose.

'I think that's enough,' I say to Ruiz, who is breathing hard.

'You all right?' he asks, taking the shotgun.

I look at the blackened palm of my right hand, feeling no pain, but I know it's coming. 'Yeah.'

He points to his left ear. 'I can't hear a thing.'

Police cars swing through the gates of Aslan House and along the driveway. Flashing lights strobe between the trees, as though an old-fashioned film reel has unspooled from a projector and is flapping against the lens.

I watch them approaching the manor house until distracted by another figure appearing from the shadows. Rosie is barefoot, wearing flannelette pyjamas, carrying the Glock. She must have taken it from Kenneth's body. Using both hands, she aims the pistol at Ruiz, who backs away, letting the shotgun fall from his hand.

Rosie tries to say something, but the words get caught in her throat. She tries again. 'I promise you, Joseph, I had no idea.'

'You drove Kenneth to Chiswick.'

'No! That was Eugene. I didn't know what they planned to do. I would never hurt William.'

'You hated him for what happened to Francis.'

'I didn't want him dead. I thought Kenneth was going

to talk to him about the money. That's all. I didn't expect . . . I didn't know . . .' Her eyes are shining. Behind her, the police cars have reached the manor house.

'This has all gone so terribly wrong,' says Rosie, dropping to her knees. She opens her mouth and slides the black barrel between her lips, angling it towards the top of her head. Her finger tightens on the trigger.

'No! Don't!' I cry, as time seems to pause. 'Listen to me, Rosie. Can you feel the rain? It's cold, isn't it? Like needles of ice. Lift your face. Smell it. Taste it. That's life. That's real.'

She's locked in an obscene pose – the ugly square barrel, glossed with spit, creating a bow in her bottom lip. I want her to focus on my voice . . . to hear me.

'I know you think that everything is hopeless, Rosie, and maybe you're right, but pull that trigger and you're not going to end the pain. You'll be passing it on to your children and grandchildren. They are going to carry the burden . . . the grief.

'I lost Julianne sixteen months ago and I didn't think I could survive the sadness. There have been days when I felt that I couldn't go on – couldn't help Charlie or Emma – but the thought of never seeing them again, of never knowing what happens next . . . Death is waiting for us anyway, Rosie. Why call on it early?'

The gun is heavy in Rosie's hands and she's struggling to hold it steady. I notice the echo between her pale skin and silver hair.

'I met two of your grandchildren the other day. David's little girl and boy. She looks like a real handful. She has your temperament, I can tell . . . and your eyes.'

433

'You think so?' says Rosie, sniffling.

'I do. What's her name?'

'Valerie.'

'And the little boy?'

'Hugo.'

'If you pull that trigger, you'll never have a chance to tell Valerie and Hugo that you love them, or to explain what happened, or to watch them grow up.'

'I don't care.'

'I think you do.'

Police are approaching. Ruiz holds up his hand, telling them to hold their ground. Nobody moves. The world has narrowed, shrinking to the size of the clearing and the firelight.

'Look at me, Rosie. I have a progressive, degenerative neurological disorder that has no cure. I need a cocktail of drugs to give me a few hours of normality. I have denied it, ranted at the unfairness, made pacts with God and crawled into the darkest of holes, but I discovered something when I was in there. I learned that I'd rather be alive than dead. Even when I'm lost, cold, lonely, hungry, or in pain – it's better than not being here. Life has possibilities. It has second, third and fourth chances. It has music and laughter and love and hope.'

I'm on my knees, meeting Rosie eye-to-eye, edging closer to her across the wet turf.

'Would I change things if I could? Of course. But would I want to miss out on what's coming? No. Never. And you know who taught me that? My dad.'

Rosie looks at me.

'Do you remember my Aunt Gracie? She burned to death in her house because she was too scared of the outside world to escape the flames. I loved Gracie and I was devastated by her death. Inconsolable. But Dad said something to me that I've never forgotten. He said, "Remember, Joseph, the worst hour of your life only lasts for sixty minutes." This is your worst hour, Rosie. Get through it and the next one will be easier . . . and the next one.'

Shuffling forward on my knees, I reach out. My hand, blackened by the flames, touches her shoulder. Rosie shudders and drops her head, lowering the gun. Her fingers are too cold to uncurl from the trigger. I do it for her, peeling back her forefinger and letting the weapon slide along her thighs to the muddy grass. I put my arms around her as the police move closer.

'Did I ever tell you that I fancied you when I was growing up?' I ask.

'Me?'

'On those holidays in Cornwall, you were so glamorous and rebellious. You didn't look like other mothers.'

'I was young.'

'You were beautiful. You still are.'

She touches her wet hair, her voice low and quiet.

'Thank you, Joseph.'

Day Twenty-Two

57

Arc lights on tripods have turned the front of the manor house into a brightly lit outdoor stage, bleached of colour and shadow. Police and paramedics have jobs to do – collecting clues and bandaging wounds. Draped in a foil blanket and shivering in wet clothes, I'm floating on a cloud of morphine. My right hand is bound in white gauze, with only the thumb showing.

A gust of wind creates ripples on puddles and shakes drops from the trees. In the distance, dressed in a reflective yellow vest, I see a scarecrow watching me from a field. Emma's Raggedy Man.

I close my eyes and picture Kenneth with blood spilling out of his neck and leaking from his mouth. His face was like a mask, plastic and unformed, childlike instead of old. Did revenge lift a weight from his shoulders, or was it death?

Ruiz appears from behind the bright lights. Wrapped in

a matching foil blanket, he reaches into his pocket and takes out a tin of boiled sweets. Unscrewing the lid, he offers me one. I choose a lemon drop, but can't pick it up with my right hand. I use my left.

'You worry me, Professor. You keep telling me you're a coward and then go charging out of the trenches, headlong into enemy fire.'

'A coward will do anything to prove he has courage.'

'Is there anything you can't rationalise?'

He nods towards DI Macdermid, who is heading our way. Behind him, I see a white tent being erected over Kenneth Passage's body.

'We'll need a full statement,' the detective says, avoiding eye contact. 'In the meantime, you're going to the burns unit to check out that hand.'

'I'm fine.'

'Argue with the doctors. The car is waiting now.'

I ride in the front seat, beside a uniformed officer who is pleasant enough. He asks me how I burned my hand and whether it was true that bullet-proof glass saved Ruiz's life. I give single-word answers where possible.

At the hospital, my hands are unwrapped and slathered with ointment. Skin grafts won't be necessary, but I will have scarring. I'm given more painkillers and a course of antibiotics before being allowed to leave.

I call Charlie from the burns unit.

'What time is it?' she asks sleepily.

'Early. I'm sorry to wake you. How's Emma?'

'Fine. She got up twice last night to check the locks. Are you coming home?'

'Soon, but I need a favour. After you've dropped Emma at school, can you bring me some clean clothes?'

'What happened to yours?'

'It's a long story. I'll tell you when you get here.'

'Are you with Granddad?'

'That's where I'm going now.'

The rain clouds have been chased away by a gusty wind that harries them eastwards towards Belgium or Holland or Denmark. Geography isn't my strongest subject.

Mum is dozing in a chair next to my father's bed. The nurses offered to get her a camp stretcher, but Mum insists that she only 'rests her eyes'. I kiss her forehead. She wakes with a start and admonishes me about my filthy clothes and how I smell, before seeing my bandaged hand and growing concerned.

I explain to her what happened, giving her a brief overview of the fraud and the attack on Dad. She's shocked that Kenneth and Rosie were responsible, but the precise details seem unimportant so long as I'm safe. Mum has never understood those who bear grudges or seek to settle scores. She'd rather believe in the goodness of people and the loveliness of things because that's her defence against the harsher realities. She has had a charmed life. Education. Wealth. Children. Friends. Faith. I used to be irritated by her rose-tinted view of the world, and her Pollyanna-like optimism; how she can find sweetness in the intolerable and beauty in deformity, while I am perpetually reaching for the unattainable. Surely hers is a better attitude. She carries happiness within her whereas Kenneth and Rosie collected resentments and polished them up like religious artefacts.

'They blamed Dad for what happened to Francis,' I explain.

'That's ridiculous.'

'It's what they believed.'

A nurse arrives to give my father his bed-bath. Mum insists on taking over, shooing the nurse away. 'I've looked after this man for more than sixty years – I think I can wash his bits.'

I laugh along with the nurse. Mum frowns at our foolishness. She unbuttons my dad's pyjamas and puts towels on either side of his chest, before dipping a sponge in warm water and running it across his face and neck.

'It wears you out – hating someone that much,' she says.

'Who have you hated?'

'That woman, of course.' She means Olivia. 'I used to wake in the middle of the night, alone in my bed, knowing William was with her. It wore me out and gave me wrinkles.'

The comment makes me smile, but also feel sad. How do I explain to someone like my mother that love and hate are not absolutes, or opposite sides of the same coin. Hate is an evil passion and love an inspired one, but they share the same brain circuitry and lead to similar acts of desperation. Then again, maybe she understands it better than I do.

I notice a suitcase in the corner.

'They're some of William's things,' she explains. 'Olivia dropped it by last night.'

'Did you talk to her?'

'It was very civil. We had a cup of tea.'

My mother raises Dad's right arm and runs the sponge down to his wrist, making sure to clean between his fingers.

'She told me that William had decided to move back to Wales. I knew he would. It was only a matter of time.'

Twenty years, I want to say, but I hold my tongue.

'She doesn't want to fight us.'

'That's good.'

Mum is humming to herself as she sponges and dries.

'We should think about when we're going to take him home,' she says. 'I thought we might turn his study into a bedroom. Take out the shelves. I won't have to go up and down the stairs.'

'Do you really want him home?'

'Of course. It's where he belongs.'

She brushes hair from his eyes and smiles. It's the look of a woman who has rediscovered her purpose in life because now she's needed. I remember my father's whispered plea to me, but it doesn't seem as clear any more. Maybe I imagined it after all.

58

My phone is ringing. I fumble in my muddy trousers, feeling the pockets in a strange dance.

'Professor O'Loughlin?' asks a woman.

'Yes.'

'I'm calling from North Bridge House. Is Emma coming to school today?'

'Pardon?'

'She missed roll call. Is she unwell?'

'No. I don't think so. Charlie was dropping her there – my other daughter. Let me call you back.'

I phone Charlie's number.

'Hi, Daddy. I'm stuck in traffic.'

'Is Emma with you?'

'She's at school.'

'She missed roll call.'

'But I dropped her half an hour ago. I watched her walk through the gates. She had her gym bag with her. They've made a mistake.'

I call the school, getting through to the office.

'There is no gym today,' says the administrator. 'None of her classmates have seen Emma. We've checked the library and the changing rooms.'

Hanging up before she can finish, I try Emma's mobile, struggling to punch the buttons with my left hand. The call goes straight to her voicemail: '*Hi, this is Emma. I can't come to the phone right now, but you can leave me a message after the tone.*'

'Where are you? You're not at school. Call me as soon as you get this. I'm worried, not angry. I promise. Please call.'

Charlie arrives, out of breath, growing more defensive as I quiz her insistently.

'How did she seem this morning?' I ask.

'The same. Quiet.'

'Did she say anything?'

'She asked where you were.'

'What else did you talk about? What did she eat?'

'She was totally normal,' says Charlie, looking at me plaintively.

I'm trying to think of who else to call. Emma doesn't have many friends. Her cousins, Lucy's children, will be at school.

'Maybe she's gone back to the flat,' says Charlie.

'You'll have to drive,' I say as we reach the car.

We argue over which way is quickest. I want to hammer

on the horn and bulldoze other cars aside, while Charlie calmly negotiates the traffic.

'It's my fault,' she says.

'No.'

'It's what you're thinking.'

'Definitely not. I'm to blame. I've been so bound up in what happened to Dad that I've forgotten the people that matter most: you and Emma. Whenever I get distracted, people I love get hurt or go missing.'

'We'll find her,' says Charlie, cursing as a cab driver cuts her off.

At Wellington Court I take the stairs two at a time, out of breath by the top floor, struggling with the keys. I shout Emma's name, running from room to room, looking in wardrobes and under beds. Obvious places. Ridiculous places.

I tell myself to relax. Concentrate. Review. Emma planned this. She dressed for school. She didn't want anyone knowing where she was going. She made her bed. Her soft toys are arranged in order from biggest to smallest. She packed her gym bag this morning or last night. What did she take?

My mind is freewheeling now, making connections. Emma's journal has gone. What else? Her beloved 'blankie' is normally folded at the end of her bed. She must have taken it with her. I pick up her porcelain piggybank, which has a rubber stopper on its pink belly. I shake the pig. Nothing rattles. How much did Emma have? It could be eighty or ninety pounds, counting birthday and Christmas money.

Charlie comes through the door. 'Is she here?'

'No.'

She wants to search in the same places, but I need space and quiet. Is Emma running away, or running towards something?

My left arm is twitching. The medication is wearing off. Charlie gets my pills and a glass of water, which she holds up to my lips to let me drink. I notice the apples in the fruit bowl. Did Emma take one? Does she have food? Water?

My gaze sweeps across the kitchen and stops on a wall above the bench, where I notice an absence, not an addition. A painting. It's a watercolour of the church in our old village, Wellow. Julianne bought it at the school fête, when they were raising money to repair the church roof. The artist, a local, had captured St Julian's on a late summer afternoon, when the trees were in full leaf and the stone-work had a soft golden hue.

'I think I know where she's gone,' I say. 'Come on.'

The next two hours are filled with the headlong rush of tar and wind, of cars and trucks and vans. Charlie has both hands braced on the wheel and her shoulders canted forwards, as though willing the traffic to part. Seated, belted and contained, I rant at drivers who hog the overtaking lanes and at lorries that lumber up hills.

The radio is on. The newsreader says a retired solicitor has been found dead at his manor house in Windsor. His wife is 'helping police with their enquiries'. No names. No mention of missing money, or my father, or Ray D'Marco.

Lowering the electric window, I gulp at the air greedily.

'Are you OK?' Charlie asks.

'Yeah.'

'She's going to be fine.'

'I know.'

I nod my head, swallowing the lump in my throat. I'm cold now, but I won't close the window. Charlie turns up the heating, blasting her feet.

'She'll have caught a train from Paddington to Bath Spa,' I say, picturing Emma trying to disappear in the crowds. 'She'll have lied about her age to get the ticket, or bought one from a machine.'

'How will she get to Wellow?' Charlie asks.

'She could catch a bus or walk.'

'That's five miles!'

'At least it's not raining,' I say, trying to make the obvious sound comforting.

We're getting close now, passing through Hinton Charterhouse on lanes that are so narrow that Charlie slows for oncoming traffic. Occasionally someone pulls over. It's not Charlie. Not today.

Wellow Lane becomes Hinton Hill becomes Ford Road. We sweep beneath the old viaduct and climb Bull's Hill towards St Julian's Church.

'Keep going straight ahead,' I say.

'But I thought—'

'Just keep going.'

Charlie drives past the church and Emma's old primary school and the Fox and Badger pub. The cottage is not far from here. Within a minute, we're out the other side of Wellow, heading towards the next village, Peasedown St John.

Ahead of us, I see a copse of tall trees surrounded by a stone wall and unkempt hedges. There are no buildings nearby. No church or crypt.

Charlie understands now and pulls off the road in front of twin iron gates. Gravestones are visible between the vertical railings.

I'm out of the car before we've stopped moving. Stepping through a pedestrian gate, I scan the headstones, focusing on a corner of the cemetery where I picked out a plot sixteen months ago. I can't see Emma. Maybe we're too early. Perhaps if we wait . . .

Following the gravel path, I near the spot. Some of the graves have fresh flowers, but most have sad-looking plastic blooms, sticking out of vases that are cemented into place.

As I get closer, I hear Emma's voice. She's sitting on her overcoat with her back to Julianne's headstone, with her legs sticking straight out. A woollen beanie is pulled down over her ears. She has swept all the leaves from Julianne's plot and used her scarf to polish the stone. Her tattered, towel-sized 'blankie' has been laid over the grave.

Emma doesn't hear me approach.

'I'm sorry I hid from you in the supermarket that time in France,' she says. 'I didn't know about Madeleine McCann or that you'd get frightened for me. And I'm sorry I made you ride the roller coaster at Alton Towers and you threw up afterwards.'

Emma's journal is propped open on her lap and she's reading from a list.

'I'm sorry I wore my Snow White dress for almost a year, not letting you wash it; and I'm sorry that I couldn't wear Charlie's hand-me-down shoes because of my odd-shaped feet, although technically that's not my fault. Daddy has weird feet too.'

She pauses and runs her finger down the page.

'Your gold hooped earring — the ones Daddy gave you on your anniversary — it was me who broke the clasp. I should have said something, but I didn't want to get into trouble.'

Emma turns her head and looks up at me. She's not surprised, or shocked. She doesn't bounce to her feet and hug me in relief.

'Hello, Squeak,' I say. 'What are you doing?'

'Talking to Mummy.' She frowns. 'What happened to your hand?'

'I got burned.'

'Does it hurt?'

'Not any more.'

I lower myself down and sit beside her. Emma shimmies across to give me room on her coat. We brace our backs against the headstone. My legs stick out further than hers.

'I only bought one apple and one juice box,' she says in a matter-of-fact way, showing me the modest picnic she has laid out on the top of her gym bag.

'That's OK. I'm not hungry. What's with blankie?'

'I thought Mummy might be cold.'

'She's not.'

'How do you know?'

'She thinks about you and that keeps her warm.'

Emma looks at me doubtfully, but accepts the explanation because it makes her happy. Shoulder to shoulder, thigh to thigh, we watch the wind bend the grasses and rustle in the leaves.

'Why did you run away?' I ask.

'I was making you sad,' she whispers.

'Why would you think that?'

Emma shrugs.

'Tell me.'

'I feel like I've lost everyone. Mummy has gone. Charlie too.'

'I'm still here.'

'Only because of me.'

'What do you mean?'

'You wake up because of me. You buy food because of me. You cook my meals and wash my clothes and go to work because of me.'

Her words are like rocks being placed upon my chest, making it hard for me to breathe.

'You're here, but you don't want to be,' says Emma.

I want to argue. I want to say she's wrong, but the words catch in my throat. I'm glad Emma isn't looking at me, while I suffocate under stones.

Sixteen hours ago, I told Rosie to choose life because it is a gift, while death is prison with no escape. I told her that life offered second, third and fourth chances, each laden with hope and possibilities. What a hypocrite I am. What a fraud. What a coward. Emma has more courage in the wax in her ears than I have in my whole twisted, decrepit body.

'Don't cry, Daddy.'

'I'm not crying.'

'Your eyes are leaking.'

'I'm watering my cheeks.'

Charlie has been watching us from a distance. She edges closer.

'What's happening?' she asks.

'We're having a picnic with Mummy,' says Emma. 'But there's only one apple and a juice box.'

'That's OK.'

Emma moves over and Charlie sits on the opposite side of her.

My eyes are squeezed tightly shut.

Emma takes hold of my good hand and asks what I'm doing.

'I'm remembering something a very wise little girl once told me when I was pushing her on a swing.'

'What little girl?'

'Charlie.'

'What did I say?' asks Charlie.

'You said, "Daddy, if you squeeze your eyes tightly shut and open them again, it can be a brand new world."'

'How old was I?' asks Charlie.

'Four.'

Emma closes her eyes. Charlie does the same.

'Do you think it's true?' whispers Emma.

'It can be.'

'Only if we pretend.'

'Let's do that.'

Day Fifty-Eight

59

I'm exercising again – my usual route down England's Lane to Primrose Hill and Regent's Park. As I walk past the parade of shops, my local butcher and greengrocer yell at me to 'slow down'. *Their idea of a joke.* I laugh and wave back to them.

I have a typical Parkinsonian gait – small shuffling steps and general slowness – and occasionally, I freeze completely, like an actor stranded in the middle of a stage who has forgotten his lines. For a moment, I will blink in panic, waiting for a prompt, until finally my limbs receive the message and begin to move.

I am not the same person as I was eighteen months ago, or even eight weeks ago. My life has been pulled out of shape and littered with debris and torn-up things, like a stretch of coastline after a storm. Emma seems happier. She no longer entertains fanciful notions that Julianne is alive in witness protection, or living on a tropical island; and we talk about her often, with more laughter than before.

It's a week before Christmas and the houses and shops are decorated with fake snow, holly, tinsel and baubles. According to the weather bureau, there's a thirty per cent chance of snow this year on Christmas Day. People place bets on such things, which rather mocks the spirit of the season.

In Regent's Park, I am passed by those who exercise more successfully: joggers who jog, cyclists who pedal and walkers who stride ahead purposefully. By comparison, I look like a man trying to walk in Wellingtons whose left arm refuses to swing, giving me the appearance of a wounded duck who can only fly in circles.

Pausing to check my watch, I wonder if Kate will be here today. She hasn't returned any of my calls, or messages, but I know she jogs most mornings. I've seen her in the distance but never close enough to wave or call to her. I have practised our first conversation. She will ask me about Dad. I will tell her that he's been transferred to a high-dependency nursing home, against my mother's wishes, of course, but she still believes she can pray him back to health. Mum says everything happens for a reason – a phrase I hate because it seems like an excuse to avoid responsibility or facing up to reality. People die unfairly all the time, from neglect, abuse, landmines, starvation, car accidents, cancer, bombs. Saying it happens for a reason is as meaningless and moronic as saying that God doesn't give us anything we can't handle (Ray D'Marco's most-loathed phrase). God

451

didn't give me Parkinson's for a reason. He didn't take Julianne away from me, or cause Ewan's schizophrenia or deprive Bethany D'Marco of oxygen in the womb as part of some grand plan. Our fates are gloriously uncertain and the arrogance of believing that human tragedy is justified because it's part of some holy blueprint is intolerable.

At the same time, I can't be angry at my mother because she has the right idea. Her soul is transcendent. She has what she always wanted – my father – in sickness and in health, for better or for worse.

As if on cue, Kate appears from the mist, running towards me. Slim. Dark-haired. Long-legged. I raise my hand. She carries on. I step on to the path. She runs around me.

I shout after her. 'I remember where we first met.'

For a moment, I think she might not have heard me, or has chosen not to answer, but she slows. Stops. Turns.

'It was at Langton Hall in Clerkenwell. I was giving a talk to a group of . . . to a group . . .' I don't finish the statement.

Colour has drained from Kate's cheeks.

'I haven't told anyone,' I tell her. 'I wouldn't do that.'

She looks past me, along the path. Two cyclists zip by us in a flash of coloured Lycra and spinning wheels.

'Can I buy you a coffee?'

'I have to go.'

'Please?'

She narrows her lips into thin lines and nods her head. We walk to a café in the park and sit on opposite sides of a table at a window, overlooking a pond. Bedraggled ducks are huddled beneath a curtain of willow branches.

'I'm sorry,' I say.

'You've said that already.'

'I'm in awe of what you've done . . . of how far you've come.'

'From prostitute to disgraced detective?' Her bottom lip is trembling.

'That's not what I meant.'

'I hate that you remember.'

'Why?'

'Isn't it obvious?'

'Not to me.'

'I have tried so hard to put that behind me. I changed my name. I went back to school, then college. I applied to the Met for four years before they accepted me. I worked hard, won promotions. Proved myself. But that whole time I've been looking over my shoulder, wondering if my past would catch up with me.'

'It hasn't.'

'It will eventually. I was convicted twice for soliciting. I didn't mention that on my application. I always feared it would be a former client who blew the whistle, or one of the girls I worked with . . .'

'Nobody else knows.'

'You do.' Kate wipes her eyes with the back of her hand. 'You're the reason I'm here, you know.'

'Me?'

'That night you came to speak to us at Langton Hall, you lectured us on staying safe and looking after each other. I remembered seeing your photograph in the newspaper a few days earlier. You'd talked a teenage boy out of jumping from the roof of a hospital. Later, when I was in Hendon doing my police training, I read the story about your daughter being kidnapped . . . and another where you rescued a girl who'd been missing for three years.'

'Piper Hadley.'

'You're famous.'

'No, I'm not.'

'Slightly famous.'

'Please don't.'

'Do you prefer, "well known"?' She's teasing me now.

'I prefer to be self-deprecating.'

Kate laughs. 'Does that work for you?' She softly clears her throat. 'They're demoting me back to uniform. It's not so bad. I like dealing with the public. Maybe in a few years I'll be forgiven and can try again – that's if the past stays in the past.' She changes the subject. 'I hear they charged Rosie Passage with attempted murder.'

'Yes.'

'What about Ray D'Marco?'

'He's home with Bethany.'

'Was it all about the money?'

'Jealousy and anger played a role.'

Kate slides her hand across the table and turns my palm, tracing her fingers over the pink scars left by the fire.

'I like you, Joseph, but you expect too much from people.'

'I know.'

The wind gusts outside, sending leaves scuttling across the grass.

'I have to go.'

'Yes.'

We are standing outside. A loose strand of Kate's hair catches wetly in the corner of her lips. She removes it with her fingertips, leans forward and kisses me on the mouth. I kiss her back, slipping my arms around her, feeling the firm muscles of her back and the soft swell of her backside as I pull her against me.

The kiss breaks and she exhales warmly against my neck.

'Goodbye, Joe.'

'Can I call you sometime?'

'If you'd like.'

'When?'

'Whenever.'

She turns away and begins running, settling into an easy stride, the soles of her shoes orange against the grey of the asphalt. I take out my phone, find her number and wait for her to answer.

Now read on for an extract of the next
Michael Robotham thriller,

GOOD GIRL
BAD GIRL

1

'Which one is she?' I ask, leaning closer to the observation window.

'Blonde. Baggy sweater. Sitting on her own.'

'And you're not going to tell me why I'm here?'

'I don't want to influence your decision.'

'What am I deciding?'

'Just watch her.'

I look again at the group of teenagers, girls and boys. Most are wearing jeans and long tops with the sleeves pulled down to hide whatever self-inflicted damage has been done. Some are cutters, some are burners, or scratchers, or bulimics, or anorexics, or obsessive compulsives, or pyromaniacs, or sociopaths, or narcissists, or suffering from ADHD. Some abuse food or drugs, others swallow foreign objects, or run into walls on purpose, or take outrageous risks.

Evie Cormac has her knees drawn up, almost as though she doesn't trust the floor. Sullen mouthed and pretty, she could be eighteen or she could be fourteen. Not quite a woman or a girl about to bid goodbye to childhood, yet there is something ageless and changeless about her, as if she has seen the worst and survived it. With brown eyes framed by thickened eyelashes and bleached hair cut in a ragged bob, she's holding the sleeves of her sweater in her bunched fists, stretching the neckline, revealing a pattern of red blotches below her jawline that could be love-bites or fingermarks.

Adam Guthrie is standing alongside me, regarding Evie like she is the latest arrival at Twycross Zoo.

'Why is she here?' I ask.

'Her current index office is for aggravated assault. She broke someone's jaw with a half-brick.'

'Her *current* offence?'

'She's had a few.'

'How many?'

'Too few to mention.'

He's attempting to be funny or deliberately obtuse. We're at Langford Hall, a secure children's home in Nottingham, where Guthrie is a resident social worker. He's dressed in baggy jeans, combat boots and a rugby jumper, trying too hard to look like 'one of them'; someone who can relate to teenage delinquency and strife rather than an underpaid, low-level public servant with a wife, a mortgage and two kids. He and I were at university together and lived in the same college. I wouldn't say we were friends, more like passing acquaintances, although I went to his wedding a few years ago and slept with one of the bridesmaids. I didn't know she was Guthrie's youngest sister. Would it have made a difference? I'm not sure. He hasn't held it against me.

'You ready?'

I nod.

We enter the room and take two chairs, joining the circle or teenagers, who watch us with a mixture of suspicion and boredom.

'We have a visitor today,' says Guthrie. 'This is Cyrus Haven.'

'Who is he?' asks one of the girls.

'I'm a psychologist,' I reply.

'Another one!' says the same girl, screwing up her face.

'Cyrus is here to observe.'

'Us or you?'

'Both.'

I look for Evie's reaction. She's watching me blankly.

Guthrie crosses his legs, revealing a hairless pale ankle where his trouser cuff has ridden up his shin. He's a jolly, fat sort of bloke who rubs his hands together at the start of something, presupposing the fun that awaits.

'Let's begin with some introductions, shall we? I want you to each tell Cyrus your name, where you're from and why you're here. Who wants to go first?'

Nobody answers.

'How about you, Alana?'

She shakes her head. I'm sitting directly opposite Evie. She knows I'm looking at her.

'Holly?' asks Guthrie.

'Nah.'

'Evie?'

She doesn't respond.

'It's nice to see you're wearing more clothes today,' says Guthrie. 'You, too, Holly.'

Evie snorts.

'That was a legitimate protest,' argues Holly, growing more animated. 'We were protesting against the outdated assumptions of class and gender inherent in this white-male dominated gulag.'

'Thank you, comrade,' says Guthrie sarcastically. 'Will you get us started, Nathan?'

'Don't call me Nathan,' says a beanpole of a boy with pimples on his forehead.

'What should I call you?'

'Nat.'

'You mean like a bug?' asks Evie.

He spells it out: 'N . . . A . . . T.'

Guthrie takes a small knitted teddy bear from his pocket and tosses it to Nat. 'You're up first. Remember, whoever has the bear has the right to speak. Nobody else can interrupt.'

Nat bounces the teddy bear on his thigh.

'I'm from Sheffield and I'm here cos I took a dump in my neighbour's VW when he left it unlocked.'

Titters all round. Evie doesn't join in.

'Why did you do that?' asks Guthrie.

Nat shrugs nonchalantly. 'It were a laugh.'

'On the driver's seat?' asks Holly.

'Yeah. Course. Where else? The dickhead complained to the police so me and my mates gave him a kicking.'

'Do you feel bad about that?' asks Guthrie.

'Not really.'

'He had to have metal plates put in his head.'

'Yeah, but he had insurance and he got compensation. My ma had to pay a fine. Way I see it, the dickhead *made* money.'

Guthrie starts to argue but changes his mind, perhaps recognising the futility.

The teddy bear is passed on to Reebah from Nottingham, who is painfully thin and who sewed her lips together because her father tried to make her eat.

'What did he make you eat?' asks another of the girls, who is so fat that her thighs are forcing her knees apart.

'Food.'

'What sort of food?'

'Birthday cake.'

'You're an idiot.'

Guthrie interrupts. 'Please don't make critical comments, Cordelia. You can only speak if you have the bear.'

'Give it to me then,' she says, snatching the bear from Reebah's lap.

'Hey! I wasn't finished.'

The girls wrestle for a moment until Guthrie intervenes, but Reebah has forgotten what she wanted to say.

The bear is in a new lap. 'My name is Cordelia and I'm from Leeds and when someone pisses me off, I fight them, you know. I make 'em pay.'

'You get angry?' asks Guthrie.

'Yeah.'

'What sort of things make you angry?'

'When people call me fat.'

'You are fat,' says Evie.

'Shut the fuck up!' yells Cordelia, jumping to her feet. She's twice Evie's size. 'Say that again and I'll fuckin' batter you.'

Guthrie has put himself between them. 'Apologise, Evie.'

Evie smiles sweetly. 'I'm sorry for calling you *fat*, Cordelia. I think you've lost weight. You look positively svelte.'

'What's that mean?' she asks.

'Skinny.'

'Fuck off!'

'OK, let's all settle down,' says Guthrie. 'Cordelia, why are you here?'

'I grew up too soon,' she replies. 'I lost my virginity at, like, eleven. I slept with guys and slept with girls and smoked a lot of pot. I tried heroin at twelve and ice when I was thirteen.'

Evie rolls her eyes.

Cordelia glares at her. 'My mum called the police on me, so I tried to poison her with floor cleaner.'

'To punish her?' asks Guthrie.

'Maybe,' says Cordelia. 'It was like an experiment, you know. I wanted to, like, see what would happen.'

'Did it work?' asks Nat.

'Nah,' replies Cordelia. 'She said the soup tasted funny and didn't finish the bowl. Made her vomit, that's all.'

'You should have used wolfsbane,' says Nat.

'What's that?'

'It's a plant. I heard about this gardener who died when he touched the leaves.'

'My mum doesn't like gardening,' says Cordelia, missing the point.

Guthrie passes the teddy bear to Evie. 'Your turn.'

'Nope.'

'Why not?'

'The details of my life are inconsequential.'

'That's not true.'

Evie sighs and leans forward, resting her forearms on her knees, squeezing the bear with both hands. Her accent changes.

'My father was a relentlessly self-improving boulangerie owner from Belgium with low-grade narcolepsy and a penchant for buggery. My mother was a fifteen-year-old French prostitute named Chloe with webbed feet . . .'

I laugh. Everybody looks at me.

'It's from *Austin Powers*,' I explain.

More blank stares.

'The movie . . . Mike Myers . . . Dr Evil.'

Still nothing.

Evie puts on a gruff Scottish accent. 'First things first. Where's your shitter? I've got a turtle-head poking out.'

'Fat Bastard,' I say.

Evie smiles. Guthrie is annoyed with me, as though I'm fomenting unrest.

He calls on another teenager, who has a blue streak in her hair and piercings in her ears, eyebrows and nose.

'What brings you here, Serena?'

'Well, it's a long story.'

Groans all round.

Serena recounts an episode from her life when she went

to America as an exchange student at sixteen and lived with a family in Ohio, whose son was in prison for murder. Every fortnight they insisted Serena visit him, making her wear her sexiest clothes. Short dresses. Low-cut tops.

'He was on the other side of the glass and his father kept telling me to lean closer and show him my tits.'

Evie sneezes into the crook of her arm in a short, sharp exhalation, that sounds a lot like, 'Bullshit!'

Serena glares at her but goes on with her story. 'One night, when I was sleeping, the father came into my room and raped me. I was too frightened to tell my parents or call the police. I was alone in a foreign country, thousands of miles from home.' She looks around the group, hoping for sympathy.

Evie sneezes again – making the same sound.

Serena tries to ignore her.

'Back home, I started having problems – drinking and cutting myself. My parents sent me see to a therapist, who seemed really nice at the beginning until he tried to rape me.'

'For fuck's sake!' says Evie, sighing in disgust.

'We're not here to pass judgement,' Guthrie warns her.

'But she's making shit up. What's the point of sharing if people are gonna tell lies.'

'Fuck you!' shouts Serena, flipping Evie the finger.

'Bite me!' says Evie.

Serena leaps to her feet. 'You're a freak! Everybody knows it.'

'Please sit down,' says Guthrie, trying to keep the girls apart.

'She called me a fucking liar.'

'No, I didn't,' says Evie. 'I called you a *psycho* fucking liar.'

Serena ducks under Guthrie's arm and launches herself across the space, knocking Evie off her chair. The two of them are wrestling on the floor, but Evie seems to be laughing as she wards off the blows.

An alarm has been raised and a security team bursts into the group therapy room, dragging Serena away. The rest of the teenagers are ordered back to their bedrooms, all except for Evie. Dusting herself off, she touches the corner of her lip, rubbing a smudge of blood between her thumb and forefinger.

I give her a tissue. 'Are you all right?'

'I'm fine. She punches like a girl.'

'What happened to your neck?'

'Someone tried to strangle me.'

'Why?'

'I have that sort of face.'

I pull up a chair and motion for Evie to sit down. She complies, crossing her legs, revealing an electronic tag on her ankle.

'Why are you wearing that?'

'They think I'm trying to escape.'

'Are you?'

Evie raises her forefinger to her lips and makes a shushing sound.

'First chance I get.'

MICHAEL ROBOTHAM
THE MULTI-MILLION-COPY BESTSELLING AUTHOR

Shatter

A terrified woman. A desperate act.
A broken mind.

A naked woman in red high-heeled shoes is perched on the edge of Clifton Suspension Bridge with her back pressed to the safety fence, weeping into a mobile phone. Clinical psychologist Joseph O'Loughlin is only feet away, desperately trying to talk her down. She whispers, 'you don't understand,' and jumps.

Later, Joe has a visitor – the woman's teenage daughter, a runaway from boarding school. She refuses to believe that her mother would have jumped off the bridge – not only would she not commit suicide, she is terrified of heights.

Joe wants to believe her, but what would drive a woman to such a desperate act? Whose voice? What evil?

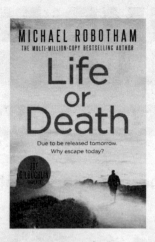

The Shawshank Redemption meets
No Country for Old Men in the breathtaking novel
that won the CWA Gold Dagger Award for 2015.

*Why would a man escape from prison the day before he's due to
be released?*

Audie Palmer has spent a decade in prison for an armed
robbery in which four people died, including two of the gang.
Seven million dollars has never been recovered and everybody
believes that Audie knows where the money is.

For ten years he has been beaten, stabbed, throttled and
threatened almost daily by prison guards, inmates and
criminal gangs, who all want to answer this same question, but
suddenly Audie vanishes, the day before he's due to be released.

Everybody wants to find Audie, but he's not running.
Instead he's trying to save a life . . . and not just his own.